THE
SAFE
HOUSE

BY THE SAME AUTHOR

You Can't See Round Corners
The Long Shadow
Just Let Me Be
The Sundowners
The Climate of Courage
Justin Bayard
The Green Helmet
Back of Sunset
North From Thursday
The Country of Marriage
Forests of the Night
A Flight of Chariots
The Fall of an Eagle
The Pulse of Danger
The High Commissioner
The Long Pursuit
Season of Doubt
Remember Jack Hoxie
Helga's Web
The Liberators
The Ninth Marquess
Ransom
Peter's Pence

THE
SAFE
HOUSE

JON CLEARY

WILLIAM MORROW & COMPANY, INC.
NEW YORK 1975

for Catherine and Jane,
of another generation

Printed in the United States of America.

1 2 3 4 5   79 78 77 76 75

Library of Congress Cataloging in Publication Data

Cleary, Jon (date)
  The safe house.

    1. World War, 1939–1945—Displaced persons—Fiction.
I. Title.
PZ3.C58Saf   [PR6053.L4]   823   74-34360
ISBN 0-688-02902-7

Author's Note

In April 1945 the Allied Forces, beating their way across Europe, came upon the first concentration camps. The pitiful, ghastly survivors of the millions who had passed through the camps staggered out to greet their saviours; and the world, seeing the newsreels of their rescue, gasped, was sickened and vowed such bestiality would never occur again. 'Horror in our time' became a phrase to mock the hollow promise of seven years before, 'Peace in our time'.

The released victims of Nazi terror took some time to accustom themselves to freedom. The smell of death gave way to the smell of DDT; disinfectant cleaned up both the walking dead and the unburied dead, made it safe for the rescuers to handle the rescued. But being sprayed with disinfectant was the least of the camp inmates' new indignities. Slowly they came to realize that, only numbers for so long, they had been issued with a new identity: Displaced Person. The phrase was not dreamed up by anyone who had to bear it: victims of the past, they were the first victims of the postwar fashion for euphemisms. But as Displaced Persons camps spread like a thin, tenuous web across the map of Europe, the DPs (victims now of the fashion for initials) came to know what they really were: nationals of Limbo, without flag, without votes, without roots.

The Displaced Persons camps were not all converted army camps. Some were empty warehouses, stripped factories, even rows of houses: but they were all abodes from which the DPs wished to escape. They were free to come and go – but go where? Many of them came from Eastern Europe: they did not want to return to their homelands to live under Russian domination. Others found themselves incapable of starting life over again in those countries where, even before the war, they had experienced such hatred and persecution. The world was full of sympathy for them; but every country found it had a quota limit when it was asked to extend its sympathy into acceptance of the Jews as immigrants into its own borders. Charity began, and too often stayed, at home.

Some DPs found work in and around the camps and made enough to support themselves; others, still shattered by what they had suffered, lived on what the United Nations Relief and Rehabilitation Administration (UNRRA) provided for them. But the camps, founded with the best of intentions, welcomed at first by the DPs, were no substitute for a home. Human dignity is not something to be gained from a hand-out, and the DPs, stripped of their dignity for so long, hungered for the opportunity to regain it.

This book is the story of a group of people who set out to find their dignity, a home and a homeland. Some of it is based on fact. But no one in it is meant to represent anyone, living or dead, who figured in such incidents.

Chapter One

'Your section goes on Friday night,' said Ben Keppel.

'We aren't ready yet!' Luise Graz felt a flutter of apprehension, tried to keep her voice calm but failed. Not so long ago she had thought she would never be afraid of anything again; not because she had conquered fear but because all feeling itself had gone. Now Ben Keppel was offering her the chance of freedom and she was afraid to take it because of what else it involved. She went on, piling up excuses like a barricade: 'You said it would not be for at least another month. It will be too cold in the mountains for the children. And two of the women are still getting over pneumonia.'

'Then you'll have to leave those women behind.'

'And who makes that decision – me? You know they'll hate me if I tell them they can't go.'

'Then put it to a vote. Prove you're a leader – explain the situation. Then do it the democratic way – no one should resent a majority vote.'

He had taken off his jacket and rolled up his sleeves. He wore only a thin sleeveless jumper over his shirt, but he did not seem to feel the chill breeze that blew down from the mountains. He was a thin dark-haired young man with an old face: the skull too prominent beneath the flesh, the eyes sometimes with that remote look that suggested the attempted counting of countless years. He had lived a lifetime before he had yet passed his majority.

He was rubbing the tattooed number on his forearm, like a child picking at an old scab. It was a habit of his that irritated Luise, who always kept her sleeves down over her own number and who always tried to avoid looking at it even when she bathed. If she got to Palestine she would seek out a surgeon and have him remove the tattoo. For her it was not a badge of honour, as it was with so many in the camp, but a searing reminder of how much, as a human being, she had been degraded.

Keppel noticed her look and said a little sheepishly, 'I keep hoping I may be able to rub it off.'

She was surprised: she had always taken him for one of those who would all his life boast of having survived Auschwitz. 'Are you ashamed of it?'

He shook his head emphatically. 'No, no. But it gives me away when I'm travelling through Italy – as soon as the English see me, they have me marked. The English in Italy are much more suspicious than the ones here in Germany.' He grinned, his teeth gaunt as tiny gravestones in the shrunken gums. He looked healthy until he smiled, but then the concentration camp grin was exposed. 'And of course they should be. Italy is so much closer to Palestine.'

Luise smiled, aware with a flicker of the old youthful vanity that by some miracle her own teeth and gums had recovered. Her beauty of face and figure, too, had survived, emerging over the past nine months, as if she had been re-born, from the grey shrunken husk that had been released from Birkenau a year ago. It had taken her, as it had taken so many others, almost three months to adjust to the fact that they were not going to die; only when that dreadful expectancy had at last been turned into hope, had she begun to live, to be Luise Graz again. There was an early tint of grey in her dark hair, but it only seemed to highlight the lustrous darkness; the liveliness of her dark eyes and her full-lipped mouth denied any suggestion of age Her skin had regained its old bloom and her body was as rounded and graceful as it had ever been. If she went back to the theatre (and even in Palestine, she expected, there would be opera of some sort) she would not be condemned to playing middle-aged women or old crones. At twenty-six, if the war had not destroyed her career and almost her life, she would now be ready to sing the great roles that all young singers dreamed of.

'You must be more careful, Ben. You've been lucky so far. How many trips have you made?'

'Friday's will be the thirteenth.'

She shook her head. 'That's an omen. Forget my section this Friday – we're just not ready to go.'

'You've been warned to be ready to go whenever we call you!' Then abruptly his voice softened, he gestured an awkward apology. 'I'm sorry. But it is orders. There is a ship at Lerici, near La Spezia. We've had to forget Bari and Brindisi for a while – it will mean a longer journey by sea, but it can't be helped. The British are checking every boat that goes in and out of Bari and Brindisi.'

'But why do we have to go at such short notice?'

'The ship was to have been filled by a section from the Displaced Persons camp near Graz –' He smiled again, the smile uglier than he meant it to be. 'Did your family own that town?'

She sighed. 'Ben, that joke isn't funny any more. We sold it to the Turks, at a discount, some time in the 17th century –'

'Now you're pulling my leg –' He was still smiling, but he looked uncertain. He felt the disparity in their ages, women were always so much older than men; even more he felt the difference of class, a feeling he despised in himself. He had thought the years in the concentration camp had eliminated all that from his thinking, but the egalitarianism of that wholesale despair was already fading, as if all memory, good and bad, had to be erased.

He became the *Bricha* man again, the underground contact man: it gave him more protection. 'The British must suspect something at Graz. They've alerted the Americans, who usually don't care, and now they're watching the camp like hawks. It is going to be tougher and tougher for us to get you to Palestine.'

Palestine: six years ago she had not known the country still existed outside the pages of the Bible. The geography of her life and thoughts did not encompass backwaters of the world; Palestine was as remote as Patagonia, places in an atlas that she never opened. *Bricha* men, more persuasive talkers than Ben Keppel, had turned her embittered eyes to the south. Six

13

years ago she would have laughed at the suggestion that she would be a volunteer to help build a new nation. But it was less than six years ago that she had seen trust, which had been her only religion, crumble and fall apart like foul flesh. The *Bricha* men, some of whom had been betrayed in the same soul-destroying way, had told her that, in the new postwar world, trust could only be found in a brand-new country.

'We're gathering groups from wherever we can,' said Keppel. 'The ship can't be allowed to sail half-empty. It costs too much, takes so much time and effort.'

She did not bother to ask how much money, time and effort. She had never been practical-minded before the war; there had been no need, everything had been done for her. Money had been so readily available she had never felt the need of it; it had occurred to her in odd moments of reminiscing that she had never seen a bill for anything. She had lived in a fantasy world where everything was seemingly free; it had been Anna Bork who had told her that only the poor ever had to pay. Time and effort: yes, she had expended those, at the *Hochschule für Musik* and at the Opera, because she had been a dedicated singer. But even there the rewards had come just as easily as the dresses and furs and sumptuous meals that were now like the haunting dreams, caught like an infection, of some stranger's life. She had expended effort, if not time (there had been no time in Birkenau: there, her mind had lost all comprehension of that dimension) in the concentration camp; one did not survive such horror by being utterly passive. In Camp 93, among the other Displaced Persons, time and effort were also necessary for survival.

'There'll be a truck on this road at eight o'clock Friday night. A small truck, so you'll be crowded a bit.'

'We're used to it.' Did she have to remind him that none of them remembered the luxury of travelling in an uncrowded truck or bus or train? Even when the Americans had brought them here to Camp 93 there had been no attempt to make them comfortable. It was not that the Americans were unkind or thoughtless, just that the U.S. Army trucks were needed for other purposes. Such as carrying stocks to the over-stocked

PX's and ferrying the German civilian workers to their comfortable jobs in the U.S. Army camps. 'I don't think we'd know what to do if we got into a bus or truck and there was an empty seat. We'd probably call for three more people to share it.'

'I'm glad you can joke.'

'So am I, even if the jokes are poor.'

'It shows the health of your mind is improving.'

'Don't play uncle with me, Ben. You have a habit of sounding like a rabbi, not a very good one.'

'I wanted to be one, once. My grandfather was a great one. The Sage, they called him. I wanted to be like him, to know the Zohar by heart, to be able to put my finger on every truth.'

She knew very little of Jewish teaching and did not want to know. There was still a good deal of her father, the non-Jewish lapsed Catholic, in her. One lived and died and that was it: God and His truths, if He and they existed, were never known. She changed the subject abruptly: 'There is a lot of traffic on this road. Have you thought of that?'

The road ran from Garmisch Partenkirchen up through Oberammergau and then on to Augsburg; it was not the main road, but it was a route that saw more than its proper share of traffic. Villages stretched at intervals along it and the overflow of Americans from Garmisch were billeted in the village inns and requisitioned houses. The fields stretched away on either side, dark copses standing on the ridges like mourners gathered around a hillside grave, and in the distance the mountains climbed towards the sky that was Austrian. Her home sky.

Keppel moved off the verge of the road as three American trucks thundered by, and she followed him. He had been walking on the inside of her and he made no attempt to take her arm and pull her after him out of the way of the trucks. She no longer expected gallantry from any man, but occasionally she felt herself wishing some man would surprise her. But not Ben Keppel, she told herself ruefully.

'The truck will be parked in that lane up there.' He nodded off to the right. 'Just behind those trees. You'll have to walk up from the camp. In small groups, twos and threes. You should not be noticed if you separate the groups. Make it look as if you're going for an evening stroll.'

'Just to freeze us up for bed.' The sun disappeared behind alps of cloud; shadow flooded across the fields. 'It's cool even now in the middle of the day – look at the snow still on the mountains. And if we're supposed to be just going for a stroll, how do we smuggle our things out? None of us has much, but there'll be things we don't want to leave behind.'

For the first time he seemed to notice her lack of enthusiasm. 'Don't you *want* to go?'

'Of course.'

'Then why – ?'

But she was saved from further answer by the arrival of a jeep. It swung in beside them and Major Dunleavy flashed his big, wide all-American smile. 'Hi, Miss Graz. You want a lift to the camp?'

Luise looked at Keppel, but his face was blank, as stiff as she had seen it once before when they had been stopped for a routine check by the military police. Major Dunleavy, who was the Assistant Provost Marshal in Garmisch, wore no MP armband, but Corporal Martin, behind the wheel, sported his: it seemed to add muscle to his arm. Luise looked back at Dunleavy, angry at Keppel for his dangerous, youthful pigheadedness.

'Well?' Major Dunleavy was still smiling: I'd love to count just how many teeth he has, she thought. She had never met such a friendly policeman, especially a military one.

'Thank you.' She felt recklessly curious, she wanted to see how Ben Keppel would handle himself when close to the enemy. After all, beginning Friday night, she and the others of her section would be in his hands and close to the enemy for perhaps weeks on end. It was time he learned the merits of diplomacy, no matter how hypocritical he might think it was. 'This is Herr Keppel.'

Keppel sat stiffly beside her in the back of the jeep as Corporal Martin thrashed the gears and took them in a quick burst of sprayed gravel back on to the tarmac of the road. Dunleavy grinned back at them, sitting half-turned in his seat.

'Corporal Martin never drove anything but mules till he joined the army. That right, Joe? You're an old Bronx Trail muleskinner, right?'

'Right, sir.' Martin chewed on his gum, politely patient with his smart-ass officer from the boondocks of Nebraska. He was a short dark man, running to fat, who hated all authority above his own rank and had only joined the Military Police as a driver because it relieved him of all the training bullshit he had experienced when he had been in an infantry outfit. 'Those Jewish Indians – !' He shook his head at the dangers he had faced.

'Are you new to the camp?' Dunleavy said to Keppel. 'I haven't seen you before.'

'There are over three hundred people in the camp.' It was the first time Luise had heard Keppel speak English.

'Three hundred and twelve, to be exact. Or that was the count on Monday's ration list. I know them all – by sight, anyway.'

Dunleavy's smile hadn't faded, but now Luise saw the sharp gleam in the blue eyes that had nothing to do with the exposed friendly teeth below it. She had never really examined Dunleavy properly, even though he went out of his way to approach her each time he came out to the camp. Twice a week he came out, Sundays to play poker with his brother Roy, the camp director, Wednesdays on his routine check; she knew he always looked for her, but she had been indifferent towards him. Still cautious about involvement, changed completely from the gregarious girl she had been before the war, she had listened politely but with only half an ear to his easy conversation.

He had told her all about himself, with that simple talent for self-cannibalism that some Americans had; but she had not really been interested and she was not to know just how much of himself still remained concealed. He was a tall good-looking man with sandy-coloured curly hair and a friendly outgoing disposition that was all at odds, to her mind, with his occupation as a military policeman. Before the war he had been a lawyer, just starting out, in some small town in central Nebraska; the boondocks he had called it, and the term itself had been no stranger to her than the territory he came from. But he was no peasant, if indeed America had any peasants.

Keppel was aware that this American was not as bluff and simple as he looked. He always tended to treat the Americans too casually, lulled by their own casualness; he knew from experience that life in the American zone of occupation was so much easier than in the other three zones, that all Displaced Persons wished they could be moved into the 49th State, as he had heard it called. He forced an answering smile to Dunleavy's.

'I've come down from Feldafing. I'm visiting Fräulein Graz. She is my cousin.'

'Oh sure.' Dunleavy nodded agreeably, then turned to face ahead. 'I can see a resemblance.'

Luise glanced sideways at Keppel: *what does he mean by that?* Keppel frowned almost imperceptibly at her, said to the back of Dunleavy's neck, 'I've never noticed it myself, major. But then families rarely look at each other closely.'

Dunleavy didn't turn round, just let the wind of the speeding jeep snatch the words over his shoulder: 'You said it! Right, Joe? Can you describe your sister exactly?'

'No, sir,' said Corporal Martin, jaw still moving in its steady rhythm. 'I'm an only child.'

Luise, watching Dunleavy closely, saw his neck stiffen; but a moment later the full-bodied laugh whipped back between her and Keppel. Major Dunleavy, she decided, was not the sort of officer who would let himself be embarrassed in front of a couple of DP's by what she knew he would call a smart-assed enlisted man. He laughed now, but Corporal Martin would be put in his place later.

Camp 93 came into sight ahead of them. It sat in the middle of a long sloping field, the remains of an ugly harvest: a dozen lines of long huts, a parade ground with a pock-marked surface, patches of vegetable gardens, washing flapping like faded flags on clothes-lines up by the latrine block. Several posts stood at odd intervals round the perimeter, all that was left of the wire fence that had once surrounded the camp. Luise had never discovered why the occasional posts had been left standing; she had also never understood why the camp inmates had not chopped them down and used them as firewood. The posts just remained, like some shorthand reminder that though the people now in the camp had once been captive, they were no longer. Like hell, thought Luise.

Corporal Martin drove the jeep in through the gateless gateway, brought it to a halt with a jerk that threatened whiplash injury to his three passengers.

'You're improving, Joe. I managed to stay in my seat that time.'

Dunleavy, ignoring Martin's sour look, got out and helped Luise down. His manners had a natural grace about them of which he seemed to be unaware; with dim memories of the mannered politeness with which she had been treated before the war, Luise found herself looking with sudden approval at Major Dunleavy. I must be recovering, she thought.

'I want to speak with Fräulein Graz,' Dunleavy said and led her away from the jeep.

She went with him, suddenly apprehensive again, but for a different reason, feeling the firm grip of his hand on her arm. She flinched and at once he let her arm go.

'You must have left a lot of bruises on Nebraska,' she said dryly.

'I wasn't a cop then.' He looked back at the watching Keppel. 'He's not really your cousin, is he?'

Her throat went dry. 'No.'

He grinned comfortingly, but she didn't trust him. 'I know how it is – you people have to keep inventing excuses if you want to move around.' He looked directly into her face. 'Is he your boy friend? Or maybe your fiancé?'

His direct stare, the direct questions, had established a sudden atmosphere of intimacy that she had not experienced with him before. 'He is a little young for me, major.'

'He doesn't look it.'

She glanced back at Keppel, watching them like a prison guard. 'He is just someone several of us met after we were all released from Auschwitz. He's come down to visit us, that's all.

I understand it's something you Americans do all the time. Visit with each other, I mean.'

'Fräulein Graz,' he said, his smile widening; he had the most incredibly beautiful teeth she had ever seen, like some sort of insult to those he came in contact with every day, 'you and Corporal Martin have a talent for taking the mickey out of me. Only with Corporal Martin I can cut him down to size when we get back to Garmisch.'

'You can do the same with me, I'm sure.'

'I never do that to ladies. Not even back in Beef City, Nebraska. But particularly not here.' He looked around the camp, at the faces in the windows of the nearby huts, at the groups standing in the thin sunlight with that dull stare of suspicion that had become so habitual to them. 'I think the women here have been taken down enough.'

'Thank you. For all the women here.'

'You're welcome,' he said, and looked back at her, silent for a moment. She recognized his look, that of a man making up his mind about a committal of some sort. Then he said, 'Friday night –'

Her throat, which had begun to relax, tightened and dried up again. 'Yes?'

'There's a dance at the Officers' Club down in Garmisch –'

She laughed aloud with relief, saw Keppel stare at her furiously and the faces at the hut windows press against the glass till they were flattened and distorted into grimaces of disgust. Dunleavy's expression, too, had abruptly changed: he looked hurt.

'Forget it, Fräulein. I didn't think an attempt to be friendly would be so damn funny –'

She was instantly sorry for him; old simple feelings were gradually creeping back into her. Turning her back on the faces at the windows, ignoring Keppel, she put her hand on Dunleavy's arm as he turned angrily away.

'I apologize, major. I'm not used to being asked out – not by anyone. It's been so long –' Her voice trailed off.

'Fräulein Graz –' Sober-faced, Dunleavy was gently sympathetic; though he could not understand why such an attractive woman had been so neglected. He pressed her hand and out of the corner of his eye saw Keppel coming towards them. 'I'll have Corporal Martin pick you up at eight o'clock. I'll be on duty till then, but by the time you get to the club I'll be waiting there.'

Then Keppel was beside them, stiff and stern and a little pompous, like an over-age school prefect. 'Luise, the children will be waiting.' He had never called Luise by her given name; somehow he managed to make it sound more formal than *Fräulein Graz*. 'She gives them speech lessons. Some of them gave up talking when they were in the concentration camps.'

Dunleavy nodded. 'Sure, I know. I've tried to talk to some of them. For a visitor, you seem pretty well up on this camp's schedule.'

Keppel wasn't caught off guard by the casualness of the remark. 'Fräulein Graz was telling me about it when you picked us up. We have organized something like it at Feldafing.'

'Good idea. What language are you teaching them? Hebrew?'

'Why Hebrew, major? I don't believe Fräulein Graz knows any Hebrew.' Keppel was growing more relaxed, looking in control of himself. He's going to be all right, Luise thought, even though he is only a boy.

Dunleavy shrugged, still casual. 'With so many nationalities ... Still, it's your problem, isn't it? When you all get to Eretz Israel you'll need a common language.'

'Eretz Israel?' Keppel's face was blank.

'Isn't that what you call Palestine?' The two men were locked together by their unblinking stares; Keppel's habitual abrasiveness invited challenge and the American had accepted it. Then Dunleavy, without surrendering, turned away towards Luise: it was a dismissal of Keppel, as if the boy had no real interest for him. 'Well, there's my brother waiting for me. Friday night, Fräulein, eight o'clock.'

He walked away, tall and straight and confident. A conqueror's walk, she thought, though she guessed he would never think of himself as such. She watched him greet Roy, his brother, slapping the older, shorter man on the back with that open display of affection that at first she had suspected of

21

being spurious, acted out for the benefit of those like herself. She had spent too long being wary of any approach by another person, man or woman: the best defence against betrayal had been self-isolation. But the Dunleavy brothers had no reason to be suspicious of each other, and she was steadily coming to admire, even envy, their deep affection for each other.

Keppel waited till the major was out of earshot, then he spun round, came towards her. His face was so tight she could see the skull behind the flesh: Ben Keppel would always have his Auschwitz face.

'Friday night?'

She told him about Dunleavy's invitation, then said sharply, 'You didn't give me time to tell him no.'

'You looked too friendly with him!'

'Herr Keppel – ' She could see the faces still at the hut windows, staring with the frank curiosity of people who were only slowly re-learning the values and rights of privacy. 'Herr Keppel, you had better stop being so distrustful of me. Too many of you *Bricha* people are the same – you think you have a monopoly on moral strength or whatever you like to call it. I'm just as determined as you that everyone in my section will get to Palestine – or Eretz Israel or the Promised Land or whatever you like to call it. But don't start treating me like a schoolgirl!'

It was typical of him that he did not apologize, just switched his attack. 'Then why are you so reluctant to leave on Friday night?'

'Friday, Saturday, next month – it doesn't matter to me!' It was a long time since she had argued so fiercely with anyone; the ghost of the old Luise Graz was taking on flesh again. 'I don't want to be responsible for all those people – you should have nominated Anna Bork – '

He changed the subject back to Dunleavy. 'You'll have to tell the major you can't go with him Friday night. Invent some excuse.'

'Such as? Never mind – ' she said impatiently, as she saw his look. 'We lead such a gay life here, I can always find a previous engagement or something.'

'Women's sarcasm is always so much blunter than men's.'

22

'I'm surprised you know the difference.' She recognized how he felt about women. She walked away, suddenly no longer wanting to argue with this man who was such a boy. 'We'll be in that lane at eight o'clock Friday night. Just be sure the truck is there!'

She walked up towards the women's shower and latrine blocks without any sense of where she was going. Then, as she arrived outside them, she smiled to herself. In the old days, at balls, parties, the theatre, the ladies' room had always been a safe retreat from unwanted attentions. This cement blockhouse was a poor substitute for those other havens, but it had its uses other than the obvious ones. She looked back through the bunting of washing strung on the sagging lines between the latrines and the shower block, saw Keppel still staring after her. She wondered if she should go into the latrines; then she heard the harsh sound of Anna Bork's singing coming from the shower block. She was singing *White Christmas* in what passed for English, without any idea of what the words really meant; in her mind's eye Luise could see the peasant woman at work on her tub of home-made schnapps, the liquor that was as rough as her voice and produced double the headache. She did not want to bump into Anna Bork, not just now.

She skirted the block and went on up the slope behind the camp. She drew her coat around her, wondering how it would protect her against the cold of the mountains when they began their trek. It had once been a very good coat, thick warm camel-hair with a Stone and Blythe label inside the collar. Before the war she had bought most of her clothes at that same store on Kärntnerstrasse. Stone and Blythe's specialized in English goods and Luise, apart from being the daughter of a passionate Anglophile, did what all discerning Viennese did, bought English goods because they were the best and because buying them was an advertisement for one's own good taste and judgement. Clothing for the DP's had been levied from the Germans and Austrians at first, before the UNRRA parcels had begun arriving from overseas with the cast-offs of those who had had a better-dressed war. Luise remembered her bitter cynicism when she and the other DP's had lined up for the distribution of the clothing; but she also remembered with a certain disgust at herself how she had raced with the others to pick over the clothing and how she had fought another woman for this particular coat and had won. She thrust her hands deep into the pockets of the coat, grateful now to the unknown woman who had shopped at Stone and Blythe's. Sometimes she wondered if the coat had once belonged to someone she had called a friend, one of those she had trusted.

She felt a chill, from the wind, from the past, she was not sure which. She turned and looked up towards the distant mountains, the borders of what had once been home. Vienna was less than three hundred miles away as the bombers had flown; a day's journey if she wanted to go by train. But she knew she would never go back, not a second time.

She had gone back to the city three months after she had been released from Birkenau. The Russians had given her papers for travelling; she had chosen to go back to Vienna because the Russians would not let her choose anywhere else. She had not known what to expect, but she had not been prepared for the ruins that she had seen; she had loved the city, with its parks and baroque palaces and rearing statues, and she had wept at how it had been smashed. But more than the city was in ruins; a society had been smashed. She had seen it falling apart, torn not by bombs but its own selfishness and lack of principles, before she had been carted off to Auschwitz. Franz Komer had been part of that society, the first and so far the only love of her life.

She had spent only a week in the city, aware all the time of the disapproving ghosts of her father and mother. She had made discreet enquiries about Franz, learned that he had been killed in the Luftwaffe, been surprised that she had felt nothing, neither grief nor satisfaction. She had enquired about relatives and friends, but she had not sought any of them out.

All her mother's relatives, the Jews, were dead or missing. Her father's relatives, the non-Jews, had survived; but she no longer thought of herself as related to them. They had chosen to live with the Nazis; they, like Franz Komer, had betrayed her when she had trusted them. In her kinder moments there were some she could not blame, the older folk who had left it too late to fight; even in the concentration camp she had seen the lengths to which some people went to survive. But she had hoped there might have been just one among her friends and relatives who might have suffered for his principles; but there had been none. Her father had died for his principles and nothing more, a hero to his daughter and a fool to those who had turned their backs on him.

She continued to look towards the mountains, the border to the past. She had stayed in Vienna a week, then left it and moved out to Feldafing, wanting nothing more than to be lost in anonymity while she found another road to the future. She had come here to Camp 93 three months ago, having at last decided upon the road she would take. Friday night it would lead over those mountains, south to Eretz Israel.

2

Beyond the mountains, beyond the Inn valley and in the mountains that were the Austrian border to Italy, Karl Besser sat in the small cluttered room that was his surgery and looked across his desk at the police sergeant who had come up from Innsbruck on his ancient motorcycle and sidecar.

'Dr Halder –'

Besser had become accustomed to his new name, responding to it as a reflex action. He had never thought of himself as a criminal and it amused him to think that all along he had had latent talents, at least as far as being able to assume a new identity with almost the same ease as some of the actors he had seen in the repertory companies that had come to Würzburg before the war.

'Dr Halder, we have a message from your friends. You are to be ready to leave Friday night.'

Besser felt a surge of excitement, got up and began to move about the room. 'At last! Jesus Christ, Pohl, you don't know how much I've been waiting for this!'

Pohl was a long-faced man who had had a wartime toothbrush moustache which had now been replaced by a more politically discreet walrus growth; by some freak chance the new growth was lighter than the old, so that the shadow of his past adornment was there under his long nose like a dark political birthmark. He had come back from a prisoner-of-war camp, convinced still that *Der Fuehrer* would have given them all a better world, and taken up his old rank of sergeant in the Innsbruck police. His superiors, conscious of the need to show the Occupying Powers that, for the time being, they were not going to favour Nazis and ex-Nazis, passed him over for promotion to higher rank. In return he had decided to contribute what he could to the small secret war that was still going on.

'I wish I could be going with you, Herr Doctor. South America – I have been reading about the Argentine – it sounds wonderful. People like us are still welcome there – they know who should have won the war – '

Besser nodded, decided against getting into a discussion on the war. He had his own opinion about who deserved to have won the war, militarily if not morally, had had that opinion since 1943 when he had begun to realize that *Der Fuehrer* should have left the running of the war to the professionals. He was a professional himself, to his manicured fingertips, and he had resented the half-trained students, classed as doctors, who had been forced on him by his SS superiors; he knew how the generals must have felt when given lessons in strategy and tactics by the Austrian ex-corporal. But he said nothing, knowing Pohl was a man who would never listen to a word said against Hitler.

'I trust the organization has been in touch with my wife?'

'Of course. You know how efficient they are.'

Besser had not learned of the existence of *Spinne*, Spider, till almost six months after the end of the war. There had been rumours in Berlin that an escape organization had been set up for the top Nazis if the worst should happen; but he had been just below the rung where those rumours could be checked as fact. Then Berlin had fallen, Hitler had committed suicide, and after that the rumours had meant nothing; he had spent the next three months trapped in the ruined city, intent only on survival. Then, risking all, tired of living like an animal in rubble caves of what had been his favourite city, he had gone back to Würzburg, to his wife and two children. He had been there three months, still undiscovered, when *Spinne* had found him, told him he was to be put on the Allies' wanted list of war criminals and that the organization would help him escape to South America if he wanted to go.

'And my wife and children?' he had asked.

The *Spinne* man, Topp, was portly, jovial, a real family man. 'Of course! Haven't you been separated from them long enough? I work for UNRRA as an interpreter – I know what it is like to see children who don't know where their parents are.'

'You work for UNRRA?'

Topp laughed at the surprise in Besser's voice. 'Half the time they don't know who they are employing. So long as we help them get the job done – ' He gestured, turned the gesture into a pat on Besser's arm. 'So long as they don't know we are also helping our own.'

'When do I go?'

'At once, tomorrow. Your wife and children will follow in a week – they will meet you in Italy, but I don't know exactly where. Nobody but those at the very top know the exact route our friends take. That way the underground route remains safe.'

'Where will I be picked up?'

'You will be telephoned tomorrow afternoon at four o'clock sharp and given your instructions.' Topp stood up. 'You don't have to worry any further, Herr Doctor. We pride ourselves on our efficiency. As far as I know, we haven't failed to get every one of our friends to their destination. Good luck. Heil Hitler!'

Besser had given a half-hearted return to the salute, wondering why they should be bothering to salute a leader who had taken the easy way out and left them to carry on the struggle. 'Heil Hitler. Tomorrow night then?'

'Without fail.'

But for once there had been something wrong with *Spinne's*

27

efficiency. The truck that had been taking him from Würzburg to the first port of call on the main road to Stuttgart had lost its way; the ports of call were only forty miles apart, but somehow the driver had managed to get himself lost. They had driven right into a military road block, the driver had panicked and tried to crash his way through, and Besser, one of four SS men in the truck, had been the only one to escape. There had been a thick fog that night and Besser, thankful for it at the moment the truck had tipped over and he had been flung out unhurt and was able to stagger away into the enshrouding mist, had later wondered why *Spinne* had not postponed the escape because of the weather. Later still he had told himself he should not have wondered: it was a German failing not to be able to change a plan once it had been put into operation. Improvisation seemed beyond the talents of his countrymen.

But not of himself. He had had no idea where the next port of call was; he had learned that no fugitive was ever told his next immediate destination and the people who ran each *Anlaufstelle* knew only the location of the previous port of call and the next, and never mentioned either to the transients they handled. But he knew that the truck had been heading south, that his embarkation point for South America was somewhere in Italy; that meant going through Austria and he knew that, pro rata, there were more Nazi sympathisers in that country than in the whole of Germany. If he could get into Austria he felt sure he could find someone who would hide him till he contacted *Spinne* again. Now that he was on the Wanted list he knew it would be suicidal to go back home.

He had made it to Austria with ridiculous ease. The Americans really were the most casual military personnel; one wondered how they had managed to be so successful in their wars. They had even given him lifts in their trucks when, daring to risk their casualness, he had asked them if they were going his way. Two days after being thrown out of the truck north of Stuttgart, he had walked into Innsbruck and the first man he had spoken to had been Police Sergeant Pohl.

He had seen the shadow of the old moustache hidden in the new one and he had taken another risk. The toothbrush moustache had long been a European fashion, but after Hitler had come to power it had blossomed fully among the lower echelons of his admirers. Pohl could have been just an apolitical devotee of the fashion or even an admirer of Charlie Chaplin. But Besser somehow felt safer in Austria than he had in his own country, felt sure that the police sergeant would not want to create a fuss by arresting a German for asking suspicious questions.

'Sergeant, I am looking for some friends –'

'Who isn't?' said Pohl dolefully. 'What name?'

'Ah, that's the difficulty. So many people have had to change their names – ' He saw the shift of focus in Pohl's gaze and at once knew he was safe. 'Circumstances beyond their control affect people – all they want is a quiet life –'

'Who doesn't?' said Pohl, still doleful but with an interested eye cocked at the big handsome German. 'Would you care for some coffee, Herr – ?'

'Halder,' said Besser, taking for the first time the name on the forged papers in his pocket. 'Dr Halder.'

'A medical man? Good. We can always find you a place in one of our villages while we look for your friends – doctors are always welcome –'

Two days later Besser was installed in a house in Kalburg, a village two miles off the Brenner Pass above Innsbruck. He had two rooms in the home of the Fricks, a dour elderly couple who never asked questions and did not object when Besser, to fill in his time, started to take in patients. The village had no doctor and the villagers were pleased at the luxury that had been presented to them; the thought of the long haul down to Innsbruck to see a doctor had, more than pills and prescriptions, kept them healthy. Now, all of a sudden, they discovered aches, pains and illnesses that had been ignored for years. Besser was kept busy and soon was making more than enough money for his needs. A French sergeant came up from Occupation Zone headquarters in Innsbruck, checked his papers perfunctorily, then went back to Innsbruck and left him alone. Then Besser sent word to *Spinne* that he was willing to try again for South America.

Sergeant Pohl had known nothing of *Spinne* when he had first met Besser. 'Spider? What is that?'

By now Besser trusted Pohl: the war would never be over for the stolid, unhurried policeman. 'Do you believe in organization, Pohl?'

'Of course. Nothing runs well without it. If *Der Fuehrer* had been allowed –'

'Exactly!' Besser had a booming voice that he had difficulty in controlling; it was not a voice for conspiracy. Forever restless, he had large gestures that kept his arms moving all the time, so that his listeners tended to sit well back from him for fear of having a point underlined by a bruise. Everything about him made him conspicuous, a poor customer for any organization that dealt in secrecy. 'It was pure bad luck, not bad organization, that –' He almost said *lost us the war*; he substituted a big vague gesture for the words. Pohl nodded, catching the meaning, if it was the wrong one. 'The war isn't over, Pohl. This is a – an intermission, a breathing space while we re-gather our forces –'

He was talking idiocies, he knew, with their leaders dead, missing or on trial in Nuremberg. But Pohl stamped a foot, an emphatic gesture of agreement, in the thin frozen snow. They had walked up from the village on this Sunday morning to the shallow narrow valley where a small frozen lake, little more than a large pond, lay like a white marble piazza before a steeply rising cathedral of dark pines on the opposite slope. A deer picked its delicate way across the snow, leaving a line of punctuation marks behind it, and disappeared into a stand of trees. Sunlight moved in patches across the whiteness; when it reached the lake both men had to turn away from it, blinded by the glare. Silence lay around them, to be felt as much as the cold air; conversation hung as balloons of mist in front of their mouths. Pohl wished they had remained in the doctor's warm surgery, but he had guessed the doctor had something to confide in him and he hadn't demurred when the walk had been suggested. He knew that Besser had had the wartime rank of major and he had always been very conscious of rank.

'What are you trying to tell me, Dr Halder?'

'About an organization called *Spinne*!' Besser took the plunge; the words exploded like smoke from his lips. He went on to explain what *Spinne* did, as far as he knew; and saw Pohl grow visibly warmer, less hunched against the cold. Excitement glimmered in the policeman's eyes. 'They could use someone like you, Pohl –'

Pohl shrugged modestly. 'Anything I can do –'

'I can't go back into Germany, to my home – I might be recognized.'

Besser had never fully confided in Pohl. The policeman only knew that he was a Nazi officer; that he had been an SS man engaged in medical research at Auschwitz, at the clinic at Sonnenstein and finally at the headquarters of T4, the euthanasia experts, in Berlin, was something that Pohl did not need to know. The SS had been the Nazi élite, but Besser had come to realize that the élite are not necessarily the most admired, even by fanatics in the cause.

'They have a file on me, perhaps even photographs. The risk is too great. But I have to get in touch with my wife – she will know whom to contact. Would you go to Würzburg for me, Pohl? If my wife gets in touch with *Spinne*, I'll have her recommend that you be their contact man here in Innsbruck. It will give you something to do, Pohl, besides keeping the peace for our enemies.'

'I'll be proud to, Herr Doctor.' Down in the village the church bells began to toll, the sound carrying clearly on the thin still air. 'It's time for Mass. Are you coming?'

'Of course,' said Besser, who was a Lutheran and hadn't been in a church in twenty years before coming to Kalburg. He had soon discovered the village was staunchly Catholic and he had decided the safest thing was not to be the odd man out. In church he prayed as long and devoutly as the best of them; or appeared to. A man on his knees was always hard to read. 'Pray that I'll soon be on my way to South America, Pohl.'

'It is time the Lord answered some of our prayers,' said Pohl with a touch of bitterness. 'One sometimes wonders whose side He is on.'

'The English have always considered Him one of themselves.

And the Americans think of themselves as first cousins to Him. Only the French and the Russians never take Him to war with them.'

Pohl nodded glumly, bemused by the political whims of God.

The following weekend Pohl took two days' leave and went to Würzburg. He found Frau Besser, having made no comment when Dr Halder had told him his wife was living under an assumed name; it didn't matter to Pohl which was the assumed name, he had become used to such camouflage in the months he had been back from the war and blamed no one for using it. He had liked Frau Besser, a good-looking red-headed woman who might have been plump had she been content instead of worried, and he had admired the two boys, fine tow-headed children such as he had seen so often in pictures with *Der Fuehrer*. Ilse Besser had wept with happiness when Pohl had told her he had come with a message from her husband; in the two months Karl had been gone she had hardly slept since the *Spinne* man had come to tell her that the escape plan had gone wrong and her husband was missing. When she had recovered, with Pohl sitting awkwardly by, rendered useless as usual by a woman's tears, she had phoned the number Herr Topp had left with her. He had arrived within half an hour, talked to Pohl, been convinced that he could be trusted, then given the policeman a name and address to contact in Innsbruck. Pohl had not been able to contain his shock, nor his chagrin that he was not going to be *Spinne's* sole contact man in his home town.

'But he lives next door to me! He works in the post office – '

'We have our men in the most strategic places, sergeant. And they don't advertise. Why should you have known that he worked for us?'

Pohl returned to Innsbruck, still put out that he was going to have to work under a man he considered inferior to himself. After all, a postal worker was a nobody compared to a police sergeant; though Fischer had been a sergeant in the SS, a rank Pohl couldn't believe he had achieved without bribery. He went to the house next door to his own and asked Fischer to go for a walk with him. They caught the bus that went up the Brenner, then walked the two miles up the thick snow-banked road to Kalburg. Fischer waited on the outskirts of the village while Pohl went in and brought out Besser. Then the three men walked back down to the main Brenner road.

'We can't get you a passage immediately. The damned English are conducting another one of their blitzes.' Fischer was a short thin man who smiled at everything with great buck teeth; he smiled now at his use of the word *blitz*. 'They have a nice sense of humour, the way they misuse our words.'

'Yes,' said Pohl, who had no sense of humour at all.

But Besser laughed. 'I can wait, Herr Fischer. Another few weeks –'

'It may be longer than that. We are examining a new route. I don't know the details – I don't even know what the old route was.' He looked at Pohl, who seemed disappointed. 'We're just cogs, Pohl, nothing more. What we don't know we can't divulge, if ever we are picked up.'

'Don't you know where our headquarters are?'

'Yes.' Fischer knew only that *Spinne's* headquarters were in Gmunden, not far from Salzburg, but he did not know the exact address and he did not know the names of the men who ran the headquarters. 'But only one of us is allowed to know it, Pohl.'

Besser sensed the friction that was growing on the part of Pohl, quickly changed the way the conversation was going. 'What about my wife and children?'

'They'll probably be moved first. We'll have them waiting for you in Italy.'

'How do you get them there?'

Fischer's teeth came out like big hunks of bone in his red-nosed face. 'Someone will take them across the border as his family, with forged papers. Perhaps me, perhaps even Pohl here. Someone who isn't on the Wanted list.' Fischer was as polite as Pohl had been: he didn't ask why Besser was on the list. 'Getting your family down there will be the easiest part. But we'll get you through, too, Dr Halder. But you'll have to be patient.'

And now on this March morning Pohl had ridden up on his

33

motorbike to Kalburg, bringing the news that Besser was once again to start on his way to South America.

'Will you miss the Fatherland, Herr Doctor?'

'Not really. Not as it is now. Perhaps some time in the future – ' Besser's voice quietened; he stood still as he contemplated the years ahead. 'One can't say goodbye to it forever, Pohl. That would be treason, wouldn't it?'

'Perhaps,' said Pohl, doleful again, envious of the doctor and his coming adventure. The last two weeks he had been busy, helping Fischer pass through three men who had come down the *Spinne* route; but instead of being excited as he had expected to be, he had only envied the men and the opportunities that lay ahead of them in the lush atmosphere of South America. 'Perhaps the Fatherland *is* dead – at least for your lifetime and mine. You have read the newspapers – they are stripping the country bare, the Russians, the English, the French. The Americans would be doing it, too, except they have so much back in their own country they wouldn't know what to do with anything extra. Reparations, they call it. Looting, more like it.'

'We'll survive, Pohl.' Besser could not quite adjust to Pohl's referring to the Fatherland; he never really thought of Austrians as Germans. He became aware of the Fricks moving about in the house, decided that he and Pohl, now they were getting down to specifics, had better take their conspiracy outside. 'I think we should go for a ride.'

He fitted his bulk into Pohl's sidecar and they chugged down the village road till they reached the Brenner road. Occasionally the motorbike skidded on the hard snow and Besser wondered what the roads would be like Friday night. He did not want to be in another truck that overturned: his luck might not be so good the next time. When they reached the road junction he got stiffly out of the sidecar, stamped his feet so that he could feel them again.

'We can talk safely here. I trust the Fricks, but as Herr Fischer said, the less people know, the better.'

Pohl outlined the plan for Friday night. 'A French army truck will meet you here at eleven o'clock. Don't worry,' he

34

said as he saw Besser's eyebrows go up, 'it will be driven by one of our men. Its trip is perfectly legitimate – it is going down to Bolzano with mail and other things for the French liaison unit there. You'll have papers that say you are a French civilian doctor, from Alsace, attached to UNRRA. Can you speak French?'

'Schoolboy French, that's all.'

'Then Fischer suggests you have a sore throat or something, say as little as possible. You can pretend to be asleep. It will be midnight by the time you get to the border check post – the guards shouldn't want to be out in the cold too long. If your papers are in order, Fischer says they rarely bother to check anyone. In any case, they are looking for Jews and black marketeers, not us. Once you are over the border the driver will not take the direct route to Bolzano, but will take you first to Merano. That's your next stop.'

'What about my family?'

'I understand they are already waiting for you in Merano. Fischer took them through last night. Good luck, Dr Halder. We probably shan't ever meet again.'

The two men were shaking hands when the truck, with its French army markings, came grumbling up the hill, slap-slapped by them on the wet tarmac of the main road and went on up round a bend of the pass. In the back of it, hunched together under the tarpaulin roof, their white faces staring back down the road like so many blank discs, were twenty or thirty young boys. The sight was too familiar, Besser had seen it so often: he felt a shiver run through him, as if he had seen a truck full of ghosts go by.

'Who are they?' For once his voice was just a whisper.

'Jews,' said Pohl.

'*Jews?*'

Pohl noticed the strained note in Besser's voice, mistook it for just surprise. 'Surprises you, doesn't it? Me, too, when I first heard of it. There's a village up there, Rennwald, that's made them welcome. They've set up some sort of farm for Jewish kids, teaching them how to farm, raise cattle, things like that. They feed themselves or buy from the villagers, so the French don't bother them. The French aren't generous with the rations they dole out to the DP's – they never were generous to anyone but their own. And even then they think twice before they give.'

Besser wasn't interested in the French and their lack of generosity. 'Who looks after those Jewish boys?'

'Some older Jews. An Austrian is in charge, but there are a few Poles there, too. It's the locals I don't like, welcoming them like that into the village. The Burgermeister there says it is a matter of conscience for what happened in the concentration camps. I don't see what it has to do with *our* conscience. We Austrians didn't build the camps. No offence, Herr Doctor.' Pohl had suddenly seceded from the Fatherland.

Besser shook his head, dismissing the gaffe as of no importance. He knew the number of Austrians who had volunteered as guards and administrators to the camps; Pohl seemed to have forgotten that Hitler himself had been an Austrian. He continued to stare up the road, saw the truck emerge again at another bend in the road. A flutter of hands appeared at the back of the truck, like a flock of birds testing their wings before being released. Without his realizing it, Besser brought his own hand up and waved back.

'You don't mind the Jews?' Pohl said and for the first time since they had met gave Besser a sour unfriendly look.

'Not any more,' said Besser. 'They're all part of the past now.'

3

Rudolph Graz died from a stray bullet from a gun that was never identified. Had the gun been identified, its user would never have been charged with any offence, except had its user been a Jew, and there were few, if any, Jews roaming the streets of Vienna with a gun on Kristallnacht, November 9, 1938. The pogrom ordered by Reinhard Heydrich had that night destroyed all the synagogues in Germany and Austria, and Jewish stores were looted and had their windows smashed. The streets were covered in broken glass, glistening like the crystal of an early frost, and the Nazis ran riot in a madness that told those Jews who had no illusions that their fate was being written that night in shards of glass on the cobblestones and tarmac of countless streets in the new Reich. Rudolph Graz, a non-Jew, had read the message six months before when the Anschluss had brought Hitler back to Vienna as a conqueror, and he had not needed the fury of a pogrom to tell him what could happen to his wife and perhaps to his daughter.

On the morning of November 9 he heard rumours. He checked them with a friend he had in the police department, then he left his office and hurried home to the apartment on Esteplatz in the Third District. Luise would remember the almost hysterical reaction of her mother, who refused to believe that her frivolous social world might come to an end; but Rudolph Graz, normally a calm man, had been fiercely adamant. The Vuitton luggage had been brought out and hastily packed. Luise had looked at it and thought of other, unhurried departures, to Waldgarten, St Moritz, Nice, always on the same dates every year. For the first time she caught the chill of her father's distraction, knew that something besides her mother's tight brittle world was coming to an end. Fifteen minutes later they were driving out of the city, heading east towards Bratislava and the country estate of Ruth Graz's parents. Rudolph himself did not go with them and they never saw him alive again.

He was found next morning on the cracked pond of glass outside a Jewish store. The police identified him from his papers and took him home. Werner, the butler, telephoned Waldgarten with the news.

Luise and her mother came back to Vienna that day. Luise's grandfather, Friedrich Wald, wanted to go with them; it was Luise, suddenly older and cautious overnight, who insisted he and Grandmama Hedy should stay at Waldgarten. When Luise and Ruth reached the apartment on Esteplatz, Franz Komer was waiting for them.

'It might have been better if you had stayed at Waldgarten.' Franz was twenty-three, very tall, very handsome, too dashing-looking for the banker that he was expected to become. Luise had had a schoolgirl's crush on him and the romance, nurtured by Ruth Graz, green-fingered in the garden of beneficial marriage, had flowered six months ago into an engagement. But the ring on her finger, like some key, had begun to open up Luise's mind to the man she was to marry. She had begun to detect flaws in him, one of them an almost abject obedience to his father, the head of the family banking firm. 'My father thinks your father was foolish to stay here in Vienna – '

'Father is dead.' The shock of her father's death had frozen Luise's natural vivacity; her cold rebuke made Franz rear back, his chin going up to make him look even taller. 'Don't insult him.'

'I didn't mean to do anything like that – ' Franz was aware of the quietness of the big apartment, a quietness that was somehow ominous; he found himself waiting for a knock on the front door. 'My father thought you and your mother should go to London for a while, till things quieten down.'

'Franz, you and your father are *frightened*! Why? Because of us?'

'We'll talk about it after the funeral.' He pressed her shoulders, but all at once his embrace had become tentative; she could almost feel him moving away from her, dissociating the Komers from herself and her mother. Numbed suddenly by his cowardice she dimly heard him say, 'Father and Mother send their condolences – '

He came to the funeral and stood beside her, but all the time he kept glancing towards the four men in leather coats standing at the side of the church. The men, faces expressionless, said nothing and made no attempt to interfere as the few brave mourners filed out.

Outside the church Franz whispered to her as she helped her grief-stricken mother into the car. 'I'll come to your place this evening. I must go now – '

'I thought I could trust you, Franz.'

He looked at her, puzzled, bridling a little. But she got into the car, nodded to the driver and had him close the door on Franz. She did not look back as they drove away.

Franz did not come that evening as he had promised. She

38

waited for him, no longer in love with him but wanting to believe in him; she looked for some rock to lean on, but Franz was not the man for it. He telephoned two days later; but Luise was out and she did not return his call. After that she did not hear from him again.

Friedrich Wald had closed up the big house on Prinz Eugen Strasse, close by the Rothschild Palais, shut down the three country houses and he and Hedy had moved into the smaller, but still grand Graz apartment with Ruth and Luise. He accepted the advice of Rudolph's cousins and uncles and offered the use of the house on Prinz Eugen Strasse and the three country estates to the government; he received a stiffly formal letter of acceptance, distinguished by the lack of any mention of thanks, and he and his family never saw the country estates again. Sometimes he would go for a walk with Luise and they would pass the house on Prinz Eugen Strasse, but they never stopped to look at it and once Luise, aware that the old man had stumbled, had seen that her grandfather had his eyes closed as they went by the house. They never enquired what use the government was making of the house or the estates. But they knew that the Rothschild Palais was the headquarters of the Vienna Agency for Jewish Emigration under the administration of an SS officer named Eichmann.

Luise went back to the Opera, to the chorus and understudying. She knew her voice was good and so did her teachers and the management; with her looks and talent it was only a matter of time before she would be moved up to at first small, then larger roles. She buried herself in study and practice, went on with her Italian language course; she began to feel safe again, sure now that the Nazis were no longer interested in her and her mother and her grandparents. At the end of August, at a pre-season charity performance, she was given her first featured role, that of Nannetta in *Falstaff*. Afterwards her grandfather gave a supper party at the Three Hussars to celebrate, the first time in almost twelve months that he and Hedy had dressed up and made themselves conspicuous in public. The party went off without a hitch, old friends and acquaintances crossing the gay, chatter-filled room to offer their congratulations to Luise. Several of the men were in uniform, the reserve having been called up, and somehow their uniforms, instead of being a sobering note, seemed to suggest the gaiety of an older, happier Vienna, a time when Friedrich and Hedy had been young and the old Emperor had smiled on them as they had danced at State balls.

Franz Komer, operatically resplendent in dress uniform, had stopped by their table. 'I was there tonight, Luise. You were wonderful.'

She was no longer in love with him; it was so easy to be cool and casual. 'I'm a year older than a year ago, Franz. It makes a difference. You look splendid in your uniform. Your father must be proud of you.'

Franz was not slow-witted; he knew when a knife was being drawn across his throat. He bowed stiffly, smiled just as stiffly. 'Good luck with your career, Luise.'

'And with yours,' she said. 'Whatever it may be.'

Franz moved away and Ruth Graz, stepping out of character for the moment, for once being serious at a party, said, 'We have only ourselves to rely upon now, darling.'

'Yes,' said Luise and kissed her mother, suddenly on the verge of tears for the frivolous woman who had turned a corner and faced reality.

They all went home to the apartment, riding close together in laughter and family warmth. Friedrich kissed his daughter and granddaughter goodnight, went to bed and never woke up. He died in his sleep, in happiness that would not have lasted had he lived another two weeks.

War broke out and the lights, and the light, of Vienna went out. Luise continued to work at the Opera, but it seemed a hopeless, empty career now. The three women, their servants called up or deserting them because it was no longer safe to work for Jews, went on living in the huge apartment. Somehow the three of them, brought up in a tradition that did not approve of women of their class learning a servant's job, learned and adapted. They were learning, if nothing else, how to survive.

On a beautiful sunny autumn day in October the SS men from the Agency for Jewish Emigration, with orders signed by an officer named Eichmann, came for Hedy Wald and Ruth Graz. No, they did not want Luise Graz. She was only half-Jewish and her father's family had spoken to higher authority on her behalf; they were prepared to certify that she had never practised the Jewish religion and was a good Catholic like themselves. But none of the Graz family appeared at the apartment, though Luise tried to call them; their secretaries or their servants, voices as impersonal as those of robots, said that their masters or their mistresses 'unfortunately, Fräulein, are not available just now.'

'I am going with my mother and my grandmother,' she told the SS men. 'You must take me, too.'

Ruth and Hedy both argued fiercely with her even while they wept with fear, and even the SS men tried to dissuade her. 'Fräulein, we have no orders that cover your deportation. We can't take you without the proper orders.'

'Then go and get them!' She tried not to sound like a bad actress, but she was learning that real life drama often looks like bad theatre.

One of the junior SS men went away and the three women sat and argued whether they should be separated. Both Ruth and Hedy continued to weep, afraid for her more now than for themselves; but Luise was adamant. She didn't mention it, but she knew what her dead father would have wanted her to do. He might have pleaded with her to stay, but in the end he would have understood that she had to go with her mother and grandmother.

She looked at the two SS men who had remained. 'My mother and grandmother are Jewish, so I, too, am Jewish. You have heard my confession. Isn't that enough?'

The SS men said nothing, turned away and went wandering through the huge apartment, feeding their hatred of the Jewish pigs who could live so well. Then the young SS man came back, a piece of paper in his hand.

'She goes with them. The truck is downstairs.'

The truck took them to a long train standing in the shunting yards. They were locked in one of the coaches, pushed in against the thick mass of humanity that already packed it. Next day the train, the coaches still locked, the people in them feeding only on what little food they had been able to grab and bring with them, left for Lodz in Poland. The train was shunted and side-tracked to make way for troop trains and it took ten days to make the 350 miles journey to Lodz. Scores of people died on the way, among them Hedy Wald.

Luise and her mother, numbed by grief and exhaustion, spent the next two days sitting in the open with the rest of the survivors, fed only on soup and bread and the wish that their fate would soon be known. Some groups were marched off on the first day; the word was that they were the lucky ones, being sent to the ghetto in Lodz. Then Luise and Ruth, along with all the women in what remained of the frightened miserable crowd, were bundled back on to another train, this time into cattle trucks. When this second train finally halted and they were ordered to get down, they found themselves standing beside a railway track that ran between two large depressing-looking camps in the middle of a vast expanse of marshland. Two words spread through the silent frightened groups of women, Auschwitz and Birkenau: but neither word meant anything to the Jewish women of Vienna.

The train drew away, no longer blocking the view, and the women looked across the track at the larger camp: that was Auschwitz, one of the less brutal guards told them, the men's labour camp. The one behind them, 'your new home and you'd better get used to it', was Birkenau, the women's camp.

Luise and Ruth clung to each other as they were herded to-wards the camp. They had one suitcase between them, one of the Vuitton bags that had known better places than Birkenau. They came to a table on the station platform where three SS guards sat; behind them stood a tall handsome SS officer. The line approached the table and only when they were twenty yards from it did Luise notice that the line was being separated, some being sent to the right, some to the left. She was only five yards from the table, only two women in front of herself and her mother when she saw that those women going to the right were all elderly, middle-aged or infirm. She clung to her mother's hand, felt the desperate panic in the fingers held in her own: Ruth had also seen how the women were being divided.

Then they were standing before the table. The officer looked at them, then at the expensive suitcase that stood between them. 'Empty the suitcase,' he said, and tapped one of the guards on the shoulder. The guard got up, came round the table, emptied the contents of the suitcase on to the ground in front of Luise and Ruth, and took the case back to the officer. The officer looked at it, nodded his head appreciatively and gestured to the guard to put it down beside him. Then he looked at the Graz women.

'We don't want the older one,' he said. 'The girl, yes.'

Ruth screamed, tried to cling to Luise; but guards came up and roughly separated them. Ruth, still screaming for Luise, was dragged away. The last sight Luise ever had of her mother was that of Ruth, head twisted back over her shoulder as the guard brutally pushed her along, calling her daughter's name with an anguish that would forever echo in Luise's memory. She learned the next day, on the grapevine that ran through the camp, that her mother and all the other women who had been sent on the line to the right had gone straight to the gas chambers.

She also learned the name of the officer who had sent her mother to her death: *Hauptsturmfuehrer* Karl Besser. He left Auschwitz and Birkenau two days later and she saw him boarding the train, the Vuitton suitcase among his luggage. She stopped for a moment, staring across the distance between them; but Captain Besser, saying goodbye to his back-slapping officer friends, did not look in her direction. Then she was hit hard in the back by one of the women guards, told to keep moving. She walked on, passed inside another fence and went to work in the squat ugly factory that housed the Union Fuse Company, a Krupp subsidiary.

She remained there till the end of the war, mixing and packing high explosives to be used against the forces that, though it was only a footnote to the Allied campaign strategy, were fighting to release them. She never forgot her last sight of her mother being taken away to the gas chamber. But gradually the face and name of *Hauptsturmfuehrer* Besser faded into the back of her mind as she concentrated only on survival.

43

Anna Bork had been in Birkenau, but had not worked in the explosives factory. In all the time they had been together in the concentration camp Luise could not remember ever having exchanged one word with the Czech woman. Their relationship, one of strong antagonism on the part of Anna and of mild indifference on the part of Luise, had only started when they arrived at Camp 93. Luise at first could not understand why the Bork woman had taken such a strong dislike to her. It was David Weill who had tried to explain it to her.

'She resents what you once had.'

It was impossible to guess at Weill's age, but Luise always thought of him as old. He had been a professor of history at Cracow University, devoted to the past and an avoidance of the present; moved to the Warsaw ghetto he had kept to himself and somehow survived. After the ghetto uprising in April 1943 he had been transferred to Auschwitz; the fortunate stroke of some SS pen sent him there instead of to Treblinka and extermination. At Auschwitz fortune had again favoured him: he had been classed as fit to work. And worked he had, determined now to stay alive; he had found a physical strength in himself that he had too long denied. But the effort of surviving, the late calling on reserves of strength that had been too long unused, had their effect. In the months after release from Auschwitz he suddenly aged; his face remained thin and lined, his hair abruptly turned white, he walked with a stoop. He was only fifty-one.

'Didn't you know her family worked for your grandparents?'

Luise shook her head. 'My grandparents, both sides of them, had so many people working for them. Which ones?'

'The ones who had the estate at – Waldgarten, was it?'

'But my grandparents treated everyone who worked for them so well!'

'Anna doesn't think so. She told me stories – ' He shook his white head, not wanting to say any more.

'Why should she tell *you* stories?'

He patted his white head with a thin hand. 'Everyone wants to confide in me – *this* makes them think I must be a wise old man. I'm not really. Neither old nor wise. But even you are confiding in me in a way, aren't you?'

Luise smiled admittance. 'You invite confidences, Herr Professor. You shouldn't look so – so receptive.'

He smiled his twisted smile that hid his broken teeth, fragile as paper sticks in his gums. 'You mistake the look. I'm not really receptive, just phlegmatic. When you come to know me better, you'll find I offer no advice.'

He had been right: he had offered her no advice. When she had been nominated as section leader by Anna Bork she had looked across at David Weill, but there had been no encouragement or even sympathy in the quiet dark eyes. He had raised his hand like everyone else when Anna Bork had called for a vote. Against her will, Luise had been made a leader. Even if she had become a great star in opera, the only ambition she had ever had, she would not have become a star in terms of wanting a production built around her. And now Anna Bork was building the section around her, surrounding her with people who would depend on her. Anna, with a peasant's cunning, was getting some sort of revenge for the sins of Friedrich and Hedy Wald, whatever they had been.

When Luise called the meeting of the section to discuss details of the move on Friday night, Anna Bork as usual had been the spokeswoman for the rest. 'Herr Keppel told us you are supposed to be going to a dance with Major Dunleavy on Friday night. Where do we pick you up – in Garmisch?'

Ben Keppel was not at the meeting; he had left the camp, telling Luise only that he would be back Friday night at the appointed time. Luise looked around the hut, searching for a sympathetic face. She knew that most of the people were not against her, that they wanted someone to think for them and take care of the details that the camp administration insisted upon; the few children were wholeheartedly on her side, but they had no vote. But there were some who were influenced by Anna Bork, who sometimes made Luise wonder why they hadn't voted for Anna as their leader. Luise looked at David Weill at the back of the group, but again there was no encouragement in the thin lined face. She was on her own, this was her first test of leadership.

'You don't have to worry about me, Anna.' She knew how to make her voice sharp and strong without shouting; the old singing training still had its uses. 'But isn't Friday night your night for delivery of your bathtub schnapps?'

'Perhaps she could set a match to it,' said Simon Berger. 'An explosion might cause a nice diversion.'

Everyone laughed and Anna Bork, no hypocrite, made a rude gesture.

'I shall be up in the lane with the rest of you when the truck comes at eight o'clock,' said Luise. 'In the meantime, Anna, I am putting you in charge of seeing that no one, and I mean *no one*, takes more than one suitcase with them.'

'Oh my God,' said Simon Berger, who could be as unhypocritically crude as Anna, 'you've just sterilized her.'

It had been a shrewd move on Luise's part; when she looked across at David Weill she saw the first reaction from him, a twinkle in the dark eyes. Anna Bork was the camp scrounger; she had a corner bunk in the hut and the corner was filled with the junk she had collected. It was as if, denied possessions all her life up till now, she was accumulating anything and everything that might come in useful in the new life in Palestine. She went down to Garmisch every morning to work as housemaid for one of the American officers and each day she never came back empty-handed. Given her own way, Anna would need a truck of her own to get her to Palestine.

Anna was on her feet at once. She was a sturdily built woman in her early thirties who might have been good-looking had she been allowed to live another life. She had thick red hair that, unlike Luise's, was not streaked with grey; good strong features spoiled only by the habitual scowl of her wide-lipped mouth; and a voice that rasped even when she joined in the songs that the hut group sometimes indulged in. She had a certain masculine vulgarity about her that put off the unattached men, such as Simon Berger: it was as if she had steeled herself against love or affection, as if neither emotion could ever be trusted.

'That's ridiculous! We can't get all we'll need into one suitcase – we can't land in Palestine with *nothing*! I've heard stories – the people there have only enough for themselves – '

'They can always steal from the English,' said Noah Malchek. 'You can do the same when you get there, Anna.'

Anna Bork made a noise with her lips and a gesture with her thumb. Some of the men laughed and most of the women gasped; the two Grunfeld sisters, their gentility revived as if Birkenau had never happened to them, had a slight attack of the vapours. Those women with children were glad their children were outside where they couldn't learn Anna Bork's universal sign language.

'My orders,' said Luise evenly, 'are one suitcase each, no more. There won't be room in the truck – we're going to be packed in tightly as it is. Everyone should wear as much clothing as they can – I don't know how long we are going to have to stop in the mountains before they move us on again. You're in charge of the luggage, Frau Bork. Next – '

'Do we have to go Friday night?' asked David Weill. 'It is *Shabbat* – '

'I am sorry, Herr Professor, but I'm afraid our organizers make no provision for the Sabbath. I don't think they can afford to. The war was fought on the Sabbath – it isn't over for us, not yet. Not till we land in Eretz Israel.'

She could feel the atmosphere changing, though she was not sure whether it was growing cooler or warmer; but she did know that the group now acknowledged her as their leader in deed as well as name. She was overcoming her own doubts of herself by plunging in at the deep end, the way her father had taught her to swim years ago at Nice.

'You'll be in charge of the food, Herr Professor. We shall need enough for at least twenty-four hours. No fancy stuff, because the food pack, too, has to be kept small.'

Weill stood up, smiled his twisted grin. 'At your command, Fräulein Graz. The Red Cross parcels come in again tomorrow, and perhaps I can persuade the Burgermeister that we need a little extra.'

'Don't let him suspect anything.'

'Even if he did, I don't think Herr Quill would say anything. He is sympathetic to us.'

'Balls,' said Anna Bork, who had learned a little English, of a quality that most of the other women did not understand; but Luise understood it and smiled. 'You can't trust any of them.'

'Just be careful, Herr Professor,' said Luise. 'And one thing – at my request, not my command. That sounds too much like what we are trying to leave behind us.'

'Perhaps,' said Weill, his face sobering. 'But where we are going they won't build a nation without commands. I think it is time we started getting used to obeying orders from our own kind.'

It was the first outright support she had had from him; and in it she recognized the tacit rebuke to Anna Bork. The group remained silent and still for a moment, then Michael Klein in the front row nodded. 'Herr Professor is right. If Fräulein Graz is to be our leader, then we do what she says.'

Luise looked gratefully at the short balding man whom she had never seen without either his wife or one or both of his two young girls. They had survived the war because they had escaped the concentration camps until the very last months; both Klein and his wife Hilde had worked for Zeiss before the war and their special skills had resulted in their being granted exemption from being deported to the camps in Poland. They had been employed as slave labour, working in one of the factories that produced binoculars for the Wehrmacht; they had never worked side by side nor been allowed to live together. Hilde had been allowed by the factory manager, a man who had known the Kleins when it had been no crime to be a Jew, to keep the children with her. Now, as if he were bound to them by some invisible cord that he dared not break, Michael Klein was never seen alone, was always accompanied by at least one of the family from whom he had been parted so long.

'Thank you, Herr Klein.' She knew that the others, with the

48

exception of David Weill, sometimes called each other by their given names, gradually trying to forge bonds; but to everyone she was always Fräulein Graz, and for reasons she had never really examined she had kept the formality of her relationship with the rest of them. 'The main thing now, besides getting ourselves ready, is to be sure that we don't give ourselves away to the Camp Director. From now till Friday evening we carry on just as we have ever since we got here. No change in our routine, no show of excitement – and please don't tell the children. We've waited so long for this, don't let us ruin it by showing impatience. We still have a long way to go yet to Palestine. This is only the beginning of our journey.'

The meeting broke up and Luise left the hut and went on down towards the camp gates, intending going for a walk up the road towards Oberammergau. Now she had assumed the burden of command, she wanted to be away from it, even if just for half an hour.

'Afternoon, Fräulein Graz. Not working this afternoon?'

Roy Dunleavy stood in the doorway of the office hut. He was a slighter, quieter version of his younger brother; his smile was not so brilliant, he approached the world sideways on, not frightened of it but diffident about its attitude towards him. Rejected by the U.S. Army because of a knee that tended to collapse under him occasionally, he had joined the Red Cross and there discovered, much to his own surprise, that he had a talent for both sympathy and administration, two gifts that Luise had found were too often not co-existent in social workers. At the end of the war he had transferred to the United Nations Relief and Rehabilitation Administration and soon, he had once confided to Luise, he had decided that his life's work would be spent with one of the United Nations relief organizations. Two weeks ago word had come through that he was to be promoted and transferred to a bigger job within UNRRA; and the camp inmates had wondered if they would be as fortunate with his successor as they had been with him. His one drawback as far as Luise and the others were concerned was his appalling taste in music. Right now he had the camp amplifiers blaring *Pistol Packin' Mamma*.

49

'I didn't think there was anything –'

'Only kidding, Fräulein.' Even he, the friendliest of men, never called her by her given name. Suddenly she wished for a friend, someone who would crack the shell of her. She was surprised when the image of the other Dunleavy, not the one in front of her now, sprang into her mind. Or perhaps she wanted more than a friend: she blushed at the totally unexpected thought, as if she had spoken it aloud.

'Have I offended you, Fräulein? You look – well, as if I trod on your toe or something.'

'No, Herr Dunleavy. It was just – just that I wondered if I *had* forgotten something you'd asked me to do.'

'No. There's nothing for either of us to do.' He looked around the camp, as if he felt there should be something for him to do, that he was neglecting his charges by having time on his hands. Then he looked back at her, lips twisted in the half-shy smile that never showed his teeth. 'I couldn't interest you in a game of poker?'

'Do I look like a poker-playing girl?'

'I've never met one. But I'm hoping. When I do, I'll marry her.'

'Thank you for the proposal, Herr Dunleavy.'

'My pleasure. When you can put a straight flush together, I'll take the liberty to come calling on you.'

She smiled, walked on, warmed by the diversion of the small flirtation. But the mood didn't last: Anna Bork saw to that.

'Fräulein Graz!' She caught up with Luise as the latter went out the gateway. 'I want to talk to you!'

Pistol Packin' Mamma had given way to another of Roy Dunleavy's selections: the Andrews Sisters, libelled by a scratched, worn recording, were celebrating with *Rum and Coca-Cola*.

'I'm going for a walk. Come with me.' Luise tried to make it sound like an invitation, but at once she saw the flush on Anna's face. She lost her patience with the obstreperous woman. 'We are being watched by Herr Dunleavy. Now if you want to talk with me, come with me or shut up and go back to the hut!'

50

She turned and walked up the road; a moment later Anna Bork fell in beside her. They walked in silence till they reached the crest of the ridge that ran down the northern side of the camp. When they were over it and out of sight of the camp, Luise stopped and faced the other woman.

'Frau Bork – ' She had determined to be as formal as possible, to give Anna Bork no advantage by trying to be friendly and then being rebuffed.

The breeze blew Anna's hair into her eyes and she swept it back with a movement of her hand that was surprisingly feminine. Luise had never thought of the other woman as having any feminity at all, as if that were a weakness or vanity that only the snobs, like Luise herself, indulged in.

'I call you Frau Bork and so does everyone else. But you have never mentioned your husband. Your name is down on the section list just like mine – our names, no Frau or Fräulein. You wear no wedding ring – '

'Who does? Or didn't they take all your gold?' She put her little finger in one corner of her mouth, pulled it aside. 'They took my gold tooth, the only treasure I had. What did you lose besides your hair and your virginity?'

'I lost only my hair. I didn't take my virginity with me to Birkenau.' They had chopped off her hair the second morning she had been in the camp, but that had been no sacrifice; they had kept her shorn all the time she had been there and she had succeeded better than most of the women in keeping the lice on her head to a minimum. 'I also had no rings or jewellery with me when they took me away.'

'It's probably all hidden away there in the big house at Waldgarten.'

Luise plunged in at the deep end again. 'Frau Bork, I've never mentioned this to you before because I didn't want to get into any argument with you – '

'Oh, we've had our arguments right enough,' said Anna belligerently, looking for another one.

Luise nodded. 'Yes, but not about Waldgarten. What have you got against me and my grandparents?'

'Your grandmother killed my husband!' She spat out the

51

words; she licked the spittle back from her lips. 'Ran over him in her damned great car!'

Luise frowned, trying to concentrate her memory. So much had happened in the intervening years it was difficult to grasp something of the pre-war years that had not directly affected herself. Dimly she recalled talk of an accident at Waldgarten that had greatly upset her grandmother Hedy and had resulted in her grandparents going away to Nice out of season, an unheard of thing; but there had been over two hundred workers on the estate at Waldgarten and she had never known more than a dozen of them and those only because they worked in the big house or in the stables. She could not recall ever having seen Anna Bork, red-haired and conspicuous though she must have been, and her dead husband.

'I'm sorry that it happened. But I don't know the circumstances and I'm sure my grandmother would not deliberately endanger someone's life. It must have been an unavoidable accident.'

Anna shook her head. 'Your grandmother didn't have to avoid anyone or anything. If a man was crossing a road, driving a herd of cows back for milking, he was supposed to get out of her way –'

'Was that how your husband was killed?'

'Yes! Run down while he was trying to save your cows from being skittled!'

Luise frowned again. 'I don't think my grandmother could drive – I'm sure she couldn't. It must have been the chauffeur –'

'Oh, he was driving all right! But he told us later it was your grandmother who made him drive so fast – she always made him drive fast.'

Luise now remembered hair-raising excursions in the Mercedes or one of the other cars, the Delage or the huge Hispano-Suiza that her grandfather had brought back once from Spain. The very names of the cars were faint echoes from a time gone forever; nostalgia gripped her for a moment, like a touched nerve. She remembered that Grandmama Hedy would wind down the glass partition and whack the chauffeur on the back with her umbrella, urging him to go faster; she also remembered that her father, not a Wald but one of the sedate Grazes, had been just as reckless in his own English-built Railton. She had seen peasants jumping into ditches on the sides of the road as they had sped by, but it had never occurred to her that their whirlwind passage might have been resented. When she had turned round and looked back at them it had seemed to her that all the quickly receding faces were laughing at the antics of her grandmother and of her father, sharing in the pleasures of the rich.

'You rich never had a thought for anything but your own pleasure –'

'No one is rich any more, Frau Bork. Least of all any of us.'

'You can go back – the Grazes have lost nothing.'

Luise knew that the Graz family, being as shrewd and cautious as they had always been, would have money hidden away in bank accounts in Switzerland. But their steel and glass works were all in the Russian Occupied Zone and she doubted that they could be any longer counted as Graz assets. When she had gone back to Vienna she had gone to see one of her uncles to ask if any of her father's estate was still intact; he had promised to look into it, but she had heard nothing from him in nine months and pride stopped her from pestering him. She would see what the Jewish Agency could do for her when she reached Palestine.

'None of us can go back. If you have any doubts about going to Palestine –'

'None – I have none!' Anna spat out the words again. Luise wished she was not so fierce; one was spattered by her wet passionate words. 'You're the one I have doubts about!'

Luise abruptly left her, walking stiff-legged and stiff-backed down the slope that led to Oberammergau. The village where they drew their rations lay in the opposite direction; the camp inmates rarely went into Oberammergau. Perhaps it was because the town every ten years performed its Passion Play, in which the Jews were the murderers; perhaps it was because it had become known that some of the leading performers in the play had been Nazis. Whatever the reason, the people from Camp 93 almost never went into Oberammergau. Which was the reason Luise chose it as a place to escape to whenever she wanted to be alone.

'Why so worried?' Major Dunleavy loomed up beside her, smiling as always.

She recovered, dropped immediately into the right role: she had been as good an actress as a singer. 'I'm trying to find something to wear Friday night.'

'Here? You should go down to Garmisch.'

'Down there, major, you Americans have made everything so expensive. Up here the prices are still a little more – Christian, shall we say? I'm told Mary Magdalene runs a dress shop. Maybe I'll find something suitable there?'

'Before or after her conversion?'

She found herself liking him more and more. There was a simple directness about him, but he would never be anyone's fool.

'I'll be discreet, major. It wouldn't do for the Assistant Provost Marshal to be escorting a loose woman.'

'Oh, we escort quite a lot of them. But for a different reason.'

'Why are you up here in Oberammergau?'

'Corporal Martin has a girl friend in the next village up the road. He asked could he go up and see her, he wants to bring her in Friday night to Garmisch. I'm waiting for him.'

'You seem a very accommodating officer.'

'That's my nature – I'm too accommodating. For a cop, anyway.' They had begun to walk up the narrow street. Townspeople went by, casting covert glances at them; they know us, Luise thought, we are both still the enemy. 'When I get back to the States, I'm going to get a master's degree. If I can,' he added modestly.

'Why?' She knew he expected the query. He wanted to throw light on another facet of himself; and unexpectedly she did not mind. She offered a little of herself, a crumb of her background: 'My father was a lawyer. He specialized in international law.'

'I know about him. I looked up some old law journals – he had some pieces in them.'

It pleased her to hear that he knew of her father. It meant that at least her father's name and reputation still lived; and it also meant that this soldier from Nebraska knew something more than what she had vaguely imagined as frontier law. She looked at him with sudden new interest.

'He used to say he was before his time, that law might never be truly international.'

'Right now, I guess he'd say he was right. But I'm a bit more optimistic. I'm going to take international law. Maybe I'll be before my time, too. But it'll come.'

'Not in Nebraska.' She couldn't help the slightly patronising note in her voice, was instantly sorry.

He grinned. 'Not in Nebraska, not unless we secede from the other forty-seven States. No, in Washington, D.C. That's where I'd like to finish up, maybe in government. Who knows, some day I may use some of your father's arguments to win a case.'

'I'd like that,' she heard herself say.

'I'd like it, too. Especially if you were there to hear me.'

She withdrew just a little. 'You sound ambitious.'

'There's nothing wrong with that, so long as you don't let it go to your head. You should get ambitious about your singing again.'

She didn't ask him how he had learned about her career. 'Do you like opera?'

'I've never heard any – seen a performance, I mean. The only classical singers I know are Miliza Korjus and Lily Pons. I saw them in the movies.'

'Do you like music at all?' She ventured towards him again, warily, as if treading on thin ice. His very affability was almost a trap in itself. 'I mean –'

He grinned. 'I know what you mean. I know what you think of my brother's taste – mine's not as bad as that. My favourite is Maxine Sullivan.'

'I hope she will forgive me – I've never heard of her.'

'I don't even know if she's around any more. But before the war I had all her records.'

'Perhaps I should start educating you in classical singers.'

'It might be an idea. If things go okay Friday night and we have other dates, I may some day ask you to marry me.'

It was a joke, of course, just as his brother's similar remark had been, and she laughed. 'Major Dunleavy, I'll start considering my answer now.'

'Do that,' he said, the joking note still in his voice; but was she mistaken or were his eyes serious, looking at her more carefully than the banter warranted? 'In the meantime, I wonder how Corporal Martin got on with his girl?'

Corporal Martin drew up beside them in the jeep, jaws working in a happy rhythm on his gum. 'Okay, major. Gretel's coming Friday night. I'll pick her up at seven-thirty, then call for Fräulein Graz, Okay?'

Dunleavy looked at Luise and she nodded. 'Okay,' she said and they all laughed at her stiff use of the colloquialism.

Dunleavy offered her a lift back to the camp, but she declined. The jeep roared off, Dunleavy's head jerking back with the sudden start; and Luise, waiting till they were out of sight, then began to walk back along the road out of the village. Mary Magdalene would not have her as a customer today.

Walking along, suddenly tired of thinking of the problems of the next few days, she let her thoughts wander off into fantasy. What might have happened if she were to have gone to the dance Friday night, if *Bricha* had not called on her and the others for another month or two? Would the sudden liking for Major Dunleavy (she didn't even know his given name) have ripened into something deeper? She had dreamed of men and love, as any woman might; she had not forgotten how she had enjoyed the physical side of love-making. She had not had a man in five years, but the memory of the *feel* of one, no particular one but an amalgam of the lovers she had known, stirred in her blood sometimes in the dark warmth of her bunk.

In the months immediately after her release her body had been too weak and shrivelled; it had revolted her to see it and she knew no man would have longed for it. But gradually, as her strength had returned, as her body had begun to fill out, the old feeling, like a sweetly remembered pain, would occasionally stir in her loins. She knew she would not say no to a

56

man if he and the circumstances were right. She would never know if Major Dunleavy might have been that man; and the right circumstances were still a long way in the future.

But suddenly she began to sing. The music of her voice burst out, in a folk song she had heard the camp children singing. Then she laughed aloud and looked around her, up and down the empty road, as if embarrassed by her lightness of heart.

5

Friday evening was suddenly upon them. Thursday had dragged as if they were going through the day in slow motion; Friday seemed even slower, everyone's watches and clocks appearing to have stopped. Barlow, the Assistant Camp Director, young and conscientious, prowled the huts all day, insisting that there had to be a clean-up; to Luise, who normally was oblivious of the lanky young man, it looked as if he suspected something unusual was going on. It was Roy Dunleavy's free day and he had gone into Garmisch and as always Barlow, in charge for the day, took himself and his duties too seriously. His musical taste was, if anything, worse than Dunleavy's and he played records all day, trying to cheer everyone up.

The ration truck went into the village and word came back that it had broken down; suddenly all the watches and clocks accelerated and Luise worried that the rations would not arrive in time. David Weill had packed some chocolate from the Red Cross parcels, but Friday was the day for the week's tinned food, the cans of soup and meat that were to form the basis of their food packages. The truck finally arrived back at dusk, by which time half the section had already left the camp.

They had been smuggling their luggage out throughout the day and it was now all hidden in the trees bordering the lane where they were to meet Keppel and his truck. With Barlow popping in and out of his office, Luise had sent off the first of the section right after lunch, to fill in their time down in the village or just walking the surrounding roads and fields. When

57

seven o'clock came, the last food package was packed and it was time to go, there were only Luise, David Weill and Simon Berger left of the section.

'*Spam* – what dreadful names the Americans have for their food.' Simon Berger was a tall man in his early thirties; he had been a miner and there was still a hint of muscle in his bony frame. He had the round head and flattened features of a Toby jug and his big hands were as hard and lumpy as the coal he had once dug. 'It puts you off.'

'No worse than some German names,' said David Weill. 'Does knackwurst sound any more appetizing?'

The meeting time with Keppel had been brought forward to seven-thirty. 'We'll be passing through Garmisch before Corporal Martin calls for me,' Luise said.

'Let's hope Herr Barlow doesn't send someone down to the hut to look for you,' said Berger. 'They'll suspect something if they find no one here.'

'We'll have to take that risk. I don't know what plans Ben Keppel has for getting us through the border post, but all we can hope is that Herr Barlow doesn't telephone the post before we get there. Herr Dunleavy wouldn't. He would guess what happened and would just wish us luck.'

'What can they do to us?' Weill asked.

Luise shrugged. 'Nothing, really. After the last five years, Herr Professor, will you be worried because they say you've broken a few of their rules?'

Weill's eyes twinkled. 'I think I may enjoy being a law-breaker. I've been a law-abider all my life, but only because the deterrents frightened me. I'm a cowardly criminal at heart.'

The food had been split into three packages. Luise took the lightest and Weill and Berger each took one of the others. Luise put on her coat over the thick sweater she wore (someone else's cast-off; she longed for the day when she would walk into a store in Haifa or Tel Aviv and buy herself, with her own money, a brand new wardrobe), wrapped a scarf round her head and picked up the food package.

'We have twenty minutes, we can't dawdle. We'll go out the back way, up over the hill.'

The chill night air bit into them as soon as they stepped out of the hut. Just before she closed the door Luise looked back at what had been home for so many months: the bunks with their makeshift screens around them, the long tables and benches down the middle of the room, the odds and ends the occupants had collected to give some personality to the hut, the stubborn pitiful attempt of a man or woman to put his or her own mark on their caves. There had been no privacy here, despite the screens: no one had had any secrets except those locked in the vault of his own skull and even some of those, in violent nightmares heard by the others, had been exposed. She closed the door firmly, hoping things would be better in Eretz Israel.

The amplifiers were blaring Barlow's choice for the night: *My Dreams Are Getting Better All The Time:* the man was an unconscious ironist, Luise thought. It evidently had not occurred to him that the rest of the camp was preparing for *Shabbat*; if it had, he probably would have been playing happy Jewish records. The music finished as the three of them crossed the camp border up the hill, walking between two of the stark useless fence posts as if making a symbolic exit. Another record scratched at the night's silence, then the amplifiers burst into song again: *Mairzy Doats* followed them into the darkness, a gibberish farewell.

'Americans,' said Berger and spat.

But Luise and Weill said nothing, just hurried on through the darkness. Prejudices were useless baggage: better to discard the one against the Americans, who were now behind them for good. From now on the British would be the enemy.

It took them ten minutes to reach the copse of trees in the lane; the truck was already waiting for them. The rest of the section were already in the back of the truck, hidden behind a stack of boxes just inside the tailgate. Luise could hear the youngest Klein child, a natural busybody, asking questions as always.

'Mama, where are we going? Mama, why is Herr Keppel dressed like an American soldier? Mama – ?'

59

Keppel, in an American greatcoat and field cap, handed Luise a similar greatcoat and cap.

'What are these for?'

'Get into them!' Keppel sounded impatient, edgy. He tapped the door of the truck and Luise dimly saw the white letters there: *U.S. Army Liaison Headquarters*. 'You ride up front with me – you're supposed to be a WAC officer. Can you do an American accent?'

'Passable.' Luise took off her own coat, struggled into the greatcoat. It was too big for her and so was the cap; she hoped she would not have to get out of the truck's cabin. In any reasonable light the ill-fitting greatcoat and cap and black slacks and heavy shoes she wore would set the sartorial image of the American army back to pre-Civil War days. 'Where did you get the truck?'

'Stole it from the transport pool in Garmisch. We have a man working there for us – he painted the sign.' He held up his wrist, flicked on a small flashlight, flicked it off again immediately. 'Seven-thirty. Let's go.'

Luise helped him pull the tarpaulin cover down over the tailgate, secured it. She heard one of the children inside the truck whimper in the blackness and Rebecca Klein said, 'Mama, why are they doing that? Mama – ?'

Luise heard David Weill begin to pray softly: as she climbed up into the cabin beside Keppel she heard the others take up the refrain: '*Shema Y'Isroel . . .*' Far down the hill there came the faint strains of Barlow taking *Six Lessons From Madame La Zonga*.

Keppel switched on the engine, let in the gears, said his own prayer: 'Let the bloody English be blind all the way from here to Palestine.'

'Amen,' said Luise, then smiled in the darkness. 'I'm sorry. The only Hebrew I know is *Shalom*.'

Keppel eased the truck slowly down the lane towards the main road. As it reached the junction the lane dipped in between high banks, so that anything coming down it was invisible to any driver coming from either direction along the main road.

Corporal Martin, driving at his usual headlong speed, came

up the main road from Garmisch. He had had trouble borrowing the staff car from the transport pool sergeant; then he had had to go around and pick up Roy Dunleavy, who had been arranging something, probably another goddam poker game, with the boss at M.P. headquarters. Gretel, who was hot-assed and said yes to the first guy who called, didn't like to be kept waiting; and Christ knew what the cold-assed Graz dame would say. Dunleavy, who wasn't a bad guy, had said he didn't mind if they went on to pick up Gretel first.

He came round the sweep of the bend in the road and saw the beam of lights striking across the road as the truck moved out of the lane and turned towards him. Its lights blazed into his eyes and he slammed on the brakes, jerking the car to the right. There was a crashing sound immediately beside him, then the car was ploughing into the ditch beside the road, miraculously staying upright. It jerked to a stop, flinging him hard against the steering wheel, and the lights in front of him suddenly went out. For a moment he thought he had been blinded, then he realized the headlamps had been smashed. There was a pain just below his chest and he could feel something warm running down into his eyes; but he was alive, he had all his senses and suddenly he was more angry than hurt. He switched off the engine, then looked at Roy Dunleavy leaning back in the seat.

'You okay? Goddam Kraut farmers –'

'I'm okay,' said Dunleavy, but his voice wheezed. 'Let's see what the damage is.'

They got out, their legs suddenly weak, leaned back against the car and looked back at the truck thirty yards away.

Ben Keppel switched off the truck engine, opened the cabin door and jumped down. He could hear the children crying in the back of the truck and someone was moaning as if in pain. He quickly examined the truck; the damage to it was slight and he would be able to drive it out of the shallow ditch without any trouble. Then he ran round to the back, to be joined by Luise. They loosened the tarpaulin, flung it up.

The boxes just inside the tailgate had been toppled over. Anna Bork's head appeared above the jumble of them. 'One of

61

the boxes fell on Frau Kogan! She sounds as if she's badly hurt!'

Keppel cursed, then spun round as Corporal Martin, legs still weak, came shambling up the road towards them. 'What's the matter with you guys? Where the hell did you think – ?' Then he came closer, seemed to recognize that things were not what they seemed. He grabbed at his waist, realized that he was off-duty and not wearing his holster and pistol, and then he swung his fist at Keppel, coming in behind it.

Luise didn't see the gun in Keppel's hand, just heard the shot. Martin fell forward, clutching at Luise; instinctively she stepped aside and he slumped down in the long grass of the ditch. Then the second man came running up from the car on unsteady legs, shouting something incoherent. He rushed straight at Keppel and Keppel shot him, too. He, too, clutched at Luise and she couldn't avoid him. She caught him, lowered him to the ground, knew who he was even before she saw his face, knew that he was already dead.

Chapter Two

===

They came down the main road into Garmisch, drove past the railway station where GI's, with weekend passes for Frankfurt or Munich, were being checked by the military police as they went through the main entrance. Luise remembered that Major Dunleavy had said he would be on duty till eight o'clock and she wondered if he was there in the station. But perhaps an Assistant Provost Marshal didn't concern himself with such mundane matters as checking a soldier's leave pass. She wondered how much he would concern himself with the murder of two men, one of them his brother.

They came to a cross street; a policeman on traffic duty in the middle of the crossing held up his hand. Keppel eased the truck to a halt, continued to stare straight ahead as he had done all the way down from where they had left the dead Roy Dunleavy and Martin propped up in the seat of the staff car. Pedestrians hurried across the street in front of them; it seemed to Luise that at least half of them were men in uniform, Americans on the prowl. A jeep drew up beside them and the driver and the three MPs with him looked up at Luise and grinned.

'Hi, honey. You want an escort somewhere?'

Luise turned her head away, unconsciously raising her shoulder, a haughty gesture that came naturally to her and would have been an asset to her in the sort of roles she had aspired to in opera. At the same time, with the turning of her head, a street light winked on the silver bar on her cap.

'Sorry, ma'am.' The MP corporal in the jeep saluted awkwardly. 'Our mistake.'

The traffic policeman waved his hand towards them and the

jeep roared off, tyres burning; its departure was a sudden painful memory of how Corporal Martin had driven. Keppel drove carefully across the junction, nodding affably to the policeman as they passed him.

Garmisch had suffered very little from the war. Luise, staring out at it, still trying to comprehend what had happened back on the road near the camp, bitterly wondered if the local citizens thought of themselves as having lost the war. Bars and cafés were open; through brightly lit windows she saw the silhouettes of people apparently without a care in the world. She knew the image was false; but at least none of them looked like murderers on the run. The Bavarians had a capacity for adapting, much more so than their fellow Germans: it was her father who had told her that, when he had brought her here in 1936 to the Winter Olympics.

'They'll always survive,' he had said, and she, too young and gay-minded then to worry about such a remote thing as survival, had nodded absently and continued to watch the skaters on the rink float beneath the banners that already darkened the future.

The truck turned down a side street, went past a cinema. *The Lost Weekend*, said the American posters on the billboards outside: just the film for GIs at a loose end on a Friday night.

'No one is taking any notice of us,' said Keppel, still staring straight ahead, 'but there's no point in making ourselves too conspicuous.'

'You made us conspicuous when you killed those two men.' She sounded a bitter prosecutor, aghast at what he had done not only to Roy Dunleavy and Martin but to herself and those in the back of the truck. She had seen murder galore, had become almost but not quite inured to the shock of that; but she had never imagined that she would be on the side of murder, would be sitting alongside a killer who had made her an accomplice. 'As soon as they have found them, they'll be looking everywhere for us.'

'We'll be over the border before then.' For the first time he turned his head towards her. 'Look, they were going to stop us. You'd have been taken back to the camp –'

64

'I'd have preferred that to taking their lives! There would have been other opportunities for us to get away – we'd have had to wait, but even that would have been preferable to murder –'

'I wasn't thinking only of you. He'd have arrested me and I'd have been charged with stealing this truck and impersonating an American soldier –'

'Herr Dunleavy would have spoken for you – we could have got him to do that –'

'I never knew Dunleavy. He didn't know me, either. Why should he speak for me?' he said bitterly. He trusted no one but Jews and only those who had been through hell like himself. 'I'd have gone to jail – perhaps six months, perhaps a year or two. The movement can wait on you and the others – it doesn't matter that much, as long as we get you there eventually. But *Bricha* needs *me* –'

'*Bricha* won't like it any more than I do when they learn what you've done. They're not a murder organization, they leave that to the extremists –'

'What's another death or two on top of – how many?' But he sounded uncertain. He had acted without thinking and he wondered now if *Bricha* would condemn him for what he had done. He went on arguing, as much to convince himself as her: 'They say six million of us have been murdered – it may be more, it may be less, a million or two doesn't matter after the first million. Or even after the first *one man* was murdered.'

She sat silent, staring at his profile as lights flickered by it outside the truck. They passed a dance hall or club of some sort: she saw it out of the corner of her eye: it could have been the club where Major Dunleavy would soon be waiting for her. The pounding beat of a dance band followed them down the street: the Chattanooga Choo-Choo was taking everyone home, away from the misery of Europe, the sour fruits of victory, the killing that wasn't over yet.

'There'll be lots more killing. I don't believe in a lasting peace – it's a myth. We're still at war, us Jews, I mean. We are still fighting the English and after them we'll probably be fighting the Arabs. The killing isn't going to stop, not in my lifetime. I'm sorry I had to kill Herr Dunleavy and that soldier.

But don't ask me if I feel any guilt – I don't. They are just another drop in the ocean of blood.'

Luise had no answer to the callous truth of what he said. She slumped down in the corner of the seat, stared ahead as they passed the outskirts of the town and the truck's headlamps probed the dark road ahead of them. It seemed to her, now in the slow whirl of a drowning person, that the darkness reached all the way to Palestine and beyond to horizons she would never know.

In the back of the truck, in blackness unrelieved by any light at all, Anna Bork and the others sat in silence, aware of each other only when the truck swayed and their bodies pressed against each other. The killing of the two Americans had affected them all, though not all in the same way. Anna Bork, though shocked initially at the sudden tragic turn of events, felt as Ben Keppel did. Another death, especially that of two Americans, meant little to her. Her own death, when it eventually came, would mean everything to her; she had not survived all that she had, gone through all the pain and grief, to surrender her life without fierce and murderous protest. And life for her meant getting to Palestine: to her it really was the Promised Land.

David Weill sat as silent as the others, but his mind was loud with prayer. *An eye for an eye, a tooth for a tooth:* the words from Exodus had never been part of his philosophy. Teaching history, he had learned that history was a cycle of proverbs that cancelled out each other. *An eye for an eye ... as ye sow ...* the cycle went on and on, words following words on a carousel where the price was the human spirit. David Weill said *Kaddish,* the prayer for the dead, for the two Americans; and he prayed also for the silent ones who surrounded him in the darkness. It did not occur to him to pray for himself: he left himself to the will of God.

Old and young all sat silently while the truck carried them through the night away from the dead Americans who might be their nemesis. None of them had expected their journey to start on such a violent note and, having lost the habit of optimism, they were filled with foreboding.

66

Keppel began to slow the truck as he saw the lights up ahead. 'The border post. Just sit tight and only speak if someone speaks directly to you. And don't forget the American accent.'

'How's your accent?' She was short and abrupt with him.

'Okay. I'm a nice Jewish boy from New York.' He spoke English now with an American accent that sounded plausible to her ear. 'You don't have to worry about me, ma'am.'

You're so wrong, she thought: we all have to worry about you a great deal.

A short queue of cars and trucks was lined up ahead of them. As the line moved slowly forward, sometimes being held up as some driver's papers were given more than the usual perfunctory examination, Luise could feel herself beginning to sweat in the greatcoat that had suddenly become too warm for her. But she could not take it off: it and the field cap were her only disguise. Then they were at the head of the line.

An American sergeant, a vapour of breath hanging like a yellow balloon from his mouth as he crossed the amber path of a car's headlamps, came up to the truck and opened the door on Keppel's side.

'Where you heading, soldier?'

'Salzburg,' said Keppel. 'A load of stuff from Garmisch.'

'Okay – inside! Bring your papers with you.'

Luise tensed, saw Keppel stiffen, his leg going out towards the gas pedal of the still-running motor. *Don't!* she screamed silently. *Don't try and crash through the barrier!*

As if she had actually spoken to him, Keppel relaxed, looked at her. 'Won't be a minute, lieutenant. Just routine, I guess.'

For the first time the sergeant saw Luise crouched in the far corner of the cabin. He saluted sloppily. 'Didn't see you, ma'am. That's all it is, just routine. Spot check on every tenth vehicle. You drew the marble.'

She nodded, took a gamble: 'That's okay, sergeant. Luck of the draw.'

The sergeant continued to look at her as Keppel jumped down beside him. She stared back at him, tensing again; then she recognized the look for what it was, a male appraisal of a good-looking woman. She gave him a smile, he smiled back, nodded to her, then led Keppel away towards the brilliantly lit office that seemed to be full of uniformed men. She could hear phones constantly ringing, saw men answering them. Why was there so much telephone traffic this particular night? Which call was the one that would tell the men in the glare of the lights there in the long narrow booth, where she could clearly see Keppel hemmed in on all sides, that two Americans had been found murdered and that any trucks carrying a load of Jewish DPs was to be detained? She watched the office with an aching stare, oblivious of anything else happening at the border post.

Then there was a tap against the door on her side. She jerked her head, snatching her gaze away from the office, looked down into the faintly smiling face of a German policeman.

'You'd better tell them to quieten the baby, Fräulein.' He spoke in German, certain that she understood him.

For the first time she heard the whimper of the child in the back of the truck; then there was the inevitable curiosity of Rebecca Klein: 'Mama, why are we stopping here? Mama – ?' Acting on reflex, Luise tapped on the back of the cabin. The whimpering stopped at once, the Klein child had another question chopped in half, as if a hand had been clapped over her mouth. Then, aware of her mistake but knowing it was too late to rectify it, Luise looked down at the policeman.

'Are you going to report it?' she said in German.

He shook his head. He was a middle-aged man, the short hair along his temples below his cap tinged with grey, his plump face ruddy with the night's cold. 'You're doing me no harm. Are they from one of the camps?'

She nodded, suddenly trusting him. Some of the Germans were to be trusted: the Burgomeister of the village where they had drawn their rations had been friendlier and more charitable than many of the Americans who dealt with them. In any event this mild-looking policeman had already guessed the truth. All he had to do, if he wanted, was to lift the tarpaulin at the back of the truck and move the boxes.

'Why are they having the spot checks?' She knew now that the news of the two murders had not yet reached the border post, but she kept a wary eye on the men on the phones in the office.

'Black market stuff. You're not carrying any?'

'No.' She ventured a tentative smile. 'That's the truth.'

Then from the other side of the truck Keppel said, 'They want to inspect the truck, lieutenant. Our papers are okay, but the sergeant says he still wants a check.'

'Just routine, ma'am,' said the sergeant, standing behind Keppel and gazing up at Luise with the same frank stare he had given her before. He just wants a closer look at me, she thought. *Damned Americans, their eyes always on a piece of ass, even when they couldn't touch it.* She knew the slang, even if her accent might have made it sound ludicrous. But she couldn't get out of the cabin, even to distract him from going to the back of the truck; she would give herself away immediately. Then out of the corner of her eye she saw the policeman move across the beam of the truck's headlamps, come round to stand beside the sergeant.

'I've already inspected it, sergeant. Everything looks all right.'

The sergeant blew out his thick lips, but the balloon of breath had no words to it. He eyed Luise a moment longer, then he shrugged as somewhere down the line a couple of truck horns were blown.

'Okay.' He repeated his sloppy salute to Luise. 'Sorry to have held you up, ma'am.'

Luise gave him her most gracious smile. She wondered if it was out of character; perhaps officers, even women officers, were not supposed to be gracious in the American Army. But the sergeant accepted it: he suddenly smiled back. 'Thank you, sergeant.' Then she looked at the policeman standing behind him. 'And you, too.'

She spoke in English to him and he answered in the same language. 'You're welcome, Fräulein.' He, too, saluted her, crisply and stiffly; it was the American style salute, she noticed. 'Good luck.'

Keppel climbed up into the truck, slammed the door and then they were driving past the barrier and down the road to the Austrian post. He slowed as they came to the second barrier, but the French weren't interested in coming out into the cold. A great-coated soldier stepped out of the booth, waved them by and stepped quickly back inside. Let the Americans carry the can tonight: they could almost read the thoughts of the lounging Frenchmen in the big-windowed office as they drove past and on into Austria.

'The policeman,' said Keppel. 'Did you bribe him or something?'

'No. He knew who was in the truck, but he was on our side.'

'Conscience,' said Keppel sourly. 'A lot of them are suffering from it now.'

'Perhaps. I prefer to think he was just a decent man.'

'You're too charitable.'

There was no answer to his prejudice: it was burned too deeply into him. She lapsed into silence as the truck began to climb towards the pass that would take them down into Innsbruck. She was in her homeland again; in the darkness she could see nothing of it but what the truck's headlamps illuminated. Memory swept over her like a physical feeling; she felt faint with the atmosphere of the past. She had loved this beautiful country when she had been young; but she had been only a child then and the children of those years were still innocent. The children behind her in the truck did not have the innocence that had possessed her. Little Rebecca Klein might be forever asking questions, but she already knew too many dreadful answers.

They passed through Innsbruck, crossed the river and began the climb up the road that led to the Brenner Pass. Above the labouring of the engine in low gear they heard the thumping from the back of the truck. They pulled up and Luise, as much to stretch her legs as anything else, jumped down before Keppel could move and ran to the back of the truck. Hurriedly she untied the tarpaulin, flung it up as Keppel anxiously joined her.

'What's up?'

Anna Bork's face glowered at them in the glow of the moon

70

rising above the mountains. 'The children want to wet. Don't you think we have bladders?'

'We can't pull up here,' said Keppel sharply.

'Don't tell our bladders what they can't do,' said Anna and swung herself down from the back of the truck, holding up her arms to take one of the children. 'Come on, love. Have your wet.'

The women went into the trees beside the road and the men stood in the shadow of the truck, raising steam from the snow by the roadside. Luise came out of the trees on the opposite side of the road, looked up at the dim signpost above her.

'Kalburg,' she said to Keppel as he came round the truck. 'Is that where we're going?'

'No, Rennwald. It's further up the road.'

'How long do we stay there?'

'Till tomorrow night. Then it's on foot, up through the woods and down to the main road on the other side of the border. There'll be another truck there to pick us up.'

'We'll never make it through the woods on foot, not in this snow. I've just come out of there – ' She nodded behind her. 'The snow's two or three feet deep.'

'We'll be on a small road most of the way – that's why we'll be travelling at night, it's used by farmers during the day.'

'How far is it?'

'About thirty kilometres.'

'We'll never do that in one night! Not with the children and some of the older people.'

'We'll stay in another safe house about fifteen kilometres from Rennwald. But we have to be down on the main road on the Italian side by nine o'clock Sunday night.'

'Where do we go from there?'

'I don't know – the driver of the truck will tell us when he picks you up. I may even have to leave you – depends on my orders.'

'I hope you do have to leave us,' she said. 'I don't want you killing any more men to help us escape.'

Then Anna Bork came across to them. 'Frau Kogan will have to be taken to hospital – she's in a bad way, poor woman.'

It was the first time Luise had ever heard Anna say a word of sympathy for anyone; the soft note in the harsh voice sounded incongruous. 'The Grunfield sisters aren't well, either.'

She spoke directly to Keppel, ignoring Luise. The latter knew she was being challenged and knew, too, that the challenge had to be accepted now. If Keppel had to leave them, it might be too late then for her to assert her leadership. But even as she spoke she was surprised at her own decision; the firm hard note in her voice was unfamiliar. But then she recognized that it *was* familiar, the faint echo of another voice: she sounded exactly as her father had sounded when he was exercising his authority.

'Frau Kogan can't be taken to hospital tonight. We'll have someone from the village where we're going take her down to Innsbruck in the morning. I'll decide about the Grunfeld sisters also in the morning. In the meantime, Frau Bork, make Frau Kogan as comfortable as you can.'

The others were clambering back into the truck. She turned away, went across and helped one of the children up into the truck: only when she had the child in her arms did she realize it was Rebecca Klein.

'Fräulein Graz, Mama won't tell me what happened to those two men? What did happen? Fräulein – ?'

'Rebecca, don't you ever get tired of asking questions?'

'No,' said the child. 'I like asking them.'

Luise sighed. 'Wait till you are old enough to have to start answering them.'

'Oh, I like answering them, too. Ask me something.'

Her father reached over, grabbed her and pulled her into the truck. 'I'm sorry, Fräulein. She's like my wife's mother –'

'Why was Grandmama always asking questions? Papa – ?'

Last on board the truck was Anna Bork. She pushed roughly past Luise and climbed up. She pushed the boxes back into place with all the strength of a man, then glared down at Luise over the top of them.

'Once we are on the ship, I'll deal with you!'

Luise reached up, took the end of the rope and jerked the tarpaulin down in front of the glowering face. There was a

72

muffled scream of rage from inside the truck and behind her Ben Keppel coughed a short harsh laugh.

Then they heard the bronchial chug-chug of an elderly motorbike coming up the main road. It swung in beside them, the weak beam of its headlamp spotlighting them as they stood at the back of the truck. The motorbike wheezed into silence and the rider dismounted and stepped into the beam of light.

'Something wrong?' he said in German. 'I am Sergeant Pohl. Police Sergeant,' he added, remembering he was not in uniform. 'I am off duty, but perhaps I can help.'

'It is nothing, sergeant,' said Keppel in German; and Luise looked at him, wondering if he realized his mistake. 'The call of nature.'

Then Pohl seemed to become aware for the first time that he was standing by an American army truck, that the man and woman were in American uniforms. 'Americans, are you? You speak German very well.'

'My parents were German, from Leipzig,' said Keppel truthfully. 'They taught me the mother tongue.'

'Where are you from?' Pohl was suspicious and uneasy. Fischer had knocked on his door half an hour ago to say that the plans for moving Dr Halder had been postponed for at least twenty-four hours. Word had come through just that minute from their man at the German border post that another blitz was on; the Americans were looking for a party of Jewish DI's who had murdered two Americans; every vehicle was being searched and the word had gone through to the Italian border post. Pohl, on his way up now to give Halder the bad news, was wishing he had ridden right by this parked truck. He was just beginning to realize that the war he was now involved in was not as simple and straightforward as the war he had come home from. Conspiracy soon lost its excitement when you found that someone else, someone you did not know and probably never would, made all the decisions. 'There are no Americans in this zone.'

'We've just moved in,' said Keppel easily. He gestured at Luise. 'The lieutenant knows more about it than I do, but unfortunately she doesn't speak German. She's one hundred

73

per cent American, you know what I mean?' he said and made it
sound like a private joke between himself and Pohl.

Pohl straightened up. He had hardly given a look to the
woman; he had a pre-war contempt for women in uniform. It
offended his sense of dignity to be told that she out-ranked
both himself and the German-American soldier. He said
stiffly, 'Ask the Fräulein Lieutenant if you are going up to
Kalburg.'

'He wants to know if we're going up to Kalburg,' Keppel
said to Luise in English. But he didn't wait for a reply from
her, turned back to Pohl and said in German, 'I can tell you
we're not headed there. We're on our way up to the border – we
have some supplies. We'd better be moving. Goodnight,
sergeant.'

He nodded to Pohl, went up to the front of the truck. Luise
hesitated, then she nodded quickly to Pohl and hurried up to
join Keppel in the driving cabin. As he started up the truck,
the motorbike chugged past and went on up the side road, its
single beam of light weaving as the bike slipped occasionally
on the hard-packed snow.

'You handled that very well,' said Luise grudgingly.

'He won't be the last who'll question us.' Keppel pulled the
truck out on to the road. 'I just hope his beat doesn't take in
Rennwald. If he comes up there tomorrow, sees us or the truck –'

'Will you kill him, too?'

'If it is necessary.'

2

'Hut 13 is empty,' said Barlow, coming into the camp
office. 'There's no one there.'

'They're probably over in one of the other huts.' The camp
clerk was a mild-looking little man named Silberstein; he
looked very un-secretive, a man open to the world. 'This is
Friday night, they get together for family suppers on the eve
of *Shabbat* –'

'I've checked the other huts – they're not there. All the

74

kids have gone from Hut 13, too. Something's going on, Silberstein.'

'I'm sure you're mistaken,' said Silberstein, who knew exactly what was going on. 'Tomorrow morning you'll find them all back there in the hut. You go off now, I know you have your date in Oberammergau –'

'I was going to wait till Herr Dunleavy gets back –'

'Don't worry. You're too conscientious, Herr Barlow. The camp won't walk away. Go on, your friends will be waiting for you.'

'Well . . . Okay. We'll check on Hut 13 in the morning. But you might mention it to Herr Dunleavy when he comes back.'

Barlow had a girl in Oberammergau. As he drove out of the camp in his jeep he heard the music stop over the amplifiers, but he paid no heed to it; he was not to know that Silberstein and the rest of the camp inmates were always glad to escape from Tin Pan Alley. He turned into the main road and two minutes later saw the staff car in the ditch, the two figures lolling awkwardly in the front seat. He pulled the jeep to a stop, grabbed his flashlight and went across to the car.

Ten minutes later the phone rang in the requisitioned house that Matt Dunleavy shared with three other officers. He had just stepped out of the bath and he knew he was going to have to move if he was to be there waiting at the Officers' Club when Luise Graz arrived. It had been one hell of a day and the phone had a warning note to it: it was more bad news. The other men had already gone to pick up their dates and he looked at the phone, wondering if he should ignore it. But, he told himself wryly, he had one weakness that over-rode all his other deficiencies: a sense of duty. Standing naked, finishing drying himself with a towel, he picked up the phone and learned that his brother had been murdered.

'Take care of it till I get out there,' he told Barlow. He felt cold, but it had nothing to do with the fact that he was still naked; he was accustomed to death and the news of it, but *this* death was different. There had been a sense of loss when his mother and father had died, but it had been nothing to what he felt now. It was so consuming that so far he felt no anger at whoever had killed Roy. Then he said, 'Has *everyone* gone from that Hut 13?'

'Everyone, major. They're the bastards who killed your brother and Joe Martin. You gotta –'

Dunleavy cut him off. 'Okay, you file your report on those missing DPs. I'll be out there in twenty minutes.'

He hung up, looked at his watch on the table beside the phone: 2010. He dialled a number, rubbing his wet head vigorously with the towel as he waited impatiently for an answer at the other end, rubbing as if trying to erase the shock in his mind.

'Headquarters? Where the hell have you been? Give me Captain Ryman . . . Jerry?' He filled in Ryman, the duty officer, on Roy's and Corporal Martin's deaths. 'I'm going out there now. Have a driver here in two minutes, get it, *two* minutes. Soon's I hang up, get on to the border post on the Innsbruck road, tell 'em to search every truck coming through – we're looking for a load of DPs, led by a woman named Luise Graz and maybe a young guy named Keppel. They probably have fake papers in other names, but the girl is about twenty-six, twenty-seven, dark-haired with a streak of grey in it, very much a good-looker – ' It hurt him to hear himself describe her so clearly. 'Get the message through to the Swiss border and to the French and Limeys up on the Brenner. Christ knows which way they're heading, but chances are they're heading south. And they won't be wasting any time!'

'Matt, you think you should handle this? Go out to the camp, by all means, but let me get some other guy to take it over officially – '

'It'll take you an hour or more to get someone.' Dunleavy, later, would marvel at how long he remained calm and impersonal; or at least managed to *sound* that way. 'I'll get things started. We'll see where we go tomorrow.'

He hung up; and the dam burst. Suddenly he thumped the table, a tremendous blow that caused him pain which was lost in the storm of grief and anger that overwhelmed him. Lulled by the fact that the war with its concomitant, sudden death, was over, he had been totally unprepared for Roy's death and

76

the manner in which he had died. As a law man he knew that killing did not stop with a war's end: Man never declared an armistice with himself. He just had not expected murder to strike so close to home.

The Military Police driver did not arrive in two minutes and Dunleavy was glad. It gave him time to compose himself. He dressed hurriedly, fumbling with buttons with unhabitual awkwardness, and was on his way downstairs when he heard the jeep pull up outside with a screech of brakes. Joe Martin used to arrive the same way; for the first time he fully realized that someone else besides his brother Roy had been murdered. He and Martin had never really hit it off, but now he knew he was going to miss the smart-ass kid.

There was a driver in the jeep and a sergeant in the back seat. 'These goddam kikes,' said the sergeant. 'They even kill one of their own. Joe Martin had his faults – '

'Like being a kike?'

Dunleavy felt both men stiffen, but the driver kept looking straight ahead. The sergeant, conceding nothing, said, 'Okay, sir, if that's the way you feel – '

'That's the way I feel.'

'They said there were two guys.' The sergeant was un-abashed, armour-plated with bigotry. 'Who was the other one?'

'My brother,' said Dunleavy, and felt a perverse, illogical satisfaction at silencing the faceless man behind him.

They drove out through the cold clear night, Dunleavy sitting hunched in his greatcoat. Slowly he was gathering the shattered mosaic of himself together again; but now there were extra pieces to be fitted in. Besides the grief he felt at Roy's death, there was the gradually growing sick disappointment at the way Luise Graz had been involved. He had never classed himself as an expert on women, but as a lawyer and then as a military policeman he had thought he had come to know something about people in general. And he would have staked his life on the decency of Luise Graz. He did not for one moment believe she had fired the murder shots, but he could not understand why she had fled, making herself an accessory to the fact.

He had been only half-joking when he had said that some

day he might ask her to marry him. Matt Dunleavy was not given to hasty decisions. He sometimes said surprising things, but they had all been thought out before he had let anyone else in on them. In Beef City, Nebraska, he had been the despair of certain girls and their mothers because he had never mentioned marriage, not even jokingly. His parents dead, his brother Roy already sending postcards from faraway places, he had even then been thinking of escape to a wider world.

The day of escape had come two weeks after Pearl Harbor. While everyone's back was turned, while everyone was torn between celebrating Christmas and bemoaning the war that had flung itself at them, he had left Beef City. He had left a note for his senior partner, a man untroubled by beckoning horizons and too old for the war, and gone to Kansas City to enlist. The Army took him with open arms, told him they wanted lawyers, and put him in an infantry battalion. He survived North Africa, Sicily and Italy unscathed except for one or two dislocated attitudes. The end of the war came, but he was not ready to go home. He was out in the wider world and he had still not seen enough of it. He had applied for a transfer to Germany when his battalion was scheduled to go home. There had been no posts offering for an infantry major, but how would he like to be an Assistant Provost Marshal? He had taken the job reluctantly and had been regretting it ever since. The one consolation had been that he and Roy had met again.

'Looks like we gonna be cops at last.' The sergeant decided to break the silence. He was an ex-boxer, a pug who still occasionally did his thinking with his fists. 'Real cops. Detective work, eh, major?'

'There won't be much of that. We're pretty sure who did it. And they'll be picked up before morning.'

'I hope you're right,' said the sergeant, but he sounded disappointed. 'You'd think those goddam DPs woulda seen enough killing.'

When they reached the scene of the accident, with the staff car still in the ditch, Barlow and Silberstein were waiting for them. Dunleavy got out of the jeep, walked across and looked at the dead Roy and Corporal Martin. They both looked suddenly small compared to how he remembered them. He gazed down at Roy, whom he had only really come to know in the past nine months, first by letter as they had learned they were both in Europe, then in person as they had been posted to the same area. Before the war Roy had been a wanderer, his search for a direction to his life marked by the occasional postcards sent from all over the United States. Dunleavy felt a sudden deep regret for all the lost years that he and Roy might have shared.

'There's an ambulance on its way out,' he heard the sergeant say to Barlow. 'Now who's this guy?'

'I know Herr Silberstein.' Dunleavy took over before the sergeant could turn this into his own little pogrom. He looked at the white-faced man wrapped against the cold in an overcoat several sizes too large for him. 'Did you know what was going on?'

'I know nothing of this, Herr Major.' Silberstein croaked, cleared his throat nervously. The overcoat heaved, a despairing movement of the thin shoulders hidden under it. 'We all had so much respect for Herr Dunleavy – '

'What about Keppel?' Silberstein looked puzzled and Dunleavy snapped impatiently, 'The guy who was here a couple of days ago, said he came from Feldafing. Did he organize the move out tonight? Snap out of it, Silberstein! Did you know they were going tonight?'

Silberstein hesitated, then nodded. 'The camp council knew. But we didn't know the route they were to take. They never give that information to those left behind.' He appeared to straighten up, grow taller; at least Dunleavy had the impression the overcoat had been filled out. 'I can tell you nothing, Herr Major.'

'Jesus!' said the sergeant and spat disgustedly.

'That's enough, sergeant,' said Dunleavy quietly, still looking at the little man in front of him. 'Herr Silberstein, were they heading south for Italy, going to pick up a ship for Palestine?'

'I'm sorry, Herr Major. I know nothing.'

'Goddam it, sir!' The sergeant was drunk with fury. 'They've killed two of our guys and he's just telling us to fuck off! Let's take him into Garmisch, question him a little –'

Dunleavy turned his head, said very evenly, 'Sergeant, go back to the jeep and wait there. You've said enough for tonight. Move!'

The sergeant hesitated, face bursting in the lights of the collected vehicles, then he abruptly swung about and stamped across to the jeep.

'Herr Silberstein is your responsibility, Leo,' Dunleavy said to Barlow. 'He seems to know his rights. Maybe he'll talk to you, if he won't talk to us.'

Barlow, all his enthusiasm gone, all at once a bewildered young man, as if it had just occurred to him how deep his responsibilities went, said, 'I believe Herr Silberstein, major. I don't think he knows where they're headed.'

Dunleavy reluctantly nodded. He wasn't sure just how much Silberstein knew, but he knew sure as hell they were going to get nothing out of the spunky little man. After five years of SS guards and the shadow of the gas chambers, an American Assistant Provost Marshal must look like Santa Claus, or whatever was the Jewish equivalent to Meir Silberstein.

The ambulance arrived and the two bodies were put into it. Then Dunleavy said goodnight to Barlow, walked across and got into the jeep beside the driver who hadn't even moved from it.

Prickily aware of the sergeant's sullen silence behind him, he said, 'Sergeant, you'll be on transfer out of this section tomorrow morning. You're going to Frankfurt for re-posting.'

'Hell, major –'

'No argument, sergeant. Nobody loves us military cops, but our image isn't improved by Jew-haters who think a little roughing up of a Jew is okay in the interests of justice.'

'We'd of got some fucking answers from him –'

'You'd have got nothing from him. That man has had five years, may be even ten years of roughing up by real experts – no American cop, military or otherwise, will ever equal a Gestapo man. The day he does, or even tries to be, I don't want to be in the same outfit as him.' He had kept his voice

80

beautifully under control. I'm learning to be civilized, he thought, right here in the country where a bunch of dogs did their best to bring civilization to its knees. 'You move in the morning, sergeant.'

'So what the fuck happens to the killers?' The sergeant was asking to be busted. Suddenly he knew what he'd do, he'd ask for a goddam transfer back Stateside, where you didn't have to pussyfoot to fucking kikes and spades, where you treated them the same as every other bum who tried to smart-ass you, you belted 'em with your billy and no questions asked, at least not by them. 'You gonna let 'em fuck off into the blue?'

'No, sergeant. I'll bring back the killers, even if I have to follow them all the way to Palestine or wherever. Now you can get out and try and get that staff car back to Garmisch. Move!'

The sergeant sat a moment, then abruptly he vaulted out of the jeep and walked quickly across to the staff car in the ditch.

Dunleavy let out his breath, sank back in the seat. 'Okay, driver. Let's go.'

The driver was a lean gangling kid whose face had shown nothing during the exchange between Dunleavy and the sergeant. But now he looked at Dunleavy. 'It ain't none of my business, major, but I think you right. It don't do us no good to look like the Gestapo.'

'Thanks. What's your name?'

'Charlie Lincoln, sir. No relation to Abe.'

Dunleavy grinned, his face muscles relaxing for the first time since he had got the phone call from Barlow. 'Keep the gas tank full, Charlie. You and I may be doing a lot of travelling.'

3

Rennwald was a village of bent streets that seemed to have found their way, rather than been planned, among houses that gave each other grudged breathing space. The village was not large, but it was old. Some houses had been occupied by the same families for two centuries; the graveyard at the back of the church had headstones dating back to the late 17th century.

The first people in this mountain redoubt had fled from the
Turks in the siege of Vienna: they knew the terror of persecution and they had passed on to their descendants their horror
and repugnance of it.

Keppel brought the truck into the village, drove down the
twisting main street and out the other end and finally turned
into a yard beside one of the larger houses on the outskirts.
A man came out of the house carrying a lantern and waved them
into a big barn where the door already stood open. Five minutes
later everyone was inside the big house, Frau Kogan the last
to be brought in. She lay on the old disused door that had
been used as a stretcher on which to carry her, a middle-aged
woman who knew she had reached the end of her road.

Luise and Anna Bork, their antagonism put aside for the
moment, knelt beside the injured woman. 'We are going to have
to send you to hospital, Frau Kogan,' Luise said. 'Someone
from here will take you down first thing in the morning.'

Gunther Kogan leaned over both women, looking anxiously
down at his wife. 'Isn't there a doctor in the village here?'

'None.' Max Lazar ran both the agricultural hostel and the
safe house. He was a stern-faced muscular man, an ex-farmer
who planted a new type of seed and raised a new sort of crop
for a nation still unborn. 'There's one down in the next village,
Kalburg. But he's a German, probably a Nazi looking for a
quiet place to retire to. They're all Nazi sympathizers down
there.'

'Why can't she be taken down to the hospital in Innsbruck
tonight?' Anna Bork asked.

'We don't know who's on duty there at night. We have a
friend on the staff, a senior doctor, but he's only there during
the day. He'll see there aren't too many questions asked when
she is admitted.'

'What are you going to tell them?'

Lazar looked at Gunther Kogan. 'You have two boys?'

Kogan nodded. 'Fifteen and sixteen. They're not very
strong, they look about eleven and twelve.'

'Doesn't matter. We'll put them on the roll here as students.
You could have been paying them a visit when you had this

unfortunate accident. But the three of you will have to stay here till your wife is well again.'

Luise left them and went to look for Ben Keppel, who was shepherding the rest of the new arrivals to the bedrooms. He turned them over to Lazar's wife, a stout happy woman who looked made for mothering families small or large, and went out to the kitchen with Luise.

'The Kogans will be staying,' she told him. 'All four of them.'

He nodded, looking depressed. 'The Grunfeld sisters aren't going to make it, either. That cuts the party down to fifteen, including you and me.'

'I told you – you should have got another group. You're too single-minded, Ben – ' She insulted him, still angry and sick at what he had done to Roy Dunleavy and Martin: 'You're more German than you think!'

For a moment she thought he was going to leap at her. Then he forced himself down into a chair, his hands gripping the edge of the table in front of him, his whole body quivering.

'You don't understand! I've got to get you to that ship! I've never failed yet – they depend on me!'

'You don't like losing your quota – ' She was exhausted to the point where she had reached the exaggeration of near-hysteria. 'You sound like some Sturmbannfuehrer delivering a load to the gas chambers! Is that all we are – a quota of bodies to help fill a ship?'

They were saved from more violent argument by the entrance of Lazar. He came into the kitchen, went to the big wood-burning stove. 'My wife has made stew and coffee – we'll feed them all in ten minutes.'

'You are very well organized here.' Luise took the cup of coffee he gave her, sat down opposite Keppel, who had lapsed into morose silence.

'We have to be, if we're not to have the French up here worrying us. We run the farming school strictly as a school should be run, discipline and all. It hides what we are doing now.' He had a soft velvety voice, like that of a man who had spent his time whispering into large dangerous silences. He sat down at the table with them, big work-scarred hands

83

wrapped round a large mug of coffee. His sleeves were rolled up and Luise could see the tattoed number on his wrist. She wondered if he had learned his organizing ability from watching the experts at it in Auschwitz or Dachau or wherever he had been. 'The boys are up at our other house for this evening – we move them up there whenever we have a group coming through.'

'Do the villagers suspect what is going on?'

'Not suspect – they *know*. But they turn a blind eye to it. It is a bit rare in the Tyrol, but there are none and never have been any Nazis in Rennwald. They're devoutly Catholic and, unlike a lot of other Catholics, they practise what Christ taught. We don't have to worry about them.'

There was a note in his voice that Luise caught, a torn thread in the velvet. 'Whom do we have to worry about then?'

'Some of our own.'

Luise looked sharply at Keppel, who sat up, coming out of his depression, aggressively defensive again. 'Who?'

'Some Poles they sent me.' Lazar didn't seem to have noticed Keppel's gritty attitude. 'Four of them, they arrived here a month ago. The Agency sent them, said they were farm workers who would help me instruct the boys. None of them has ever been on a farm in his life before.'

'Then how – ?'

'I think these four men stole the original men's papers.'

'What would have happened to the other men?' But with a sickening feeling Luise had already guessed the answer.

Lazar nodded. 'It wouldn't have been the first time it's happened. Not all Jews are good men, Fräulein. It took me a couple of weeks to wake up to these men –'

'What would they be planning? Not to give you away, surely?'

'Nothing like that. This is a perfect cover for them. I think – but I've got no proof, not even any evidence – that they are in the black market. If they are, and the French get on to them, that will be the end of us here.'

'Why haven't you contacted the Agency?'

'I haven't been able to get away and there's no one I could trust to take a message. The Agency would never forgive me if

84

I had one of the villagers get in touch with them – I'd trust completely one or two of the villagers, the priest, for instance. But the Agency trusts no one outside its own ranks. Perhaps I could have sent one of the boys, but they're too young, the eldest of them is only fifteen. They've been through enough. I want them to stay here till Eretz Israel is ours and they can go out then and be the farmers we hope they'll be.' He put down his mug, looked directly at Keppel. 'I knew you'd be coming soon. I want you to take the message to the Agency contact in Merano – you'll be going through there again. Tell them to send someone here to deal with these men.'

'Why can't we deal with them?' Keppel said. 'There are enough of us – you, me, Simon Berger –'

'I heard how you dealt with the two Americans,' said Lazar quietly. 'That, too, has to be reported to the Agency. Do you tell them yourself or does Fräulein Graz have to do it?'

Keppel, hands on the table, closed them into tight fists. 'None of you has any right to judge me! I know what my job is – I've done it too many times –'

'How many others have you killed?'

Keppel stared at the older man, then shook his head in despairing argument. 'None. But it had to be done this time – it *had* to be!'

Then Frau Lazar opened the door of the kitchen, ushered in the still-cold and hungry others. None of them noticed the tense atmosphere at the table; Lazar broke it up by suddenly rising and offering his chair to Hilde Klein. Luise stared at Keppel for a moment, silently telling him that his argument would never convince her; then she, too, stood up and gave her seat to one of the other women. Soon everyone was warmed and revived by thick hot stew, home-baked bread and apples brought up from the cellar. When Luise went up to bed she found she had been put in a room with the two ill Grunfeld sisters and Anna Bork. She busied herself making the two frail women comfortable, not wanting to have any conversation at all with Anna Bork. She was worn out with the abrasions of other people, wanting only to escape to bed without further argument.

85

Ruth, the elder of the Grunfeld sisters, looked up at her out of eyes that had no light in them, were sunk in the darkness of the skull that showed through her thin grey hair. 'We shan't be going with you tomorrow night, Fräulein. You should have left us behind – someone else, someone younger, should have taken our place.'

'We had hoped – ' But Luise knew it was a lie and Ruth Grunfeld knew it too.

'All that worries my sister and me is where will they send us? Back to the same camp?'

'Is that where you'd like to go?'

'Yes. At least there are familiar faces there – we have no friends or family anywhere else.' She took a thin claw from under the blanket, held Luise's hand. 'If you can arrange it, Fräulein Graz – please? We don't want to die among strangers.'

Oh God, Luise thought. She was powerless, she knew; getting the two older women back to Camp 93 was beyond her control. But the hand that clutched hers was an expression of faith in her: someone *trusted* her. She looked across the room at Anna Bork watching her closely from her bed: there was someone who had no faith in her, would never burden her with trust. And felt a perverse sort of gratitude towards the bitter selfish Anna. But, equally selfish, shut her mind against the thought that perhaps she had been wrong in burdening the friends of the past in Vienna with her own trust in them.

'I'll do everything I can, Fräulein Grunfeld. But go to sleep now – you'll need all your strength for the journey back.'

She went across to her own bed, took off her shoes, lay down and pulled the blankets over her. Keppel had warned them all that they would not have the luxury of taking their clothes off for the first forty-eight hours, not till they were over the Italian border; they had to be ready to move at a moment's notice, and a moment's notice didn't mean while they got dressed and gathered up their belongings. But Luise was so tired, it was a luxury *not* to undress. She looked across again at Anna Bork, but the other woman had turned her face to the wall, was already asleep. Luise turned down the oil lamp, stared up at the darkness. The journey had at last begun, but

86

her mind refused to look ahead. She fell asleep and dreamed of the past, the black winter of the last five years.

She woke depressed, disturbed by the sound of church bells down in the village. The other three women were still asleep. She got up, putting on her own coat instead of the army great-coat she had worn last night, and went downstairs. Keppel, Lazar and another man were in the kitchen eating a breakfast of boiled oats, sausage and bread.

'Did the church bells wake you?' asked Lazar. 'That's the only thing I have against the priest here – he has some idea that God gets up early. Every morning in the week he rings those damned bells. Oh, this is Zalman.'

Luise noticed that Lazar did not give the third man a given name nor introduce him with the customary polite *Herr*. There was no intimacy between the two men, none of the camaraderie one would have expected in a community as small as this. Zalman was of medium height, bony-bodied and bony-faced, with pale cold eyes that weighed everything like a pair of scales. Luise had seen his type before in the larger camps, the man who could count the money in your wallet before you had even shown it to him, the sort who had been exploiting their fellow victims as soon as the concentration camps had been opened and the walking skeletons had staggered out. She shivered and drew her coat around her.

He stood up, poured her a cup of coffee, handed it to her with a slightly mocking graciousness. 'That will warm you up, Fräulein. Though you shouldn't be shivering in a coat like that. Camelhair, isn't it?'

'How would you know?' Keppel said. He seemed surer of himself this morning, as if he had spent the night convincing himself that his argument would convince the *Bricha* men when he had to face them. 'Herr Lazar said you were a farmer.'

'I was, too. A successful one. I bought my wife a coat like that, once.' He had the quick mind of the easy liar. He sat down again at the table, put a slice of sausage on some bread. He smiled at Keppel, almost as if taunting the latter to chal-lenge him. 'You'd have been a boy before the war, Keppel. You wouldn't know how well some of us lived then. Even Poles.'

87

Keppel looked ready to argue, but Lazar jerked his head warningly, pushed back his chair and got up. 'You and I had better go for a walk, Herr Keppel. We have to arrange for Frau Kogan to be taken down to the hospital.'

Luise stood up hurriedly: she didn't want to be left alone with Zalman. 'I think some of her things were left in the truck last night. I'll get them –'

'There was nothing in the truck,' said Zalman. 'I came down last night, took it up to the other house. Our own truck is out in the barn now.'

Keppel, about to go out the door, spun round. 'Who gave you permission to touch that truck?'

'It's an American Army truck. Who gave *you* permission to use it?' Zalman stood up, unhurriedly, chewing on the sausage and bread. But he kept his hand on the heavy coffee mug, as he might grasp a stone to throw it. 'The truck is safer up at the other house, Keppel. We're too close to the village here. Right, Herr Lazar?'

Lazar nodded reluctantly. 'It is safer up there. But you had no right to move it without telling Herr Keppel.'

Zalman shrugged. 'From what I gather, he won't be using it again. It's left to us to get rid of it. He and his friends will be gone tonight. What happens to us if we're caught with it?'

He is far too smooth, Luise thought: he is always one jump ahead of the rest of us. All at once she wanted to be gone from Rennwald as soon as possible. Zalman was dangerous, in a subtler but just as vicious way as the other dangerous men she had known.

She abruptly left the men to their argument, went to prepare Frau Kogan for the trip down to the hospital in Innsbruck. The rest of the day she managed to remain busy within the house; it was a pleasure to be in a *house* again instead of a camp hut. Now she enjoyed the simple diversion of wandering from room to room through Frau Lazar's big house, wrapping around herself once more the atmosphere of a place that, irrespective of what other uses it was put to, was a *home*. Some of the other women followed her example, touching furniture, fluffing out cushions, dusting ornaments, taking in through their fingertips the feeling of a memory that had almost faded. Frau Lazar, an understanding woman, left them to their enjoyment.

In the afternoon Luise sang to the children, the first time she had ever done so. It was Rebecca Klein who got her started. 'Fräulein Graz, were you a singer? What did you sing? Why don't you sing any more? Fräulein – ?'

It was easier to sing than to answer questions: she was surprised just how easy it was. But there were no adults around and the children were not going to ask her why her voice might quaver. But it didn't quaver, was as true and beautiful as it had ever been; but not strong enough, she knew that, and she stayed with simple songs that were no real test. Then she saw several of the adults standing in the doorway of the big room where she had been entertaining the children.

'Beautiful,' said Judith Winter. 'You should sing more often.'

'Do you know any cowboy songs?' said Simon Berger. 'I used to sing them to the pit ponies in the mines. American songs are so good – '

'You should have stayed with Herr Dunleavy,' said Noah Malchek, and then suddenly everyone was quiet. The squat-bodied Malchek seemed to deflate; he ran his small woman's hand over his bald head, then down over his good-looking face with its dark woman's eyes. Before the war he had owned one of the best china stores in Dresden, but his tongue sometimes had the delicacy of a bull's foot among his prewar stock. 'Sorry.'

Luise gathered up the broken moment, turned to the children. 'Everyone to bed for a sleep. You have a long walk tonight. Come on, into bed.'

Frau Kogan had been taken down to Innsbruck by Lazar, her husband accompanying her. Luise had arranged for the Grunfeld sisters to stay here in the house for another week, then they were to be taken down to Innsbruck, put on a bus for Garmisch, where Luise told them they were to give themselves up to Major Dunleavy, who would see that they were returned to Camp 93. By then she and the rest of the party would be aboard the ship that was waiting for them and they would be headed for Palestine. The Grunfeld sisters would be subjected to questioning about the deaths of Roy Dunleavy and Martin, but that couldn't be helped. It would not be the first time they had been questioned.

Irma Grunfeld, the younger sister, spoke to Luise as she came into the bedroom. 'Fräulein Graz – my spectacles. They were in their case – I dropped them in the truck last night when we were getting out – '

Luise tried to hide her annoyance: why hadn't the woman mentioned her loss earlier in the day? Then she saw Anna Bork eyeing her, waiting for another chance to criticize her.

'It means I'll have to go up to the other house, Fräulein Grunfeld – '

'I can't read without them. But it doesn't matter – ' Irma Grunfeld had a semi-invalid's self-pity that her sister would never have.

'It's all right. I'll go.'

She put on her coat, went downstairs and asked directions from Frau Lazar. 'You should rest, Fräulein Graz. I'll go and get the spectacles.'

But Luise insisted and then Keppel came into the kitchen. 'I know where the house is – I was up there this morning.'

He put on the army greatcoat, but Luise noticed there were no insignia on it today. He had discarded the army cap and now pulled on a knitted balaclava from which his thin face peered out like that of a starving knight from a rusty chain helmet. He nodded to her and led the way out of the house. Ever the gentleman, she thought, and followed him.

The road led up through snow-covered fields. Luise heard shouts and laughter and saw some boys driving a herd of cows down a path below a thick stand of trees. In the fields themselves the snow was ridged on the ploughed earth; but, a city girl in her education, she had no idea what crops the fields would produce in summer. But she did appreciate the cold clean beauty of what surrounded her. Cities now were just ruins, the harvest of war.

'What do the boys learn up here? When they get to Palestine they'll be farming desert land.'

'They'll adapt. We'll all have to. It'll be just as strange there for you as for them.'

90

The second house was at the end of a lane, surrounded by a cluster of sheds and a huge barn. Luise was surprised by the quietness of the place; she had expected it to be like any other school, loud with the noise of boisterous boys. Then she remembered this was a *work* school.

'Some of the boys work with the local farmers,' Keppel told her as they turned in through the farmyard gates. Then Luise became aware of a distant buzz that occasionally thinned to a scream and Keppel nodded up towards the thick forest behind the farm. 'They have a sawmill up there, too. Some of them are being trained in forestry.'

Then suddenly he stopped, one arm going up in front of her to hold her back. Luise stood stockstill in the mud of the yard, staring at what had stopped Keppel. The door of the big barn was open and Zalman and another man were loading cardboard cartons into the back of the army truck.

'Let's go back,' she said softly.

But they were too late. Zalman turned, saw them, said something to the man up on the back of the truck. The second man, short and burly with a shaven head and naturally flat features that had been flattened still further by fists or a gun butt, jumped down and stood beside Zalman.

'We're loading stuff that has to be taken down to the village,' said Zalman. 'They buy from us and we buy from them.'

'What do they buy from you that's in American Army EX cartons?' said Keppel. He still had his arm across Luise's front, as if he had forgotten to lower it, and she could feel the rigidity of it. Then the arm started to quiver as anger took hold of him. 'It's black market stuff! Cigarettes or something!'

'Don't shout, son,' said Zalman quietly, as if talking to one of the schoolboys, and came out of the barn. 'It's really none of your business –'

Keppel abruptly dropped his arm, shoved his hand into his greatcoat pocket. Luise knew what he was going to do, was not surprised when his hand came out with the gun in it.

'Ben, put it away!'

'Stay where you are, Zalman,' Keppel said, taking no notice of Luise. He motioned with the gun at the other man at the back of the truck. 'Come out and join him. Put your hands up.'

The burly man, watching Keppel closely, moved forward and stood beside Zalman. He half-raised his hands, then saw that Zalman still had his by his sides; he dropped his own, but still stood tensed. Zalman looked unperturbed, smiling thinly; Luise waited for him to shake his head at Keppel's melodramatics. Yet she knew Keppel would shoot if one of them made a move: he was – she remembered the phrase from an American movie they had shown at the camp – *gun-happy*.

'Ben, please – '

'You don't belong here,' said Zalman: he, too, ignored Luise. 'You'll be gone tonight, so what's all this got to do with you?'

'If you're caught, the French will close this school – '

Zalman shook his head. 'They wouldn't do that, Keppel. The French are practical-minded, they pride themselves on that. While this school remains open, supports itself, the boys here are no worry to them. If they closed the school, they'd have to set up a camp for them somewhere – ' He shook his head again, his expression still mild; he was still treating Keppel as a boy, giving him a lesson. 'Put the gun away. Go back to the other house and mind your own business.'

'The French would keep an eye on the place – '

'You mean about smuggling people like you through here? The French don't care – every Jew in Europe can go to Palestine as far as they're concerned – they turn a blind eye to it – '

'That's in France. Not here they don't. The English put too much pressure on them – ' Keppel wasn't giving up; the gun quivered slightly in his hand, his voice trembled with the fury he was suppressing. 'We could never use this farm as a safe house again, once they had to raid it – '

'You'd have to find another port of call then.' For the first time Zalman's voice hardened; Luise realized with a sense of danger that he had not been patiently amused, he had just been very much in control of himself. Which Keppel was not. 'We have our organization, too. We have money invested in this – '

He started to move forward, but stopped as Keppel brought the gun up. 'Fräulein Graz, quick! Go back to the other house

– Frau Lazar will tell you where her husband is! Bring him here!'

Luise turned, slipped in the mud but managed to stay on her feet, and ran quickly out of the yard. She did it all by instinct, not to help Keppel in his confrontation with Zalman but to prevent more bloodshed. She was halfway down the lane towards the road when she heard the shots. There were two shots, then three more; even her inexperienced ear told her the last shots came from another, heavier gun. She stopped, torn between going back to see what had happened to Keppel and running on for help. Then she heard the truck roaring out of the yard, heard two more shots. She looked back and saw the truck come skidding out of the yard and speeding down the lane towards her. She hurled herself backwards into some bushes as the truck, spraying mud over her, swept by. She caught a glimpse of Zalman at the wheel, but he didn't even look at her. The truck braked, skidding again, then swung out on to the road and was gone from sight.

Luise, her face spattered with mud, sick with the sudden turn of events, started running back up the lane. Then she saw Keppel, covered in mud, come out of the gates and walk unsteadily down towards her. She pulled up, gasping for breath in the thin cold air, as Keppel reached her.

'I'm all right.' He walked right by her and she had to turn and run after him. She saw that he was limping, but he was ignoring it, hurrying as fast as the damaged leg allowed him. 'We'll have to get started now! If they're picked up by the French or the local police – !'

'Were you hit?' She had to keep breaking into a run to keep up with him.

'Only by the truck – ' Abruptly he stopped, felt his leg and swore. 'There's nothing broken, but it's going to slow me up. I should have killed them at once!' He was weeping with rage; she could almost feel the heat of his anger. 'You can't talk to people like that – '

'Ben, you can't go on killing people just to get us to Palestine –' He glared at her, turning his anger on her; suddenly she lost her temper, refused to be bullied by this headstrong boy. 'You're not laying down the law for me or any of the others! We're fed

93

up with killing – so shut up about any more of it! Your job is to get us to that ship – but do it without using your gun again!'

He stared at her a moment longer, then he turned his back on her and went hobbling off down the lane. As she went after him she saw the boys running down across the fields towards the house, the herd of cows forgotten. She wondered how many of them would reach Palestine without someone having to commit murder for *them*.

4

Karl Besser, coming back from a house call, heard the five shots. The reports, coming up a dip in the ridge that separated the shallow valleys of Kalburg and Rennwald, carried clearly on the still air. He knew guns and he recognized the shots as those of pistols; no one around here went shooting game with a pistol. He paused, then shrugged and went walking on down the road past the lake.

He had conducted his surgery this morning and had hoped that would be the last call on him as a doctor by the villagers of Kalburg. Then in mid-afternoon had come the call from the farmer whose wife had developed pneumonia. Besser had accepted the call, even though it meant a two-mile trudge from the village to the farmer's house. He wanted no suspicions aroused that this was his last day in Kalburg. His hosts, the Fricks, knew that he was leaving tonight, but true to their habits ever since he had arrived, they had asked no questions. Fischer, through Sergeant Pohl, had told him that *Spinne* preferred to keep the movements of those it aided as secret as possible.

Down on the main road from Innsbruck Sergeant Pohl was coming up to say his farewell to Dr Halder. He enjoyed the thrill of being part of an underground movement, but there was a natural caution to him; he did not want to take any more risks than was necessary. The secret war might be a long one, its victory might not come till long after he was dead; in the meantime he had to go on living, and making a living, in the aftermath

94

of the war that had been lost. He preferred to say goodbye to
Dr Halder in Kalburg this afternoon rather than tonight when
the French Army truck would pick up the doctor at the road
junction. Someone might, just might, follow that truck up from
Innsbruck. The trouble with belonging to an underground
organization was that you never knew who was watching you,
that they, too, often worked underground.

'You don't have to worry about the French,' Fischer had
told him, 'or even the English. And particularly the Americans
– they trust everyone who isn't a Communist. It's the others.'

'What others?' Pohl had been puzzled.

'The Jews. They're already using their influence again.
You only have to look at how many are working with the War
Crimes Commission. They're the ones you have to watch out
for, believe me. They have their agents everywhere.'

Pohl, lost in thought, letting the old motorbike find its own
way up the long curving road like a farmhorse that could be
trusted, came round the bend and saw the truck speeding down
towards him in the middle of the road. He jerked the handle-
bars and the motorbike swung out of the way, its sidecar wheel
skidding a little in the slush piled up at the side of the road. The
truck went rushing by and Pohl caught a glimpse of the sign on
its door: U.S. Army something. He growled a curse after it as
he turned into the Kalburg road. Damned Americans, what
were they doing here in the French Zone? The Brenner road
carried a lot of military traffic, but most of it was French and
English.

Then, like a late developing photograph, another glimpse
registered: that of a face behind the wheel of the truck. It had
not been that of an American: it had been a familiar face, that
of one of the Jews up at Rennwald. He pulled up the motorbike,
but kept the engine running. He didn't know the man's name
and he had avoided going up to Rennwald; it was not part of his
beat and he wanted nothing to do with a village that harboured
Jews. But one of his junior officers had pointed the man out to
him down in Innsbruck, said he was from Rennwald but spent
several nights a week in Innsbruck, always with certain charac-
ters who were on the books at police headquarters. They had

95

nothing on the man himself and they did not intend making work for themselves by picking him up and questioning him. But they were watching him because any man who kept the company he did would eventually be up to no good.

Pohl rode on up the road, got to the Frick house as Dr Halder came down the street, his tall figure striding along in the gathering dusk with the jauntiness of a man with his work day behind him and a night of entertainment ahead of him. And of course that's what he's got, Pohl thought enviously, a wonderful night ahead of him. A party that's going to stretch all the way to South America.

'You look worried, Pohl.'

'I wonder if Herr Frick would mind if I used his telephone? I want to call headquarters.'

'About me?' Besser crackled with good humour, the ebullience that fired off bad jokes as indiscriminately as good ones.

Pohl looked pained: jokes, good and bad, bounced off him like rubber pellets. 'Why should I do that, Herr Doctor?'

Besser slapped the policeman on the back, followed him into the house. He would be glad to leave the lugubrious Pohl and the dour Fricks; he wondered what sense of humour he would find in Argentine. He left Pohl by the phone in the hall and went into the room he used as his surgery. He put down his medical bag, looked around at what he wanted to take with him. Nothing: this had been no more than a railway waiting room where he had filled in time till the word had come from *Spinne*. There was nothing in the room that would identify him. He carried all identification within himself; that, he had learned, was the safest habit one could adopt. His working at his profession was a partial identification, he supposed; but it had also been a useful disguise. A community was more suspicious of the recluse who did nothing than it was of the man who worked amongst it: work wove its own camouflaging pattern.

He sat down at his desk, trying to restrain the impatience and excitement he had felt since Pohl had come to him and told him he was to be on his way again at last. Ilse and the children were already in Italy; Fischer had taken them over the border last night and they were now waiting for him in Merano.

96

He felt a stirring in his balls at the thought of Ilse; he hoped he and she would not have to share a room with the two boys in Merano. Despite all the opportunities that had presented themselves, and Berlin had been full of willing women, he had remained faithful to Ilse; there was no woman who could give him the pleasure she could give him, not just sexually but in every way that a woman could make a man's life better. He loved her with a devotion that had been a mild joke among his fellow officers at T4; and he knew that she loved him with the same devotion. Even the children, on whom she had lavished her love while she had been separated from him, had not diluted any of the feeling she had for him.

It was Ilse who, unwittingly, had fired his ambition. When the Nazis came to power he had just finished medical school and, just married, was intent only on building a career as a family doctor. He had had no political inclinations; he was in favour of the National Socialists if they could make the new Germany that they promised, but he was not infected by the fanaticism of the party supporters. Then Ilse casually remarked one day that Dr Palmbaum, a neighbouring doctor, had emigrated to Australia or some strange place and wouldn't it be nice if Karl could take over Dr Palmbaum's patients. Neither of them mentioned that Palmbaum was a Jew and that was the reason for his going; the Jewish question had never been one that they had discussed, not even after he had come back to Würzburg for those few months after the war ended. He had absorbed most of Palmbaum's patients, though none of the Jewish ones came to him and he shrugged away the loss of them, and gradually his practice had grown. Then, just as gradually, he had begun to see that Nazism was Germany's future and his own future lay with the Nazi Party. He had joined it and from then on doors had begun to open for him. When war broke out he had been about to join the Wehrmacht when it was suggested to him that the SS could offer him more advancement.

'Herr Doctor?' Pohl knocked hesitantly on the door, then edged into the room. The class distinctions encased Pohl more rigidly than his uniform; he was, in a way, Besser's rescuer, but he would never impose on the relationship. Besser, a gregarious man when he wanted to be, was glad in Pohl's case of the pre-war formality that bound the policeman's behaviour towards himself. It made the relationship so much easier, at the same time was a reminder that the whole world hadn't fallen apart. 'Forgive me. I had to make that telephone call – a police matter. Someone we want to pick up for questioning. One of the Jews from Rennwald.'

Besser raised an eyebrow, but didn't mention the shots he had heard coming from the direction of Rennwald. When he left here tonight he wanted to take nothing of this district with him, not even memories. He had trained himself over the past few years, ever since the SS had told him what they wanted him to do as a doctor, to block his mind off from what really did not concern him.

'Well, it's goodbye,' said Pohl. He smiled, tried for one of his rare jokes: 'If you see an opening out there in the Argentine for a good policeman – '

'Goodbye, Pohl.' He shook the policeman's hand. He did not feel sorry for Pohl: the unimaginative man didn't realize how well off he was here in his home district. He wouldn't survive twelve months anywhere where ambition was the requisite for survival. 'Be patient. The French will be gone eventually and things will be just as good again as they used to be.'

'Perhaps.' But Pohl's doleful tone didn't suggest any optimism. 'But we need you Germans to lead us – '

'We'll do that again,' said Besser, but didn't expect it in his lifetime; better to head for South America, the land of the future. 'The truck will be on time tonight?'

It was, exactly on time: *Spinne*, on this occasion, was as efficient as it had boasted. Besser, the collar of his overcoat, turned up against the night cold, had been waiting at the road junction no more than five minutes when the truck came up the Brenner road from Innsbruck. His two suitcases were put in the back of the truck among the mailbags and boxes for the French liaison unit at Bolzano, then he climbed up into the cabin beside the driver. The latter, a middle-aged man with grey hair and a broken nose, introduced himself as Metz, said he

was an Alsatian and left Besser to work out for himself where
his sympathies lay.

'Anyone see you leave Kalburg?' He spoke German, but like
a man whose use of it over the past few years had been sparse
and careful.

Besser shook his head. 'I don't think so. The people I've
been staying with, the Fricks, will keep quiet till Monday.
Then they'll just say I was called away unexpectedly.'

'Good.' But Metz sounded as if the query about Kalburg
had only been a conversation-opener. He drove in silence for a
while, then he looked at Besser. 'It may be sticky up at the
border post. They still have their alert on.'

'But they're not looking for me.'

'No.' Metz never asked why the men he drove were wanted
by the Allies; he did the job for money and too much knowledge
might bring some moral responsibility. 'I gather you were told
they are looking for some Jews who killed two Americans over
near Garmisch?'

'Yes.' He really wasn't interested in the Jews, unless they
threatened his own escape.

'Police headquarters down in Innsbruck picked up two
Polish Jews carrying black market cigarettes in an American
Army truck. The truck, unfortunately, seems to have been the
same one that carried the Jews over from their camp near
Garmisch.'

'Where are they – the Jews, I mean?'

'Nobody knows. The Poles were from Rennwald – we just
passed the road to it back there.' He nodded backwards. 'The
police and the French are up there now looking for the other
Jews. If they've caught them by the time we get to the border
we may be lucky.'

'Where did you learn all this?'

'Your friend Sergeant Pohl. He came to warn me just as I
was pulling out. It was too late to cancel the trip.'

Besser laughed drily. Good old Pohl, the conscientious
policeman who couldn't leave well enough alone. 'He was the
cause of this alert, you know.'

'I gathered that. He said to apologize to you.' Metz looked in

99

his driving mirror, stiffened a little. 'There's something coming up behind us very fast. If we're pulled up, don't say more than you have to. They told me your French isn't very good.'

Besser felt himself suddenly beginning to sweat. He was not afraid of any physical risk he might have to take in the next few minutes; but all at once, after the lulling safety of the past few months in Kalburg, he was afraid of capture. He had never thought that he would not make it to South America: as he had blocked his mind against the morality of what he had done in the SS, he had also blocked out any thought that he might be captured. All one needed was a certain amount of caution and the same amount of luck. And already it looked as if the luck had run out.

He saw the beam of the overtaking vehicle's headlamps sweep up beside the truck; he waited for the warning hoot of the horn. The road curved and Metz kept the truck's speed steady; the other truck or whatever it was dropped back as both vehicles came to a blind bend. Then a straight stretch opened up ahead and Besser, suddenly pessimistic, knew this was there they were going to be stopped. Would he have to run or would Metz be able to cover for him?

Then the headlamps behind swung out and a moment later a jeep went speeding past. In the beam of their own headlamps Metz saw the markings on the rear of the jeep, suddenly laughed with relief. 'Just Americans! They have no authority in this zone – we're all right.'

Besser relaxed, wiped his gloved hand across his damp brow. 'Have you lost any of your – er – clients so far?'

'Not yet. The English are the main hurdle and they're more concerned with stopping Jews. You'd almost think the English had fought the whole war just to hang on to Palestine.'

'One never understands the English.' Besser had recovered, donned his sardonic cover again. 'They're so unlike us – we're so predictable, they never let anyone guess what they are going to do. We'd have made an admirable team had Hitler been able to get together with Churchill – both ends of a pole. We'd have baffled the world between us, conquered it and ruled it forever. The English Thousand-Year Reich.'

'You didn't conquer it with the Italians,' said Metz, equally sardonic.

'Ah, they're unpredictable, but everyone understands them. Children are very easy to understand.'

Metz said nothing, just flicked a pitying glance at the man beside him. If Dr Halder didn't get out of Italy quickly he was in for a few shocks, especially if the Communists in the north stumbled across him. There were no children among them.

Then they were approaching the border post. Both of them sat up again, apprehensive of all the activity that suddenly confronted them. The casual midnight crossing that had been hoped for might have occurred on another occasion; but not tonight. Trucks and cars were queued up at the barrier; soldiers and police moved up and down the line. They were stamping their feet and swinging their arms to ward off the cold, but they still looked very much alert. Every driver and passenger was being made to alight from the vehicles and every vehicle was being searched.

'All this for a truckload of Jews?' said Besser. 'Even if they did kill a couple of Americans?'

Metz shrugged. 'The English and Americans have no sense of values.'

'What about you French?'

'*Us* French. No more German now till we get over the border.'

The first man Besser saw when he got down from the truck, on a French corporal's orders, was Sergeant Pohl. He stood beside a tall American major who stared with stony-eyed disappointment at each vehicle as it was released and drove away. Pohl looked at Besser and his hand started to lift in a salute; Besser turned his head before the stupid policeman gave him away. *He* had caused all this trouble, with his damned punctilious sense of duty, his automatic reflex to any infringement of the law. If Pohl had left the Poles to their black market, this border post wouldn't be looking like a Nuremberg rally.

'You are with UNRRA, Dr Vence?'

Besser gave his attention to the corporal, who was examining the passport and travel documents Besser had given him. When Besser had been handed the papers by Metz, he had noted the name by which he was to be known but he hadn't spoken it aloud. Now that the corporal had called him by name he had to adjust to the sound of it: it was to be his name from now on, at least till he reached Buenos Aires.

He coughed, made his voice hoarse, apologized for his bad cold. His French sounded passable in his own ears; behind the corporal he saw Metz nod approvingly. The corporal handed back the papers, nodded that they could move on. Besser climbed back into the truck with Metz. The latter was about to drive off when the American major, with Pohl coming hesitantly up behind him, appeared on the passenger's side and looked up at Besser.

'Sir, do you speak English?'

The word *yes* was already on Besser's tongue: his English was better than his French. Then he swallowed hastily, shook his head. 'No, major. Do you speak French at all?'

Dunleavy shook his head, looked at Pohl, who also shook his head. Then Dunleavy shrugged, nodded and moved back towards the next truck. Metz let in the gears and the truck moved off. At the British post down the road they were stopped again by Italian police and some British soldiers. Then they were peremptorily waved on by a British sergeant whose French ran to, 'Rightio, *mon ami*, piss off.'

Besser sat back, took off his gloves, lit cigarettes for himself and Metz. 'How far to Merano?'

'About forty kilometres. It's all smooth riding from here on.'

'The worst is over,' said Besser and sat back to enjoy the rest of the journey.

Back at the border post Dunleavy, trailed by the police sergeant he had picked up in Innsbruck, walked across to his jeep, got in beside Charlie Lincoln and looked out at the policeman.

'That French doctor, sergeant – do you know him?' His German was lame, stilted and wobbly. 'I thought you recognized him. You were going to salute him.'

'No, Herr Major,' said Pohl, his own voice stilted and wobbly with his effort to lie convincingly. 'I have never seen him before.'

'Okay,' said Dunleavy and seemed satisfied. He looked at his driver. 'Let's go, Charlie. The sergeant can get a lift back to Innsbruck.'

'Where are you going, Herr Major?'

'I don't know that it's any of your business, sergeant,' said Dunleavy evenly. 'But I'm going to Merano. Where that guy we questioned down at your headquarters said those Jews might be headed.'

Chapter Three

It had been a long hard day for Dunleavy. He hadn't got to
bed till after midnight last night and he had been woken at
seven this morning by the sergeant on duty at the Provost
Marshal's office.

'Major Dunleavy? A report in from the transport pool – one
of their trucks is missing. We did what you asked, checked all
our trucks going south into Austria. At the border post on the
Innsbruck road, eleven US Army trucks passed through last
night after twenty hundred hours. Ten of them check out okay.
The eleventh was our missing truck. The serial number of it
was the same, but it's marked down on the border post's transit
list as belonging to the US liaison outfit in Innsbruck. I've
checked with them and they say they had none of their vehicles
on the road last night.'

'How did it get through? I mean, if it had our DPs in it?'

'Search me, major. Someone wants his ass kicked.'

At 0830 Dunleavy and the Provost Marshal, a greying
lieutenant-colonel named Sinclair, were closeted with the
Garmisch area commander, an officer from the Judge Advocate's
division and two officers on detached duty with the Control
Commission.

'I want to go after these DPs, sir,' Dunleavy said to the area
commander, 'even if it means chasing them right to the bottom
of Italy.'

'It's not that easy, sir,' said the Judge Advocate man, dry-
voiced and jaundice-coloured, like a brief that had been left too
long on a shelf. 'Our jurisdiction ends at the border –'

'To hell with jurisdiction! With your permission, sir,'

Dunleavy hastily added and was relieved to see General Folkard smile.

'What do you fellers think?' Folkard, short, wiry and always open to the advice of experts, so long as they were experts, looked at the Control Commission men. 'How do we stand with the British and French?'

'I don't think we have to worry about the French, sir. If the DPs have passed through their zone in a hurry, they'll look the other way. The British –' He looked at his colleague.

They were both young men, eager and enthusiastic. They're on my side, Dunleavy thought. And so they should be. Back home they'd just be starting out at the bottom in some ward in Boston or Butte or wherever, ten years of running ahead of them before they'd get to wield any influence at all; it had been a young man's war, but back home the country was still run by old men who suspected youth. But here were these two, twenty-five, twenty-six years old, helping run half a goddam continent.

'The British,' said the second Commission man, face smooth and snow-tanned under his crew-cut, looking like a high school corps cadet, 'are a bit browned-off with us, sir.'

'Browned-off?' Folkard had arrived late in Europe from the South Pacific and had had nothing to do with the British.

'Pissed off,' said Sinclair, an ex-lieutenant of detectives with no respect for any authority but his own, 'sir.'

Folkard nodded his thanks for the language lesson. 'Go on, Captain Griggs.'

'They feel we haven't been tight enough with our security. The DPs have been moving pretty freely through our zone into Italy and Yugoslavia. The British seem to think we don't care if the Jews take over Palestine.'

'Do we?'

'The Zionist movement is very strong back home, sir.'

'Who do we serve, the Jewish vote back home or the British government?' But Folkard didn't want an answer to his rhetorical question. He looked at Dunleavy. 'You're sure you're not too close to this – personally, I mean? Maybe you should hand it over to someone else.'

105

'I'd rather you didn't, sir.' Dunleavy knew he had control of his emotion. 'It is personal, I'll admit. But I happen to know the people we're after better than anyone else does. I'm sure I can bring them back.'

Folkard gazed at him steadily, then he nodded. 'Okay, that's your first priority – but don't let your personal involvement cloud your judgement, understand? Your second priority is to show the British Army we're still on their side, at least till we're out of sight of the people we're supposed to have beaten in the goddam war. We'll worry about the Jewish vote when we're all back home and running for office.'

'But you're a career officer, sir,' said the Judge Advocate man.

'Exactly,' said Folkard. 'I get easily pissed-off with politicians. Browned-off,' he added for Sinclair's benefit.

'So I can go after them, sir?' said Dunleavy.

'As soon and as far as you like, so long as you observe protocol all the way – I don't want you acting like some bounty hunter. Give my regards to the British. I bet if one of their soldiers had been murdered, they'd have been through here like Attila the Hun and asked permission afterwards. There's something to be said for the old imperialist attitudes.'

'Maybe it's time we started learning from them,' said Sinclair.

'I thought we already were,' said Folkard.

Half an hour later Dunleavy was on his way south with Charlie Lincoln.

'How far we going, major?'

Dunleavy waved his hand towards the mountains south of them. 'Your guess is as good as mine.'

Charlie Lincoln beamed. He hoped they wouldn't catch up with the goddam DPs till Italy ran out into the sea. Charlie had grown up on the waterfront between the Mississippi and the high bluffs of Memphis, Tennessee. Though the river had been an escape route, to New Orleans and the sea or to the cities to the north, he had never thought of taking it. He had been content with his narrow horizons, uninfected by ambition; the living had never been easy, but even in the Depression his old man had somehow always managed to earn enough to feed them. Then Uncle Sam had sent Charlie Lincoln a letter and Charlie had suddenly, to his surprise, discovered a whole new world. Or rather an old one, called Europe.

'What do you know about women, Private Lincoln?'

Charlie Lincoln kept the smile fixed on his face. What sort of smart-ass officer have we got here? Another of them thinks us Joes don't do nothing but hump all the time? Part of the attraction of Europe had been its women, some of whom fell on their backs for a bar of candy or a pair of nylons far quicker than the girls back home in Memphis ever had.

'You want the truth, major?' he said cautiously.

'Sure, that's why I asked.'

Charlie Lincoln relaxed. He'd give the major the truth. Well, almost: it never paid to be real honest with officers.

'I had my first gal when I was nine years old. She was twelve and she knew all about it.'

'Well, there's nothing like an early start in life. How old are you now?'

'Twenty-one.'

'Twelve years of them. What do you know about them?'

'Only that you never able to satisfy 'em.'

Dunleavy shook his head, convinced now that he should have kept his mouth shut. 'Just what my old man told me. Only he meant it in another context.'

'They's only one context for women, major, and I don't mean humping. They look at everything, the whole goddam world, and they fits it all into one little context. Theyselves.'

'Who taught you the word *context*?' Dunleavy could feel his leg lengthening as it was being pulled: he'd drawn another goddam smart-ass just like Joe Martin.

'My teacher. My last year at high school, she helped me with my homework.' Charlie Lincoln smiled his big bright smile, and after a moment Dunleavy found himself returning it. 'And I helped her with hers.'

But though Dunleavy was smiling, the conversation hadn't helped at all with the angry confusion he still felt about Luise Graz. Sure, she had offered him no encouragement; the fact that she had stood him up on a date meant nothing. But he had sized her up as a woman with principles. And a woman with principles didn't run off after she had seen two innocent men killed, especially one who had been as sympathetic to the DPs as Roy had been. Not unless she would bend all those principles in favour of just one. He would never understand the Jews and their dream of Zion.

He checked in at French headquarters in Innsbruck where the French were politely correct but not really interested in two dead Americans and some fleeing Jews. He was free to travel in their zone, they told him, but if he found his quarry he should come back and ask them and the local police to do the arresting.

'Protocol, major,' said the French captain. 'It is one of our national habits – and handicaps.'

Christ, thought Dunleavy, how much protocol am I going to be able to bear? The grid of bureaucracy was being fitted back over Europe again. The bureaucrats never lost a war; once they were back in their chairs, the task of re-building could begin.

'We haven't learned it yet, captain, but I'm told you Europeans are teaching us fast.'

'I hope it comes in useful, major. It's only a handicap when you're a victim of it.'

'Like a dame's morality,' said Dunleavy.

'Why, yes,' said the Frenchman, surprised that an American appreciated a woman's subtlety.

By one o'clock in the afternoon Dunleavy was at the Brenner border post. He was still there at six o'clock when the message came through from Innsbruck that the truck he was looking for had been picked up with two Jews in it. By seven o'clock he was in police headquarters with the French captain and two Austrian policemen interrogating the two Jews.

He had been disappointed to find that neither of them was from Camp 93, but at least they had had contact with those other Jews: the truck was the link. 'You'll make it easier for yourselves if you tell us where we can find Fräulein Graz and her friends, especially a guy named Keppel.'

'Perhaps we should use Gestapo methods on them. No offence, gentlemen.' Captain Corbot, punctiliously polite, looked at the two Austrian policemen who bowed their head stiffly.

Both men kept their faces expressionless. Schmidt, the senior officer though the younger, had no known political bias: the sort of man that any Occupying Power could use like a puppet in his role as policeman. Pohl, being only a sergeant, did as he was told.

'We been through it with the Gestapo.' Zalman, the thinner of the two Jews, spoke English with an American accent. 'I was also in Chicago, eight, ten years ago. I been through it with your guys, too.'

'So you know what to expect.' Dunleavy knew he would only use force as a last resort; but he wasn't against using the threat of it. 'We go to work on you, you still keep your mouth shut, then you get five to seven years – '

'Five to seven? For a little black market stuff? Don't make me laugh, major. We ain't in your territory. We'll get a year at the most. They ain't keen on filling up the jails here in Austria, major.'

'Were you as cocky as this all the time you were in Auschwitz or wherever?'

'Treblinka. Me and Rawicz, we got by.'

'Collaborating?'

Zalman shrugged. 'Call it surviving.'

'Okay, try a little surviving now. You'll get more than a year in jail, Zalman. We can dream up quite a few charges – accessory after the fact of a murder, aiding and abetting the escape of a murderer – '

'Hey, wait a minute, we dunno anything about any murder! Jesus, they didn't say anything about killing anybody. Who was it?'

'The Camp Director and my driver.'

Zalman looked at Rawicz, said something to him in Polish, then looked back at Dunleavy. 'That's different. I swear to you we didn't know anything about that. This guy Keppel, he took some shots at us and we just took off – '

'Keppel's the man we want.' Dunleavy knew it was a wish as much as anything else. Maybe Keppel had killed Roy and Martin, then forced everyone else to go with him. Including

109

Luise Graz. 'Where can we find him? Are they up in – where is it? Rennwald?'

'Maybe they're still there. If they ain't, then you better start looking over the border. I didn't talk to any of this lot, but Merano is usually the next stop.'

Out of the corner of his eye Dunleavy saw Pohl, the police sergeant, tilt his head on his stiff neck, blink, then resume his mask. But this wasn't the moment for questioning an Austrian policeman about Merano. He concentrated on Zalman, who was collaborating like crazy now. Jesus, what a son-of-a-bitch you must have been in Treblinka, Dunleavy thought. How the hell had Zalman survived the hatred of his fellow Jews?

'How do you know? You been to Merano?'

'Sure. We been working both sides of the border – we take our stuff wherever we got buyers. But I dunno where the safe house is in Merano. Lazar, the guy up at Rennwald, he let slip, one day, we had people in Merano. But we never went near them. You know how it is, you can't do business with our people, they ain't got any dough. The Jews are the real losers in this war.' He looked up at Schmidt and Pohl, repeated the remark in German.

Schmidt ignored him, looked at Captain Corbot. 'Shall we hold them for you, Herr Captain?'

Corbot looked at Dunleavy. 'Do you want them any further, major?'

'No. I'll have someone come down from Garmisch to pick up the truck. I'm going up to Rennwald, if it's okay with you.'

'I'll send four men with you, just in case there's some trouble.'

'Sergeant Pohl can go, too,' said Schmidt; then for the first time sounded political: 'Just so that the villagers won't think the war is still on.'

Corbot gave a thin smile, looked at Dunleavy. 'You see, major? The last shot hasn't yet been fired.'

Dunleavy took Pohl with him in the jeep, squeezing him in between the valise and kit bags in the back. He said nothing to the policeman till they were entering Rennwald, then he looked back at him casually. 'Do you know Merano, sergeant?'

'No, Herr Major. I have never been down into Italy.'

'Never? You live only a few miles from the border – '

'My father was killed by the Italians at Caporetto. One doesn't forget.'

Caporetto: the name meant nothing to Dunleavy. Then he remembered something from one of Hemingway's books; but that had been another war, one he had never really been interested in. 'The First World War? You still hold grudges about that? How are you going to feel about us in this war?'

'Only time will tell, Herr Major,' said Pohl, but Dunleavy read the right answer at once.

The search of Rennwald was fruitless. Lazar, the man who ran the Jewish farm hostel, was quite adamant there had been no party of DPs staying at the hostel. Yes, he knew Zalman and Rawicz, a couple of criminals he was sure, and liars to boot; he wouldn't believe their story of how they had come to be in possession of a stolen US Army truck. The hostel was nothing more than a training centre for Jewish boys. Ask the Burgermeister or the village priest, both of them honest men. Which Dunleavy did and got the same reply. As far as the Burgermeister and the priest knew, Rennwald was not a staging camp for DPs.

Frustrated, believing nothing of what he had been told in the village, he at last gave up. 'Okay,' he said to the French sergeant in charge of the soldiers who had accompanied him, 'they were here, all right. But they've gone and they won't be coming back. Thank Captain Corbot for his co-operation. I'm going up to Brenner, see if the DPs try their luck through there in another truck. If nothing shows by midnight, I'll be on my way to Merano. You can come with me, Sergeant Pohl.'

'To Merano?' Pohl's voice cracked a little.

'To Brenner,' said Dunleavy, wondering again how much Pohl knew about the Jews and their safe house. If he held grudges, as he obviously did, was he still conducting his own private war against the Jews? 'What use would you be to me in Italy?'

'None, Herr Major. I don't see what use I can be to you up at Brenner.'

'You can help me arrest the DPs if they come through.'

But the DPs did not come through and by midnight Dunleavy was ready to continue the trail south into Italy. But as he and Charlie Lincoln drove the road now towards Merano he was again wondering what connection there was between an Austrian police sergeant and a French doctor who pretended not to know each other and why Sergeant Pohl, who said he had never been into Italy in his life, should have been afraid of going down to Merano.

2

'I'd suggest singing,' said Luise, 'but I don't think any of us have enough breath.'

'Remember the films before the war?' said Hilde Klein. 'Lilian Harvey used to run around the mountain tops singing like a bird. Even then I never believed it.'

They had been walking for four hours and Keppel had told Luise they had probably another two hours to go before they would reach the farmhouse where they would rest till tomorrow night. The group, now an attenuated line, was not only physically exhausted but their spirits seemed to be going out of them with every breath they expelled. Luise had kept walking up and down the line, urging everyone to keep going, trying to inject into them some of the *ersatz* confidence that she had difficulty in brewing in herself. The road, no more than a wide track, had fortunately been traversed by some traffic since this morning's snowfall; it was slushy, but so far they had not had to trudge through any thick snow. But the slush was turning to ice as the night cold settled on it and Luise had already had to stop and help several of those who had fallen to their knees.

The departure from Rennwald had been hurried, some of the group on the edge of panic. Most of them had had to be roused from sleep and now all of them were feeling the effects of not having had enough rest.

They had paused now for their second rest in half an hour. They were in among trees and some of the men had gathered branches and small logs for the weary women and children to sit on. A small handcart had been borrowed from Lazar and it was piled with the luggage; Keppel and the two men who had been helping him pull it leaned against it and smoked cigarettes. Luise and Hilde Klein rested against the back of it, staring at the dim figures squatting in the shadow of the trees.

'When the troops were going east in the early part of the war, they used to sing.' Hilde offered Luise a cigarette, but the latter shook her head. 'We used to watch them from the factory – we used to hate them for sounding so confident and strong. It was different this time last year when they were coming back, with the Russians chasing them – they weren't singing then. I think it only happens in films – I mean, people singing to keep their spirits up. Did you like singing?'

Luise had been only half-listening. 'What? Singing – you mean before the war? Yes. Yes, I loved it very much.'

'Is it true you've lost your voice? Your opera voice?'

'I don't know.' She hadn't talked about it with anyone before. 'I've lost my confidence and perhaps that's the same thing. I have nothing left in here – ' She tapped her breast. 'I couldn't sustain a note.'

'Perhaps re-training – ? Another year or so, when you're fully recovered – '

'Perhaps,' Luise said, but she couldn't think that far ahead. She was finding it difficult to think even two hours ahead. 'I guess we'd better start moving again, before they all fall asleep.'

They started off again, some of them, especially the children, having to be cajoled, scolded and even bullied to their feet. Keppel, still limping, had been relieved by Michael Klein on the cart; he walked now with Luise at the tail of the line. She sensed that for the first time the strength was beginning to drain out of him.

'Are we over the worst of it?'

He nodded, but she didn't see the movement of his head and she repeated the question. He snarled, 'Yes! For God's sake – yes!'

She lapsed into silence, angry at him but not wanting to waste her precious breath on abusing him. The road ran through a narrow pass, the mountains climbing steeply on either side. With an effort she lifted her head and looked up at the mountains, a crumpled mass of rock and ice, blue-white light and deeper blue shadow; the moon rested on a peak, balanced there like a silver coin in the moment before falling heads or tails. Let it be good fortune, Lord: but she couldn't remember that the moon had ever influenced her life one way or the other. She was just surprised that her mind, with a will of its own, had said a prayer. It had been that way in Birkenau: at the worst moments, when she had had nothing else left to draw upon, she had found herself praying.

A star moved from one peak to another; then she heard the faint hum of an engine and recognized the navigation lights of a plane. Oh, to be in it, to make the journey south with such ease! She had never been in a plane in her life. All the journeys before the war had been made by train or car and always to the same places, to Waldgarten, St Moritz, Nice, Paris, London; people of her class did not fly, one took one's time and travelled in privacy and comfort. Her father had been something of a rebel and had encouraged her in the flouting of certain conventions; he drove his cars at breakneck speed, but never to get to a destination sooner, only for the sheer thrill of speed. She remembered now his admonition to her once when she had been impatient to reach Paris: 'Destinations are better for being delayed, my dear. Arrival is sometimes only another form of disappointment.' It was the first time that she had seen that her gay debonair father had a dark side to him, that he mocked life because it was his only way of dealing with its shortcomings.

She was jerked back to the present by a yell up ahead. At the same time she realized they were going downhill; the road sloped towards a bend cut into a steep ridge. They were out of the timber and the snow-reflected moonlight showed shapes clearly if not in detail. She saw the hand-cart running down the road, the three men trying to hold it back but sliding helplessly on the ice-crusted road. One man fell, skidding over the ice into the snow at the side of the road; the people ahead of the cart stumbled out of its path. A second man lost his footing, let go of the cart and fell headlong, sliding into two women at the side of the road and sending them sprawling. Michael Klein was still clinging to the cart, trying to halt it but being pulled along faster and faster as it gained momentum from the slope. Ben Keppel tried to run after the cart and the frantically yelling Klein, but he slipped almost at once on the ice and crashed to the ground.

Luise stood frozen, watched as the cart reached the bend in the road, saw it plunge off out of sight. She would never understand why Michael Klein did not let go; he was still clinging to the cart when it disappeared. There was a scream from Hilde Klein, then she went running down the road, slipping and falling, clambering back to her feet, calling her husband's name in a shrill continuous scream that came back as a pain-filled echo from the mountains around.

When Luise reached the bend the group had congealed again, were staring down the slope. Anna Bork was struggling with Hilde Klein, holding the distraught woman back from flinging herself down the steep incline. The long wall of snow was pockmarked with bags and bundles that had been hurled out of the cart as it had plunged down; but there was no sign of the cart itself or of Michael Klein. Then Luise saw the long smear in the snow that ended in the black border of trees at the bottom of the slope.

Luise looked around, jerked her head at Simon Berger. 'Come on, Herr Berger. You and I must go down there.' Ben Keppel limped forward, but Luise barred his way. 'Stay where you are – you can't go down there with that leg of yours. If Herr Berger and I need help, we'll call out.'

It took her and Berger ten minutes to get down to the trees. They had to go carefully for fear of starting a snow slide; several times as she came close to the weaving path of the cart she felt the snow move around her. Then she and Berger were in the shadows of the trees, standing above the disintegrated cart and the shattered body of Michael Klein.

'Do we take him back up to the road?'

Berger shook his head. In the coal mines he had seen the crushed and mangled bodies of other men and he had known the correct if cruel rule that no miner's wife should see her husband's remains. 'It would do Frau Klein and the children no good to see him like that. Let them remember him like he used to be.'

The darkness under the trees was not complete; some light was reflected from the snow. Luise looked again at the black lump of clothing wrapped round the base of a tree; the face was turned towards her but it too was black, with blood. This corpse was no one she had known, it bore no resemblance to Michael Klein.

Berger picked up the tarpaulin that had covered the baggage that had been in the cart. 'We'll wrap him in this, leave him here. I'll come back with one of the men in the morning and bury him.'

Luise, shutting her mind if not her eyes against the wreck of what had once been a smiling hopeful man, helped Berger lift Klein on to the spread-out tarpaulin. Berger then rolled the tarpaulin expertly round the pitiful shape, tucking in the ends; he had done the same thing years ago in the mines, but he mentioned none of that to Fräulein Graz. He recognized that she was having difficulty in retaining control of herself; if he treated her carefully she was not going to crack. He had had his doubts about her, the countryman's contempt for the soft ones of Vienna, but she was not as soft and vulnerable as she looked. She had survived Birkenau, which was more than his wife, poor damned woman, had managed to do.

Leaving the tarpaulin bundle at the foot of the tree, they climbed slowly back up to the road. Hilde Klein had quietened down, stood with her two children clinging to her; for once young Rebecca was silent, had no question to ask. As Luise shook her head to the unspoken query of their mother, both children cried aloud, then buried their faces against their mother's hips. Hilde Klein shook her head dumbly.

'Herr Berger will come back in the morning,' Luise said. 'We can't bring your husband up now –'

'No!' It was an animal shriek; the mountainside shivered with the echo of it. 'No, no, no!'

Anna Bork and two of the other women moved in, took Hilde

and the children gently but firmly, began to lead them down the road. Luise mustered the others, told them to go on. Everyone stared down the slope, saying a silent farewell; then the tiny procession got under way again, moving faster now as if the unexpected tragedy had somehow frightened up reserves they had forgotten. David Weill was the last to go, the mutter of his prayers dying away down the road.

'What about the baggage?' Luise said.

'It will have to stay there tonight,' said Keppel. 'We couldn't get it up now, we're all too exhausted.'

'Perhaps we can borrow a truck or something in the morning,' Berger said. 'When we come back to bury Herr Klein.'

Herr Klein. All our months together in the camp, the events of the past twenty-four hours: all of it, Luise thought, and we are still almost strangers to each other. Would Zion unite them all into a whole?

It took them another hour and a half to reach the farmhouse run by the Bonetti family, a tough leathery old man and his two wiry muscular sons. On the way the group passed a deserted border post, a small hut and a striped post hanging from a broken hinge; up here in this lonely pass it seemed that both travellers and officialdom had decided that the international boundary had no meaning. The faded sign on the northern wall of the tiny hut was in German, that on the southern wall in Italian: an illiterate would have passed from Austria into Italy without knowing it. It was a mocking echo of how meaningless arbitrary boundaries had proved in the war years just gone.

The Bonettis were not welcoming hosts. They hustled the group into the big low stone barn at the back of their farmhouse, pointed to the piles of straw that would be the beds, then brought in several piles of rough army blankets and dumped them on the dirt floor.

Luise looked at Keppel. 'And that's all? What about a meal?'

'The old man says we'll have to cook our own. His contract is only to supply us with shelter, so he says.'

'Contract?'

'These men are professional smugglers – we *pay* them.' Keppel was smoothing out straw for a bed, covering it with two blankets. 'You and I will have to sleep together, Herr Professor – there aren't enough blankets to go around.'

'Any bed is welcome, even any bedmate. No offence, Herr Keppel.' Then David Weill looked at Luise. 'Do not look so angry, Fräulein Graz. These men here on the farm were probably untouched by the war. Why should they worry about us? They are peasants trying to scratch a living – we are just money to them, another cash crop, the same as the goats and sheep I heard in the other barn across the yard.'

'But it's making money out of misery!'

'I agree with Fräulein Graz,' said Anna Bork unexpectedly. She had been making Hilde Klein and her two children comfortable in a corner of the barn; now she came across and stood beside Luise. The latter looked at her, wondering if she had missed some sarcasm in the Bork woman's remark, but Anna had turned her head and was staring fiercely at the younger of the Bonetti sons who was standing by the half-closed door. 'They shouldn't be paid till they have given us something hot to eat – some soup or something for the children!'

'They have already been paid.' Keppel sounded exhausted. He sank painfully down on to the straw, easing out his injured leg. 'Go to bed, ladies. We'll bring the food down with us in the morning, when we collect the baggage. But don't expect any service from Signor Bonetti and his sons. They are giving us exactly what they have been paid for and no more.'

Luise looked around the barn, dimly lit by a couple of smoky lanterns, at the women and children lying exhausted and shivering on the straw. The menfolk seemed dispirited by the ordeal of the past hours, unable to conjure up any real anger and rebellion against the callous bargain of the mercenary Bonettis. Luise, exhausted and frozen herself, understood their apathetic surrender: they had no strength to attack the Bonettis physically and they had long ago learned the futility of verbal protest. But she could not herself surrender: those days were gone forever.

'Were they paid for Michael Klein? And the Kogan family and the Grunfeld sisters?'

'I suppose so,' said Keppel wearily.

'Then they owe us something. Food or a refund!'

Drawing her coat about her, trying to warm herself with her anger, she strode across to the Bonetti son still standing by the door. He held a lantern in one hand and he lifted it as she approached him, like a sentry scrutinizing someone who might attack him. He had a long thin face, aged beyond his years by deep lines, and black close-cropped hair that started growing just above his thick eyebrows; in the yellow light of the lantern his face was a leathern mask behind which the dark suspicious eyes watched her resentfully, the slow mind quick enough to anticipate that this woman was going to battle with him. Luise did not disappoint him, attacking him at once.

'Do you have any soup cooking in your kitchen?'

Surprised by her ability to speak Italian, he was trapped into nodding. Then he recovered and shook his head. 'Only for us.'

'Then we'll make more.' She looked around; only Anna Bork was on her feet. 'Will you help me, Frau Bork?'

Anna Bork, for the moment anyway, had someone to hate more than Luise. She glared at Bonetti, nodded to Luise. 'I'll cut off his balls if he tries to stop us.'

Bonetti shook his head, tried to slip out of the door immediately behind him. But Anna was too quick for him. She pushed him aside, catching him off balance, and flung open the door. She looked back into the barn at the people sitting up in their rough beds.

'Stay awake! We'll be back with some soup!'

Luise was grateful for the other woman's forceful support; she knew she would not have had the physical strength to stop Bonetti slamming the door in her face. The support had come from the most unexpected quarter, but now all at once she was glad; she did not care whether it would heal the breach between herself and Anna Bork, she only knew she was glad that it had not come from Ben Keppel or one of the other men. She had more faith in the power of women in this circumstance.

'You will have to talk to my father.' Bonetti was in retreat, already beaten by these two foreign women. 'He's in the house –'

Luise and Anna were ahead of him, striding across the frozen mud of the yard and into the low-roofed primitive house. Old Man Bonetti and the other son, seated at a rough table eating their supper, looked up in angry surprise as Luise flung back the door and she and Anna strode in. She couldn't help but remark the theatricality of their entrance and it, too, delighted her: she was something like the old Luise Graz, the one who broke the conventions. The other Bonetti son followed them in, looking sheepishly at his father and brother.

'Signor Bonetti, I want some soup – now!' Luise saw the big black pot hanging from its hook over the glowing coals in the open fireplace; the kitchen was thick with the smell of the bubbling soup. 'Enough for the children. I'll take that over to the barn now, while you give meat and vegetables to Frau Bork to make some sort of meal for the rest of us!'

Luigi Bonetti didn't stand up. He looked at the son who had come in behind Luise and Anna. 'Idiot! Why didn't you lock them in the barn?' Then he looked at the two women. 'You get nothing more without paying for it.'

Luise stepped quickly to the table and before either of the men seated there could stop her picked up the big bread knife and handed it to Anna Bork.

'When we were released from the concentration camp, Frau Bork, personally, castrated four SS men. Right, Frau Bork?'

Anna Bork knew a good lie when she heard it. She nodded and ran her thumb along the edge of the big sharp knife.

'Do you want that to happen to one of your sons?' said Luise. 'He's still young enough to cherish what he's got.'

Anna had caught the mood: she swung round, held the knife menacingly close to the belly of the younger son. The older son rose from the table, but his father shook his head and he sank back on his chair. Luigi Bonetti, bald head shining like speckled marble in the light of the lamp hung above the table, stared calmly at Luise.

'You are a lady – why do you talk like that?'

'Because Frau Bork and I know what men value most – even the men who don't have women in their house. We have killed other men, signore – ' *What am I saying?* But the words came easily to her: she sensed the power of her threats. The old man was unafraid, but his sons were apprehensive, both of them looking with scared eyes at the glinting knife in Anna Bork's hand. 'If you had a wife here, she would see that our women and children were fed. If you won't give us the food out of your own charity, then give it to us in your wife's name. If you don't give it to us, Frau Bork will give the knife to your son's belly!'

Anna jerked the knife and the Bonetti son shrank back, drawing in his stomach. It's so easy to be threatening when you have someone else to use the knife, Luise thought; she was doubly grateful now that Anna Bork had come with her, knew that Anna would have no hesitation in using the knife. But what would happen to them if she did? The two of them could not possibly fight off Old Man Bonetti and the other son; out of the corner of her eye she saw the three hunting rifles leaning in a corner, saw the Bonetti son at the table glance quickly at them. But the son against the door proved their trump card.

'Papa, let them have the food!' The dark eyes were now popping out from under the heavy brows; his stomach kept shrinking away from the knife. 'There's enough – give it to them!'

Luigi Bonetti didn't even look at his son, just kept staring calmly at Luise. Other than for the glance when she had first turned the knife on his son, he had ignored Anna. Thirty years of married life had taught him nothing more about women than that one would never understand them; but he had never been afraid of them and had beaten his wife whenever she had abused or puzzled him. He recognized the woman with the knife for one of his own kind, a peasant; but the younger woman, the one who had done all the talking, was another kind altogether. He had seen the upper class women holidaying down in Merano in the days before the war and he had recognized instinctively that you could not treat them as you treated a woman like his Isolina. The peasant woman had the knife, but this was the one he had to deal with. If she were not handled properly she could ruin the business he had. The men who had come to make the contract with him had told him there were thousands of Jews in Germany and Austria wanting to make the journey south through Italy to Palestine. Though illiterate and uneducated, he had a farmer's approach to business: it was like early spring sowing, you took the long view.

'You can have the soup,' he said. 'There's more in the other pot that can be warmed up. You can have it all for two thousand lire.'

'For nothing,' said Luise, determined not to let the old skinflint make another penny out of them. She had no idea what he was being paid by *Bricha* for their accommodation, but it was irrelevant; she was now extracting charity from the old man, at the point of a knife. 'And we'll want to use the kitchen tomorrow for cooking.'

'You are a hard woman.'

'You are a hard man, Signor Bonetti. Your wife, if she is in heaven, must be looking down with contempt on you.'

For the first time there was a flicker in the old man's stare. He abruptly crossed himself, stood up. 'My sons will bring the soup over to the barn.'

'We'll want bowls. We have nothing of our own.'

Bonetti spat disgustedly on the dirt floor. 'What else?' he asked sarcastically.

Anna Bork dropped the knife on the table, picked up the large coarse loaf of bread. 'This. And another couple of loaves, if you have them.'

'Jews,' said the old man sourly.

'Yes,' said Luise, and wondered how Bonetti, isolated in this remote region, probably never having met a Jew in his life till six months ago, had been infected by the old prejudice. 'And you had better accept us, Signor Bonetti. Those of us who are left are never going to let you forget the millions of us who died.'

But there was no reaction on Bonetti's wrinkled face and she realized he knew nothing of the gas chambers, of the pogroms in the ghettos; he was infected by anti-semitism, but he was ignorant of what the sickness had done in the countries north of these mountains. Illiterate, not having a radio, he knew nothing of what had happened in Germany and Poland; and though he must have met scores of Jews in the past six months it seemed that none of them had spoken of the Final Solution. His imagination was strictly one of cash-on-the-table-and-no-questions-asked.

Luise and Anna Bork went back to the barn. Crossing the yard Luise said, 'Thank you for helping me.'

'I did it for the others.' Now they had scored their victory, Anna went back to her other conflict. 'I don't want your thanks.'

You bitch, Luise thought; and suddenly wanted to scratch the other woman's face. But she knew her anger was hysterical; she was on the point of collapse. She walked on groggy legs into the barn, told those there that they were going to be fed, then sank weakly down on to a blanket-covered patch of thick straw.

'I made your bed,' said David Weill, hovering over her. 'It was the least I could do, seeing our roles have been reversed. You the bread-winner, I the bed-maker. I am ashamed.'

'Herr Professor – ' She smiled wanly up at him, lay back against the straw piled up against the wall. She drew the blanket up around her, wondering if she would have to share the bed with anyone. She was too exhausted to care, even if it should turn out to be Anna Bork. 'I have been playing Brünnhilde. I don't think I am the right casting for the part.'

'I think you are.' Weill smiled gently. 'Perhaps not as stout as some I have seen, but you have the strength. By the time we reach Palestine a lot of us may be playing unaccustomed roles. We were all glad you spoke Italian so well.'

'Not well, just fluently. Whenever I could, I used to come down to La Scala in Milan with my father. He hoped some day to see me playing Violetta in *La Traviata*. But that would have been wrong for me, too. I'm not the tragic type.'

'I hope not,' said Weill. 'It would be a waste.'

'Herr Professor, were you a ladies' man when you were young?'

He smiled, shook gently with quiet laughter. 'I have always been scared of women. A ladies' man? I'm a misogynist, Fräulain Graz, but only out of fear.'

Later, when the second pot of soup arrived, he brought her

a bowl of it and some bread. He sat down on an upturned broken wheelbarrow, looked at her while she ate greedily. 'Do you ever think of the meals you had before the war? I give myself indigestion remembering a meal I once had at Sachers. I went to Vienna for a conference and disgraced myself by over-eating and getting drunk. Some day I dream of disgracing myself again in the same way.'

'At Sachers?'

'No. I am saying goodbye to Europe.' There was a sadness in his voice that she had remarked before; he still lived in the past and she wondered why he was going to Palestine, to help build a future where optimism would be one of the major necessities. He smiled down at her, a sad grin that matched the note in his voice. 'I should always have indigestion if I remained here, no matter how little I ate.'

When she woke in the morning he was the first person she saw, standing in a corner facing the wall, his shawl over his shoulders as he began the day in the only way he knew how, in prayer. She gazed at him a while, envying him and feeling a little ashamed. Cobwebs of prayer had hung in the corners of her mind for the past five years, ever since she had realized that survival was a matter of luck. But religion, as a total commitment, was beyond her. God, in whom she had come to believe, would have to accept her on personal terms.

She went across to see if she could coax breakfast out of the Bonettis. But Old Man Bonetti had done some thinking during the night, balancing the small profit against the larger one: this contract with the Jews could run on for a year or two, perhaps even longer. Without argument he offered more soup and bread, ordered his surly sons to take it across to the 'signorina's friends.' Luise thanked him graciously, giving the old man the sort of smile he had not had from a woman in years; she had learned from her father the advantages of being magnanimous in victory. *You never know*, he had said, *your next client may be the lawyer you have just defeated in a case*. But she had known that, as always, Rudolph Graz had been disguising his natural charity behind his gentle mask of cynicism. It was her own charity that made her smile at Luigi Bonetti, though she was cynical enough to wonder if he appreciated charity of any sort, even that in a simple smile of thanks.

She insisted on going back up the pass with Simon Berger, Noah Malchek and the younger Bonetti son. Ben Keppel argued that he should go, but Luise, her authority now totally acknowledged by the rest of the group, told him he should stay at the farm and rest his leg. He would be needed that night to guide them on the next stage of their journey.

'God help us,' he said, 'if ever a woman becomes head of Eretz Israel.'

'None of you men will let that happen,' she said sweetly. 'Jews are even worse than the Catholics at keeping women in their place.'

Hilde Klein wanted to accompany Luise and the men, but Luise, feeling more and more sure of herself but being gentle with her authority, told Hilde to stay with the children. The small party set off back up the pass, Berger and Malchek hauling a small cart with them. Aldo Bonetti led the way, never looking back at them, doing only what his father had told him to do and offering not the smallest dividend of friendship.

The morning was clear and brilliant; the mountains glimmered with white flame. Occasionally there would be a sharp crack, the sound of gunfire; it occurred several times before Luise recognized it as a noise from the peaceful past, that of ice or rock breaking off the side of a mountain. The ice on the road had melted under the morning sun; they passed some bushes where buttons of green dotted the branches. Suddenly Luise realized that spring was coming up from the south, creeping up the mountains like a slow beautiful tide. Michael Klein had died in the season when hope began anew.

They brought his body and the baggage back down to the farm. He was buried in a corner of a field, in the angle between two low walls built of stones like fossilized bones. The Bonetti men stood aside, looking on from a distance, resenting this permanent intrusion on their land by a stranger they had never met; but Luise knew they would never disturb the body, recognized the superstition that would always make them skirt this spot with their plough. David Weill said *Kaddish*, the words as melancholy as the keening cry of a dying bird; tears turned cold on the chilled cheeks and the frozen clods of earth thudded like blows on the tarpaulin-wrapped body. Hilde Klein let out a wail of anguish that wounded the silence of the mountains: they echoed with the sound of pain. The grave was left unmarked: Michael Klein could not be allowed to betray the other Jews who would follow him through here. Luigi Bonetti had argued the point, careful not of the Jews but of his own continued profit, and Luise had conceded it.

The day passed, the shadows flowed down from the mountains like silent avalanches, and then it was night and time to be moving again. Hilde Klein and the children hung back, but Luise and Anna Bork gently but firmly steered them after the others.

'You have the girls to think of now,' said Luise. 'You must get them to Palestine.'

Hilde reluctantly nodded, but her face was turned back towards the far corner of the moonlit field. 'Will I ever come back to put flowers on his grave?'

Luise had no answer, so attempted none. She took Hilde's arm and they went on down the road after the others, all of them now carrying their baggage and Simon Berger and Joachim Winter, another of the men, also burdened with the two food packages. Luigi Bonetti had refused to lend them the handcart.

'I have given you enough.'

'Let us buy the cart.' Luise knew the group had very little money to spare, but she hoped that if she bought the cart *Bricha* would re-imburse her.

But Bonetti wasn't interested in selling. 'Goodbye, signorina,' he said flatly.

Luise wanted to swear at him, but restrained herself. Ben Keppel, when she told him of Bonetti's refusal to sell or lend them the cart, had wanted to walk off with it anyway. But she pointed out to him that though there were five men in their group, they were really not a match for the Bonetti men if it came to a fight.

'They are in much better condition than you are, even the

126

old man. And they have three rifles back there in the house – all we have is your pistol. And you've used that enough.'

Now they were heading down the winding road, between the pale blue fields of snow, the doors and shutters of the Bonetti farmhouse already closed against them: no chink of light showed and the low stone house soon faded in the pale glare of moonlight, was slowly bleached out like an already fading memory. Luise wondered how long any of them, with the exception of Hilde Klein and her children, would remember this stop on their long journey.

It took them an hour and a half to reach the main road. They came down the gravel track they had been traversing through a long stand of dark pines; long before they reached the Merano road they could hear the hum and whine of traffic on it. After the mountain silence that had surrounded them for the past twenty-four hours the sounds down on the main road made some of them apprehensive. The whine of engines, the hum of tyres, were a hint that they were coming out into the open again, that they were now approaching territory where the British lay in wait for them.

The plodding line came together as they came down through the trees. Luise was at the head of the group as they came round the last bend and almost walked into the truck parked in the shadows. Two men appeared from the darkness on the other side of the truck, one of them flashing a torch on the ground in front of him.

'Keppel?'

Ben Keppel stepped forward and the man who held the torch turned it up into his own face. He was plump-cheeked, with a thick black moustache under a hooked nose and amused eyes; and he wore the uniform of a British army sergeant. Luise caught her breath and heard the gasps behind her.

Keppel said, 'You are Elkin and Strauss? This is Fräulein Graz.'

Sergeant Elkin switched off the torch, said in English, 'Welcome to Italy, Fräulein Graz. And your friends.'

Luise could feel the panic simmering inside her, felt the empty sickness welling up. All this way, and Michael Klein dead, to be betrayed by Ben Keppel. 'How much do they pay you, Judas?'

It was a moment before Keppel realized she was speaking to him. 'Judas? What are you talking about?'

'Why bring us all this way to sell us to the English?' Her voice was hoarse with the effort to keep it down; but what did keeping quiet mean now? The panic behind her had given way to growing anger at the treachery of Keppel. Simon Berger moved up alongside her, was ready to leap at either Keppel or the two British soldiers, or all three of them.

Sergeant Elkin must have sensed the threat: the torch flashed on again. 'Now settle down, all of you. Get into the truck – we don't have any time to lose, there are patrols all up and down this road. Come on, get a move on!' He still spoke in English, in the abrupt tones of an n.c.o. giving orders to a bunch of slow-witted recruits. 'Come on, no mucking around – up in the truck! Move!'

The group, still puzzled and frightened, moved forward, clambered up into the truck: they recognized the voice of authority when they heard it. Elkin counted them as they got aboard.

'Is this all? Where's the rest of 'em?' Keppel explained what had happened to the rest of the section and Elkin spat into the darkness. 'Christ, it hardly seems worthwhile. Okay, into the truck!'

Luise and Keppel were the last to get aboard. The tarpaulin was pulled down and they sat in darkness as the truck pulled out on to the main road.

'We're waiting for an explanation,' Luise said into the blackness.

Keppel said nothing for a moment and there was a growl from one of the men. Then, his voice pained and shocked: 'How could you believe I'd do such a thing – betray you to the English? These men are on *our* side. We couldn't use this route without them.'

Luise was aware of the quiet in the black interior of the truck; everyone was waiting for Keppel to go on. The trouble with this underground emigration was that *Bricha*, for reasons of security, told its charges so little. She felt the unease of someone who had judged another too hastily, but she was still puzzled. Why should British soldiers want to smuggle Jews to Palestine? Were Elkin and Strauss mercenaries just like Luigi Bonetti and his sons?

'Do we pay them, too, just like the Bonettis?'

'No, no.' There was now also a note of exasperation to Keppel's explanation. 'They belong to *Bricha* –'

'How do they get English uniforms?' said Simon Berger. 'And this is an English truck.'

'Didn't you see the Star of David on their sleeves? They are English soldiers – they belong to the Jewish Brigade, from Palestine. They were here in the war, and in France, too.'

'You mean they fought for the English?'

'Why not? They were fighting the Nazis – I'd have done the same if I'd been in Palestine when war broke out. Elkin and Strauss were born in Palestine – what else could they have joined but the British Army? They've just changed sides now, but it's in our interests for them to stay with the English. We have scores of them working for us.'

'What happens to them if they're caught?'

'It's an embarrassment to the English. So far they've just been discharging those they've caught, sending them back to Palestine. None of them have minded – it is a sort of honour. But just before Christmas they moved most of the Brigade to Belgium – they knew what was happening and they thought we'd be out of the way there. There are only two units left in Italy now, the one Elkin and Strauss are from, a transport company over at Udine, and another one down at Caserta, further south.' He was silent for a moment, then he said, 'I've told you too much.'

'It might have been easier if you had told us more at the start,' said Luise.

'I just don't know why you thought I'd betray you –' There was a youthful whine in his voice: he was still young enough to be hurt by the knowledge that people he had thought were friends could distrust him.

'We're sorry about that,' said Luise and everyone in the

truck echoed her. They knew how distrust and suspicion could weaken the collective strength of them all. No one was more ashamed than Luise, who had placed some value on trust. And now she had been found wanting.

The journey to Merano did not take as long as they had expected. Soon the truck was slowing, turning up a side road and climbing a hill. Then it halted. The horn was tooted, they heard a gate being opened on hinges that creaked, the truck drove in and the gate was slammed shut behind it. A moment later the tarpaulin was flung up and Private Strauss, short, thin and happy, stood below them in the light that came from a nearby window.

'All out!' He sounds so cheery, Luise thought, like some of those tram conductors in Vienna. 'End of the line!'

The group clambered down from the truck, slowly, cautiously, still apprehensive. Luise, having helped all the children down, turned as a hand touched her arm.

'This way, signorina,' said a woman's voice.

Then Luise and the others saw that they were surrounded by nuns, ten or twelve of them. Luise looked up and around her, saw the tower against the night sky and the tall cross on the gable of the building that formed one side of the high-walled yard in which they stood. She looked back at the nun, an older woman whose face was as white as the coif above it.

'A convent, Sister? You are hiding Jews?'

'We hid them during the war.' She was leading Luise and the women and children towards the house; other nuns clucked and fluttered along behind like domestic penguins. 'Charity shouldn't have any armistice, do you think?'

'I don't think the English would equate themselves with the Nazis and the Fascisti.'

'Oh, some of us were Fascisti. I was a great admirer of Mussolini. For a while, that is.' She led them into a large kitchen where other nuns had set places at a long wooden table. 'I am Sister Teresa, the Mother Superior. We are Sisters of Charity – or at least we try to be.' She smiled, looking surprisingly young; dimples made deep shadows in the white cheeks. 'It isn't always easy.'

'Too true,' said Luise and thought how much more difficult it was for someone like herself whose charity was incidental rather than dedicated.

3

The reunion with Ilse and the boys had been everything Besser had hoped for. Early on the Sunday morning Metz had brought the French Army truck down through the moon-bathed mountains into Merano. He had pulled up by a bridge and Besser had got out. The roar of the torrent below them kept their farewell just to gestures; neither had really liked the other and their parting was brief. Besser picked up his suitcases and headed in the direction Metz had pointed out.

The streets were deserted; he passed some gardens, dark and silent as virgin bush. Three unfamiliar trees loomed above him: palm trees here in the mountains? He had never heard of Merano till it had been mentioned as his next destination after Kalburg; then with his usual attention to detail he had gone down into Innsbruck to the library and made himself knowledgeable about the small town south of the border. He knew now that it had been a health resort, that its soil was remarkable for the variety of what it could grow, and that it lay at the junction of four valleys. But he had learned nothing of the people who lived there and so he walked warily now through the silent dark streets, wanting to meet no one till he reached the address he had been given.

It was a three-storied house on the corner of a street of similar houses built in the Tyrolean style; somehow he had expected the houses to be more Italian, plain-fronted and washed in pastels. He had never really been interested in Italy or the Italians, not even after Hitler had made the pact with Mussolini; he could remember reading only one book about Italy, Goethe's account of his journey to Rome, and that hardly applied to the present situation. He wished now he knew more about this country he was in.

The familiar gables and balconies of the house reassured

him a little, as if telling him he was still in friendly territory. The sign on the ornamental gate said: *Pensione Maddalena.* He pushed open the gate and at once a dog, deep-throated and threatening, barked inside the house.

The barking stopped almost at once, as if the dog had been hushed by someone who had been waiting for Besser to arrive. A light appeared behind the tiny barred window in the front door, then the door opened and a man's head was silhouetted against the lighted hallway behind him.

'I am Dr Vence,' Besser said softly in German.

'Come in, Herr Doctor.' The man's German was good, but he was an Italian. 'Madame Vence and your boys are waiting for you. Welcome.'

Besser, not normally emotional in public, wept when he saw Ilse and Hans and Paul waiting at the foot of the stairs that led up from the hall. He gathered them into his arms, held them as the promise of life itself.

The proprietor of the pensione, Signor Fiesco, with an Italian sense of the occasion, had given Besser and Ilse a back room, well away from the boys, where they could enjoy their reunion without interruption. They went to bed and tore at each other with that passion where love stops just short of murder. Their stamina had always been remarkable; it was no less so after this long separation from each other. Alternating with talk that was aimless and comfortable and love-making that was direct and had a sweet agony to it, it was dawn before they fell asleep. They slept wrapped in each other's limbs, secure in that other love that went deeper than anything that lips and hands and genitals could express.

Besser was woken by the sound of church bells, opened his eyes and saw Ilse drying herself by the bidet in the corner of the room. She smiled at him. 'Why don't you doctors invent something *safe* for us women? We always have to go through *this.*'

'We should have worked on it, a pill or something. But *Der Fuehrer* wanted more and more kids. Come back to bed,' he said and threw the covers back.

Then there was a thumping on the bedroom door. 'You had

better put something on,' Ilse said, putting on a robe and getting back into bed. 'The boys are old enough now to notice things. And *that* is very noticeable.'

The thumping on the door was growing more insistent. Still smiling at her, he put on pyjamas and let the boys in. They flung themselves at him and he tumbled back on the bed with them. 'Easy, easy! You're going to bruise me!'

'You smell funny,' said Paul, the seven-year-old, sitting astride him.

Besser twisted his head, grinned at Ilse, then looked back up at his son. 'I need a bath – I've been travelling. What time is it?'

'Ten o'clock.' Hans, nine years old and well on the way to self-importance, looked at his wrist-watch. 'Herr Fiesco said we were to let you sleep. But there is a man downstairs to see you, Father.'

Besser knew who the man would be. 'Tell him I shall be down in ten minutes – I'll have a quick bath. Where did you get such a good watch?'

'Captain Gerstein gave it to me. He said he had taken it from an American soldier in France.' Hans looked at his mother, then back at his father. 'Mother said I wasn't to wear it any more, but I wanted to show it to you.'

'Why didn't you want him to wear it?' Besser looked at Ilse.

'It was taken from a dead man.' She seemed to shudder, drawing her robe tighter round her neck as she sat up in bed.

'Who was Captain Gerstein?'

'Oh, a nice man,' said Hans, and Paul nodded enthusiastically. 'He used to tell us stories of the fighting –'

'All right, go down and tell the man downstairs I'll be there soon.' Besser didn't look at the boys as they went running out of the room, but continued to gaze steadily at Ilse. He could never remember her, a direct uncomplicated woman, being ill at ease before. And felt the unease welling up in himself, the sick gas of betrayal. 'Who was Gerstein?'

'He came to the house only a few times –' She got out of bed, turning her back on him, making a business of looking for her slippers. 'He was in the same regiment as Gerhard Naumann. They came home on leave together –'

'When was this?'

'Oh, early last year, January or February. You'd better have your bath – that man is waiting –'

'Where is he now?'

'Who?'

'Gerstein.' He was almost choking on the gas now; he could feel a trembling in his hands. 'Look at me!'

She found her slippers, put them on, stood up and faced him. Her red hair hung down about her face, her lips were slack and puffed from last night's passion, the green threadbare dressing gown hung shapelessly on her: she suddenly looked old and undesirable. 'Why don't you say it, Karl? Did I go to bed with him? Yes! Once – once in five years, the only time I wanted another man! No, not another man – *any* man! I wanted *you*, but you weren't available – you had your diversions in Berlin, we women heard all about them –'

'That's a lie!' His arm quivered, he had to hold himself back from striking her. 'I never touched another woman – and you know it! Jesus Christ – !' He slammed a hand down on the brass bedstead; it shivered with the force of the blow, an echo from last night's passion. 'How *could* you? How many times have you seen him while I've been – while I've had my *diversions* in Austria?'

'He was killed the last week of the war – the same day as Gerhard. I never heard from him after that one night – I told him I never wanted to see him again and he understood. Tilly Naumann told me he had been killed – I went round to console her when I heard of Gerhard's death. It didn't mean a thing to me – Heinrich's death, I mean –'

'Heinrich?' His sarcasm was as thick as the sour taste that was still choking him.

'When you go to bed with a man you don't keep calling him by his rank. Not unless you're a paid army whore, the girls I thought you were having in Berlin –' Abruptly she sat down on the side of the bed, began to weep. 'I wouldn't have minded if you had had them – I know your appetite, how much you like it. I wouldn't have wanted to know, that's all –'

He didn't bother going to the bathroom. He washed his

hands and face in the basin in the room, dressed hurriedly, his back to her all the time. Then, still smelling of her, still sick with the thought of what she had done to him all those months ago, he went downstairs to see the *Spinne* man.

He was surprised to find he was an Italian: without really thinking about it, somehow he had expected a German. Signor Lucca was a fat bald man with cold pale eyes and a cold air of efficiency. He wore a dark expensive suit and a white silk shirt of a quality that Besser, once something of a dandy, had not seen since before the war. Lucca looked a man untouched by the war and its subsequent shortages, but he also looked a man who would not welcome questions about himself.

'I have new papers for you, your wife and your family, doctor.' His voice was gruff and coarse, as if his windpipe might once have been trodden on; he spoke German with a sort of studied fluency. 'The heat has got a little more intense in the past couple of days and the organization thinks you might cause too much suspicion if you are stopped and pretend to be Dr Vence – I'm told your French is not good.'

'How did you learn that?'

'The organization knows all about you, doctor. Your new name is Karl Ludwig and you are an Austrian national, born at – 'He looked at the papers in his hand. 'Ah yes, at Linz. Do you know it?'

'No.'

'No matter. If ever the matter arises you can say you left there when you were a child. We have changed your wife's maiden name to Fischer and she was born in Vienna. The children were born in Innsbruck. If you want to practise medicine where you are going, there are new medical papers made out for you, from your old university but in your new name. And your army discharge, dated last September in Innsbruck where your wife lived all the time you were away on the Russian front.' He held out the papers. 'Everything has been thought of, doctor.'

'You are most efficient, Herr Lucca.'

There must have been an inflection of surprise in Besser's voice, for Lucca's thick lips twisted in a caricature of a grin. 'Some Italians *are* efficient. Some of us in the north, that is.'

Besser acknowledged the reprimand, changed the subject: 'Did our friends in Germany mention money? I understood there was to be some – ?'

Lucca took out a large bulging wallet from the briefcase he had set down on the table. They were in a small parlour, with the door closed, and Lucca seemed confident that they were not going to be disturbed by any guests who might be staying at the pensione. Besser had the feeling that this house, under Lucca, was run as efficiently and smoothly as any SS office he had ever entered.

'Fifty thousand lire for your immediate needs, plus two thousand dollars for your use when you arrive in Argentina – dollars are more negotiable there. I understand that once you arrive, there will be someone else to look after you. This money, you know, is a loan from the organization, re-payable direct to its agent in Buenos Aires on terms you will discuss with him when you see him. Sign this receipt, please.'

Besser went to sign, then saw the amount on the piece of paper. 'This is not for the full amount.'

'You pay me ten per cent.'

'Doesn't the organization pay you?'

'Yes. But you do, too, doctor. Those are *my* terms – the organization understands that no one can operate in this area without my permission. The war is over, doctor. We are no longer comrades in arms.'

Besser looked into the cold pale eyes, then nodded resignedly. The enemies were more numerous in peacetime, it was dog eat dog and no one could be trusted. 'What name do I sign?'

Lucca shrugged. 'That's up to you. The organization will know who you are, no matter what name you use.'

'Do you know who I am?' Besser paused with the pen above the paper, looked up at the unsmiling fat face.

'Yes, Dr Besser. But you don't need to worry. I am a business-man, not a blackmailer.'

Besser signed the receipt in his new name. 'What business are you in, Herr Lucca, besides this one?'

136

'I have a factory that makes religious statues. Business is very good at present, with so many ruined churches to be built.' He did up the straps of his briefcase, held out his hand. 'A word of advice, doctor. Don't ask such questions of other people – in case they start asking you the same. The SS were not popular in Italy.'

Besser shook the plump strong hand. 'Is there any charge for that advice?'

There was no expression at all in the cold eyes, neither of amusement nor resentment. 'It's the only thing I ever give free, doctor. Good luck. My compliments to Frau Ludwig.'

Frau Ludwig: he remarked the irony of the new name for Ilse, who was already becoming another woman for him. 'Thank you, Oh, one thing, Herr Lucca – you have forgotten to tell me how we leave here and where we go.'

The eyes flickered, there was a momentary air of flusterment. 'Of course – ' You aren't so efficient after all, thought Besser; and felt a malicious pleasure tinged with nationalism. 'There is a train leaving tomorrow morning. Your tickets are with your papers – you go to La Spezia, changing at Milan and Genoa. You will be met at La Spezia – the schedule is also with the papers. They will let you know when you are to board your ship for Argentina.'

'Travelling by train? Is that safe?'

'Dr Ludwig, you have to come out into the open *some* time.' Lucca had recovered his composure; the crack in it had been almost imperceptible, but he would never forgive himself for having lapsed in front of the German. He had always prided himself on his efficiency, his attention to detail. It was so necessary with the business he was running. 'You are just an Austrian doctor and his family who are emigrating to South America – a lot of people are doing it these days, including Italians. You will be safe, so long as you don't wear your guilt on your sleeve.'

'I have no guilt,' said Besser stiffly. 'Good day, Herr Lucca.'

He let Lucca find his own way out of the house, certain that it was he and not Fiesco who owned the place. He went upstairs to the bedroom; Ilse, smelling of talc and the freshness of a hot bath, came in immediately behind him. He threw the papers on the bed.

'We leave tomorrow morning,' he said. 'If you still want to come –'

She slipped off her robe, began to dress. He gazed at her for a moment, at the full breasts with the marks of his teeth still showing on them, at the ripe belly and the thighs . . . He turned away, angry at the feeling welling up in him. The crotch had no loyalty.

'I am sorry you found out about Gerstein.' She began to dress, taking her time about what she put on. Her calmness added to his anger, she was showing new sides to her every moment. He had made the mistake of thinking that in the five years he had been away from her she had not changed. She was five years older, if nothing else, and that made a difference in anyone. He wondered what changes in himself were apparent to her. 'If you hadn't known about him, nothing between us would have been changed. I still love you – I thought last night would have shown that.'

'Bed proves nothing. It's a breeding ground for lies.'

'You never told me you had become a philosopher.'

'Only since this morning.'

They had been reduced to blunt barbs; they hadn't the sophisticated weapons of long-time domestic combatants. Ilse said, 'I am coming with you. If you don't want me to, it'll be for you to say so. I'm not staying behind of my own accord.' He remained silent and after a moment she repeated, 'I still love you.'

Awkwardly, somehow now at a disadvantage, he said, 'There are the children –'

She loved him but she was not prepared to surrender everything: 'If you tell me you don't want me, they stay with me. I've been the one who's had to raise them.'

He nodded angrily, knowing she had defeated him, at least for the time being. 'We have to stick together, for their sake. Make a pretence –'

'I shan't be pretending.' She began to do her hair, leaning forward to look into the dressing-table mirror by the window.

A taper of sunlight touched flame to her hair; he shut his eyes for a moment against the temptation of it. He loved her, always would, but she had planted a worm that could never be eradicated; it was like the bite of the iguana, that he had read never healed. She turned, hair done, lipstick covering the bruised mouth, looking as attractive and desirable as he had ever remembered her. 'Have your bath, then we'll take the boys for a walk.'

Later, as the four of them walked down through the town, through the promenading Sunday crowd, he saw that Hans was no longer wearing his watch. He was about to query what the boy had done with it, then changed his mind. Already he was retreating: any further argument with Ilse, he knew, would be useless. He looked at her above the heads of the boys between them and she smiled at him as if nothing in the whole wide world had happened to their happiness. Christ, he thought, whatever became of the simple uncomplicated girl I married? And was angry at the perverse attraction she had for him as a woman who was proving more interesting, more puzzling than the old Ilse had ever been. Had Gerstein done that to her?

They sat in the gardens, admired the flowers already in bloom, looked up at the sun striking the snow-capped peaks behind the Tschigat, watched the parading crowd watching itself.

'I like the Italians,' said Ilse. 'They have a nice honest vanity.'

'Did you fight with the Italians in the war, Father?' asked Hans.

'No. Doctors don't fight.'

Hans and Paul looked disappointed. 'But you were a major, Father. You should have been fighting!'

'If all soldiers carried a gun, who would look after the wounded?'

'Women,' said Hans, nine years old and already decided on the status of the sexes. 'What did you do in the war, Father?'

The recurring question of postwar generations, Besser thought: he had asked his own father the same question after the Great War. 'Run along. Go over there and see the Passirio

– you have never seen water run so fast as it does in a mountain river.'

The boys, disappointed in a father who had done little or nothing in the war, left them. Ilse moved close to Besser, but kept her eyes on the boys as they leaned over the wall above the torrent of the river.

'What *did* you do, Karl?'

'That's behind us,' he said shortly.

'Is it? When Herr Topp came to tell me you were missing after you had left us, I asked him why you were wanted by the Americans. He seemed embarrassed and wouldn't tell me.' She turned her head, looked directly at him. 'Are you what they are calling a war criminal, Karl?'

'I told you – it's behind us.'

A street musician stood in front of them playing an accordion. A thin chain from his wrist held a skinny freezing monkey in a red knitted vest; it was jumping up and down on stiff legs, like a tiny wizened old man who had been pumped full of some elixir he couldn't handle. Ilse felt in her handbag, dropped some coins into the rattling tin box the monkey held. The musician touched his hat and moved on, playing not an Italian tune but one that Besser had heard on the American forces radio: *Till The End Of Time*. The Americans had conquered everyone, even the musicians.

'Perhaps it isn't behind us,' Ilse said. 'Herr Topp seemed to think the hunt for war criminals might go on for years.'

'Stop talking about war criminals! It's a ridiculous term.'

'It's not my term, Karl.' She was still looking at him; it was he now who was staring across at the boys, avoiding her eyes. 'I don't care what you did – in a way, I'd rather *not* know. But –'

'But what?'

'I know you were at Auschwitz – I still have the letters you wrote when you were there, though you never said what you were doing.'

'You have the letters – *with you?*'

'Every letter you wrote – they are in one of the suitcases.'

He shook his head, looked at her at last. 'You'll have to burn them. Just in case – '

'There's nothing in them, nothing incriminating – I was reading them again last night while I was waiting for you to arrive. Just that you were at Auschwitz and then in Berlin.' She licked her lips tentatively, as if feeling the bruising of last night; but she was feeling future bruising, something that might happen to her in the next minute or two: 'Karl, were you involved in the killing of the Jews at Auschwitz?'

He hesitated, then nodded. He had never been able to lie to her; he realized that, in his own way, he was just as simple as she was. Or had been. 'An order is an order. We were told some of them had to be got rid of. But I was disgusted by it – '

'Disgusted? Only disgusted?'

'Horrified, then. I applied for a transfer – ' Now he *was* lying. He had applied for a transfer long before September 1941 when the first experiments in gas chambers had started. But it would sound better if he made the gas chambers his excuse for going. 'I left Auschwitz a month after the exterminations began – '

'Exterminations? God, what a horrible word!'

'It's not my term – it's like that one you've borrowed, *war criminals*. You sound like a prosecutor,' he said accusingly.

She turned her head away from him: horrified by him or just to look at the boys, he wasn't sure which, 'What did you do in Berlin then? I just wrote to you at headquarters there.'

Should he tell her? He decided to make it a half-truth, tried to sound like a merciful doctor: 'I was with T4 – it was the code name for our operation, we were at Tiergartenstrasse 4 in Berlin. We dealt in euthanasia – mercy deaths, if you like. It was purely medical research, to help people who were suffering, who were more dead than alive.'

It was not the truth and suddenly he hoped she would never find out. He knew the programme had been correct, the *Vernichtung lebensunwerten Lebens*, the destruction-of-lives-not-worthy-of-living. He remembered the briefing he and the other officers had been given by the Director, Professor Heyde; the Director had been a professor of psychiatry at Würzburg

University and Besser had been almost childishly pleased when Heyde had recognized a former student. Heyde had explained that the 'useless eaters', the incurably sick, the mentally retarded, the very old, those who ate precious food but contributed nothing in the way of production, had to die in the interests of the Reich.

At first there had been no Jews on the lists sent from the hospitals and asylums; the operation had only been extended to the concentration camps after the supply from the hospitals and asylums had run out. He had not been one of those doctors who had indulged in only paperwork euthanasia, just marking an X on the personal files of 'useless eaters' that arrived from all over Germany, Austria and the occupied countries. He had worked as a doctor should, trying to see as many of the patients (he had always thought of them as patients) personally as possible, experimenting constantly with the quickest and cheapest way of inducing death. There were times when he had dreamed, if the war had ended another way, of being Germany's top euthanasia expert, a man who would be honoured for his work in relieving the suffering of prolonged dying. He had only become disenchanted when the work had been extended to the Jews in the concentration camps, when the killing had been reduced to paperwork, when it was no longer a work of mercy but a necessity to rid the Reich of the Jews, those who were least worthy of living.

Ilse looked back at him, frowning, wanting to believe something that was beyond her comprehension. She had never been a lover of Jews, but as the war had gone on, as she had seen Jews being carted off, as rumors of the concentration camps had begun to filter back, she had begun to think of Dr Palmbaum, the fortunate one who had escaped to Australia. She had seen the pictures the British and Americans had released of the skeleton dead and skeleton living in the camps and had been physically sick: at what she had seen, at the guilt she had felt as a German, at the thought, that she had tried so hard to deny, that Karl had somehow been involved in such murderous horror.

142

'I *want* to believe you –'

'Please do. You *must*.' His hand reached for hers, took it; it was a moment before he realized what he had done, but he did not withdraw it. 'For the boys' sake. I am not a – a war criminal. Whatever that is,' he added, genuinely puzzled: war was war, not a crime.

'I believe you,' she said and made it sound sincere enough to convince herself as well as him. 'Here come Hans and Paul.'

That night there was no love-making. She turned for his goodnight kiss and he gave it to her, but when she put her hand on his belly all he said was, 'I'm worn out.'

She smiled, playing dumb. 'No stamina. Never mind, there will be plenty of time on the boat to South America. I'm told the warm weather does wonders for one.'

'Yes,' he said and tried to remember if the mind was blank when one made love, if the thought of another man could come between their struggling bodies.

In the morning Ilse burned his letters in the grate in their bedroom; he was surprised at the size of the ribbon-bound pile of letters she had. 'Do you want me to read some of the things you used to say to me? Do you know you had never used dirty words to me till you started to write?'

'Were you offended?'

'I *loved* them. They are so much more – more *honest*. Do you want me to read something you say in this one?'

'No.' She was tempting, like a whore, smiling up at him above the letters as the flames licked at them in the grate. She had already returned to their old relationship, as if Gerstein had never occurred; but he couldn't accept that, at least not yet. 'We must hurry – the train could be early.'

'Mussolini boasted that Italian trains always ran on time.'

'Mussolini is dead.'

When they were ready to leave he looked at the three suitcases she had brought. 'The Vuitton – why did you bring that?'

'It's such a good one. Vanity, if you like – not everyone can afford luggage like that. I was going to take the initials off it, but it would have spoiled it. R.G. – if anyone asks,

I'll say it was my mother's. Say my name used to be Gersbach or something.'

'Or Gerstein.'

She threw another letter on the fire, watched it burn. 'Where did you get it? From some Jew?'

He winced. 'I got it from another officer.' He searched for a name: he was now lying to her all the time. 'Rudy Gunter. He owed me some money, but couldn't pay me. He gave me that instead.'

'I'm glad he did.' She stood up, the last of the letters burned. 'It's beautiful, and so well cared for. He must have had servants – it looks as if it had saddle-soap or something rubbed into it regularly.'

He looked at the bag, wished she had left it behind. It was the only memoir he had of Auschwitz and, after yesterday's talk, he wanted no reminders. But it was too late to throw it away, go and buy another. He picked it up and two of the others, shoving the smallest up under his arm. Ilse took the other two cases, the ones he had brought with him, they said goodbye to Signor Fiesco, and they left for the station. Fiesco, watching them go, thought they looked a nice family group who could be going on a holiday; they looked *German*, but there were plenty of people of German descent here in the Italian Tyrol. He closed the door and wondered when Signor Lucca would telephone him to say that *Spinne* had some more customers on the way.

The train was almost half an hour late in starting: Mussolini was indeed dead. The delay made Besser edgy, as if it were some sort of omen that now they were out in the open, travelling freely just like all the other passengers on the train, things might begin to go wrong. *Spinne* had provided him and his family with first class seats; he knew that the organization still treated him as a serving officer and afforded him travel and accommodation suitable to his rank. He put the luggage up on the racks of the compartment, left Ilse and the boys in their seats and walked along the corridor to the carriage door. He stepped down on to the platform and stood there smoking a cigarette, growing more impatient every minute as the train showed no signs of departing.

He became aware of a young woman standing some distance away who seemed to be observing him; but each time he looked in her direction she turned her head away. She was an attractive girl, some might have called her beautiful, though he preferred them plumper in the face; she was not well dressed, though she was wearing a coat that looked as if it might once have been expensive. There was an air of distinction to her and he wondered if she was a daughter of one of the better families of the town. Her face was unfamiliar, but she did seem to be paying him more than usual attention; surely she was not a whore, looking for some man to pay her fare down to Milan. His unease increasing, he wondered who she might be.

Then the train whistle blew, there were shouts at the far end of the platform, and the train slowly began to move. Besser stepped aboard, slamming the door behind him. He looked out of the open window at the girl as he drew abreast of her. She stepped forward and looked directly at him, but she was still a stranger to him.

'Dr Besser?' she said.

Chapter Four

Luise slept so soundly that when she woke on the Monday morning she had difficulty at first in recognizing where she was. She lay on the straw pallet in the tiny cell staring up at the stone walls and ceiling; she turned her head and saw the small barred window high up in the end wall. A prison cell? She felt the panic of disorientation; then she saw the crucifix above the plain wooden door. As she looked at the door it opened and Mother Teresa came in.

'I hope you had a good night's sleep. I'm afraid most of the others were rather crowded – we had to bed them down in our dining hall.'

'You shouldn't have favoured me, Sister.'

'I don't think they minded. I've been talking to them and they all think you deserved the best night's rest.'

'All of them?' said Luise, thinking of Anna Bork.

'Well, not *all* of them.' Mother Teresa smiled. 'Even here we rarely have unanimity.'

When Luise went along to the dining hall for breakfast the first sound she heard was a child coughing harshly and almost uncontrollably. Judith Winter was leaning over one of her twin daughters, trying to get the child to suck an orange.

'She's got bronchitis – she's always had it.'

Judith Winter was a small thin woman who might once have been pretty, but suffering had made her plain. She and her husband Joachim had survived Treblinka because they had been wig-makers, had been able to work in the factory where the hair shorn from the inmates was utilized in a score of ways as cloth for blankets, coat linings, dresses and, plaited, as whips for some of the more individual guards at the camp. The children had survived because they were identical twins and SS doctors at Auschwitz had been looking for twins on whom they could conduct experiments. By a miracle the Winters had found their seven-year-old daughters alive and almost healthy and they were as devout in their prayers now as David Weill.

'We must get some medicine for her.' Joachim Winter was as thin and plain as his wife; to Luise, the beauty of their two chubby daughters was almost a mockery of the parents. 'The nuns have nothing – '

Luise went looking for Mother Teresa, explained the situation. 'Would I be conspicuous if I went down into the town to a chemist's?'

'Only the rich are conspicuous these days,' said Mother Teresa. 'I shouldn't worry if you think you look Jewish – you could quite easily be Italian. In any case, there is a TB clinic just outside the town and there are a number of Displaced Persons there, including Jews.'

'Do the English watch the clinic?'

Mother Teresa nodded. 'Yes. Some of your people used to pass through there, but not any more. That's why they came back to us.'

'Do the English suspect you?'

Mother Teresa spread her hands. 'Who knows? We just trust in God.'

Luise ate her breakfast quickly, soup, bread and bitter coffee; then she put on her coat and went out into the yard. The army truck had gone and she wondered what their next transport would be. Ben Keppel limped across the yard to her.

'The nun told me where you are going. I'll go with you.'

'Don't you think you should rest your leg?'

'I want to get some liniment or something for it. And I have to look up our contact man here, find out who's picking us up and when. Sergeant Elkin couldn't risk staying around, he said, so he's gone back to Udine. The English are still putting the heat on.'

147

'Did you tell him about what happened at Rennwald?'

'They already knew. Zalman and the other Pole were picked up in Innsbruck.'

'How did *Bricha* know?'

He shrugged, looking depressed: he knew he was going to be disciplined. 'They *know*, that's all I know. They sent word that Major Dunleavy was in Innsbruck and Rennwald.'

'Do you think he'll come after us, all this way?'

But he didn't answer that and she knew now that he had begun to worry, to regret his hastiness with his gun.

They walked down the long narrow road towards the town spread out below them on either side of the wide loop of the river. Turreted castles looked down on them from surrounding hills; one of them, with a square tower rising above it, was a shivering reminder of the guard towers of Birkenau. Luise wondered if these images would forever keep recurring and she turned her eyes away from the tower, aware now that the imagined familiarity of the castle tower was too far-fetched. Better to look at the gun-cotton almond buds ready to explode on the branches, at the corduroy pattern of vineyards on the southern slopes, at the river glinting like a twisted silver sword on the green jacket of the valley. The sun was suddenly warmer, like a promise one knew would be fulfilled.

The town closed around them, but they didn't feel trapped. Nobody hurried, but Merano was busy; this was a working day and it did not have time to stop and gaze curiously at the strangers in its midst. It was marvellous to walk through a town seemingly untouched by the war; what ruins there were stood on the hills outside, castles and fortresses destroyed by time, not bombs. Luise looked at Keppel, who seemed to be responding to the relaxed air of the town, seemed even to be limping less.

They found a chemist, bought cough mixture and liniment, then came out again into the sunlight, turning their faces up to it as to a blessing. Luise had always loved the sun, it had been one of the few attractions that had made her accompany her parents every year to Nice.

Then Keppel, as if to relax and enjoy something as simple

as sunshine were some sort of sin, straightened up. 'Now I must go and find our contact man.'

'Do you know who he is?'

'He's a local business man, his name is Lucca.'

'Another mercenary like the Bonettis? God, how did we Jews get the monopoly reputation as money-makers?'

'That sounds good coming from a Wald.' But Keppel went on quickly before she could reply: 'Will you go back to the convent?'

'I'll wait for you. Where shall I meet you?'

'Make it the station – it's just up there. I'll see you there in half an hour. Fräulein Graz – ' He looked awkwardly down at his feet, like a young boy stumbling over his first approach to a girl. 'Thank you for what you have done since we left Kalburg.'

Luise put her hand on his arm, felt like a mother towards this brave, bitter boy who could so easily make her angry. 'Ben, I'm glad I've done something for the cause of women. We're not a bad sex, really. After all, if it hadn't been for Eve's initiative, we'd all still be bored stiff in the Garden of Eden.'

He half-smiled, looking at her suspiciously. 'You're pulling my leg.'

'It might do it more good than liniment. You should smile more, Ben.'

But he wasn't prepared to relax entirely, not yet. 'There will be time for that when we get to Palestine.'

He went off up the street, limping again, and she watched him sadly. He would never relax, never laugh outright, not even when he got to Palestine; the spring of him had been wound too tightly, he would never survive in a world where there was no enemy. If the British ever allowed them to settle freely in Palestine, whom would he have left to fight? The Arabs? But she knew nothing of them.

She went into a shop, bought some chocolate and candy for the children, taking pleasure in the splurging of her meagre money. Extravagance, even minor, was an echo of the past and she delighted in it. She bought some chocolate for herself and, eating it like a schoolgirl, smiling to herself at the thought of what one of her governesses would have said if she had seen such vulgar behaviour, she walked up the street towards the railway station.

She came to the corner of the sidewalk, paused to let several cars pass before she crossed the road. The last car went by, like a screen drawn aside, and on the opposite side of the road the entrance to the station was exposed. A tall man, a good-looking red-headed woman and two small blond boys had just arrived outside the station. The man put down the three suitcases he carried, eased his arms up and down, then felt in his pockets for their tickets.

Luise, still eating the chocolate bar, crossed the road leisurely. She looked once again at the family, idly thinking what a handsome group they were, wondering how they managed to be so healthy and well fed; then she saw one of the boys, the taller, trying to pick up the biggest suitcase. And suddenly the past rushed back at her like a train: she leaned back as if she had been hit.

The boy wobbled under the weight of the suitcase, put it down again with a bump. She stared at it, saw the initials on it as clearly as if they were luminous and in letters four times as big. Then she looked at the man as he put the tickets back in his pocket and picked up the cases again. He was not as easy to place as the Vuitton bag: he had been a landmark in her life, but the fog of years best forgotten surrounded him. She had seen him only twice, if he *was* the man: in those few moments when he had condemned her mother to death, in that minute or two when he had stood waiting for his train to leave Auschwitz. They seemed destined to meet only at railway stations.

She stared at him, trying to picture him in uniform, to take the grey out of his hair, to surround him with other SS men instead of this happy healthy family. But it was difficult: she was sick with shock, neither her memory nor her eyesight seemed to be functioning properly. The family went on into the station and she looked wildly around for Ben Keppel. *He* would remember, his memory was etched in steel.

But there was no sight of him. On legs that were all at once weak she went into the station, pushing her way through the crowd that had come either to travel or to farewell the travellers. How the Italians seemed to love farewells; everyone she passed seemed to be in an ecstasy of weeping. No one had come to farewell the tall man and his family: did that mean they were strangers like herself in Merano? She went out on to the platform, saw them getting into a first class carriage. She dropped the half-eaten chocolate bar into a waste basket, didn't see the two ragamuffin kids who instantly salvaged it. She moved on down the platform, paused as she saw the man come out of the carriage again, light a cigarette and stand looking about him.

She stood by a signboard, trying to be inconspicuous; behind her the peeling faded posters invited the ill and ailing to take the local waters. The tall man kept glancing about him and it abruptly struck her that he was nervous; almost, it seemed, *afraid*. He kept looking at his watch, then at the station clock. She looked at the clock herself, wondering how soon Ben Keppel would arrive. She needed him; she had no idea what she could do about the tall man. Two carabinieri were standing by the inner gate; but what could she say to them if she went to them? 'There is a man over there who was once an SS doctor at Auschwitz and sentenced my mother to death. Would you arrest him, please?' She knew of the war crimes trial that was going on at Nuremberg, but was the tall man (his name evaded her, as if her memory was telling her the past was best forgotten) a big enough fish to interest the prosecutors at Nuremberg? Would they, could they, respond to the plea of everyone who pointed his finger at his own private war criminal?

Then the train's whistle blew. The tall man threw away his cigarette, walked across and swung aboard the train, slamming the carriage door behind him. She felt the sickness of shock drain out of her; all at once she was tingling with excitement, as if her fingers had touched some electrical charge. And then, as if her memory had had a sudden change of mind, as if it conceded that the past should not be forgotten, the tall man's name came to her, clear and distinct as a shout.

She stepped forward as the train began to pull out.

'Dr Besser?'

The man swung his face back towards her. The train went

down out of the platform, Besser's face turned back towards her like a blank disc from which her question had wiped all markings.

She watched till the train went round a bend, Besser's face disappearing round the long curve of the train; then she turned and walked slowly back towards the station gate, wondering what, if anything, she should have done. The two carabinieri looked at her, but their interest was not official: she was a pretty woman, to be admired not arrested. She passed them and went on out to the street where Keppel was limping up and down like a crippled picket.

'Where have you been? Good God, we don't have time for sight-seeing! I couldn't find Lucca –'

'Ben,' she said quietly, 'do you remember a doctor at Auschwitz named Besser?'

The indignation on his thin face set, then changed gradually into puzzlement. 'Besser?'

'A tall good-looking man. He was one of those who used to sort us out when we first arrived at the camp –'

'I remember him. Why?'

'I've just seen him and his family – they went out on the train.'

Keppel said nothing, then he began to walk down the street, not looking at her, taking it for granted that she would follow him. She wanted to clout him over his superior male ear, but the cause of women was unimportant right now. She fell into step beside him.

'He nominated my brother for the gas chamber.' Keppel's voice sounded mechanical; he walked staring straight ahead of him. 'Kurt was only fifteen, he wasn't very strong and he had poor eyes. Besser decided he was useless –'

'He condemned my mother, too. For no reason at all, except perhaps that she wasn't young.'

'I was outside the station when the train went out. You should have come and got me – I'd have killed him.' He touched the pocket of his threadbare overcoat where she saw the bulge of his gun.

Yes, he should be killed. Then she was horrified at what her

152

mind, with the irresponsibility of pure hatred, had said. Reason came back: 'And got both of us arrested? Don't be so stupid!'

Keppel at last looked at her, stopped on the edge of the sidewalk. They were opposite a church: a few people flowed down the steps, coming from daily Mass, everything right for the moment with God and their world. Keppel looked at their faces, varnished with piety, their faith whole, if only for the moment. Then he looked back at her.

'If I came face to face with him – do you think I could stop myself from killing him?'

She shook her head, not in answer to his question but in bewilderment at the thought of what he was saying: murder, she told herself, was beyond her. But it had not been a moment ago.

'We should leave it to others – '

'Who? The Italians? The English? What would they do to him, unless we stayed behind to be witnesses against him? He'll go free,' he said bitterly. 'The English are more concerned with us. And the Italians couldn't care less – they've already forgotten they had anything to do with the Germans.'

They crossed the street, began to walk back along the street that led out of town. Luise, her mind tortured, wanting more time to think about Besser, changed the subject: 'What about Lucca?'

'He was out on business, they said. They told me – ' Then he looked beyond her, spun round and limped away, shouting over his shoulder, 'Tell him nothing!'

She stared after him, utterly bewildered; then the jeep swung into the kerb beside her. Dunleavy grabbed her arm, shouted, 'Get him, Charlie!' and she saw the young soldier running up the street after Keppel, who had already turned a corner and disappeared. Trembling, she looked up into Dunleavy's face.

'You can let go of my arm, major. I am not going to run away.'

'You feel as if you might fall down if I let you go.' But he freed her arm, stood back a little from her. 'I didn't think it was going to be so easy, catching up with you, I mean.'

Luise said nothing, aware of the passers-by stopping to look at her and Dunleavy with the frank curiosity of the Italians. So far she had seen no British army personnel, but now she saw a small truck, a desert buggy, though she didn't know it by that name, come down the street and stop in front of a large building. The two soldiers in it got out and disappeared into the building. Dunleavy watched them.

'Afraid I'll hand you over to them?'

She still said nothing, because she could think of nothing to say; her mind was numbed by the successive shocks of the past half-hour. Then the young soldier came back, panting a little, sweat glistening on his bony face.

'Sorry, major.' Charlie Lincoln took out a handkerchief and wiped his face. 'He just disappeared. Aint no sign of him.'

Dunleavy nodded dourly, bit his lip. He stared across at the British desert buggy; then he looked at Luise. 'You want to make a deal?'

'What sort of deal?' she said in surprise.

'Get in.'

He half-pushed her into the back seat of the jeep and they drove off up the street as the two British soldiers came out and got back into their vehicle. Charlie Lincoln, on a word from Dunleavy, swung the jeep into a side street and headed up a hill out of town. They drove in silence till they were out in the countryside, had turned into a lane that ran between two vineyards. Then Dunleavy told Charlie to pull up.

'Go for a walk, Charlie. I'm going to do some unofficial bargaining. I wouldn't want you to hear something that might be prejudicial to military discipline.'

'Sure, major.' Charlie grinned. 'You just holler when everything's official again.'

He went ambling off up the lane, loose-kneed, ungainly. Luise watched him go, concentrating on him till she was sure of what she was going to say to Dunleavy. But when the words came out they were utterly banal, the clichés of sympathy: 'I'm sorry about your brother. And also Corporal Martin.'

'I'd like to think you mean that.'

'What makes you think I don't?' She knew as well as anyone the sense of loss one could feel.

'Forget it.' Now that he was beside her, aware of her once again as he had never been of any other woman, he knew she could not have been directly responsible for the deaths of Roy and Corporal Martin. But he also knew, just as surely, that she was not going to hand over Keppel to him. A row of almond trees bordered the lane and, avoiding her gaze, he looked up through the bud-studded branches. 'The deal I mentioned . . . If I let you and the rest of the group go, will you tell me where I can pick up Keppel?'

'I don't know where he is.'

'Jesus!' Normally he never swore in front of women; but now he didn't even apologize. 'Stop horsing around! You were all with Keppel when he killed my brother and Joe Martin —'

'We didn't kill as a group.' She knew the pain he must be suffering from the death of his brother, but she could not betray Ben Keppel.

'I know that, goddam it!' A bud fell off a branch, hit him over the eye and dropped into his lap; he picked it up and hurled it away as if it were a pebble that had actually hurt him. 'Keppel is the one with a gun —'

'You have no proof it was Herr Keppel.'

'If it wasn't him, it had to be one of the others. I've got their names — ' He took a sheet of paper from his pocket. 'Gunther Kogan —'

'He stayed behind in Innsbruck with his wife — she is in hospital there. He had nothing to do with the death of your brother and Corporal Martin.'

'Michael Klein —'

'He is dead — he was killed Saturday night.' He looked up sharply and she added, 'An accident.'

'David Weill, Simon Berger, Noah Malchek, Joachim Winter —' He put the list back in his pocket. 'We picked up a couple of guys in Innsbruck. They said Keppel had a gun, had taken a coupla shots at them. If any of the others has a gun, tell me who it is. Tell me where I can pick him up, or Keppel, and the rest of you can go on your way and I'll say nothing about you to the British.'

She said nothing, gazing up the lane to where Charlie

Lincoln lay on a bank, chewing grass and staring at the peaceful sky, unbeset by choices, a long long way from home and troubles. Somewhere a cow bellowed; a bird sang among the almond buds; then there was silence. The air was so still that she could hear the distant sound of the river as it tore over rocks down below them. The setting was idyllic, no place for betrayal.

'I am not telling you where anyone is, major. You can hand me over to the English, if that will give you any satisfaction.'

He stared at her in silence, his eyes narrowed, his mouth tight over the hidden teeth: this man was nothing like the smiling Major Dunleavy who had invited her to the dance in Garmisch. At last he said, 'You know damn well I won't do that.'

'Why not?' But she knew the answer and felt a curious thrill: one that she was ashamed of, as if it too were a betrayal, of herself. Emotion heightened, she turned her face away from him.

Dunleavy, for his part, wasn't going to answer the direct question she had put to him. He had already surrendered enough of himself. Looking at her, even while still angry with her, he realized that he was in love with her; or anyway as much in love as could be expected from their limited acquaintance. He knew she stirred him more than any woman he had ever met, that to know her further, say for the rest of his life, would offer more possibilities than he had seen in any of the others who had interested him. But he was not just plain Matt Dunleavy: he felt the tightness of his uniform jacket, like an official reminder.

'Why the hell did you run – I mean, after you saw my brother and Martin killed? I thought you had some decency in you –'

She recognized the disappointment in his voice, turned to him. 'Major Dunleavy, don't you know how much some of us want to escape from Europe?'

'I know living in those camps is pretty hellish –'

'It's not just the camps – though they are degrading enough. It's that we can't see any future. Not all of us – a lot of people have gone home, are trying to start all over again. But there are a lot more of us – ' She looked away again. 'We couldn't stay – it would have meant more interrogation, perhaps even prison for some of us – ' She faced him once more. 'We're a headache nobody wants, but that nobody wants to do anything about. UNRRA tries, but the military would rather not have anything to do with us. We're the spoils of war they wish someone else would claim.'

'That's not true – '

'Don't kid me, as you Americans say. You still see yourselves as something apart from us, you wish you could go home and forget us. If it had not been two Americans who were killed, if it had been two Germans, say the Burgermeister and someone else from the village – would you have followed us all the way down here to take us back?'

His honesty surprised her: 'No, I guess not. But then it would have been a matter for the Germans, wouldn't it?'

'Major Dunleavy, I am truly sorry for what happened – '

'You said that.' They would be burying Roy today, he guessed. They had asked him if he wanted the body sent home, but Roy had no one to go home to. Perhaps he should have stayed at Garmisch to make the final formal farewell, but that would have been an empty gesture. Better to take off after Roy's murderer and bring him back.

'I understand how you feel. But you must understand me – I have a duty too. The only thing we have that binds us, besides our being Jews, is trust.'

He put two fingers in his mouth, let out an ear-splitting whistle that made her jump. Charlie Lincoln came trotting down the lane, fitting his cap on his close-cropped head.

'We official again, major?'

'No. Drive us back to town, Charlie, while I think.'

They drove back to town, pulled up outside the church.

'I'm sure it was Keppel who killed my brother and Joe Martin.' Dunleavy helped Luise out of the jeep. 'I got no proof, just a hunch. When you see him, tell him I'm going to take him back to Germany with me. That's a promise.'

'Are you going to follow me now?'

'That's a chance you got to take.'

But when she walked off the jeep did not follow her. She walked around town, hurrying up and down side streets; but each time she looked back over her shoulder she could see neither Dunleavy nor Charlie Lincoln. At last she took the risk and headed up the road that led to the convent. At the gate she paused and looked back. There was still no sign that she was being followed.

She rang the bell and a moment later a young nun opened the small gate set in the larger gate. She stepped through and almost bumped into the fat well-dressed man standing behind a truck from which two workmen were unloading a large statue of the Virgin Mary.

Luise saw Ben Keppel standing at the corner of the truck. She handed the paper bag full of chocolate and candy to the young nun. 'Would you give this to the children, sister? See they don't make themselves sick on it.'

The young nun went away and Keppel came forward. 'Did you get rid of Major Dunleavy?'

'For the time being.'

Keppel frowned, looking worried, then he introduced her to the fat man. 'This is Signor Lucca.'

Luise looked at the truck, at the half a dozen Virgins wrapped in sacking and lying on the floor of the truck. 'Is this the truck we'll be going in tonight?'

Lucca's cold eyes were appraising her with the look of a man who would have no time for virgins, plaster or otherwise, unless they gave him some return. 'Not this one, signorina. It will be another army truck. I am just the contact.'

'Are there no *Bricha* men in Merano?'

'There were, but they were both arrested by the English two days ago.'

'Did you know that?' Luise looked at Keppel, who nodded. 'You're safe then – till we meet up with the next lot.'

'They will understand –' Then Keppel shut up.

Luise looked back at Lucca, who had watched the small exchange with no expression on his face. 'Something personal, signore. If there were *Bricha* men here, why were you needed?'

Lucca's expression remained unchanged. 'Your friends in the British Army only provide transport. I provide all accommodation – where you stayed last night at the Bonettis', here, where you will stay tomorrow night. There always has to be a middleman, signorina. Jews should know that.'

She kept her own face under control, but she saw Keppel's stiffen. 'We don't stay anywhere tonight?'

'No. It will be a long journey, over five hundred kilometres, but it cannot be helped. Something is going on down in La Spezia, where you are going, and the English are on the alert.'

'Wouldn't it be better if we waited?' Luise said to Keppel.

'We can't. The ship is waiting. I don't know what else is going on – perhaps the *Bricha* men could have told us that. But unless we're told tonight to postpone our trip, we have to go on.'

'I'm afraid so,' said Lucca. 'I have contracted to put you up for only one night here.'

'The nuns wouldn't put us out,' said Luise.

'No,' said Lucca reluctantly, as if charity was something that shouldn't get in the way of business. 'But there is another group due through early tomorrow morning, a much larger group than yours. The nuns couldn't accommodate all of you and there's nowhere else in town for you to go.'

'I'm sure you have somewhere else, signore,' said Luise. 'A man of your business acumen.'

For a moment the pale eyes glinted: she could have been mistaken, but it was almost as if he were suddenly afraid. Then he turned his head sharply away as one of the men, handing down another statue, carelessly bumped it against the edge of the truck floor.

'Careful, Paolo! That's the Saviour.'

The second man took the Saviour over his shoulder, like a butcher carrying a side of beef, and went across the yard and into the main house, preceded by four young nuns in a flutter of anticipation. Mother Teresa came out of the house and crossed to the truck.

'I've looked at the statue of the Virgin, Signor Lucca. It is not very good work.'

159

Lucca shrugged. 'Nothing is these days. You can't expect miracles.'

'I don't.' Mother Teresa's smile, Luise decided, was just the right mixture of sweetness and ice; and admired the older woman for it. 'I just expect value for money. I want you to take back both statues.'

The expression in Lucca's eyes changed once again. 'You gave me a definite order for them, Mother Teresa! You can't refuse them now. They are good statues, maybe not as good as pre-war but still good. You are not worshipping quality, you are worshipping the spirit –'

'I am *paying* for quality,' said Mother Teresa. 'The spirit comes free.'

The nun and the statue merchant moved away, taking their argument with them, and Keppel looked at Luise. 'What about Major Dunleavy?'

She told him, flatly and briefly, about Dunleavy's threat.

'What are you going to do?'

'We'll have to hold a meeting.'

They held the meeting in the convent dining hall, a room as stark as the choice before them. The nuns discreetly left them alone, as if what they had to discuss was a religious question, one beyond their own beliefs. Luise felt a momentary envy of them: they had found *their* Promised Land. But then she knew she could never live here in this haven of piety, chastity and an innocence that was in its own way a deceit. They would never be entirely safe from the outside world, not while they had to deal with the likes of Lucca, the wholesale purveyor of worshipful objects, the middleman of safe havens for fugitive Jews.

Luise looked around the small gathering. The children, with the exception of the sick Winter child who was in bed, were all playing outside under the care of a young nun, whose laughter came through the open window as light and childlike as that of the children themselves. The group looked pitifully small. Twenty of them had started out from Camp 93 only three night ago (was that all it was?) and now there were only thirteen of them left, including the children outside. It hardly seemed all worthwhile; she could understand the sharp irritation last night of the two men from the Jewish Brigade. Yet, she told herself, all the ships that sailed for Palestine were full of such groups, big and small. It was her and Keppel's job to see the group was not diminished further. Yet it seemed that they must already lose Keppel himself.

'We must take him with us,' said Simon Berger. 'We're all in this together.'

'He should not have killed Herr Dunleavy and that other man,' said Joachim Winter. 'But it's done and nothing can undo it.'

'I don't agree,' said Anna Bork. 'If what Fräulein Graz says is true, that the American is not interested in the rest of us if he can have Ben, then we have to look out for ourselves.'

'Are you suggesting we should turn Herr Keppel over to the American?' asked David Weill.

'No. I'm suggesting he should make his own way to wherever the ship is. We don't need him any more – '

'I don't think you need to be so brutally frank,' said Luise, watching Keppel sitting stiff and silent at the far end of the long table.

'There is nothing personal in it.' Anna Bork bobbed her head at Keppel, the closest she could come to making an apology. 'But we have come too far, gone through too much, to risk being sent back – '

'We owe it to Michael Klein to see that his wife and children get to Palestine,' said Noah Malchek.

The argument went back and forth, with Luise saying little and Ben Keppel saying nothing. But the look on his face exposed his thoughts to Luise: for all his ruthless talk, he was still shattered to find that the others could think him dispensable. It was not selfishness or arrogance: he was still young enough, despite the forced-feeding of experience in the past six years, to have illusions of trust in those he thought friends. Twice in two days he had been declared the odd man out. Luise, the one who more than any of them was seeking the climate of trust, felt Ben Keppel's sick disappointment.

'I suggest we vote,' said Luise when she realized the argument might go on endlessly. 'Those for Ben leaving us and making his own way?'

Anna Bork put her hand up without hesitation. Noah Malchek looked around, then raised his hand. Hilde Klein said, 'I am sorry, Herr Keppel,' and raised her hand. Judith Winter looked at her husband, then put up her hand, saying to her husband and the table at large, 'It is for the children.'

'Those for Ben staying with us – ' said Luise and raised her hand, to be followed at once by David Weill, Simon Berger and Joachim Winter.

'I am thinking of the children,' said Joachim Winter in answer to his wife's half-puzzled, half-accusing look. 'But if we do not stick together now, how can we work together in the future? His won't be the only mistake any of us will make.'

Too true, thought Luise. 'Four to four. You have the deciding vote, Ben.'

'He can't vote!'

'He can, Frau Bork, and he shall. I am still the section leader and I say he gets a vote!' Luise stood up, looked down the long table at Keppel. 'Ben?'

Keppel did not look at those who had voted against him. He looked straight down the table at Luise and for the first time she saw a naked look of gratitude on his face, an admission that she might be the only one he could trust.

'I'll make my own way.' He stood up. 'I'll see you on the ship.'

'You're not going *now?*' Luise moved down towards him. 'Ben, at least wait for tonight, for darkness. And what about your leg?'

'I can travel faster and more easily alone.' There was no mistaking the bitterness, the contempt in his voice. 'They are your problem now, Fräulein. Good luck.'

Despite his limp he was gone from the room before anyone could stop him. Luise turned to the group still seated around the table. 'Well? I thought we Jews were always supposed to stick together.'

'Only a half-Jew would say that,' said Anna Bork. Oh God, how single-minded she is, thought Luise, delicacy is never going to trouble her. And half-envied the peasant woman: her malice and selfish determination for her own survival was almost another sort of innocence.

'We're just the same as anyone else,' Anna went on. 'Only sometimes more practical.'

'Being charitable isn't always practical, but it is more rewarding in the eyes of the Lord,' said David Weill.

'Then you pray for Herr Keppel,' said Anna. 'Old men can afford to be charitable. The rest of us can't.'

'Frau Bork,' said Luise, 'I'm sure you'd have re-written the Torah if you had been around at the time.'

'I don't have any time for books. People have to live with people, not books.'

'There is something else I have to tell you.' Luise was aware of the uneasiness around the table; Anna Bork was going too far for some of them. 'This morning, down at the railway station, I saw one of the doctors from Auschwitz. Dr Besser.'

She had expected more reaction from those who had been in Auschwitz; the one who showed the least was Anna Bork. The peasant woman put a hand to her face, but it looked no more than an idle movement, as if she were brushing something from her cheek; then she got up from the table and, still quiet, went out of the dining hall. Luise looked around at the others.

'He was with what I took to be his wife and children. He caught the train that was going to Milan.'

'Did you try to stop him?' Simon Berger said.

'How? Call out for the police? Herr Berger, I wished there had been some way of having him stopped –'

'Have you thought what it would have meant? Staying here to give evidence?' David Weill shook his head. 'Even if they had been interested in him ... We can't afford the idea of vengeance. Not now.'

'When?' Noah Malchek did his polishing act on his bald head, rubbing his hand gently back and forth as if he were handling a precious piece of his old stock of china. 'It will be too late when we are in Palestine and he and the others like him are spread all over the world.'

'An eye for an eye – ' said David Weill. 'No one gains in the end. Two half-blind men who'll lose their world to some other man with both eyes.'

'You're talking from books again,' said Anna Bork from the doorway; she had come back without anyone seeing her. She stared at them, then just as quickly was gone, flinging back over her shoulder, 'There's too much ink in you, Herr Professor, not enough blood!'

The group sat silent for a moment, then Hilde Klein and Judith Winter stood up: they could hear the shouts and laughter of the children outside, they were not interested in academic talk of vengeance. They went out, followed by the men, leaving Luise and David Weill alone together.

'Perhaps Frau Bork is right,' said Weill.

'Half-right. If a half-Jew may say so.'

'How do you tolerate her? Sometimes I feel I'd like to borrow a little of the wrath of God and whack her across her rump.'

Luise smiled at the frail man. 'A whack across *that* rump would probably snap your arm off.' Then, sober again, she said, 'Do you think we should have let Ben go off on his own?'

'Do you think you could have stopped him?' Weill had learned long ago the easiest way to answer a question: ask another one. 'Fräulein Graz, I went to a lot of places before I settled in Cracow. France, England, Germany, America. A friend in America, when he learned I was going home to Poland, called me the Wandering Jew who had learned nothing. He may have been right. I haven't learned to influence my fellow man. That was why I was such a poor teacher.'

'Why do you keep belittling yourself?' Luise was a little angry with the white-haired man: he had been degraded enough, by experts.

Weill shrugged. 'It simplifies existence. Nobody expects anything of me, least of all myself.'

'Isn't that cowardly?' She couldn't help the accusation.

'Of course. But, who knows, some day I may be of help to someone. All the dead heroes aren't any help to us. I am denying what the books tell us,' he said with a twinkle in the eyes that had given up hope.

'The memory of them is a help,' she said, remembering her dead father. 'If you think like that, I'm surprised you read the Zohar –'

'Another form of cowardice, a retreat. I am tired, Fräulein, that's the whole truth of it. Tired of being a Jew.' He looked around the big room, careful of his treason. 'You don't know what it has been like –'

'I have been Jewish for five, six years.' But she knew her argument was weak. She could always walk away from what she had opted to be: no stranger would know her for Jewish, she did not have the mark of circumcision. Once, in Vienna in the early days, she had seen a man stripped in the street, his race and religion exposed on the end of his fear-shrivelled penis. It had been a joke with her father that he, too, was marked, but for hygienic reasons: for a while she had been haunted by the thought that some strange mob, not knowing who he was, might strip him.

'But not a lifetime,' said Weill. 'That is why I long for Palestine. To be a Jew among Jews, to be able to forget.'

'You'll never forget your religion.'

'No,' he said, burdened by faith. 'That is the only thing that makes the rest of it bearable.'

She left him, wondering if it would be possible to forget one's Jewishness when surrounded by it; in Feldafing she had seen the Orthodox, safe again, turning their backs on the worldly; there would always be Jews to remind others of what they were. For the first time she began to have doubts about where she was going.

She went to look for Ben Keppel, but he had already gone. She was angered by his abrupt departure; he might at least have left her some instructions. Then, calming down, she realized that all their forward instructions came from *Bricha*: all she had to do was keep the party together. Something that, in the case of Ben Keppel, she had not succeeded in doing.

Lucca and his truck of plaster effigies had gone when she went out into the yard. But he came back that night with two more soldiers in another British army truck. He raised his hat to Luise and Mother Teresa, the only nun who came out to say goodbye to the convent's guests.

'Signor Keppel came to see me, told me he was going. I got in touch with our friends.' He gestured at the two soldiers. 'Sergeant Katz and Private Engels.'

'Are you from the Brigade?' Luise asked.

'Sort of, miss – ' The voice was straight Cockney: Sergeant Katz had been brought up on the Mile End Road. 'We've come up from Milan. A long way for just half a load.'

'I'm sorry you've been troubled.' Luise turned back to Lucca. 'Have you paid Mother Teresa for our board and lodgings?'

'Naturally.'

'Signor Lucca is scrupulous about our arrangement,' said Mother Teresa. 'Our only disagreement is about statues.'

'Whatever they are paying you,' said Luise, 'I wish we could pay you more.'

Mother Teresa smiled. 'Sisters of Charity with money to spare? We shouldn't know what to do with it.'

The nun said goodbye to the Jews, shaking hands with each one and wishing them God speed: God, Jehovah, Elohim, made no difference, they were all just names for The One they believed in. Or so Mother Teresa thought: she could not accept that, deep within himself, anyone could deny the existence of God.

She said goodbye to Luise last of all. 'I only learned at supper that you were a singer. I wish you had sung for us.'

'I wish I had, too,' Luise heard herself say.

'Don't neglect your gift. God bestows talent on so few of us.'

'Perhaps in Palestine – ' But she would need something to sing about: it was no longer enough just to sing for singing's sake.

When the truck drew out of the yard Mother Teresa and Lucca were resuming their argument about the proper price for statues in a post-war, post-quality world.

Dunleavy was not to know it, but his quarry had already fled. When he had let Luise Graz go this morning he had not made the mistake of trying to follow her at once. Merano was a small town; he felt pretty certain he would soon pick up her trail again. He had left Charlie Lincoln in the jeep, walked up a side street parallel to the one Luise had taken, turned down the next cross street and seen her turn in the same direction a block ahead of him. After that it had been easy to keep her in sight, even when she had started doubling back. She was an amateur at trying to lose a tail; he was no expert, but he remained one jump ahead of her. Each time she looked back he had slipped into a doorway or lane; she telegraphed when she was going to look back, slowing her stride in mid-block or pulling up dead at a corner. At last he had seen her walk up the long road towards the convent and from the side lane at the bottom of the hill seen her knock on the gate and be admitted.

Twenty minutes later a truck came out of the convent and came down the hill. It was an open truck, the back of it filled with sacking-wrapped statues; at first he thought the statues were people and he almost took off after the truck as it passed the end of the lane. But it slowed to turn into the main road and then he saw the dozen Saviours staring frozenly back at him. He relaxed, went back to waiting, staring up the hill. When Luise did not re-appear in the next hour he knew where she and the rest of the DPs were hiding.

Whether Keppel, too, was there was anyone's guess. What to do? He could go back into town, look up the British Field Security men and have the convent raided. That might or might not mean capturing Keppel; it would certainly mean that Luise and the rest of the DPs would be sent back to Germany or be confined in one of the camps here in Italy. And he couldn't bring himself to being a party to that.

Banking on the DPs not leaving the convent in daylight, he went back into town, found Charlie Lincoln and the two of them drove back up to the side lane at the bottom of the hill. At mid-day Charlie went down into town, bought some food and gassy lemonade and brought it back. They spent the next two hours burping and re-tasting the stale mortadella rolls.

'Charlie, if you are going to stay with me, you'll have to raise your food standards. Since I've been in Europe I've become a gourmet. Almost.'

'I'm just an enlisted man, major. Standards are different for officers, I guess. I ain't ever met no gourmet private.'

'Another smart-ass,' said Dunleavy.

Charlie Lincoln grinned, already sure of his relationship with this officer. This was one of them who wouldn't kick your ass in for trying a little fun talk.

It was a long day and they took it in turns to doze in the warm sun, getting out of the jeep to lie in the grass beside the road. As the sun went down it got suddenly chilly and Charlie got out his own and Dunleavy's greatcoats.

'We gonna stay here all night, major?'

'If we have to. You better go down and get us something else to eat. Something hot, if you can. Here, take our mess tins. If you pass a hardware store, buy a flask and get us some coffee somewhere. Well?'

'What'll I use for dough, major? I'm just a poor enlisted man.'

'Charlie, give me any more of that enlisted man crap and I'll personally promote you to officer rank.'

'Anything you say, major. Can I be a colonel?'

Dunleavy gave him some money and he went off down the road whistling *Boogie-Woogie Bugler Boy*. Dunleavy grinned, settled back in his seat, drew his collar up round his neck. He hoped they would not have to spend the whole goddam night here. If nothing had happened by 2300, he'd go up to the convent and root them all out of bed, nuns, DPs, Luise and Keppel. How he and Charlie Lincoln would handle them all, he didn't know. But he wasn't going to sit here all night and have his ass frozen off.

Charlie had been gone less than ten minutes when the

168

British army truck went up the road. Dunleavy got out of the jeep and watched it as it slowed at the top of the hill. In the deep dusk that was now almost darkness he could barely make out the shape of it as it pulled in at the gate of the convent. On the still evening air he heard the short hoot of its horn; a moment later it disappeared into the walls of the convent. What the hell was going on up there?

He looked down the road towards town for Charlie, but there was no sign of him. Suddenly Dunleavy was impatient, edgy. He paced up and down at the entrance to the lane, stopping every now and again to stare up through the darkness towards the top of the hill. The moon was not yet up and the starlight was as useless as a lighted match.

Then he heard the truck coming down the hill, in low gear and without lights. He got back into the jeep, waited till the truck was almost opposite the end of the lane; then he switched on the headlamps and drove out into the road. The truck jerked abruptly to a halt as Dunleavy, pistol in hand, got out of the jeep and stepped quickly up to the driver's side of the cabin.

'Okay, out! Both of you! No tricks from your buddy, driver, or you get a bullet in you!'

'Blimey, mate – ' Sergeant Katz pulled on the brake handle, switched off the engine. 'Righto, Mickey, come around this side and see what the Yank wants. You're a bit outa your territory, ain't you, mate? Or are you playing funny buggers?'

Private Engels, hands up, dark eyes white-rimmed with surprise, came round the front of the truck and joined Katz as the latter got down.

'There's nothing in this lot worth pinching, mate.' He, too, had a Cockney voice; but he had inherited it from his mother and father, East End émigrés who had worked for Spinneys, the Middle East provisioning agents. Dunleavy knew nothing of the Jewish Brigade and for the moment he was just as puzzled as the two men in front of him. What the hell were these two British Tommies doing here, driving down from the convent in a truck without lights? 'If this is a whatyoucallit – a hijack like them gangster things – '

169

'Blimey.' Fred Katz was a balding barrel of a man whose uniform seemed several sizes too large; it hung on him in folds, giving him a concertina effect. 'A gangster major.'

'Knock it off,' said Dunleavy testily. 'Let's go around the back. Okay, move!'

Katz and Engels seemed reluctant to do what they were told, but when Dunleavy raised the pistol and pointed it at Katz's chest the sergeant shrugged. 'Okay, you win, sir. You are an officer, straight up?'

'I'm an officer,' said Dunleavy. 'And not a gangster one.'

The back of the truck was soon emptied. Luise and the others, the children huddled close to their mothers, young Ruth Winter coughing into her mother's muffling hand, came round into the glare of the jeep's headlamps, stared silently at the frustrated and angry Dunleavy.

'Okay, Fräulein Graz, where is he? Keppel, I mean.'

'I told you this morning – I don't know. This night air is cold, major – may the children get back into the truck?'

Dunleavy gestured with the pistol, forgetting that it was still in his hand. 'Okay, they can get back in with their mothers.'

Then Charlie Lincoln, hands full of food and coffee, came up the road. 'How about that, major? You got 'em all, huh?'

'No, Private Lincoln, we haven't got them all. The guy we want isn't here.'

'So what you gonna do, major? You want me go downtown, get them British officers? I seen their office when we were driving around today. Field Security, ain't that it?'

'There's no need for that.' Fred Katz cleared his throat, looked at Luise, then back at Dunleavy. 'It's a fair pinch, sir, we'll admit that. But if you hand us over to those blokes down in town, it's going to cause a lot of bloody trouble. All around.'

'That's the idea,' said Dunleavy. 'But you tell me where I can find Keppel and there'll be no trouble for anyone. Except him.'

'I dunno where Keppel is, sir, and that's the truth. My orders was just to pick up twenty bods. When we got up here this evening, there was just this lot. Twelve of 'em. Hardly worth the trip.'

'You said that,' said Luise, who hadn't taken to Sergeant Katz.

'Who gave you your orders to pick them up?'

'I'm afraid that's all I'm going to tell you, sir.'

Then Luise said, 'Are you offering us an alternative, Major Dunleavy?'

'I wasn't aware that I was. I don't have any alternative, except to follow you all the way to where you're going.'

'You think that will lead you to Herr Keppel?'

'It might or it might not. But I don't see any other way of picking him up, unless I turn you over to the British down in town and one of you decides to talk. Anyone want to do that?'

Luise looked at Anna Bork standing with her back to the truck. But the latter just glared back at her and Dunleavy: there was a limit to her selfishness. The men, standing beside her, said nothing: their mere expressions were a flat refusal to talk.

'Will the major be in the way if he follows us?' Luise asked Katz.

'Oy,' he said and hit his forehead with the palm of his hand; he acts more Jewish than any of us, Luise thought. 'He's not going to be any help.'

'If we hang about here, with those headlights blazing,' said Mickey Engels, 'we ain't going to help ourselves, either. We got no option, Fred. We take him with us.'

'What are they going to say when we turn up with him down where we're going?'

'Then the problem's going to be outa our hands, ain't it? It'll be up to them what happens next. It's just our job to transport, not decide policy.'

'Where are you going?' said Dunleavy.

'You'll find that out when we get there, sir,' said Katz. 'But if you wanna change your mind, it's over three hundred miles from here.'

Dunleavy waved the pistol. 'Okay, I'm coming with you. I don't intend to kill any of you, but I won't give a second thought about putting a bullet into the leg of anyone who gets smart. Just so you'll know I'm not fooling.'

171

'Will you put a bullet into the legs of the women, too?'

'I thought you'd ask that,' said Dunleavy, pained. 'Yeah, the women, too.'

A minute later the two-vehicle convoy started down the main road that led through town and on south. Dunleavy drove while Charlie Lincoln ate the now-just-warm tortelloni he had brought up from the restaurant in town and drank the hot coffee from the flask he had bought. When it was Dunleavy's turn he ate at the wheel, driving one-handed.

'You ain't enjoying that, major. And I ain't enjoying watching you getting us around these curves one-handed.'

'I'm not pulling up while we change seats. Those bastards would be outa sight as soon as they saw us stop. I'm not that hungry.' He handed his mess tin to Charlie. 'Give me some coffee. Then try and get some sleep. I got an idea we're going to be driving all night.'

At midnight the truck ahead pulled up and Katz and Engels got down as the jeep pulled in in front of them.

'Let everybody stretch their legs,' said Katz. 'We've got some bully-beef sandwiches in there if you'd like some, sir.'

'Next time. What's our route?'

'You're really coming all the way with us?'

'All the way.'

Katz sighed, looked at the group as they got down from the back of the truck and found shadowed spots beside the road where they could relieve themselves. 'Why persecute them? Don't you think they've been through enough?'

'All I want is the guy who killed my brother and my driver. I think these people should be allowed to go anywhere in the world they want to. But I don't think that gives them the right to murder two Americans, one of them who was doing everything he could to help them. Would Private Engels here just shrug and turn his back if one of them took it into his head to put a bullet into you?'

Katz looked at Engels, shook his head. 'I'd come back and haunt the bugger if he did. Okay, sir. I think you're on our side – up to a point. But if we meet up with that bloke Keppel, don't expect me and Mickey to help you take him.'

Dunleavy nodded. 'Now which route do we take?'

Katz produced a map, flashed a torch on it. 'We're by-passing Genoa. There's a blitz on down there – they're looking for an SS Nazi named Eichmann and a couple of others who worked with him.'

'I've heard of Eichmann.' He remembered the name from the latest Wanted list that had been sent to the Provost Marshal's office only a month ago. There had been an accompanying page, marked Confidential, that had shown Eichmann as a monster, one whose crimes Dunleavy, case-hardened though he was, found difficult to believe.

'The Nazis have an organization just like ours – it's called *Spinne*, Spider. They're smuggling their blokes out just like we're doing with ours.'

'How do you know about them?'

Katz winked. 'There's nothing we don't know. But we've got too much else to do without worrying about them. Mickey and I bumped into one of 'em one night up in Milan – our blokes had passed the word he was on his way.'

'What happened?'

Katz ran his finger across his throat. 'Summary justice, ain't that what they call it?'

Dunleavy looked at the stout, baggy-trousered Jew who appeared more an amiable uncle than a killer. 'That's what they call it.'

It was four o'clock in the morning, they had just come down on to the coast road south of Santa Margherita, when they ran into the road block. They came round a bend in the narrow tortuous road and there were the two desert buggies blocking their way. The truck slammed on its brakes and the jeep almost ran into the back of it.

Dunleavy jumped out and hurried forward, shaking his head warningly at Luise as she looked out of the back of the truck's canopy. A short boyish British lieutenant, a corporal and two privates moved forward from the desert buggies as Sergeant Katz got down and joined Dunleavy.

'Good morning,' said the lieutenant politely. 'What have we here?'

'A load of Eyetalian slave labourers, sir,' said Katz quickly before Dunleavy could fumble out an answer. 'They've been in Germany and we're taking 'em down to Livorno for dispersal back to their homes.'

'What unit are you from, sergeant?'

'114th Transport Maintenance, sir, in Milan.'

Only then did the lieutenant look at Dunleavy. 'I don't wish to be rude, sir, but what is an American officer doing with this lot?'

'I'm on my way to Rome to join our liaison staff there.' Dunleavy tried to be relaxed, to sound plausible. 'These people were in my area at Garmisch in Bavaria and I was asked to escort them. It's all okay, lieutenant.'

'Then you won't mind awfully if I look at their papers?'

Bloody British politeness, thought Dunleavy. They can make you feel so goddam – *uncivilized*.

'I have all our papers here.' Luise appeared out of the darkness behind the headlamps of the truck, held out a small bundle of papers. 'The children are asleep and their mothers don't like to disturb them. Do you mind, lieutenant?'

'Not at all. Awfully sorry to bother you at all.' He took the papers, glanced through them perfunctorily. 'Who are you, signorina?'

'Luise Graziani.'

'Where from?' said the lieutenant in Italian.

'From Rome.' Dunleavy had to admire the way Luise immediately dropped into the other language. He couldn't tell how good she was, but she sounded as fluent as the young Englishman. 'I was taken to Germany in 1943 because I was suspected of anti-Fascist activities.'

'Were you? Anti-Fascist, I mean.'

'Just as much as you, lieutenant.'

'And the others?'

'The same. But they don't all come from Rome. There are only twelve of us, including four children, and all we want is to get home to our families.'

'I'm surprised they've kept you so long.' In the truck the Winter child had begun to cough, going on and on as if coughing up her lungs. The lieutenant paused, listening to the painful hacking, then he handed back the papers. 'Rightio, you may go.'

The desert buggies were pulled off the road. Dunleavy stood by the lieutenant while the road was being cleared.

'Why the road block?'

'The French have been letting Jewish DPs through over their border and they've been using this road. I'd be careful when you get down to La Spezia.'

'How's that?' Dunleavy was suddenly aware that the lieutenant had dropped his voice.

'That girl is no more Italian than I am. But if you want to risk your neck for them, then it's no business of mine – I'm going home in a week. But down in La Spezia they're awfully stuffy about the Jews on their way to Palestine. Cheerio.'

Dunleavy and Charlie Lincoln drove on, speeding to catch up with the truck.

'Charlie, if I'm picked up when we get to La Spezia and I can't talk my way out of it, I'll see that you're okay, that you didn't know what this was all about.'

'I'm an enlisted man, sir,' said Charlie. 'We never know what nothing's about.'

At last they came down the winding road into La Spezia. The small gulf spread out below them, the arm of Porto Venere locking it in against the sea. The sun had come up out of the mountains, climbing into a cloudless sky, and the light slanted across the blue waters, filling it with shoals of gold on which a fishing boat crawled like a red-winged insect. Tiled roofs splashed colour along the shore, like rusted flotsam, and on the hills behind the city olive groves climbed in terraces of giant steps.

'Peaceful, ain't it?' said Charlie Lincoln and began to whistle *O Sole Mio*. He broke off in mid-note, said, 'That's Eyetalian, I think.'

But ten minutes later they were driving through the bombed-out port area and they were back in familiar territory. Jagged walls, ugly as broken teeth, lined the route. Some of the walls, with huge cracks in them, looked held up by the graffiti painted on them. *Viva Il Duce* in white had been besmirched by black, but the black paint must have run out because the message still showed through. *Kilroy Was Here* said another wall; beside it Chad peeped over a drawn wall, asked *Who's Kilroy?* They passed a cinema standing miraculously undamaged, like a holy place that had been spared. American films were advertised, part of rehabilitation aid: the Italians were being shown how the other side had won the war: Errol Flynn threw a punch to the chin of Helmut Dantine.

'Geez, they took a pounding here, major.'

'This was one of their major naval ports. Forget the scenery – keep an eye on the truck. The traffic's getting thicker. They may try to duck us.'

Then they were out of the city again, passing through several villages, finally coming to a loop that led round a small bay. A newly painted sign said Lerici: Italy was being identified again.

Dunleavy saw the castle on the headland above the village, the strip of beach below the promenade, the long stone jetty with the fishing boats crowded against it like multi-coloured piglets nuzzling into the belly of a giant grey sow. Then they had swung round a corner, skirting a small piazza, and were following the truck up a winding road out of the village. The truck swung into a narrow side street, crawled up between tenements that shut out the sunlight, came into a lane that ran between stone walls bordering olive groves on either side. At last it pulled up outside big ornamental gates set in a high crumbling wall. Chipped and barely distinguishable letters carved in the wall said this was the Villa Fontana. Mickey Engels got down, opened the gates and the truck and jeep drove through. A winding drive led up past a small guest house, shuttered and unwelcoming to any guest, through gardens that were overgrown to jungle density, past trees that had broken branches; Dunleavy had the feeling they were driving into some sort of wilderness, ruined Pompeii was going to pop up ahead any minute. Then the drive suddenly finished in a wide patio in front of a huge four-storied villa that looked like a small palace. A big dry fountain stood in the middle of the patio, a final commentary on the rundown state of the Villa Fontana.

Dunleavy got out of the jeep, went forward to help the women and children down from the truck. Everyone, including Dunleavy, looked around them in puzzled surprise.

'It could do with a coat of paint,' said Dunleavy, 'but it sure as hell beats Camp 93.'

'I was born in a house bigger than this,' said Luise matter-of-factly. 'It was still no protection.'

A wide flight of chipped and broken steps led up to a terrace that ran right along the front of the villa at the first floor level. A grey-haired woman, plump and short, stood there watching them suspiciously.

'You'd better come up and meet the Contessa,' said Fred Katz. 'She's wondering what's going on. I don't blame her – bringing a coupla Yanks with us. No offence, major.'

They went up the steps, treading carefully to avoid turning an ankle. Dunleavy, examining the villa more closely, wondered why something had not been done to put it back into shape. The walls were spattered with bullet and shrapnel marks, war-pocked; one whole balcony on an upper floor had been shot away; and most of the windows were boarded up, the eyes of the house closed against the neglect surrounding it. That was all war damage, Dunleavy thought, and maybe the Contessa, whoever she was, was waiting for some sort of compensation. But at least some attempt could have been made to clean up the place.

When they reached the woman Dunleavy saw that she was not as old as she had appeared from the patio. She could not have been more than forty, if that; her skin was unlined and her full pretty lips were as soft as a young girl's. But her figure, encased in a mould like a half-set jelly, was matronly: the young girl she had once been was buried under layers of flesh. She spoke English with just a slight accent, in a voice a little below a shout.

'Are you under arrest, Sergeant Katz?'

'No, Contessa.' Katz had obviously been here before. He took the woman's hand and clumsily, perfunctorily, kissed it; but the Contessa didn't seem to notice that the gesture was half-mocking. Katz introduced Luise and Dunleavy. 'The major is a sort of friendly escort – you don't have to worry about him. The Contessa Fabolini, your hostess.'

The Contessa gave Dunleavy her hand. It was held too high for him to shake it; he saw Luise looking at him, the hint of a smile in her eyes. He took the outstretched hand, bent his head and kissed it. He did it awkwardly, his lips landing smack on the back of the be-ringed hand; the Contessa withdrew it and he waited for her to wipe it on her stout rump. But she was a lady, despite her raucous voice, she just turned the hand over in a graceful gesture and motioned towards the house.

'Won't you come in? I'm afraid you will all be quartered in the cellars, but we have to be as discreet as possible.' Dunleavy wondered how anyone with a voice as loud as hers could be discreet. 'The English officers sometimes pay me a visit, so my guests must remain out of sight.'

Dunleavy looked at Katz. 'What happens to you now?'

'I'll come back tonight when I find out what the final plans are. I don't even know if the ship has arrived yet. I'll see your driver puts the jeep away outa sight.'

He went down the steps, began ushering Anna Bork and the others round to a side door that led down to the cellars.

'What about her?' said Anna, nodding up at the disappearing Luise. 'Why does she go in the front door and we go in this way?'

'That's just the way it is,' said Fred Katz, who had gone in side doors and back doors all his life. 'Some people just naturally go in the front way.'

'She's got no more right than we have –'

'Pipe down, love, willya? I got to get that bloody truck outa here before it starts drawing the flies. Relax. She's going to finish down in the cellar just like you, no matter what door she's gone in.'

Up on the first floor, in the big shabby over-furnished salon where she had led them, the Contessa Fabolini was saying, her voice bouncing off the high walls, 'You understand that no one is to come up out of the cellars unless I give permission. It is much too risky.'

'What about your servants?' Luise said.

'I have only two. They have been with me for years and they keep their mouths shut. But I couldn't trust others if I had them here – that is why my house is so neglected.' She beamed at Dunleavy, shouting at him as if he were at the other end of the big room: 'I saw you looking at it, major. But if I had workmen here cleaning up the place, I couldn't do what I'm doing now. This house was SS headquarters in the last year of the war – I was down in Rome fortunately. There was a three-day battle right here in my gardens before the SS men surrendered.'

'Then it's a sort of poetic justice that the villa should be sheltering Jews, isn't it?'

The Contessa blinked, as if she hadn't quite got Dunleavy's meaning; then she nodded vigorously, her second chin wobbling like a wavering underline. 'Yes, yes.' She lowered her voice a decibel or two, ignored Luise, turned into a heavyweight coquette. 'Major, I don't think there is any need for you to spend all your time in the cellars. The English won't be looking for you, will they?'

Before Dunleavy could accept or decline the invitation Luise said, 'Why do you have the English here, Contessa? Isn't it dangerous?'

'Oh, they invite themselves. They just telephone and say they'd like to visit me. After all, they *are* our conquerors.' For just a moment the plump pretty face hardened, like suet pudding turning cold; then she raised an eyebrow, woman to woman: 'But it is always nice to have men around. If one keeps them in their place, of course.'

'Which isn't always easy,' said Luise and smiled at Dunleavy.

Then an elderly man, gnarled and scruffy as one of the trees in the gardens outside, came hobbling in on bent legs. '*Scusi, signora* –'

The Contessa waved a hand at him, brushing him out of the room ahead of her as she might wave away annoying smoke. There was an animated conversation out in the large entrance hall, the Contessa's voice this time reduced to a hoarse whisper. Dunleavy gazed about him, at the peeling paint on the walls, the flaking gold on the picture frames, the worn and faded silk on the chairs and couches.

179

'Some of them never did care much about their houses,' said Luise. 'When I was a girl I came down once with my father to a villa on Lake Como. Much grander than this, but I don't think it had had a lick of paint in a hundred years. It is the middle classes who worry about the *bella figura*, the good image. The middle classes everywhere.'

'The Contessa doesn't strike me as upper class. I wonder where the Count is?'

'He was killed in the war, in Libya,' said the Contessa, coming in from the hall. 'No, I'm not upper class, major. My husband found me in the chorus at La Scala. He liked music and pretty women – he got both in me. I was pretty once,' she said challengingly.

'I'm sure you were,' said Dunleavy, no man to pick a fight with a woman if it could be avoided.

But the Contessa had something more on her mind than her lost looks; the conversation out in the hall had disturbed her. 'I'll have to ask you to stay down in the cellars after all, major. There has been a complication –'

'What sort of complication?' Luise said sharply. 'Has something gone wrong with our arrangements?'

'Not with yours, no, no – at least I don't think so!' The Contessa was shouting again. If she was in the chorus at La Scala, Luise thought, however did the audience hear the principals? 'All you have to do is stay out of sight till your friends come for you – they should come early tomorrow morning, if everything is all right –' She had begun to run out of breath; her bosom heaved up and down and the be-ringed hands fluttered about her pink face like jewel-studded birds. 'Please go down to the cellars now. Giulio will show you the way –'

The old man stood in the doorway, jerking an officious hand at them. Dunleavy bowed his head slightly to the Contessa, stood aside for Luise to go out of the door ahead of him. But she paused. 'I'd like a word with the Contessa, major. If you don't mind –?'

Dunleavy hesitated, then he nodded and followed the old man down a corridor towards some back stairs. Luise waited till he was gone; this echoing room was no place for a secret conversation. She lowered her voice to a whisper.

'Contessa, if Herr Keppel should arrive –'

'Herr Keppel?' The Contessa dropped her voice in midbreath; it finished as a hoarse gasp in her throat. 'I was wondering why he didn't come with you.'

'He has been here before?'

'Several times. A dangerous boy, too headstrong. The English are looking for him –'

'So is Major Dunleavy.' The Contessa looked puzzled, but Luise was not going to waste time explaining. 'If he comes, don't bring him down to the cellars. Tell him the major is here, that he must go somewhere else.'

'I wish you'd all go somewhere else!' The shout, though muffled, escaped again. 'It's not worth it –'

'Do you do this for charity or money, Contessa?'

The Contessa looked at her, eyes suddenly as hard as the diamonds on her fingers. 'Both.'

'Then I'm sure it's worth it,' said Luise. 'And don't let yourself forget it, at least not till we're out of here tomorrow or whenever we're supposed to go.'

3

Besser stood at the train window for at least twenty minutes after the train left Merano. At last Ilse came out and stood in the corridor beside him, closing the door of the compartment and shutting in the boys.

'Something is worrying you, Karl. Who was that girl?'

'I don't know.'

He racked his memory, trying to place her. Even if he had not slept with them, he had looked at other women; surely he would have remembered a girl as attractive as that one back there on the platform. He had examined no pretty girls when he had been with T4; there had been only the old and the very sick and the mentally unbalanced, none of them attractive enough to make him give them a second look. And Auschwitz was too far back in his memory, he couldn't possibly drag a face out of the thousands in the lines that had passed before him . . . And then behind Ilse's shoulder, distorted by the glass of the door so that it looked bigger than it was, he saw the Vuitton suitcase on the luggage rack.

'What's the matter, darling? Are you ill?'

'No, no.' He brushed off her solicitous hand, snapped irritably, 'I'm all right, I tell you!'

'For a moment I thought you were going to faint.' Ilse turned away from him, stared out of the window. But she saw nothing of the countryside as it rolled by: river, fields, mountains were just a blur, scum against the eyes. 'I don't know why. You never used to be the fainting kind.'

'Perhaps I'm getting old.' He was still shaken, was taking out his shock on her. 'It happens.'

'Oh, indeed it does. That was what I used to think every night, lying in our bed alone.' She looked at him, steadying herself against the swaying motion of the train; the wheels drummed beneath her, like an audible migraine. 'You used to write and tell me the war might go on forever. I often wondered what your superior officers would have said if they could have read your letters – '

'I'm surprised you didn't show them to Captain Gerstein.'

'Oh Karl.' She shook her head, smiled with rueful patience. 'You sound no older than Hans.'

'Ilse – ' He wanted to reach out for her, to brush away all the bitterness he felt; all at once he felt insecure, almost afraid. 'Please – '

But then the compartment door opened and Paul poked his head out. 'Father, come and play cards with me. Hans says he can't be bothered.'

'Cards? When – ?'

Ilse guessed the question in his mind. 'No, they didn't learn to play cards from any – visitor. I taught them. It was another way of filling in the time.'

Cards, reading, sleeping filled in the time as the train, stopping at every station, rumbled on towards Milan. There they changed to another train for Genoa. Besser found a porter, gave him the suitcases, draped his topcoat over the Vuitton. He would throw it away when they reached La Spezia, buy another case.

'We change again at Genoa, for La Spezia.'

'Is that where we board the ship, Father?'

'Perhaps. We shan't know till we get there.'

'Nobody seems to know anything.' Whose son is this? Besser wondered. How did I sire such a questioning know-all?

'Was it always like this, Father, I mean before the war?'

'Was it?' Besser looked at Ilse, who smiled and shook her head. 'No, everything was almost perfect in those days, Hans.'

'Then why did the Fuehrer start the war?'

'Always asking stupid questions,' said Paul disgustedly.

'No, that's a good question.' Then Besser realized he was talking to a much-too-talkative nine-year-old boy; out of the mouths of babes and innocents could come betrayal. 'Just be quiet for a while, Hans. Until we are on the ship just pretend you are Hans Ludwig from Innsbruck and you've never heard of the Fuehrer. Why doesn't the train start?' he snapped to no one in particular. He glared out at the candidly curious Italians standing on the platform and staring at the foreigners who could afford to travel first class 'It's getting on.'

'It isn't time yet.' Hans lifted his wrist, showed his watch. 'It doesn't go for another three minutes.'

'I thought you were told not to wear that watch!'

'Hans, give it to me,' Ilse said gently and, over the boy's protests, took the watch from him and put it in her handbag. 'Father would rather you wore one he'd given you. He will buy you one in Buenos Aires.'

'I am teaching myself Spanish. Do you want to hear me, Father?'

'Some other time, Hans.' The war hasn't touched him, Besser thought, looking at his self-confident, bright-eyed son. Are there enough like him back home to drag Germany out of the ruins? All at once he felt nostalgic, wanted to go back: to the solid old towns with their baroque architecture that he loved so much; to the mountains and their green forests, like the loden-coated shoulders of giants; to the good stolid people who believed in themselves. But he was dreaming of a Germany that was gone ... The train began to pull out, starting with a jerk. The suitcases tottered on the edge of the rack and he had to reach up and push them back. The Vuitton seemed the hardest to make secure.

He sat down in a corner seat, closed his eyes. There in the dark truth of his lids his fear condensed into tears of anger. Christ, he had thought it was all behind him! He felt no guilt about what he had had to do: as he had told Ilse, orders were orders. And the orders had been correct at the time. He believed he had no hatred of the Jews just because they *were* Jews; that sort of prejudice was a form of moral stupidity. But as enemies of the State they had to be eliminated if they contributed nothing; and if they had been left to volunteer they would have contributed nothing. All the elimination (he had never used the word *extermination* in his mind; sometimes it slipped out in conversation, like a fashionable phrase) of the useless Jews, the useless Gentiles, had been necessary; so he had believed up till the last year of the war. Then nothing had been necessary that didn't bring to an end the war that couldn't be won.

The train was an express, but half an hour before it was due in Genoa it suddenly began to slow, the wheels shrieking on the rails as the brakes were applied. Hans pressed his face against the glass of the window, peered slantwise ahead.

'We're pulling up at a station! Is it Genoa? It's so small!'

Besser saw the small country station slide by, felt the train bump to a halt. Hans and Paul were already out in the corridor, heads hanging out of a window.

'Policemen and soldiers are getting on! English soldiers!'

'Come back in here!'

Besser's voice was so sharp that the two boys whipped back into the compartment and sat down so quickly that it was almost as if he had threatened them physically. Ilse looked at him but said nothing.

It was twenty minutes before the carabinieri and the British soldiers, three of each crowding into the corridor, came to the Bessers' carriage. Besser heard them moving down the corridor and it was all he could do to keep himself in his seat. Hans, after a cautious glance at his father, stood up and looked out the compartment door; Paul, also watching his father warily, stood up and joined his brother. Besser was about to order them to sit down again, then realized the scene would look more natural if the boys were allowed to show their curiosity at what was going on. They didn't want to be sitting here like a well-drilled German family when the British came to their compartment. He wasn't sure how an Austrian family would behave in such circumstances, but that was what they were supposed to be. An ordinary Austrian family free to travel to a new life in South America . . .

'Your papers, please.'

A red-faced British captain stood at the door, a British corporal and a carabinieri sergeant just behind him. They looked a formidable group packed in the doorway, all threatening uniform and authority.

'I have travel papers only.' Besser's English was only what he had learned at school and he had had very little occasion to use it since.

'They will do – we are just looking for proper identification.' The captain's German was impeccable: had he been prepared for victory or defeat? Besser wondered. He perused the papers Besser gave him, stroked his thick blond moustache, looked back at Besser. 'A medical doctor, Herr Doctor?'

'Yes.'

The captain, with his plump red face and his slightly pop eyes and his too-large moustache, had a slightly ridiculous look, almost a stupid one. One wonders how we lost the war to these pompous asses, Besser thought; and felt a little safer. Then saw that the captain was turning to Hans.

'Do you want to be a doctor like your father?'

'Yes, Herr Captain.' Hans had retreated to stand with his back against the window.

'What sort of doctor was he?'

'I don't know, sir. Just an ordinary doctor.' Hans rubbed a nervous hand against his nose, looked at his father.

'I am just a general practitioner,' said Besser.

The captain looked at the papers again: Besser was suddenly

aware of the shrewdness behind the pop-eyed image. 'You're going to the Argentine. Plenty of opportunities there for doctors, I should imagine. Were you in the Wehrmacht?'

'Yes.'

'Where did your husband spend the war, Frau Ludwig?'

The question was so abrupt, the change of direction so unexpected. And Besser noticed that it was the first time the name *Ludwig* had been used, as if the captain expected it to be a false one. But Ilse was not caught off guard.

'He was on the Russian front most of the time.'

'Stalingrad?' The captain looked back at Besser, who nodded. 'Must have been pretty bad. For both sides. Here are your papers. Good luck in South America. I'm told you may find a lot of your old comrades there.'

The captain was about to close the compartment door when Hans said, 'Why are you searching the train, Herr Captain?'

Besser could have killed his son on the spot; even Ilse looked ready to slap him across the mouth. Stiffly, like mechanical dolls, they forced their faces away from their son, looked up at the captain who stood in the doorway, pop-eyed face chopped off by the half-opened door.

'We are looking for a monster, my boy. One who is disguised as a man named Adolph Eichmann.'

'I don't believe in monsters,' said Hans.

'Stay that way,' said the captain and looked down at Besser. 'A charming innocent boy, Dr Ludwig. How are you going to protect him from the truth?'

He closed the door, nodded to the soldier and the carabiniere and they went on to the next compartment. But one of the soldiers remained standing outside the Bessers' compartment, leaning negligently against the corridor window, winking smilingly at Paul as the younger boy stared out through the compartment window at him.

'Father –' said Hans.

'No more questions.' Besser kept his voice low, tried to keep the grit out of it. 'You've asked enough questions for one day. Let's play cards.'

'I don't want to play cards –'

'Neither do I,' said Paul.

Besser looked across at Ilse, sitting stiff-backed on the opposite seat. 'You've spoiled them. They could do with some discipline.'

'There'll be time for that.' Ilse's voice was soft, controlled; but sweat was now breaking on her forehead and upper lip. She was not meant for conspiracy, for deceit: it came to him now how easily, willingly, she had confessed to the affair with Gerstein. 'But not now – not unless you want that officer coming back.'

'What is the truth, Father? What did the English captain mean by that?'

Besser closed his eyes again. 'Hans, no more questions – please!'

'Your father is tired,' said Ilse. 'He'll answer all your questions some time – but not all at once.'

'Do you ever ask Father questions?'

Besser opened his eyes, gazed across at his wife. 'Sometimes,' she said, not looking at him. 'But only important ones.'

It was another half hour before the train got under way again. By then Hans and Paul were once more out in the corridor. As the train eased out of the small station the two boys stood at the window and waved to the British captain and his men as the carriage went past them. The captain waved back, said something to the corporal beside him. Then the enemy and the station dropped out of sight round a bend in the track and Besser, who had come out of the compartment to stand behind the boys, felt a sick spasm of relief flood through him. He went quickly back into the compartment, flopped down on the seat opposite Ilse.

She closed the door deliberately, said quietly, 'You knew the man they were looking for. I saw it on your face.'

'I met him once – in Berlin.'

'Who was he? A monster, like the Englishman said?'

'Yes.' At least he couldn't hide the truth from her. 'He was the one in charge of the – the extermination of the Jews.'

It was her turn to close her eyes, but as a retreat: it was a reflex of exhaustion, as if she was learning more than she could bear. 'Oh God!' It was a minute or so before she opened her eyes again, then she said in whispered bitterness, 'And you are horrified by *my* small sin!'

'That was different. It was personal – between you and me – '

But he knew it was no real answer, could tell by the look on her face. He turned his head, looked out at the boys in the corridor. Both of them smiled at him, pointing at something in the passing countryside, and somehow he managed to smile back. It seemed to him, seeing the dim reflection of it in the dusty glass of the compartment window, that his face was broken and splintered, a mask that would forever show the cracks in it.

The hour's delay of the train resulted in their missing their connection at Genoa. He had been given no *Spinne* man in Genoa to contact; he had to make his own arrangements for the night's stop-over. It was a simple task that, uncharacteristically for him, became a major effort; he could not make up his mind whether to stay near the railway station or go somewhere quieter. When he did choose a quiet side street he could not decide among the half a dozen pensiones that offered accommodation. It was Ilse, tired by the journey, tiring of his unnatural irresolution, who made the decision for them.

They ate with the family who owned the pensione, exchanging nothing but smiles since neither family knew anything of the other's language. Then they went to bed, the boys to one room where they shared a double bed, Besser and Ilse to another where they did the same. They lay side by side under the big patched quilt, like strangers sharing a shelter from a common danger. When they finally fell asleep their legs entwined of their own volition, like mating snakes; Besser woke in the middle of the night with an erection, but Ilse was still sleeping soundly and he immediately turned away from her. He still had the erection when he woke in the morning, but he let her get up first, get dressed and go down the hall to the boys before he got out of bed. A stiff cock, he had once heard a misogynist fellow officer say, was only a flag of surrender.

They caught a train for La Spezia in the afternoon and arrived in that city just on nightfall. They stood on the platform until all the other passengers had passed through the gates; Besser hoped that the *Spinne* man, whoever he might be, might see them and come forward to meet them. But no one approached them and Besser realized they had suddenly become suspiciously conspicuous standing there in the middle of the empty platform. When he reached the gates he wished they had hurried through with all the other passengers.

'Can I help you, sir?' said the British major stepping out from behind the ticket collector's booth. 'You appear to be expecting someone to meet you.'

'Thank you.' Besser wished he had kept up his English; but then he had never imagined he might need it so much as now. 'We are all right.'

'May I see your papers?' He was in his late twenties, a handsome slim young man who had the weathered tan of someone who had spent most of his life in the open air. 'Austrian, eh? Were you in the war, Dr Ludwig?'

'The Wehrmacht. Medical corps.'

'I see you and your family are booked on the *Rio Blanco*. I'm afraid you have missed it, Dr Ludwig. It sailed this morning.'

'This morning?' Besser had been speaking quietly; shock now made his voice boom out in its natural volume. 'Today?'

'I'm afraid so. We've had a bit of a flap on here these last two days —'

'Flap? What is that?'

'Nothing, Dr Ludwig.' The officer handed back the papers, seemed uninterested in any further conversation. 'Check with the shipping company. If you are going to remain in La Spezia longer than twenty-four hours, you must report to the police.'

He saluted and walked off, swagger stick tucked up under his arm, his head tilted slightly forward so that the peak of his cap shadowed his eyes, a conqueror in the first year of the new world of peace: his doubts were still ahead of him, like his pension.

'What do we do?' Ilse said frantically; she was suddenly on the edge of panic. 'Where do we go now?'

'Let's get out of here first.' Besser tried to sound calm,

but he could hear his voice booming in his own ears, like that of a man shouting for help, any help. 'There must be some mistake –'

They walked out into the street and a man moved up beside them as they stood on the edge of the kerb wondering which way to go.

'Herr Ludwig? No, don't look at me – just in case we are being watched.' He spoke in heavily accented German. 'Go down to the first corner on the left, turn into that street. There is a taxi waiting outside the Bar Sport. The driver is expecting you.'

The man slid away into the darkness. Besser didn't catch even a glimpse of his face; all he saw was a thin overcoated figure disappearing into the night. Gathering up their luggage, they went down the street, feeling as strange here in this alien city as they had expected to feel on another continent; the noise and chatter of the Italians, the dirtiness of the streets, was something for which they had been unprepared. How could Germans have been partners with these people in the war?

The taxi was standing outside the bar, a pre-war Fiat with a massive dent in its back; the spare wheel, still on its mounting, was embedded in the body of the car like a giant seal. The driver must have been watching for them in his driver's mirror; he got out as soon as he saw them turn the corner. He held open the door of the taxi, waved them in like a man herding slow sheep into a pen. 'Quick! Quick!'

Ilse and the boys were pushed into the back seat, the luggage was flung on to the roof rack and tied down with rope, Besser got into the front seat beside the driver and they were off, tearing down the narrow street like a shell being shot out of the barrel of a gun. The boys laughed with delight, but Besser and Ilse clung to the side of the swaying car and waited for the inevitable accident to happen. They went round corners on screaming tyres and Besser began to wonder if the driver was trying to draw attention to them, was hoping to be chased by some British military vehicle.

Then, after what seemed like miles of headlong driving, they were speeding, though less recklessly now, along a road that bordered the sea. Besser saw the glint of water on his right, smelled the salt air coming in through the open window of the taxi. As if he were no longer afraid of pursuit, the driver sat back from the wheel and at last looked at Besser.

'What happened to you, Herr Ludwig?' he said in good German. 'You should have been on the early train this morning.'

Besser explained what had happened. 'Has the ship really gone? An English officer at the station said –'

The driver nodded. 'It left. Don't ask me why – we have no control over the ships.' He sounded angry, as if someone somewhere had fallen down on the range of their controls. He was a young man, short and thickset, with dark hair cut *en brosse* and thick eyebrows raised in perpetual surprise, as if he would never quite believe whatever was presented to him. 'My name is Ricci, Giovanni Ricci. It used to be Richter – my father was German. He came here before I was born, to work in the shipyards – he married my mother, an Italian, and changed his name. He was killed in the air raids. My mother, too.'

'Is that why you are working for us?'

Ricci stared straight ahead. 'This situation can't last. We'll get Europe back from – *them*. It may take some time, but we'll get it back.'

Besser gave the expected nod of agreement. 'Where are you taking us? What do we do about another ship?'

'I don't know about the ship – I'll have to find out about that. There's none going to South America from here, not for another month. You may have to go further south, to Naples or somewhere. Tonight you will be staying just along the gulf here. In a way it was fortunate you did not arrive this morning. The place we were going to take you to while you waited to board the ship was raided by the English.'

'Looking for Eichmann?' Besser didn't look back at Ilse as he said the name, but he sensed that she had leaned forward.

'Who? I've never heard of anyone by that name.' Ricci slowed the taxi, fell in behind a convoy of six British army trucks. 'No, they were looking for Jews. There's a ship out in the harbour, the *Fede*, that's supposed to be waiting to take a load of them on board for Palestine. The English have been raiding all the likely safe houses. Including ours.'

'Will we be safe where you are taking us now?'

'The safest house for miles around, so long as you stay out of sight. We've used it before, but only for VIPs.'

'Thank you,' said Ilse from the back seat, trying hard for a smile. 'We'll try not to lower the tone.'

Ricci speeded up the taxi, cursing in Italian as the convoy ahead kept him back. Suddenly he swung out, dangerously overtook the convoy on a much-too-short stretch of road, tooted his horn derisively as each of the British truck drivers tooted angrily at him; he screeched round a corner, cutting in front of a military policeman on a motorcycle to avoid a car coming in the opposite direction. Then they were coming into a village, skirting a piazza and starting to climb, suddenly turning off into a side street as the first truck of the convoy swung into the piazza below them. They went up the narrow street, turned into a lane, finally came to some tall ornamental gates. Ricci got out, pushed back the heavy creaking gates.

Besser caught a glimpse of the chipped letters cut into the wall. He got out, went across and peered at the name: he always liked to know where he was. He came back, got in beside Ricci as the latter slid under the wheel again. As he got into the taxi he saw the single headlamp, heard the chug-chug of a motorcycle down at the end of the lane; but then it turned off, probably into a side lane. He became aware of the stiffness of his hand on the taxi door; then he shrugged, got in and slammed the door. Exhaustion was making him too nervous.

'Who owns the Villa Fontana?' he said.

Chapter Five

Luise heard the car come into the courtyard and drive round to the back of the villa. The windows were too high in the cellar walls for her to see out and they had been curtained over with dirty sacking – 'It's our own blackout,' the Contessa had said. 'The war isn't completely over, is it?'

'I try to convince myself it is,' Luise had said and was glad Ben Keppel hadn't been there to argue with her.

The cellar, or rather cellars, underlay the whole of the villa and part of the courtyard: a series of dark rooms, connected by archways, in which the junk of two centuries had been dumped. The main cellar, in which Luise and the others had settled down to wait, contained three huge wine vats and several rows of empty racks: if the Contessa had a wine supply, she did not keep it where it could be sampled by her paying guests. The rest of the cellar was furnished with a couple of dozen rough wooden beds, covered with mattresses and army blankets, a long table and two long benches; the big room was lit by two dirty electric globes that threw a light as weak as the Contessa's charity. In an inner cellar, so dark that none of the children would go there without one of their parents, a rough toilet had been set up, its smell lost in the general dankness of the whole big basement. They had become literally underground people, Luise thought, travellers in the dark. She began to yearn for the yet-to-be-experienced heat and glare of the Palestine sun.

'We'll have to get you out of here,' Dunleavy said. 'This is no place to keep kids cooped up.'

'*We*? You're on our side now?' She smiled at him.

'I don't know,' he said, only half-smiling.

'Do you wish you had gone home right after the war?'

'I don't know that, either. Sometimes, yes – ' America would be well at peace now. The casualty lists would have been replaced by batting line-ups: spring training would have begun down there in the South and Musial, DiMaggio, Williams would be taking the winter stiffness out of their muscles. He suddenly longed for the sound of a bat against a ball, to feel the thump of a ball into his glove. He stirred with the memory of it. 'Things keep cropping up that I'd like to see – you'd probably think them unimportant, frivolous. Baseball, for instance.'

She wrinkled her nose. 'I was never interested in sport. I used to ride and ski and swim. But as for team sports . . . Were you any good? All Americans are supposed to be good at sport. I can remember how angry Hitler was in Berlin when the Americans won so many events at the Olympics. Especially the Negroes.'

'I was never any good. I played ball and tried out for high school football, but I was too awkward to be any good. I'm the only guy you've met who can trip over, standing still.'

They had spent most of the day together and, leavened by the presence and occasional remarks of the others, they had eased into a relationship where suspicion had finally evaporated. He had taken off his jacket and under his tight shirt she really saw for the first time the bulk and strength of his chest and shoulders. She became aware of his maleness, that physical quality that had attracted her to men in those days and nights in Vienna when love-making had been a natural part of living. She stretched her legs out in front of her, cat-like, easing the feeling that had stirred in her.

'Getting stiff?'

She smiled to herself: that was the least she felt. She went back to the subject they had been discussing. 'How did you feel last January, when those American soldiers rioted and demanded to be sent home?'

'I understood them. But I had to go out and crack a few skulls. That's the tough part of being a cop – you sympathize with the guys breaking the law, but you've got to uphold it.'

He looked at her. 'You probably think I'm wrong, but I some-times am on the side of the British. Their soldiers, I mean, not their politicians. They've got themselves out on a limb with Palestine. It happens all the time when a country starts shoving its nose into another country. The politicians start it, but the poor goddam military have got to carry it out.'

'It might happen to America some day.'

'Could be. Depends which way our politicians and our military go. Some of our generals, they're pretty fascist-minded. I didn't know it till the end of the war. But they've tasted power and they're not going to give it up easy.'

'What about your politicians?'

'I don't know. Harry Truman is from the Mid West and we're pretty isolationist out there.'

'Are you an isolationist?'

'Would I still be here if I were?'

'No, I suppose not. What about your driver?'

'Charlie?'

Dunleavy looked across at Charlie Lincoln who was enter-taining the children with music on a mouth-organ he had produced from somewhere. The music, blues and swing, had originated a long way from the children's birthplaces, but somehow it communicated itself to them; they had heard so little music in their short lives, their ears had no prejudice against it. But behind them, in a corner, David Weill had his eyes closed as if in pain.

'I don't know. Even Charlie himself won't know that till he goes back to Memphis.' He looked across at the boy, foot pumping away in rhythm to his music, whose life seemed so uncomplicated. 'At least he can go back.'

'You can't?'

'Not to Beef City, Nebraska. I don't belong there any more.' He anticipated her question and smiled: 'I'm not sure where I belong. But that's one of the things you and I have in common, isn't it?'

Then they heard the car come into the courtyard and drive round to the back of the villa. Dunleavy held up his hand and everyone quietened; Charlie Lincoln's mouth-organ cut off in mid-note. David Weill opened his eyes, but there was no sign of relief in them at the shutting off of the alien music; he glanced fearfully up at the sack-covered windows. In the silence the dank smell of the cellars seemed to thicken.

'The English?' Luise whispered.

'Could be.' Dunleavy stood up, head cocked. 'But why the *back* of the house?'

'The bitch of a Contessa has given us away!' Anna Bork almost strangled herself trying to keep her angry voice down.

Luise could see the group moving closer together, congealing into a mood of half-fear, half-resignation; only Anna Bork looked ready to fight anyone who might come down the steps to arrest her. She wanted no violence if it could be avoided, but she knew she had to keep the group from giving up.

She took command, even of Dunleavy. 'Go upstairs and find out what's happening. You're the only one who has a legitimate right to be here.'

Dunleavy looked at her in surprise, then he grinned. 'That an order?'

But he put on his jacket, went across to the steps at once. Luise waited till he had quietly slipped through the door at the top of the steps, then she picked up one of the two torches Sergeant Katz had left with them.

'Herr Berger, would you come with me? I'd like to see if there is another way out of here. We can't go out the way you came in – that leads right into the courtyard in front of the house. And we can't go up those steps, through the house itself.'

'If there is another way out and we have to run,' said Simon Berger, 'where do we run to?'

'We'll find somewhere,' she said doggedly. 'Don't be defeatist, Herr Berger.'

They were moving through the smaller cellars, following the probing yellow shaft of the torch's beam.

'Just tiredness, that's all it is, Fräulein. And this – ' She sensed rather than saw him nod up and around at the black ceilings pressing down on them. 'I spent fifteen years of my life in the mines. When the Nazis took me away, had me working

196

out in the open air at Auschwitz, it was almost like a release. For a while, anyway.'

'We shan't stay down here a minute longer than we have to. I just hope –'

But she really didn't know what she hoped for: she couldn't see beyond this succession of black rooms in which they stood. They found no other exit, turned back towards the main cellar.

'If it's the English upstairs, then we're trapped.'

'They'd already be down here if it was them,' she said. 'The English don't play cat-and-mouse.'

Upstairs Dunleavy, one hand smoothing down his crew-cut, the other straightening his tie, trying not to look like a man who had spent all day in a cellar, was moving through the main floor of the villa. He was at once cautious and casual, a house guest not sure of his environment. But each of the rooms he wandered through was deserted and he knew now that the new-comers, whoever they were, were not the British come to arrest the Jews down below. As he moved into each large room he searched for the switch and turned on the lights; gradually he brought the whole main floor of the villa alight in a blaze of chandeliers. The great shabby house glowed like a memory of past glory; once, he guessed, it had been rich and opulent, full of rich opulent people with no care in the world but that of creeping age and the dying of an era. He wondered how long ago that careless time had been, if it had been in the days when the Contessa had been young and slim and pretty.

She came into the furthest room of the house, as ablaze with indignation as her chandeliers with light. 'What are you doing? Who gave you permission – ?'

'No one, Contessa.' He wasn't disturbed, he felt he could handle her. There was some mystery about her, but she was basically a simple woman. And simple women had never really been a problem for him, not even as a lawyer back in Beef City. 'I was just looking around, admiring what you have here. It's a beautiful house. You must have enjoyed it before the war.'

She calmed down, taking his admiration of the house as some sort of compliment to herself. She was dressed in a purple dinner gown that thrust her plump bosom up like a serving of two over-ripe melons; four strands of pearls fell into the cleavage like frosted sugar crystals. Her fingers were small chandeliers in themselves; he had never seen a woman who wore so many rings. The English might still be the enemy, but when her eventual surrender came it would be in style.

'Il Duce came here several times – he loved our balls.'

Il Duce, balls and all, were gone forever: Dunleavy wondered how many other heroes the big house had survived.

'Perhaps some day we'll have them again,' she said and the wish glowed pathetically in her face like a child's dream.

They had begun to walk back through the rooms, the Contessa turning off the lights as they went. They passed the big dining room and Dunleavy nodded at the elegantly set table.

'Are you having someone to dinner?'

'The English officers telephoned, invited themselves again. They do it – such an un-English thing. But how can I refuse them?'

'I heard a car – '

If he hadn't been watching her so closely he might have missed the slight hesitation. The tip of her tongue ran along her lips like a large globule of blood. 'Just – just a tradesman from the village.'

'I didn't hear him drive away,' he said casually.

She switched out another light, another room died into darkness behind them. 'He sometimes stays and has a drink with Giulio. You know what servants are – '

'Of course,' said Dunleavy. 'My mother used to have the same trouble with our Indians.'

'You had Indians working for you?' But now they were in the big entrance hall and someone was clanging the heavy knocker on the front door. 'Oh, there are the English! Giulio! Rosanna!'

She shouted towards the back of the house: she was no more than ten feet from the door but she couldn't open it herself, she had to greet her guests as a Contessa should, regally at ease in the comfort of her salon. She left Dunleavy in a rush, tripped light-footed across the marble floor of the hall. He followed her leisurely into the big salon, found her hastily arranging herself like a giant purple seal on the green velvet rocks of a chaise-longue. Out in the hall Giulio clumped across the marble, swung open the big front door. The English officers came into the house in a babel of high light voices and loud laughter, some joke brought in with them and divested at once with their trenchcoats.

Then they were in the doorway of the salon, three young men and an older man, assured and confident but not arrogant. They're on their own, thought Dunleavy, they'll never worry about the warmth of their welcome outside England. No wonder they had made such a success of empire-building.

'My dear Contessa – ' Then they saw Dunleavy, an *American*, and they pulled up, all at once cautious, even suspicious.

The Contessa raised a fist of diamond knuckles: the rings sparkled so much it was difficult to focus on her fingers. 'Gentlemen – my house guest, Major Dunleavy. Major Shell, Captain Miller, Lieutenant Bankhead, Lieutenant Updyke.'

The senior man, Shell, was not the balding older man: that was Miller. Major Shell was younger than Dunleavy, in his late twenties, a handsome man who appeared to have spent too long in the desert sun; there were already wrinkles around the blue eyes and small sun cancers just below the line of his hair. He had a light pleasant voice with the public school accent that Dunleavy, who had grown up among flat nasal twangs, sometimes had difficulty in catching.

'We're Field Security,' said Shell. 'You're from – ?'

'Then you're the guy I'll be coming to see in the morning.' Dunleavy explained who he was, why he was here, only leaving out that one of the murdered men had been his brother. All he had to do was play it straight with these Englishmen. 'Maybe you can help me.'

'With Keppel?' Shell looked at the other three officers, who all shook their heads, then he looked back at Dunleavy. 'We've been after him for three months now. We had him once and let him go, without realizing who he was.'

'I didn't know he was on any Wanted list. He wasn't on our list in Bavaria.'

'Why should he be? The Jews are our problem, isn't that what you chaps think?' Shell was smiling as he spoke, but Dunleavy felt the needle. 'President Truman worries about the Jewish vote back home, doesn't he?'

'Could be.' Dunleavy could feel the Jews beneath his feet, Luise and the others down in the cellars who, denied the vote so long, had forgotten what it was for. 'It's some time since I heard from him.'

The Contessa must have sensed she was losing control of her own party; she shouted to Giulio to bring in drinks. A moment later the old man, now wearing a white jacket and white gloves, wheeled in a large double-decker tray, handed out drinks that had the potency of secret weapons. Dunleavy coughed on his Scotch, but the Englishmen seemed unaffected by theirs.

'Giulio is rather heavy-handed.' Miller was a type Dunleavy recognized from any army; the man who had reached the limit of his promotion potential, who might have been a captain for the past five years and would remain one for the next ten. 'The Contessa has a jolly good source of supply, the way Giulio throws it around.'

'Where does she get it?'

'Black market. The Jewish Brigade – chaps who were always in our hair, we had to send 'em north to Belgium – they used to levy their chaps a bottle a week from their issue, sell it to finance their smuggling of the DPs. Shouldn't be surprised if this is some of it.' He held his glass up to the light. 'But good Scotch always tastes the same, black market or otherwise.'

'It doesn't stick in your gullet, if it was Jewish Brigade stuff?'

'Good God, no! One can be too bloody ethical, y'know. We shouldn't be dining here with the Contessa if we felt like that, eh?'

The Contessa and Shell had drifted towards the other end of the room. Dunleavy sized up Miller as a talkative type and invested some time in him. 'What's with her? Was she a Fascist?'

'Oh, absolutely. One of the best of 'em, I gather. But she's useful to us, she knows everyone for miles around. And, of course, it's jolly nice to come up here once a week or so for a spot of gracious living.'

Bankhead and Updyke joined them, nodding agreement at Miller's opinion of gracious living. They were both younger than Shell, eager-looking and a little too casually smart in their dress: Dunleavy wondered if either of them had seen anything of the war, if they were not late postings here to Italy. Bankhead, who couldn't have been more than twenty, said, 'We've been frightfully busy all day. Raids all over town, looking for the damned Yids.'

'There's a ship out in the gulf, y'know,' said Updyke, who had a long blond moustache that stretched halfway across his face. 'Had our eye on it ever since it put in here a week ago. There's movement afoot, y'know.'

'Hundreds of bloody Jews around La Spezia.' Miller sipped his drink, nodded appreciatively at it. 'We've been picking 'em up all day. Poor buggers.'

'I suppose so,' said Updyke. 'One can't blame them for wanting to get away from Germany and Poland, put those dreadful camps behind them. But why Palestine? You've been there, David. All bloody sand and flies, isn't it?'

'Bloody horrible,' said Miller. 'Can't understand why they're flocking there. We should get out, too, just leave it to the Wogs.'

'Oh, I don't know,' said Bankhead, twenty years old and ready to build a new world. 'I think we owe the Arabs something. After all, we did let them down after the last show.'

'Bloody Lawrence of Arabia,' said Miller, winking at Dunleavy. 'Timothy spent a week in Cairo, fell in love with the Wogs and their burnouses. You can't trust any of the buggers. Give the Empire away, that's my motto, and let's all go home and occupy Piccadilly Circus.'

The Contessa and Shell drifted back, her voice drowning out anything he was saying. 'Let's go into dinner,' she shouted as if bursting into an aria. 'I have a surprise for you!'

'She always has surprises for us,' Miller whispered. 'Usually stuff she's had pinched from our own stores. Incredible bloody woman, y'know.'

'Come and see us in the morning,' Shell said. 'Our office is in La Spezia. But we live here in Lerici, in Shelley's house.' Dunleavy looked blank. 'Shelley, the poet. Percy B. *A dream has power to poison sleep* and all that. Poor blighter drowned himself, just down the coast.'

'Never had much time for poets, I'm afraid,' said Miller.

'Where I went to school we got Edgar Guest.'

'Afraid I've never heard of him,' said Shell. 'Place reeks of literary types around here. Used to come here to dodge people like Miller. Shelley, Byron, D. H. Lawrence, Baroness Orczy. She wrote *The Scarlet Pimpernel* in a villa just up the road, y'know. Probably interest your chap Keppel, if he knew. I suppose he sees himself as some sort of Pimpernel.'

'I doubt it,' said Dunleavy.

Down in the cellars Luise stood at the bottom of the steps, her back against one of the huge wine vats. She and Simon Berger had come back into the main cellar just in time to hear the second car arrive in the front courtyard. They had heard the clanging of the knocker on the door, then the Contessa's shout for Giulio; a moment later they had heard the tread of men's heels on the marble floor above. She knew now that *some* English had arrived; she could hear their voices. But who had arrived in the first car?

She shook her head warningly at Judith Winter as her daughter began to cough. The child, catching the urgency of the adults, put her hand over her mouth, went red in the face as she tried to muffle the cough. Judith Winter put her arm round her daughter's shoulders and led her into the darkness of the inner cellars. Luise, watching the suffering child and her mother disappear into the blackness, said softly, 'Sometimes I wonder if we should be putting the children through this.'

'Kids have more stamina than you think. You'd know, if you'd had any.'

Luise had not been aware of who was standing next to her: it annoyed her to find that it was Anna Bork. 'Where are *your* children?'

'Dead,' said Anna Bork. 'Both of them. When I got to

Birkenau they took them away from me. We got off the train and there was Besser – ' Suddenly she began to weep, the tears streaming down her freckled cheeks.

It was so unexpected that Luise acted automatically: her arm went round the other woman's thick shoulders. They stood together, backs against the wine vat, like sisters sharing a common grief. David Weill turned his head towards them and his eyebrows went up in comical surprise. Then Luise became aware of the rest of the group staring at them. But she did not draw her arm away, tried to put silent sympathy into the pressure of her hand on Anna's shoulder.

It was Anna who broke the momentary bond between them. Her eyes cleared of tears and she saw that they were the centre of attention; she frowned in puzzlement and wiped the tears from her face. Then she felt Luise's arm across her shoulders and she abruptly stepped away from the wine vat as if Luise had pushed her.

Luise let her arm drop, kept her voice calm. 'Was that why you said nothing yesterday when I told you I'd seen Besser?'

Anna wiped her eyes with a tattered handkerchief; she glared angrily at Luise, as if the latter had taken advantage of her with the show of sympathy. 'I swore I'd never forget him. When the War Crimes people came to the camp I gave them his name, but I never heard any more. I hoped he was dead!' she said savagely. 'I hoped the Russians had got him and killed him horribly!'

'He's still very much alive, unfortunately.'

They could hear the clack-clack of boot-heels on the marble floor above their heads. A faint shout came down to them, the Contessa playing the gracious hostess.

'I wish you hadn't told me – ' The tattered handkerchief was lost in the suddenly clenched fist. 'I'd told myself he was dead – I dreamed of the Russians torturing him before they killed him – ' She looked at Luise as if disappointed in her. 'Don't you wish he was dead?'

'I don't know – yes, I suppose so. Unless, of course, they catch him – '

'Who? Who wants to catch him? Those upstairs?' She jerked

a contemptuous thumb at the roof of the cellar. 'All they are interested in is us.'

'We should let them know he is alive –'

'How? Drop them a note?'

'I should have told Major Dunleavy about him. Perhaps he could tell them.'

'What's he doing up there anyway?' Anna, suspicion clouding her face again, looked up towards the top of the stairs. 'He's been gone a long time. Surely he's not having dinner with that bitch and the English?'

'Why not? Perhaps he can learn something –' But Luise herself was curious: what *was* going on upstairs? 'Tell everybody to keep quiet. I'll sneak up there and see if I can find out what's going on.'

She reached for her coat automatically, put it on, as if she were going outdoors on some errand; or as if she now had always to be fully dressed, ready to escape. She went cautiously up the steps, pausing at the top while Noah Malchek put the lights out. Then she slipped out through the door into the long narrow corridor that led from the entrance hall to the kitchens at the back of the house. She was not awed by the size of the Villa Fontana; as she had told Dunleavy, she had been born in a house bigger than this. Twice as big: for a moment she wondered who ran through the corridors of Waldgarten now as she had done, if the huge old house knew even an echo of the laughter that had once filled it.

There was laughter in this house; she heard it as soon as she stepped out into the corridor. She looked towards the back of the house; she could hear the rattle of dishes in the kitchen back there. Then she moved quickly and quietly towards the front hall, towards the sound of the laughter. The hall and the main salon were in darkness; the light and the laughter came from the big dining room on the other side of the hall from the salon. She stood for a moment in the shadows, looking through the high archway. The Contessa sat at one end of a long narrow table, Dunleavy at the other end and four English officers, two on either side, in between them. Light was reflected from the lace snow of the table-cloth, glittered on the crystal glasses and the cutlery. It was years since Luise had seen such a scene and another memory came back pricking her like a thorn.

The Contessa picked up a small silver bell and rang it, just as Luise remembered her grandmother doing. The tinkle of the bell seemed to be too faint to be heard at the back of the house; but the old man Giulio must have been standing at the door of the kitchen waiting for it. Luise heard him coming down the long corridor, wheeling a trolley

She looked wildly around her, turning for a moment towards the salon. But she could be trapped in there when the Contessa brought her guests back to it after dinner. She ran up the stairs, slipped into an alcove on the landing halfway to the gallery that ran round the upper floor level of the high-ceilinged entrance hall. She brushed against dusty velvet curtains, felt her blood run cold as her nails touched the cloth; then she turned sharply, startled, as the voices and laughter came up behind her more clearly than she had heard them down in the hall.

She was in a small musicians' gallery that looked down on the dining room. Rusted music stands stood in a dark corner of the gallery like the skeletons of storks; sheet music was stacked on the floor, yellowed and dusty. Luise, hidden by the faded red drapes, looked down through the white sun of a chandelier at the dinner party below.

'I'd love to go back to La Scala to sing,' the Contessa was saying, 'but I'm much too old to start all over again.'

Too true, thought Luise.

'Oh, I don't know,' said one of the young English officers, a pink-cheeked boy with a huge blond moustache. 'Don't opera singers go on and on?'

'How gallant you English are,' said the Contessa. 'I envy Englishwomen. They must be spoilt by all the charm you lavish on them.'

'She's got your measure, Walter old boy,' said the bald-headed officer sitting just below Dunleavy. 'One up to you, Contessa.'

Walter blushed, stroked his moustache nervously. 'Wasn't

trying to offend, Contessa, absolutely not. Peter will tell you –
I'm a great admirer of women, especially Italian women.'

Peter, whoever he was, was slightly obscured by the chandelier. Luise craned her head to one side, saw the tanned handsome young major smiling at the still-blushing lieutenant.

'He's a problem, Contessa. Falls for every Italian girl he
meets.' Luise, watching him closely, saw him turn his wrist
over, glance at his watch; it seemed an odd thing to do at such
a moment in the conversation, but she thought no more of it as
he went on, 'What are the girls like in Germany, Dunleavy?'

'Willing – maybe a bit too much.' Dunleavy waited while
Giulio put a steaming soup plate down in front of him. 'If
you'll forgive me saying so, Contessa, the Germans don't live
as well as we are tonight. You sit down in a restaurant or café
and before the waiter gets to you, you got a girl for company.'

'It was like that in Naples when we first landed there – '
The young major looked at the Contessa. 'Are we offending you,
talking like this?'

'Why should you, Major Shell? I know what it was like –
war is always worse for women. Or worse than you men
think.'

'I saw you looking at me – '

'I was wondering why you keep looking at your watch. It
is not very polite, not when we are only at the soup course.'

'Force of habit,' said Shell; and Luise, all at once sensitive
to something in the atmosphere down at the dinner table,
noticed that he did not bother to apologize. 'I've been looking
at it all day.'

'The raids on the Jews?' said Dunleavy, and Shell nodded.
'What about Nazis?'

'What about them?'

'Just wondering. There are a lot of them still on the loose,
trying to get out of Europe. Some of them must come down this
way looking for a ship.'

'We don't give ourselves any more work than we have to.'
Shell began on his soup. 'It's bad enough chasing these Jews.
In theory we should leave them to the Italian police, but the
Italians don't want to be bothered. So we've had to come back

on the job. We certainly don't want to have to go looking for escaping Nazis.'

'Absolutely not,' said Miller. 'Jolly nice wine, Contessa.'

'I wanted to serve you sherry with the soup, but there was none available.'

'Can't have everything. But I'm sure you'll have some next time we come.' Miller winked at Dunleavy.

Then Miller and the other officers sat up straight in their chairs. Luise heard the trucks drive into the courtyard. Major Shell put down his soup spoon and stood up; the other three officers did the same. Dunleavy and the Contessa remained seated, the former relaxed but watchful, the latter suddenly stiff and frightened.

'I'm sorry, Contessa,' said Shell. 'We have to search the villa. All right chaps, get cracking.'

The other three officers hurried out of the dining room. When they opened the front door Luise heard the clatter of boot-heels out in the courtyard, the rattle of rifle bolts, some shouted commands. She sank down on to her haunches, huddling closer into the dusty velvet, stared down through the marble railings of the gallery at Dunleavy, the Contessa and Major Shell in the room below.

'We knew you were up to something, Contessa, but we thought it was just buying on the black market. It never occurred to us that you might be a Jewish sympathizer – you were too much of a Fascist for that.'

'I don't know what you are talking about.' The Contessa hadn't moved from her chair. It was as if she had become paralysed, even her voice had lost its volume. 'This is insulting, major –'

'How do you know there are Jews here?' Dunleavy was still sitting relaxed at his end of the table; but Luise, sharply alert to him, caught the strain in his voice. 'I've been in the house all day.'

'They got here less than an hour ago,' said Shell. 'A taxi passed one of our convoys on the way out from La Spezia, turned off down in the village and came up here. One of our MPs who was with the convoy followed it on his motorbike – he wanted to tick the taxi driver off for overtaking the convoy the way he did. Then he got suspicious when he saw it coming in here – the Jews have been spreading their people all around town. He went back and waited for us till we came through the village – he knew we were coming here for dinner, we always leave word where we can be found.' He looked at the Contessa. 'That was why I kept looking at my watch – I sent him back for those men who have just arrived. Sorry about that.'

'Just one taxi full of Jews?' said Dunleavy. 'It's hardly worth the bother, is it?'

'There'll be more of them. There always are.'

'What are you going to do?' The Contessa stood up at last, moving stiffly, as if all her fat were turning to bone. 'You have no right –'

'We're going to search the house, madam.' Shell's voice was crisp and hard; the languid accent had gone. 'And, believe me, we have the right.'

2

Besser held up a warning hand, silencing the boys as they began a low-voiced quarrel. Ilse, lying on the bed, sat up, looked enquiringly at her husband as he switched off the attic light. The Italian, Ricci, crossed to the narrow window, pulled back the thick black curtains and looked down past a tall ornamented chimney into the courtyard below. Three trucks were parked there, lights blazing directly at the front of the villa. Soldiers, heavy boots hammering on the stone pavement of the courtyard, were running to take up their positions all around the house. Then a voice belonging to someone Ricci and Besser could not see shouted, 'Righto, sergeant-major – search the house!'

The blaze of headlamps was reflected on the low ceiling of the attic. Even in the dim glow Ilse could see the strain and fear on Karl's face as he turned away from the window. She got off the bed and crossed to him, putting her hand in his.

'What do we do?'

208

Besser looked at Ricci. 'I thought you said, when those English officers arrived, that there was nothing to worry about? That they came out here all the time.'

'They do – they have. Something's gone wrong – they've never raided this place before.'

'Is there some way out of here?'

The Italian shrugged. 'I don't know.'

'You should know! You should be better organized!'

'It has been organized well enough for the past six months,' Ricci said sharply; there was enough Italian in him to resent this officious German. 'We've had no trouble at all.'

'Father – ' Hans had crept to the window, hoisted himself on to the sill to look down. 'All those soldiers – have they come just for us?'

'Get down!' Besser snatched at his son, felt the boy flinch with pain as he gripped his arm and dragged him away from the window. Struggling to keep control of himself, he shoved Hans at Ilse. 'Keep him quiet and out of the way!'

'Who brought the soldiers here?' Ilse said. 'That woman downstairs? I knew she couldn't be trusted.'

Besser looked at Ricci and the latter shook his head. 'She is only interested in money. What would she make out of informing on you?'

Besser didn't know if there was a price on his head; perhaps war criminals (the term was bitter, like poison, in his mind) were not honoured by having a value placed on them.

'How many other Germans have you brought here?'

'I don't know – fifteen or twenty. I haven't been the contact man in every case.' Ricci opened the door of the attic, stood listening. 'They're not coming upstairs. I'll go down, find out what's happening?'

'What if they grab you?'

Ricci spread his hands, gave a thin smile. 'I'm an Italian, I work for the Contessa, I've brought some things out from La Spezia for her in my taxi. They have nothing on me – my record is clean.'

'It's a pity your taxi is still down there.'

When the taxi had pulled round to the back of the villa and

they had all got out, Besser had looked up at the big house towering above them and marvelled at the variety of *Anlaufstelle* that *Spinne* had managed to organize. 'The Villa Fontana,' Ricci had said with a flourish, as if he had built it himself. 'It belongs to the Contessa Fabolini.'

'One of us?'

'Up to a point,' said Ricci. 'She is paid well.'

A door opened and an old man, scurrying towards them on bowed legs, came out of the house. He said something to Ricci in Italian in a croaky whisper, grabbed two of the suitcases and hurried back to the house, jerking his head for them to follow him. Besser took two of the other suitcases and Ricci picked up the Vuitton.

'Why the whispering?' Besser said. 'Who else is here?'

'There's an American officer and his driver. The Contessa is having to billet them. She can't pick and choose all the time, Dr Ludwig.'

They followed the old man into the house, Ilse with her arms round the shoulders of the two boys. They were led through the kitchen, along a long narrow corridor and up a wide flight of stairs. They caught glimpses of huge rooms, saw numerous doors opening off the gallery above the two-storied entrance hall, climbed another flight of stairs, were led along another corridor towards the front of the house, then climbed a final flight of narrow winding stairs to the attic. Besser had not been inside a house as big as this since he had left Berlin; Ilse and the two boys had never been in anything like it. Hans kept whispering, 'Father, it's so big! Who lives here?'

'A great lady,' said Ilse, hushing him to be quiet, wondering at the luck of a woman who could be mistress of a house like this.

They were in the attic only a minute or two when the great lady came puffing up the stairs, pushed open the door without knocking and walked in on them. She waved a be-ringed hand in front of her flushed face, gasped for breath, put a steadying hand on the plump bosom that rose and fell under the tight purple dinner gown. I was wrong, Ilse thought, this is no great lady.

'You must be quiet!' the Contessa hissed after Ricci had introduced the Bessers. 'And don't leave this room!'

Besser bridled: he was not used to being given orders by a woman, especially one who was so peremptory. 'Will you explain – Do you speak German?'

'Yes, yes.' The Contessa closed the door; it was obvious that she would choke if she continued to speak in whispers. 'I learned it when I was singing – and then I knew so many Germans during the war. The Wehrmacht officers used to come here, before the SS took over the villa. I had no time for them – Were you in the SS, Dr Ludwig?'

'No,' said Besser, not looking at Ilse. 'But you have not explained why we have to be so quiet. Is it because of the American? Why is he here?'

The Contessa shrugged, smiled at the boys, patted Paul's head. 'Such healthy-looking boys! I have no children – ' She looked up at Besser. 'In Italy, Herr Doctor, you will do better as a German not to ask questions. Herr Ricci should have warned you.'

The atmosphere in the small room was suddenly chill; even the two boys shifted their feet awkwardly. Ilse, suddenly disliking this arrogant vulgar woman, snapped, 'If you take our money, we are entitled to ask questions. Why are you harbouring the American? Is he a deserter? Or your lover?'

The Contessa had taken no notice of Ilse up till now. She looked at the good-looking red-headed German woman. 'It's not a subject to discuss in front of the children, Frau Ludwig.'

Ilse smiled: if the fat cow wanted an American for a lover, it was no business of theirs. 'You should have asked him to come another night. You have made it dangerous for all cf us.'

'I am doing you a favour,' said the Contessa coldly. 'I was not expecting you or anyone else this week. But when Herr Ricci rang, explained the circumstances – '

'You didn't sound too willing,' said Ricci. 'Only when I threatened you would get no more business – ' He looked at Besser. 'You have no idea how much she charges. You'd think she was a Jew, she's such an extortionist.'

'Everyone has their price,' said the Contessa calmly; but her look at Ricci was deadly. 'Just stay up here till I tell you it is safe to come down. There will be other visitors tonight – English officers.'

'You seem to run a League of Nations,' said Besser.

'So long as they have the price,' said Ricci.

The Contessa gave him another killing stare. She put out a hand, ran it over Paul's head again, then turned and went out of the room. Not even her wide tightly-girdled bottom spoiled the cold dignity of her exit.

'She's no longer on our side,' said Besser. 'You've just made her an enemy.'

'Money will always win her over,' said Ricci. 'She'll never hate any of us as much as she hates the idea of being poor.'

But now, as he prepared to go downstairs and find out why the soldiers were here at the villa, he paused and looked back at the Bessers.

'Just in case – I mean, if she has betrayed us – don't mention anything about the organization. All this was a personal deal between you and me.'

'What about her? Won't she tell them?'

'She knows what would happen to her if she did. We give all our contacts the same warning when we first use them.'

Ricci went out of the attic, closing the door after him, and Ilse sat down on the bed, all the strength gone from her. She could not believe the situation which was swiftly and steadily enveloping them; a web was tightening around them that had the gossamer strands of a dream but the unbreakable strength of real chains. When Topp, the *Spinne* man, had come for her and the two boys, told her that they must now start their journey south to join Karl, he had warned her that there might be danger ahead, for Karl if not for Hans and Paul and herself. She had accepted the thought of *danger* as possible imprisonment for Karl if he were caught; it had never crossed her mind that any of them might face the possibility of death. But she had come, reluctantly, fighting against the thought ever since yesterday on the train, to realize that if Karl *was* captured, he might be sentenced to death.

'Father – ? What did Herr Ricci mean? What would happen to the lady?'

But Besser, staring out the window, hadn't heard his son and Ilse said, 'Ssh, Hans. Please be quiet.'

She had been shocked, like most Germans, when the Nuremberg trials had begun and the death penalty had been demanded by the prosecutors. Karl was not a war criminal in the class of Goering and the others, but she knew the extent of the need for revenge by the enemy. Karl might die, if he were captured: it was a thought that tortured her like a tumor. It only added to the agony, to the disbelief, that the organization that was helping them escape, which (idiot that she had been) she had seen as some sort of charity organization, would cold-bloodedly kill anyone who might betray them. She had seen little but death and destruction for the past four years, had not known a day when she hadn't felt a sense of despair; but she was still a *hausfrau*, still believed in the decencies her Lutheran father and mother had taught her, still thought of violent death as something one experienced only in war and not in one's everyday life. Then she looked up and around her again, heard the shouts down in the courtyard, took in, as if for the first time, where she and the boys and Karl really were. This was not their everyday life: that had finished six and a half years ago, in September 1939.

'Father – ?' It was Paul who asked the question.

'Yes?' Besser, silhouetted against the window, staring down at the courtyard, did not turn his head.

'Father, why do we have to hide? What have we done wrong? Isn't the war over?'

'Of course it's over!' Then he felt ashamed of how he was treating his sons; the war had not been their war. He looked back into the room, saw his family in the gloom, Ilse sitting on the bed and the two boys standing close beside her. They're judging me, he thought, and hated the guilt he suddenly felt. 'It's the English who want to carry it on. Boys, look –'

But then there was a commotion down in the courtyard, louder shouts, the cry of a child and the scream of a woman. He leaned out of the window, risking being seen, peered down past the tall chimney at the scene below. The soldiers were pushing a group of civilians down the front steps, men, women and children, not treating them brutally·but acting with that brusqueness of men who were doing a job that was distasteful to them. The civilians were bundled up into the waiting trucks, the soldiers lifting up the children. One soldier looked up and Besser hastily withdrew his head.

'What is it?' Ilse stood up.

'They are taking away some civilians. I can't see who they are –'

A woman's voice came up from one of the trucks, shouting abuse, amplified by the canopy over her head. Ilse looked at Besser, frowning. 'They're German!'

'I don't understand it –'

He went to the door, opened it slightly and listened: he could hear voices far down in the house, but there was no sound of footsteps coming towards the upper floors. He closed the door again, stood staring at the still-unpacked suitcases on the attic floor.

'I wonder if it would be better if I left you –'

'No!' Ilse grabbed his arm. 'We must stay together! I can't look after Hans and Paul on my own, not in a strange country –'

The two boys stared at their parents, frightened bystanders who knew that everything depended on the two adults who, Hans had dimly begun to realize, had already failed them.

Besser saw the look in his elder son's face, recognized it. He had all at once developed the perception of the guilty man, the frightening capacity to read judgement in another's face. He felt sick, felt an urge to tear open the door and run. But where to run to?

Then the door opened and Ricci came in, pushing a girl ahead of him.

'I found her hiding downstairs in a music gallery. I don't know who she is. The other lot down there are Jews –'

'Dr Besser and I have met before,' said Luise calmly.

Dunleavy felt queasy, as if the soup he had eaten had turned to fat in his gullet. Normally he had what he remembered his father's calling 'a poor man's stomach': anything that filled him didn't upset him. But this meal of the Contessa's, no more than half a dozen spoonfuls of soup, would never have been digested. He had seen Major Shell look at his watch even before they had sat down at the table, seen him glance at it only a few minutes later as Giulio had brought in the soup. He had sensed that something was wrong, that Shell and the other British officers had not come out here tonight for just their usual spot of gracious living. He had looked down the table and seen that the Contessa, light flashing from her fingers like an hysterical code lamp, was even more on edge than himself.

He was not really surprised when he heard the trucks drive into the courtyard and Shell and the other officers stood up. The soup did rise up in his stomach, but it was not shock that caused that: only distress at what was going to happen to Luise and the other Jews and his absolute inability to do anything to help them. They would be back in Germany or Austria within the week.

For a moment he and the Contessa were left at the table alone. They stared down the long white tablecloth at each other. He saw the woman suddenly age, years flooding into her face, her hair, by a trick of light from the chandelier above her, turning totally white. She had reached the end of some road: he could only wonder how far she had hoped that road might stretch. But he could feel no sympathy for her.

He stood up, moved down to her. 'I'm staying on here, Contessa. I'm still your guest – don't forget it.'

Then he went on out to the entrance hall, stood at the bottom of the wide stairs and waited for Luise and the others to be brought up from the cellars. The hall and the long corridor running off it echoed with the footfalls of the soldiers and the shouted commands; he was impressed with the efficient way the British soldiers went about their business, as if cleaning out the cellars of large villas was a routine job they did every day. Out in the courtyard he could hear other soldiers as they took up positions around the house. A carabinieri lieutenant and two carabinieri stood just inside the front door, looking like reserves who knew they would not get into the game and were glad.

'Your men look as if they're used to this sort of thing,' he said to Shell standing beside him.

'It's not the first time we've had to do it, probably not the last, either. Personally, I don't think it's soldiers' work. I don't like playing policeman.'

'Then why are you in Field Security?'

'Posted to it. It was that or go home to England, be cooped up in some bloody barracks there. You see, I'm permanent army – they don't demob us when the shooting stops. I'm going out to join my regiment in India next month. Though I suppose we'll be playing policemen out there, too, with bloody Attlee giving away the Empire.'

'You believe in the Empire?'

'Not really. But if we give it away, what's the point of staying in the army?' He smiled wryly. 'Trouble is, I'm trained for nothing else and don't really want to be. I enjoyed being a soldier. But not a bloody policeman!'

'Would you let the Jews go if you had your choice?'

Shell looked at him out of the corner of his eye. 'Are you trying to make some sort of bargain with me?'

'Why would I want to do that?' said Dunleavy, heavy innocence caked on his face.

'You've known all evening those Jews were down in the cellars. There's more of them than just the lot who were spotted in the taxi.'

'You're wrong about the taxi – whoever was in it, they weren't Jews.'

'Well, whoever they were – ' Shell dismissed them with a wave of his hand. 'What's your connection with the Jews?'

Dunleavy chose frankness again: this Englishman was no fool. 'They are my only lead to Keppel. They were with him when he killed our two guys.'

216

'He's not with them now?'

'He wasn't when they arrived here this morning.'

Shell half-smiled, looked the American up and down. 'Y'know, I should take you in with these people. Accessory before or after the fact, take your pick.'

'Think of the complications it would cause. They might even send you home to those barracks for causing an international incident.'

'You really think you're so important?'

'Neither of us are.' Dunleavy smiled; he knew now that Shell was not going to be a son-of-a-bitch. 'You take these people in, but just let me know where you're going to keep them.'

'Why?'

'They are still my only lead to Keppel,' he repeated, wondering if he sounded as obsessed to Shell as he had to Luise.

'If you do catch up with him, we may still have first call on him. Have you thought of that?'

'If I've got a murder rap against him, your guys might hand him over without any argument. It would solve their problem for them, wouldn't it? Get him out of their hair and let us do the dirty work.'

'You're developing a devious mind, Dunleavy. I think you must have been in Europe too long. Ah, here they come!'

The women and children came down the long corridor first, huddled close together. They stood in a tight group, staring across at Shell and Dunleavy; some soldiers brought their suitcases and bundles and placed them beside the group. Dunleavy looked for Luise, frowned, then looked at Anna Bork.

'Who told them we were down there, major? Her?' Anna nodded viciously at the Contessa, who had come to the door of the dining room.

'I don't think so, Frau Bork. They followed you out here.'

'Then why did they wait all day to come and get us?'

Dunleavy looked at Shell. 'Like I said, you were wrong about that taxi you mentioned. That must have brought someone else here.'

'Sergeant-major!'

'Sir!' A tall muscular soldier with a broken nose, who looked as if he might have been a heavyweight boxer when he wasn't fighting a war or arresting Jewish DPs, came to attention beside the frightened women and children. He slammed down his boot-heels and two of the children jumped as if a gun had gone off beside them.

'Is that taxi still here?' Shell said.

'Out the back, sir. It's a La Spezia registration – we'll have the driver first thing in the morning.'

'Perhaps,' said Shell to himself; only Dunleavy heard him. Then he raised his voice again: 'Search the rest of the house. Something worrying you, Contessa?'

The Contessa, still standing in the doorway, still looking old, shook her head. 'Nothing except these people, Major Shell.' Her voice was not her own, a whisper more than a shout. 'I feel I've let them down –'

Anna Bork said something in German that Dunleavy didn't catch, but that seemed to offend the women standing around her; Judith Winter put her hands over the ears of her daughters, pulled their heads against her hips to block their free ears. But Anna was too angry to apologize. She was about to harangue the Contessa when there was a noise down the corridor and the Jewish men were pushed up out of the cellars.

Dunleavy leaned forward, looking for Luise; then he looked at Anna Bork again, querying her with his eyebrows. But the red-headed woman just stared back at him: it was impossible to tell whether she was angry with him or trying to protect him from too much involvement with them.

The men, carrying their own bundles, were hustled out through the front door; then the women and children were told to follow them. The two small groups moved with long-accustomed obedience: such orders had become part of the routine of their lives. There was no pushing or shoving by the soldiers; they looked as if they did not relish the job they had. Little Ruth Winter started to cough and one of the soldiers slung his rifle over his shoulder, picked up the child and carried her down the steps. As the last of the group went out the front door the sergeant-major barked an order and half a dozen soldiers went clumping off through the house, three towards the back rooms, the other three going up the stairs to the upper floors.

Shell crossed to say something to the carabinieri lieutenant, who still looked as if he did not want any of this to be his business. Dunleavy moved over to Charlie Lincoln, who had followed the last of the Jewish men up out of the cellar. Shell looked at the young soldier, then left him to his own officer.

'Charlie, where's Miss Grazi?'

It was the first time he had seen any expression of concern for the Jews cross Charlie's face. 'She ain't outside with them other women?' Dunleavy shook his head and Charlie sucked his lip and shook his own head. 'I dunno, sir. She come up here about ten, fifteen minutes ago. I ain't seen her since.'

'Okay, keep it quiet. If they don't know about her, they aren't going to go looking for her.'

Charlie glanced up the stairs, towards the noise of running boots and slamming doors. 'They sure as hell looking for *something*.'

'All I hope is they don't find her.'

In a few minutes the soldiers who had gone upstairs came clattering down again. Shell was still talking to the carabinieri officer as the three soldiers came down the stairs, but Dunleavy was watching the Contessa closely. He saw the mixed look on her face (relief? puzzlement?) as the men came down empty-handed; then she saw him watching her and at once her face became as blank and bland as only a fat face can. Dunleavy tried to assume the same bland look, in case Shell should glance at him.

But Shell was interested only in the report of his men. 'Nothing upstairs, sir. We searched every room and up into the attic. Nothing, sir.'

The other three soldiers came through from the back of the house. 'Not a blooming thing, sir. The bloke who drove the taxi musta skipped it over the wall when he heard us drive up.'

Shell hid his disappointment well: he, too, was good at the blank face. 'You had better get your coat, Contessa. I'm afraid you will have to come in with us for questioning.'

'Why? What have I done wrong?' The Contessa wasn't going to give in without a fight. 'These are just ordinary people – they are not criminals. All I've done is give them shelter. After all they have been through, isn't that the least one can do?'

She even makes her charity sound convincing, Dunleavy thought. And he had heard a lot of good liars in his time.

Shell must have heard some, too: he looked unconvinced. But there was no mistaking the reluctance in his voice as he said, 'Indeed they have been through an awful lot. But the fact is, Contessa, they are prohibited aliens in this country. I'm sure we'll find they are travelling on false papers and that is an offence. Will you please get your coat?'

'I am an Italian citizen –'

'That is why Lieutenant Taviani has come along.'

Taviani said something in Italian that Dunleavy didn't understand; whatever it was, the Contessa knew she had lost for the moment. She tossed her head in an extravagant, operatic way and made for the stairs. Shell nodded at the sergeant-major, who at once fell into step behind her. She stopped some way up the stairs, looked back at the sergeant-major, then down at Shell.

'The sergeant-major will help you on with your coat,' said Shell. 'English gallantry. You remarked upon it at dinner.'

The entrance hall cleared, leaving only Shell, Dunleavy and Charlie Lincoln. Halfway down the long corridor Giulio and his wife stood flattened against the wall, faces turned fearfully towards the front of the house; but Shell was not interested in them, they were only servants doing what their mistress had told them to do. He put on his cap and trenchcoat, his evening of gracious living finished.

'I can get you a billet back in La Spezia –'

'I'll stay here,' said Dunleavy. 'It's comfortable and those servants back there can look after me and my driver. Besides, there's always the chance that Keppel will come looking for his friends.'

Shell nodded, but there was a hint of suspicion in his face. 'You'll be in to see me in the morning? I shouldn't want you starting any independent action of your own.'

'Strictly according to the letter of the law,' said Dunleavy amiably. 'I won't put a toe out of line.'

'I'll be leaving four men to keep an eye on things. If Keppel should turn up, you can call on them for any help you need. Remember, he's our pigeon first. After we've plucked him, you can have him. Ah, here comes the prima donna.'

The Contessa, a rich purple cloak about her, came down the stairs, head high, hand held out at a distance on the arm of her escort, the sergeant-major. She swept past Dunleavy and Shell and went out the front door, making an exit that Dunleavy knew would lead nowhere. As he passed the two officers the sergeant-major, face stiff, head held as high as the Contessa's, winked at Shell.

'Poor old trout,' said Shell. 'She might have been better off if she had stayed in the chorus.'

A minute later the British trucks drove off and Dunleavy and Charlie Lincoln, except for Giulio and his wife, were left alone in the big house. Or were they? 'Charlie, I'm promoting you from cop to detective, just for tonight.'

'Thanks, major. But I've never been a cop, not even in our outfit. I'm just a driver.'

Dunleavy didn't query Charlie's niceties of distinction. More than ever now he wished that he himself was not a cop. But it would need some detective work to find out what had happened to Luise. He led Charlie down the corridor.

Dunleavy stopped in front of Giulio and the old woman. 'You speak English, Giulio?'

The old man shrugged. '*Poco.*'

'Do you speak German?' Dunleavy said in German.

'I speak German better, sir. I worked for the Germans here in this house.'

Well, at his age I guess he had to get through the war any way he could. 'Who else came to the house this evening? Who came in that taxi out back there?'

'I do not know, sir.'

'Come *on*, Giulio!' Dunleavy tried to keep his patience; he always tended to get impatient when he could not converse in his own tongue. 'The Contessa said it was a man delivering something, someone you know. He stopped to have a drink with you, she said.'

The old man and woman exchanged glances. Both had lined and worried faces, gullied by the erosion of the years and the struggle just to stay alive. Once they had believed in Il Duce and Fascism, the hope of the poor; now one was dead and the other was just another Italian ruin. Illiterate and uneducated, they could still read the writing on the wall: when the crunch came, there would be no one to speak up for them but themselves.

'It was a man named Ricci. He brought a German family to the house.'

'Germans?' Dunleavy saw the second look of surprise on Charlie's face in ten minutes; he felt his own brow furrow. 'Who were they?'

'I don't know, sir. It was a man, his wife and two small boys.'

'Have you had any other Germans here in the house? Lately, I mean.'

Giulio nodded and his wife repeated the movement of the head. They were going to hold back nothing now; there was no guarantee the Contessa would be back tomorrow. 'German one week, Jews the other week. It has been like that for six months, sir.'

Dunleavy looked at Charlie Lincoln. 'You understand what he just said?'

'I got most of it, sir. That Contessa, she sure know how to make a buck. Regular hotel she's been running here.'

'Where did you hide the Germans?' Dunleavy snapped at Giulio.

The old man no longer hesitated. He jerked his head, then led Dunleavy and Charlie along the corridor and up a flight of back stairs. They climbed to the top of the house and at last Giulio flung open the door to a large attic and switched on the light. 'They were in here, sir. We always brought the Germans up here and put the Jews in the cellars.'

Dunleavy looked around. A worn rug on the floor, a chest of drawers, a wardrobe, two armchairs with broken springs, a double bed and a smaller bed: the Contessa didn't believe in selling luxury to her guests.

'Someone's been sitting on the bed,' said Charlie. 'Look how the cover is wrinkled up.'

'Charlie, you sure you were never a cop?'

'Elementary, major,' Charlie grinned. This was better than sitting on your ass in Garmisch waiting to drive some horny officer around to see his girl friend. 'I remember seeing Basil Rathbone in one of them Sherlock Holmes movies.'

'Okay, they were here all right. But where are they now? And where's Fräulein Graz?' And suddenly he was afraid for Luise. He spun round on Giulio, his concern for Luise coming out as anger at the old man. "Take us through the rest of the house! And don't miss a goddam room or a hole in the wall!'

He spoke in English, but the old man got the message.

4

Ben Keppel stood in the shadows of the guest house at the end of the drive and watched the trucks come down and pass out through the gates. He looked at Sergeant Katz as the latter came out of the darkness and slipped in beside him.

'Did you hide your truck?'

'It's in an olive grove down the lane. We were lucky we didn't drive right into them up there at the villa. What's happened?'

'I caught a glimpse of the back of one of the trucks. They've got our people.'

'Bugger!' Katz spat into the darkness. 'When you get them all this way without a hitch, you begin to hope – '

'So far this has been the easiest stretch,' said Keppel, fifteen years younger than the other man but just as much a veteran in this smuggling game. 'Once we get within sight of a ship, that's when the hard part really starts. That's why the English concentrate on the ports.'

'I know,' said Katz, annoyed at this attempt at education by this kid. 'But every day they aren't stopped, you hope the luck is going to continue.'

Ben Keppel didn't believe in luck or God's blessing or whatever men hoped for: you had to make your own way. Then he saw the staff car coming down the drive and he held back until it, too, had gone through the gates.

'Where do they take the people they round up?'

'There's a camp over near Sarzana – they've just set it up, temporary-like.'

'Any of our men there?'

'Not a Jewish soldier in the camp. They've got the Eyetie police helping out. The Eyeties don't like it, but they've got to play along.'

'We've got to find out how much the Contessa has told the English.'

'If you'd been with them –'

'If I'd been with them, I'd probably have been caught, too. What use would I have been then?'

Keppel's trip down from Merano to La Spezia had been simple and without incident. The British were not looking for single men but for groups; he had just been another of the countless travellers moving around northern Italy. Only when he had reached La Spezia had he received a setback. He had reported to the local *Bricha* man with some trepidation, wondering what lay in store for him for what he had done to the two Americans outside Camp 93. But the *Bricha* man had had too much on his mind to worry about disciplinary action. A confrontation with the British had been decided upon: a ship was going to sail openly from La Spezia with a full complement of immigrants for Palestine: world opinion, it was felt, was on the side of the Jews and the British would have to face it. Meanwhile Keppel would have to look after his own small party, get them to *their* ship which, he was told, was in a small cove just south of the La Spezia gulf.

'Righto,' said Katz. 'But if you're thinking of busting into that camp over at Sarzana, forget me, matey. I'm more use driving a truck, ferrying 'em down from the north. There's a couple of hundred thousand more of 'em still up there in Germany and Austria. I'm not going to forget them, and risk me neck for a dozen who've been unlucky and got themselves nabbed.'

'You'll do what *Bricha* says,' said Keppel.

'Up yours,' said Katz, with a suitable gesture. 'Don't start giving me orders, sonny. You've caused enough trouble as it is. Our outfit is more important than you or your little party.'

Keppel said nothing, suddenly reduced by the word *sonny* to being a boy; he felt a wave of anger, was glad of the darkness that hid the tears he could feel in his eyes. He knew the truth of what Katz said and that didn't make him feel any better. Katz belonged to the famous 'phantom unit' of Milan: famous, that is, only to those in *Bricha*. Jewish Brigade soldiers, detaching themselves from the movement order that had sent the Brigade to Belgium, had set up their own unit in Milan, complete with forged papers; they had been operating there for several months, their presence never once queried by British headquarters, not even by the supply depots from whom, with more false papers, they drew their rations and supplies every week. Taken at face value, on their uniforms, their papers and their exemplary conduct as good smart soldiers, they had been accepted by the British army as part of itself. But they were even more a part of *Bricha* and Keppel knew that to jeopardize them would bring more trouble on his head than the killing of the two Americans would.

He abruptly stepped out on the driveway, began to walk quickly up towards the villa, still limping on his sore leg. He had gone almost twenty yards before Katz caught up with him, grabbed him by the arm.

'Don't be a bloody fool! They'll have picquets there – Christ, what do you think the English are? Idiots?'

Keppel jerked his arm free, angry at having made a fool of himself. 'I was going to look around,' he said lamely. 'I wasn't going to just barge straight in there –'

'Righto then.' Katz softened his tone; he recognized he was dealing with a kid here. These concentration camp ones were all the same: they were always so bloody *desperate*. Sometimes he wondered how they were going to fit into Israel when they finally got the new country started. 'Let's have a scout around first. No sense in us all finishing up down in that camp in

Sarzana. And if that Yank is still here, you could finish up back in Germany with a rope around your neck.'

It took them a few minutes to locate the picquets. Three were sitting in a taxi at the back of the villa; the other, rifle slung over his shoulder, was slowly circling the house. The British might not be idiots, but the men left on duty here were being as casual as it was possible to be.

'A taxi?' Keppel whispered. 'What's that doing here?'

'Search me.' The presence of the taxi didn't worry Katz; nothing in the post-war world in which he lived surprised him any more. 'There's a door leads down to the cellars. We can make it next time that bloke comes around – soon's he's gone round the corner we can duck across.'

They waited behind a large untidy clump of oleanders; the garden was ideal for anyone wanting to break into the villa. Keppel stared at the front of the house, the scars on its wall distinct in the bright moonlight, the shrapnel and bullet holes doubled in size by their shadows. He wondered how many English troops had been hidden here in the garden when they had first attacked the SS headquarters in the villa. He hoped there had been enough of them to kill every single SS man in the big house. Each time he had entered it over the past months he had almost felt the presence of Nazis in the house, as if they had infected it.

The picquet, cigarette end glowing and dying in front of his mouth as he drew on it, came round from the back of the house. He was short and small, wrapped in a greatcoat that squared him off; he looked slightly ridiculous, no threat at all. Except that he had his rifle over his shoulder and, if he gave the warning, he had three mates in the taxi at the back of the house.

The picquet paused, looked straight at the clump of oleanders; then came ambling towards them, rifle still slung over his back. Keppel put his hand on the gun in his pocket; beside him he felt Katz go tense. The picquet paused, looking directly at the oleanders behind which they were hidden; then they heard the splash of water on a stone, saw the picquet holding back the front of his greatcoat. The splashing stopped, the soldier adjusted his trousers, then he turned and walked on.

Keppel let out his breath in a long gasp. 'Okay – now!'

Then the front door opened, light flooded out into the courtyard. A man stood silhouetted against the brilliance in the entrance hall behind him. The picquet stopped, came back and stood at the foot of the front steps.

'You want something, sir?'

'Nothing, soldier. Where are your buddies?'

'Round the back, sir. They're having a kip in the taxi. We're doing one hour on and three off.'

The picquet waited a moment, gathered that the American officer wasn't interested in further conversation, and, a little more smartly this time, marched off round the corner of the house. Dunleavy stood in the doorway looking after him, then he turned his head and the light behind him fell on his face.

'Let's go,' said Keppel. 'We can't go in the house now. Not while that American is there.'

'Where do we go?'

'To the camp at Sarzana. I've still got to get that group of mine to our ship.'

'Not tonight, mate. The British will stay on guard with them there tonight. Tomorrow maybe they'll leave it to the Eyeties to keep an eye on 'em – that'll be the time for you to go in. The Eyeties can turn more blind eyes than a busload of statues. I'm pretty done in, mate. I'm going back to the truck, kip down for the night.'

Keppel looked up at the big house. Were the American, Dunleavy, and the Contessa alone there in the villa? Was it they who, between them, had betrayed Luise Graz and the others to the English? He felt the weight of the gun in his pocket, like a growth that would always plague him. If Dunleavy and the Contessa *had* betrayed the others, he would kill them just as he had killed the other two Americans, but with more sense of purpose.

Chapter Six

'Dr Besser and I have met before,' said Luise.

She sounded calm, but inside she was a whirlpool of shock; far down below she could hear the shouts and thudding boots of the British soldiers as they ran through the ground floor. She knew now that the group down in the cellars was doomed; their long journey had been fruitless. When she had recovered from the initial shock of the arrival of the truckloads of soldiers, she had slipped out of the music gallery and run back up the darkened stairs, keeping close to the wall. She had just reached the main gallery at the head of the stairs when the entrance hall below was flooded with light as someone switched on the chandelier there. The light swept up at her, exposing her; she stumbled back into the darkness of a corridor. Right into the arms of the stranger who, clamping a hand over her mouth and pushing a gun into her back, had brought her up here to the attic. The shock of encountering him had been swamped by the almost paralysing emotion she felt when she faced Besser.

She seemed to be standing outside herself. As a child she had suffered occasional attacks of *petit mal* in which there had been moments of frightening detachment, as if she had become two persons; she had the same feeling now, but there was none of the giddiness or the sense of unreality that had affected her as a child. Some instinct had taken over her external faculties: her voice, her expression, were those of someone in full command of the situation in which she found herself. But the other self, her true inner self, knew she was in more danger than at any time since she had been released from Birkenau.

'Jesus Christ!' Besser was anything but calm; he looked like a man on the verge of a stroke. 'Why did you bring her up here?'

'What else was I going to do with her?' Ricci had acted instinctively when the girl had stumbled into him; the German was right, but he wasn't going to admit it. 'She came out of the music gallery, straight up to where I was. Who is she, anyway?'

'It doesn't matter – ' Besser went to the door, listened to the noise downstairs. 'We have to find a way out of here. A house as big as this, there must be some back stairs!'

'What do we do with her?' Ilse said.

'We'll have to take her with us – ' Besser looked at the girl, hating her as he had never hated anyone, not even the never-seen Gerstein; she was still a stranger to him, a dim fragmented memory, but he with absolute perception knew that she was his nemesis. 'If she tells them I've been here – '

Ilse grabbed two of the suitcases, reacting to the panic in her husband in a practical way. 'We must hurry! Anything is better than just standing here waiting to be taken by the English!'

Besser grabbed the two largest suitcases, the man with the gun took up the fifth case; then Luise was prodded in the back with the gun and she followed the Bessers out of the attic and down the narrow winding stairs. She could still hear the shouts and noise downstairs, suddenly heard the raucous voice of Anna Bork swearing at someone. For a moment she was tempted to scream for help, to bring the soldiers rushing up here; she had a wild frantic hope of some bargain being struck, twelve harmless Jews for a Nazi monster. Then the gun dug in her back again and she knew she would be dead before the sound of her scream died away. The stranger would kill her without a second thought, would kill on impulse: he was a twin to Keppel. And for the moment he was much more dangerous than Besser, the bureaucratic killer who had put people to death much as he might have put them on a pension.

At the bottom of the narrow stairway they turned right, hurried quietly towards the back of the house. They heard the footsteps clumping up the main staircase: the house echoed and re-echoed with the sound of the search, footsteps running, voices shouting, doors being slammed; but always the sound was behind them, they ran ahead of it as before a wave that could not quite catch up with them. It was the elder of the two boys who found the back stairs. Running ahead, he jerked open a door and there was the steep stairwell, lit only by moonlight coming in through a dirty uncurtained window. They went down the stairs, the elder boy pausing to close the door and turn the key in the lock. Luise heard Besser whisper, 'Good boy, Hans!', but he didn't look back, was leading the way down into the bowels of the house.

They came to the foot of the stairs, were now in utter blackness. Besser blundered into something, cursed as if he had hurt himself; the younger boy whimpered and was told by his mother not to be afraid of the dark. Luise stood on the stairs, feeling the gun still pressed into her back; she could see nothing, could hear nothing but the heavy breathing of the others close by her. The noise of the searching soldiers had faded away.

Besser was fumbling in the dark. Then there was a creak as he swung open an invisible door. Luise at once caught the acrid smell of coal, knew this was a cellar she and Simon Berger had missed in their search of the basement. There was a scratching sound, then a match flared.

'Wait here.'

Besser lit another match and went ahead into the coal cellar. They heard him stumbling over the coal, saw the flare of other matches. Then he came back.

'There's a door that leads into a basement garage. There is an American Army jeep there and a big limousine.'

They were in darkness again. Luise felt that the stranger shook his head; she felt the gun move in her back. 'We'd never get away in either of them. They'd catch us before we were halfway down the drive.'

'We could stay here till they have gone.'

'Too risky. They could come down here any minute.'

Besser gave the box of matches to Hans. 'You'll have to lead the way, Hans. I have to carry the suitcases.'

'Yes, Father,' said Hans eagerly. 'Follow me.'

230

The boy led them, match held aloft, across the cellar, finding a less rocky route than his father had and skirting the huge heap of coal that lay like a landslide against one wall of the cellar. They went out through a second door and were in a large garage, one big enough to have contained at least four cars. The jeep and a magnificent but dusty and rusted pre-war limousine stood side by side.

Some moonlight filtered in through three shallow windows set high up in one wall of the garage. Besser put down his suitcases, crossed to a small door beside the larger doors. He opened it cautiously, looked out, then shut it again. He came back and picked up the suitcases.

'We're at the side of the house. There are no men in sight at the moment. There are trees and big bushes just across the courtyard. You go first, Ilse, with Hans and Paul. If we move quickly – ' He looked at Luise. 'I'm afraid you'll have to come with us, Fräulein. Please don't make it difficult for yourself or us.'

'Please – ' Ilse leaned almost conspiratorially towards Luise. 'There are my boys – '

The woman's plea and the gun in her back decided Luise. Her death became something too terrible to contemplate, the thought more horrifying to herself than the witnessing of it would be to the two young boys. She had suffered a great deal, there had been times when she might have been glad to give up what had passed for living. But not now: she was no longer a heroine, not when confronted with the possibility of her own death. She would cling to life as long as she could.

'I shan't be difficult,' she said.

'Thank you.' Besser's wife sounded genuinely grateful.

She and the two boys were first to go. The boys, though frightened, might also have been in a game; they raced across the courtyard like sprinters in some school sports on Parents' Day. Ilse followed them, moving as fast as she could but hampered by the two suitcases she carried. She had just reached the protection of the trees when four soldiers came round the corner of the house, grumbling among themselves, and walked by the garage doors towards the back of the villa.

'Foocking hell,' said one of the soldiers in a thick accent that was unintelligible to the Germans and the Italian who heard him. 'Nowt boot foocking guard dooty.'

His companions echoed his grumbling, then the four of them had disappeared round the far corner. At once Besser left the garage, hurried across the courtyard, the two heavy suitcases banging against his long legs. Then Luise was jabbed in the back by the gun.

'Our turn, Fräulein. And don't be difficult. I've never shot a pretty girl before, but there is always a first time for everything.'

Luise had no argument to such a proposition. Her legs felt weak, but she knew they would carry her; they had always kept her on her feet when the rest of her had been ready to capitulate. She looked at the face of the stranger, dark and implacable in the dim moonlight coming through the half-open door; only the peculiar eyebrows, as if he were surprised at the situation in which he found himself, stopped him from looking thoroughly evil. 'Just be careful with that gun.'

'That's up to you, Fräulein.'

They made the shadows of the trees with no trouble. The six of them moved on through the small jungle of the garden, Ricci leading the way. The elder of the boys, whispering a question to his father as to where they were going, had said the stranger's name. Luise had now identified them all; she wondered if they knew who she was. Even Besser had not recognized her, she was now sure.

They were still in the villa garden when Ricci suddenly stopped, held up his hand. Low voices came up from up ahead in the bushes: at once she recognized the voice of Keppel. Her first instinct was to cry out; but Ricci was too quick for her. He put down the suitcase he was carrying and whipped his hand over her mouth. All six of them stood stockstill while the voices up ahead argued in low whispers. *Ben, Ben!* Luise never thought she would plead for Keppel's help: now she desperately wanted him and whoever was with him to come charging out of the bushes. There might be shooting, but that was a risk she was now prepared to take.

Then, every nerve strained, she heard the voices drift away.

There was the snap of a twig under a foot; then silence. Ricci still kept his hand over her mouth, the gun still in her back. Then at last he relaxed, took his hand away.

'I'd have shot you, Fräulein,' he whispered in her ear. 'You had better take me seriously.'

They moved on, going more cautiously now, came out through a side gate of the garden and went down a side lane. Then they were going up a long stepped alley in which the moonlight was suddenly blocked out by the bulk of a turreted castle. The village lay below them, lighted windows staring up at them like unblinking yellow eyes; the shouts of children came up from the megaphone of an alley and down at a bar on the waterfront a radio blared out music. More American music: someone at the radio station, Luise thought, had the same taste as the dead Roy Dunleavy: some Italian had a girl in Kalamazoo.

Ilse, a good German mother, shook her head at the screams and shouts of the children coming up at her out of the alley. 'Why are the children up so late?'

'Why not?' said Ricci.

'They should be in bed, it is ten o'clock – ' She stumbled on the slippery cobbled path they were negotiating; she stopped and put down the two suitcases. 'It's no way to bring up children – '

'Neither is this,' said Luise and picked up one of the cases. '*Your* children are still up.'

Ilse looked at her, then picked up the other case. 'Thank you. You are right.' She looked over her shoulder at Besser, who had paused behind them. 'Perhaps Hans and Paul and I should have stayed in Würzburg.'

'No,' said Hans and Paul together. 'We had to come with Father.'

'Just a few more days.' Besser, exhausted by the climb with the two heavy cases, sounded uncertain, his voice almost petulant. 'You must be patient – '

'I've been patient enough – all the war years – '

Ricci looked back at the Bessers. 'This is no place for a family row. Please shut up!'

'Don't talk to me like that!'

But Ricci ignored Besser, pushed Luise ahead of him, and after a moment the Bessers fell in behind him. Divisions, Luise thought: this tiny group was even more divided than her own. The atmosphere was abruptly taut, as if a touch of ice had settled on the night air. They walked on in silence.

They climbed a hill through olive groves, the trees crouched like arthritic ambushers on either side of them; then Ricci pushed open a rusted gate and they were climbing a flight of rough steps to a low stone cottage that clung to the steep hillside like an outcrop of rock. They went into the shadows of a grape arbour; new vine leaves rustled in the night breeze. Ricci knocked on the door, then opened it and almost pushed the others in ahead of him. He came in, closed the door and faced the elderly couple who had risen to their feet as their home was invaded.

'I've brought you some visitors, Grandfather,' Ricci said in Italian. 'Just for tonight.'

The old man, face as knobbed and rough as the bark of the trees in the grove outside, said nothing. The old woman, a past handsomeness buried under a creeping ivy of wrinkles, glared at Ricci and the adults with him. Then she looked at the two boys, faces bright, innocent and uncertain in the yellow glow of the lamp hanging from the beamed ceiling, and the wrinkles took over her face completely as she smiled. She threw up her hands.

'Ah, the children!'

'They are my mother's parents,' Ricci explained to Besser as his grandmother took Ilse and the two boys under her care. She looked at Luise, then seemed to dismiss her as another of her grandson's girl friends; Ricci had put the gun away in his jacket pocket. 'They are not on our side, but I'll have you out of here by morning. I'll go and see our friends, get new instructions on you, but I'll leave you the gun.'

'The gun? Why?'

Ricci looked at his grandfather, still silent and hostile. 'My grandfather is a Communist. He fought with the partisans against the Germans.'

'And you expect me – ?' Even Luise felt some of Besser's shock.

'There's nowhere else to take you,' Ricci said impatiently. 'I told you – they raided our other safe house this morning. All you have to do is watch him – I'll be back in an hour, two hours at the most.' He took the gun out of his pocket, handed it to Besser, who took it reluctantly. Ricci looked at his grandfather, his voice grating as he spoke in Italian again: 'Don't act foolish, Grandfather. You're more use to the Party alive than you would be dead. Togliatti won't give you any medals for capturing some harmless Germans. The war's over, Grandfather.'

The old man spoke for the first time, a voice as rough as the sound of stones rubbing together. 'Then why the gun?'

Ricci glanced at Besser. 'He just asked the same question as you – why the gun?'

'Do you expect me to shoot him – your own grandfather?'

'He'd have me shot tomorrow if the Communists ever got into power. He is still fighting the war against the Fascists. Only my grandmother might save me.'

He crossed the room, kissed his grandmother's cheek. The old woman and Ilse, the two boys between them, had frozen in their attitudes as Ricci had produced the gun. Stiff and wide-eyed in the yellow light, they looked like a faded sepia portrait of a three-generation family group. Ricci shook his head at his grandmother's cold reception of his kiss.

'Remember my mother, Grandmama,' he said quietly. 'You owe her something.'

It was one of those remarks that the bystanders would never fully understand, something secret between Ricci and his grandmother; yet Luise, if not the others, knew somehow it guaranteed their safety. The look on the old woman's face was an insurance, a grimace of pain in which the wrinkles seemed to widen till her whole face threatened to fall part. Whatever she owed her dead daughter, she would repay it somehow with charity towards these strangers thrust upon her by her grandson.

Ricci left, repeating his promise to be back in no more than two hours. The old man glared at the door as it closed on his

235

grandson, then he jerked his head at Besser and made for an inner room off this big kitchen where they all stood.

Besser seemed embarassed by the gun in his hand; he awkwardly stuffed it into the pocket of his coat. Then he picked up the suitcases and nodded to Luise. And for the first time she gestured at the Vuitton case.

'You've looked after it well, Dr Besser. My mother would be pleased – if there was any way of her knowing.'

Out of the corner of his eye Besser saw Ilse's head come up. He didn't turn his head, just nodded at the open door where the old man stood.

'In there, Fräulein.'

She went into the room, a small bedroom, and he followed her and put down the suitcases. The old man stiffened as Besser brushed past him, almost as if he could hardly contain the rage within him, as if violence wanted to burst out of him at the German *here in his house*. But Besser paused, looked down at the old man, towering above him. Then the old woman snapped warningly at her husband and the bone went out of him. Shoulders slumped, he shuffled back into the kitchen.

Besser stared after him, then turned to Luise. 'The past is past, Fräulein,' he said softly; behind him, beyond the doorway, his wife stood with head still cocked, trying to hear what was said. 'I am sorry if something happened to your mother. But orders were orders. It had to be done, whatever it was –'

'You don't even remember her, do you?' But Luise felt no real shock. Six million dead: she remembered what Ben Keppel had said: just another drop in the ocean of blood. But it hurt her to think that her mother's death went unremembered by this man.

'I wish I could remember –' But Besser lied; he wanted to forget all of them 'But it's all past now –'

'It's not! It can't be rubbed out, like some dirty mistake –' She looked beyond him, saw his wife and two boys staring at her; behind them the old woman had turned from the big wood-burning stove, was looking in at her. Suddenly she wilted: she could not bring them into her war against this murderer. She waved a weak hand, began to weep for the first time in years, remembering her mother and her grandmother, her father and her grandfather, the good decent past that was gone forever. 'Please leave me alone.'

Besser hesitated, then he went out of the room, leaving the door open. Luise lay back on the narrow bed, let the tears run down her cheeks, wept as she had not wept since she was a small girl. She felt weak and alone and afraid; she remembered the apartment on Esteplatz, the huge house at Waldgarten; she would go back tomorrow, touch the reassuring comfort of the past. But the tears rolled down into the corner of her mouth, she tasted the salt of reality. She would find nothing in Vienna but ghosts.

She must have dozed off. Someone was shaking her gently; she opened smarting eyes and looked up at the strange woman bending over her; it was a long confused moment before she recognized Frau Besser. She sat up, wiping sleep and dried tears from her face as she might have rid it of cobwebs. She had been dreaming – but her mind, too, was cobwebbed, she could not remember what the dream had been.

'I want to put the boys down. Do you mind? They are so tired.'

She stood up and Ilse put the two boys, still dressed but for their shoes, down on the bed and drew the big quilt over them. Almost at once they fell asleep, their faces as blank and innocent as those of plaster saints. They have no past, Luise thought enviously; and wondered when their disillusion would begin, when their father's past would catch up with them.

The old woman brought in a bowl of soup and some rough homemade bread. Luise sat on one of the stiff-backed reed-bottomed chairs and Ilse sat opposite her; through the open door Besser, eating at the table in the kitchen, watched them. It was some time before Luise realized that he was watching both of them with equal suspicion. Chewing on the bread she looked at Frau Besser with new interest.

'You knew my husband?' Ilse said at last; she bit her lip as if afraid to ask the next question: 'At Auschwitz?'

Luise nodded, glanced towards Besser out in the kitchen.

237

He had stopped eating when he had seen his wife speak; but he could hear nothing, the old woman was rattling pots on the stove behind him. The old man sat in a far corner of the kitchen, sullenly staring at the German.

'You should get your husband to tell you about it, Frau Besser.'

'He won't. I don't know that I want him to – ' Her hands clawed at each other. 'Does that sound cowardly?'

'Yes.' Then Luise's natural kindness weakened her; she felt sorry for the woman: 'But natural.'

Ilse shook her head, a shadow crossing her face that had nothing to do with any trick of light. She *wishes* there was no past, Luise thought; but felt no satisfaction at the torture that the other woman appeared to be going through. Her war was with the man at the table out in the kitchen, not with his family.

'I knew about the camps. We all did. But we never thought they were – were as bad as – ' She shook her head, as if still unable to believe the evidence she and the other innocent Germans had been given.

Luise had heard it all before, the denial of any knowledge at all or the guarded qualified admission: *we never thought they were as bad* . . . She sighed, losing some patience and sympathy for the woman.

'Please don't make any excuses, Frau Besser. It all happened, it's a fact of history. Six million of us – you all have to bear some of the guilt. You knew your husband was in the SS – '

'He was my husband – I loved him. You make excuses to yourself when you really love someone. Didn't you have a lover, a boy friend?'

'Yes. But I didn't make excuses for him.'

'Then you didn't love him.'

Luise realized the other woman wasn't accusing her, just stating a fact. She looked out at the watching Besser, wondered how any woman could love a cold-blooded murderer.

'What did he do?' Ilse said suddenly, taking the plunge, face tight for the expected blow.

Why should I spare her? 'He sent my mother to the gas

238

chambers. Her, and I don't know how many others. That was in October 1941. Then he left Auschwitz and what he did after that – ' Her voice trailed off; she couldn't bear the look of agony on the other woman's face. She looked away, staring out at Besser without seeing him. 'I can't forgive him, Frau Besser. I'll never be able to do that.'

'If they catch him, will you – will you testify against him?'

Luise looked back at her. 'I should have to. You see, I loved my mother.'

Ilse sat silent and unmoving for a long moment, then she nodded dumbly. At last she stood up, awkwardly, as if she had been sitting for hours on the hard uncomfortable chair.

'I'll help you get away.'

Luise gazed at her steadily. 'You can't buy me, Frau Besser. I'd still testify if they wanted me as a witness.'

'They have to catch him first. What I don't want is for you to testify in front of my two boys, say something that will tell them the truth about their father. I want to protect them, not him.'

Luise stood up, held out the empty soup bowl; it was not a begging bowl, more an offertory cup. 'I shan't hurt your children, Frau Besser.'

Ilse took the bowl, looked down at the sleeping boys. What was it, she thought, that the English officer had said in the train? *How are you going to protect them from the truth?*

'I don't know how you can get away – you will have to take the chance when it comes. But I promise you – I shan't let my husband come after you. But you will have to go before Herr Ricci comes back. I don't trust him.'

Could she trust Frau Besser? What if the other woman just wanted her to make a break so that Besser would have an excuse for shooting her? But Ilse Besser looked too shattered, too uncomplicated for such trickery. She might try to delude herself because of love for her husband, but she was an honest woman. Luise nodded her thanks.

'Try and get him outside, find some excuse. I'll run for it then.'

Ilse went out to the kitchen, taking hold of the door to

239

close it behind her. But Besser rose from the table, pushed the door wide open again. 'Leave it.'

'I don't want the boys disturbed –'

'Leave it! They'll sleep – ' He stood in the doorway, silhouetted against the yellow lamp in the kitchen; he looked huge, threatening, but his voice had a frayed edge to it. 'I don't even know your name –'

'It doesn't matter, does it?' She did something she thought she would never do, pulled back her sleeve and showed the tattoo on her arm. 'We were all just numbers, weren't we?'

She couldn't see his face, but his head went back as if he had been hit. 'Don't try to escape!' he snapped and swung round and went back into the kitchen.

Luise looked about the room, at the sparse furnishings, the stone slab floor. Ricci's grandparents were the peasant poor who never profited from war or peace: a whole new world had begun to open up for her, one that touched her heart. She looked out at the old woman washing pots and dishes in a battered iron tub beside the stove: what chance would *she* ever have to escape? A faded picture of the Madonna hung on one wall of the bedroom; the old woman saw that religion prevailed in the private rooms of her house. Luise had seen the portraits of Lenin and Togliatti on the wall by the stove: politics was for the kitchen. She pulled a chair to the doorway, sat down and composed herself, gazing out at the four people in the outer room.

'Do you have to sit there?' Besser said irritably. 'Go back into the bedroom.'

'I'm keeping an eye on you,' said Luise. 'I don't trust you, Dr Besser.'

'Trust me? Why do you have to trust me?' Besser, exhausted and afraid, was puzzled; his normally clear mind didn't respond, he looked for a trick but was too slow to catch one. 'Don't joke, Fräulein –'

'Oh, I'm not.' Luise all at once felt in command; until Ricci came back she was safe. 'I gave up joking some years ago. October 1941, to be exact. The day you took that suitcase away from my mother and me – ' She nodded back at the Vuitton case, a gravestone, standing on the floor beside the bed where the boys slept. 'No one was laughing that day, remember? Not even you.'

'That bag,' said Ilse. 'Was that yours?'

'My mother's. A birthday present from my father. I hope your husband didn't give it to you for *your* birthday.'

She knew she was being cruel, throwing stones at the defenceless woman; but it worked. Ilse suddenly stood up, dragging on her husband's arm. 'Let's go outside – please, Karl!'

Besser went to protest, then changed his mind; he looked as if he, too, wanted to escape from this Jewish bitch who knew so well how to wound. He stood up, looked at the old man in the corner, then took the gun out of his pocket and gestured with it.

The old man snarled in Italian and Luise smiled.

'What did he say?' Besser whirled on her.

'He said to shoot yourself with it.'

Besser flushed with anger, then he clutched Ilse's arm and led her out of the cottage, leaving the door open behind them. He and Ilse stood beneath the grape arbour, cut off from Luise's view by the door; but she knew from the old man's hard hateful stare that *he* was being watched by Besser. Quietly she rose from the chair and moved back into the bedroom, shaking her head warningly at the old woman as the latter paused in her pot washing.

Please don't give me away!

The old woman heard the silent scream for help. She went back to her washing-up, banging the pots more loudly in the tub. Luise backed across the room, still watching the doorway, every nerve tight now. She backed into the wall, spun round and fumbled with the catch of the window. It came undone at once; she opened the window and cautiously unlatched the shutters, pushed them back. She lifted herself on to the sill, looked back into the room. And saw the boy sit up in the bed, stare at her wide-eyed.

It was the younger boy, Paul: the quiet one who had said almost nothing all evening. *Dear God, let him say nothing now!* She knew that the other boy, the bright precocious one, would have shouted for his father at once. She and the younger boy stared at each other; then Paul suddenly closed his eyes and lay down again. She would never know whether he had been awake or not.

She dropped down off the sill, landing more heavily than she had expected; a stone rolled away from beneath her foot and she stood flattened against the wall, waiting for Besser to come lurching round the corner. Then she heard the angry murmur of voices in German: the Bessers were arguing. She moved off quickly across a narrow yard, clambered over a low stone wall and in a moment was in the shadows of an olive grove.

She was almost a hundred yards down into the grove before she heard Besser shout. She didn't panic; somehow she knew that Ilse Besser would stop him from coming after her. But she kept running, stumbling over the rough earth between the trees, clambering over two more stone walls. Then she found herself in a lane that ran downhill, its surface cobbled and slippery as glass, and she turned down it. She could see the village below her, the castle rising like a giant broken-knuckled fist against the moonlit gulf. The scene was beautiful, but she had no time to admire it.

She slowed to a walk, treading carefully on the ice-smooth cobbles. She knew where she was going: back to the villa. If the soldiers had not gone, she would hide in the garden; she had to see Dunleavy, there was no one else to turn to. She had no idea where she might find Keppel; or the man who had been with him, who had probably been Sergeant Katz. So there was only Dunleavy. What she would do after she met him, she did not know. For the moment she wanted no more than someone to lean on, someone *to trust*.

She used the castle as her landmark, found her way back to the Villa Fontana. Down in the village the children still played in the streets and alleys. She passed a group of youths as she went down the long stepped alley; they spoke to her, turned and whistled after her. The world was so normal: laughing children, flirting youths, a love song on some radio . . . Then she came to the gates of the villa.

She walked cautiously up the drive, the gravel crunching

loudly beneath her shoes. She was just within sight of the villa when the two men stepped out of the bushes. She almost fell over in shock; one of the men rushed forward and caught her. She looked up into the face of Sergeant Katz.

'We saw you when you passed my truck down the lane there. You'd have walked into strife up there at the house. There's still four guards there.'

'Where have you been?' Ben Keppel said. 'Were you in those trucks with the others?'

She was still getting over her shock. She leaned against a tree, looked at the black shape of Keppel almost lost among the shadows of the bushes.

'Besser was in the villa,' she said. 'What sort of safe house does *Bricha* run?'

'Who the hell's Besser?' said Katz.

Keppel had gone abruptly quiet. Luise, calm again now, told them what had happened to her, told Katz who Besser was. 'He's in a house up on the hill back there, he and his wife and two boys. We can get him – !'

'Can you lead us there?' said Keppel.

'Now hold on a minute!' These bloody Jerries, Katz thought; they were worse than the bloody Eyeties at flying off half-cocked. 'Has this bloke Besser got a gun? Anyone else with him besides his wife and kids?'

'Yes, he has a gun. It belongs to an Italian named Ricci, a Fascist, I think. Ricci wasn't there when I got away, but he could have come back by now.'

'Why did he leave?'

'He went away to get instructions on what to do with the Bessers. Why?'

'Take it easy, Fräulein, will you?' Katz said testily. 'Look, if he went away to get new instructions, chances are he'd come back there with help. Who knows, perhaps half a dozen blokes like himself. There's still a lot of Fascists left in Italy – all the Eyeties ain't mandolin players glad to have us around instead of Musso or the Nazis. If we got up there and some shooting started, we'd have our troops up there before you could say Jack Robinson.'

243

'Who's Jack Robinson?' said Keppel.

'Blimey,' said Katz. 'Never mind, mate. What I'm saying is, we've gotta tread careful, like. The ideal thing would be to arrange a swap with the Army – this bloke Besser for our people who've been grabbed. Only thing is, we dunno if he's on the Wanted list. They've been looking for a bloke named Eichmann and one or two others, but I aint heard anything about a Besser.'

'He must be on the list!' Luise said fiercely; every moment she could feel Besser slipping away from her. 'Some Wanted list *somewhere!*'

'There ain't time to find out. Look, take us back to the house where he was. You and Ben can keep an eye on it while I nick back –'

'You ain't gonna nick anywhere,' said a voice from the darkness. 'Put your hands up, all of you, and step out there where I can see youse.'

Before Luise could raise her hands she was knocked over by Keppel. He plunged past her into the bushes, disappearing into the darkness. The sound of his crashing progress as he stumbled through the undergrowth was abruptly blotted out by the loud crack of the sentry's rifle as he fired two quick shots in the general direction of the fleeing Keppel. A moment later there were shouts, boots thudding on paving stones and then the other three picquets came round the corner of the villa on the run.

'Over here!' yelled the man who covered Luise and Katz. Arms above their heads, Luise still deafened by the crack of the rifle as it had gone off right by her ear, she and Katz stepped out on to the driveway. The three new arrivals, rifles at the ready, eager for a bit of action, pulled up in front of them.

'Hallo,' said one of them, two stripes on the arm of his greatcoat, 'what you got here, Herbie? Who was you shooting at?'

'One of 'em got away,' said Herbie. 'I dunno who they are, but something funny's going on. This geezer in one of our uniforms, for one thing.'

'Righto,' snapped the corporal. 'Up to the house. You parla Inglese?'

'Just as good as you, mate,' said Fred Katz. 'What part of London you from?'

'Tottenham,' said the corporal. 'But we'll have all the questions when we get you into the house.'

The front door of the house had opened and Dunleavy and Charlie Lincoln stood there. Leaving two of his men outside, the corporal marched Luise and Katz up into the entrance hall, Herbie bringing up the rear. Dunleavy closed the front door and, without a glance at Luise, looked at the corporal.

'What's going on, corporal? Those shots –'

'Private Coogan here caught these two out in the garden. There was another one of 'em, but he done a bunk. Righto, sergeant. Let's see your paybook, if you got one.'

Katz produced his paybook, the corporal looked at it, then handed it back.

'Looks okay. But you don't belong around here, do you, sarge?'

'No. Milan.'

'Yeah, well, we'll leave it to the boss to ask what you doing outa your territory. Righto, miss. You got an identity card or something?'

'Of course.' Luise took her papers from the pocket of her coat. 'I am Luisa Graziani. I was in a forced labour camp during the war and now I'm on my way back to my home in Rome.'

'Nothing doing, miss,' said the corporal. 'We picked up a load of Jewish DPs in this villa tonight and they were all supposed to be Eyetie forced labourers. And it don't look good for you, either, sarge. You being Jewish and all.'

'You anti-Semitic?'

'I'm just anti-everything, mate, till they tell me I can go home. Is there a telephone in the villa, sir?'

'There's one down the hall there, I think,' said Dunleavy. 'As for Signorina Graziani, I can vouch for her.'

The corporal looked suspicious: you couldn't trust these bloody Yanks when it came to women. 'How's that, sir?'

'She came from a camp in my area in Germany. Matter of fact, I gave her a lift down here. That right, Private Lincoln?'

Charlie Lincoln nodded, face impassive. What the hell was the major up to, why was he putting himself out on a limb for this Kraut Jewess? Not for a piece of ass: this girl wouldn't put out for anyone, not even for someone trying to keep her out of trouble.

The corporal was still unimpressed. 'What's she doing with the sergeant then, sir?'

'I don't know,' said Dunleavy blandly. 'What was she doing with you?'

Katz was not dumb. He read the Yank's message: *we've both got to get Fräulein Graz out of here.* 'I picked up Miss – what you say your name was?'

'Graziani,' said Luise.

' – Miss Graziani down in the village. I stopped there for a cuppa. Tell you the truth, mate – excuse me saying this, miss – I thought I mighta been on to something. You know what it's like. But nothing doing – she put me in my place right off, you know what I mean? So I brought her up here to the villa, just like she asked. My truck's down the road, in a lane just outside the gates.'

'What were you doing out there in the garden?' The corporal was still suspicious; he wasn't dumb, either. 'What about the bloke who buzzed off? Who was he, someone else you give a lift to?'

'Search me, mate. He just stepped outa the bushes and pulled a gun on me and Miss – Miss Graziani.'

Don't get carried away, thought Dunleavy.

'He said he was one of the DPs you picked up here tonight – except he got away.' Katz knew the value of telling some of the truth; it made the rest of your story sound more convincing.

'He wanted to know where the rest of 'em had been taken – I think he thought I was with you lot. I told him I'd nick down to La Spezia and find out. Then Herbie here butted in.'

'You hear what they were saying?' the corporal said to Herbie.

'I didn't waste any time listening, corp. Soon's I heard 'em, I moved in on 'em.'

The corporal looked at Dunleavy. 'I'll leave it up to Major Shell, sir. Can I use the phone?'

Giulio was waiting down the corridor, watching this clash between the foreigners. Dunleavy nodded towards him and he came forward and led the corporal down to the phone. Private Coogan was left in charge of the two prisoners. Dunleavy took Luise's arm.

'Excuse me, sir, where you going?'

'I'm taking Miss Graziani into that dining room there. I'm not going to let her get away. Relax, soldier. I just want to ask her some questions.'

Private Coogan looked uncertain. 'I dunno –'

'Major Shell knows who I am and he knows why I'm here. He'd okay me putting some questions to Miss Graziani.'

As if taking it for granted that Private Coogan wasn't going to argue any further, Dunleavy led Luise into the dining room. Coogan looked after them, doubt knotting his square young face; then he glanced at Katz and shrugged. He wasn't paid to argue with officers, Yank or otherwise.

Dunleavy and Luise stood beside the table, still bright and gleaming beneath the blaze of the chandelier. This whole house was more brightly lit than any house Dunleavy had ever been in, yet he knew it was full of dark corners. The Contessa, who sounded so silly and loud, had her own mysteries.

'You shouldn't have spoken up for me,' said Luise quietly; through the big open doors she could see Herbie Coogan watching them suspiciously. 'I don't want you to get into trouble on my behalf.'

'Where were you? How come they didn't pick you up when they took the rest of them?'

Luise told him what had happened to her.

'Yeah, I know the Contessa has been sheltering Germans

247

here – Giulio told me. But Jesus – you mean this guy – Besser? – he actually sent your mother to the gas chambers?'

'Not just my mother. Other people lost relatives – Frau Bork lost her two children. He's a monster. Why are the English bothering with us when they should be arresting someone like him?'

'Everyone's got their own priorities,' said Dunleavy. 'Who was the other guy out in the garden, the one who got away? Keppel?'

'Yes. But why are you so obsessed with him? You should be going after Besser –'

'Christ Almighty, Luise, Keppel killed my brother! I didn't come all the way down here to get sidetracked into chasing some Nazi.' Then he added lamely and awkwardly, 'Even one who – who was responsible for murdering your mother.'

She turned sharply away. Her hand knocked over a glass: wine spread in a dark stain over the snow of the cloth. 'I'm sorry. One tends to forget other people's losses. I've seen so many – ' She turned back to him. 'I do regret your brother's death, and I'm not pleading for any sympathy for Ben Keppel. But I can't turn him over to you, even if I knew where he is.'

He gazed at her steadily. 'In other circumstances I'd help you all I could to find Besser. But – '

'I understand. But tonight, when I was there with the man who killed my mother – ' For the first time he saw how vulnerable she might be if she lost control. 'We mustn't fight, not you and I.'

The corporal came to the door. 'I've gotta take 'em both in, sir. Major Shell wants to see 'em.'

'Okay, corporal,' said Dunleavy quietly, still looking at Luise. 'I'll follow you in.'

'Yes, sir.' The corporal's tone suggested that he wasn't really interested in what Dunleavy did. He nodded at Katz. 'Righto, sarge. We'll go down and get your truck, if it's where you say it is. And no funny stuff, understand? You're under close arrest, the major told me to tell you.'

'You're making a mistake.' Katz sounded almost philosophical.

'It won't be the first. Me biggest mistake was joining the army in the first place. Everything else is just a matter of proportion, like.' The corporal, too, could be philosophical.

As they followed Katz' truck into La Spezia in the jeep, Charlie Lincoln said, 'You sure you ain't making a mistake, too, major?'

'Charlie, I know you've got my welfare at heart, but in your outfit did they teach you to ask your officers if they were right or wrong?'

'We didn't have to ask, sir. We knew they was wrong all the time.'

'I'm not going to ask what outfit you were in.' Dunleavy sighed. 'Okay, what mistake am I making?'

'Putting yourself out on a limb for them DPs. Vouching for Fräulein Graz ain't gonna help 'em any.'

'Private Lincoln, I think you're imposing on my friendly disposition.'

'Okay, sir,' said Charlie Lincoln, face abruptly sullen. 'Just trying to help was all I was trying to do.'

They drove in silence round the curve of the gulf. Out on the silver-blue sea the fishing boats carried their own tiny yellow moons; the lights seemed more substantial than the boats, which were only faint shadows on the brilliant sea. The fishermen had no troubles out there, except storms and empty waters. Their real problems were here on land, Dunleavy thought, back here among the people who insisted on being a part of your life.

They were passing the shipyards, coming into La Spezia, when he said, 'Okay, what would you have done?'

Charlie Lincoln took his time. 'About Fräulein Graz, sir, or the DPs?'

'Both.'

'Play it safe, that's my motto. Don't start being responsible for nobody till you seen if anyone else wants to be responsible for 'em.'

'You're a smart-ass enlisted man, Charlie. What do you want to be when you get out of this man's army?'

'I think I might be a smart-ass politician, sir.'

'I think you just might be that, too. Don't ask for my vote. You sound just like every other politician I've listened to.'

But he knew that Charlie Lincoln was probably half-right. Back before the war he had had as clients farmers who had been forced off their land by drought, poor markets and banks that thought a broken-down dirt farm was some sort of asset. The farmers had come to him and told him they couldn't pay their bills; then they had headed west to the Promised Land of California. He had felt sorry for them, but sympathy didn't pay the mortgage or cause the sky to rain. He heard of the Okies moving west further south, saw pictures of them: refugees in their own country, not poor stateless sons-of-bitches shuttled back and forth between countries that didn't want them. Christ, he thought, no wonder Luise and the others wanted to get to Palestine. But even there the British would still be with them . . .

The truck pulled up outside a large building and Charlie slid the jeep in behind it. 'Good luck, sir.'

Dunleavy grunted, got out and followed Luise, Katz, the corporal and Private Coogan into the building. It was like any commandeered army headquarters Dunleavy had seen, suggesting nothing but temporary authority. There were patches on the walls where pictures had been removed (Mussolini? King Victor Emmanuel? The walls of history are full of blank spaces, the paint or wallpaper just a bit brighter than the surrounds, like a reminder of the hopes for the hero when his picture had first been hung). An attempt had been made to cover one patch with a portrait of King George the Sixth, but the picture, fly-blown and with its glass cracked, had seen better days and better places; George looked out on his subjects and foreigners alike with a slightly pained look, as if he wondered what he was doing up here on this foreign wall. The building's air was stale and so was the air of the staff lounging about in the corridors and offices: they had been here too long, peace was already a bore and a bind.

'We'd hoped to be gone from here by now,' said Shell. 'But the local carabinieri weren't too happy with the number of Jews coming in here and we had to come back. Bloody bore, really.' He led Dunleavy into his office, nodded at a faded pre-war London Underground poster: *Visit Epping Forest.* 'Home. My parents live just near it. Wouldn't mind being back there. For a while, anyway. So we've got two more, eh?'

'If your Private Coogan had been a bit sharper, we'd have had three. Keppel was there tonight, but he got away.'

'Christ!' Shell slumped down in his chair, waved Dunleavy to another. 'That must have disappointed you.'

'There was someone else at the villa, too – that taxi brought them out. The Contessa has been harbouring Nazis, too.' Shell raised his eyebrows and Dunleavy went on, 'There was an SS doctor there tonight, with his wife and kids. He was at Auschwitz. He killed the relatives of some of those people you're holding outside.'

Shell swore again, a mutter this time. Abruptly he reached into a drawer of his desk, flipped through some papers, took out a printed sheet. 'What was the chap's name?'

'Besser. Karl Besser. I don't know his rank.'

Shell ran his eye down the paper, shook his head. 'Not on this list. But this could be months out of date – ' He turned it over, looked at the bottom of the page. 'Last October.'

'You don't really care two bits about these guys, do you?'

The two men stared sourly at each other: their common war was over. Then Shell sat up in his chair, put the Wanted list away, slammed the drawer shut. 'Let's have our two latest arrivals in.'

'First – where's the Contessa?'

'She's in another room being questioned by Lieutenant Taviani. She insisted on being an Italian citizen, so I turned her over to him – and was glad to. I have the feeling he wishes she were Bolivian or Tibetan – anything to be rid of her.'

'How do you feel about her? Now you know she's been playing landlady to Nazis.'

'I'd like the job of escorting her to Tibet. It would get me out of this mess. Corporal!'

The corporal brought in Katz and Luise, got his orders from Shell to return to the villa, about-turned with a great thumping of boots and went out. Shell, looking tired and fed up, a young man growing old in the night, looked up at Katz first.

'You are in trouble, sergeant. I'm afraid I don't believe a word of what you told Corporal Taylor. Has this man Keppel been in touch with you before?'

'I dunno anyone named Keppel, sir. This bloke tonight, the one held up me and Miss Graziani, he was a complete stranger, never seen him in my life before.'

Shell sighed, his irritation not strong enough to come up through his weariness. 'You're lying, sergeant. However, I'm not going to load myself with you. You'll be sent back to H.Q. in Milan under close arrest and they will deal with you.'

'What'll be the charge, sir?'

'Between now and when you get there, I'll have thought of something. I'll signal it through and they'll tell you when you get there. You can think up your answers then.'

'Is that what they call British justice, sir?' Katz seemed to know the game was up: he was Jewish and rebellious now, a defiant Zionist.

'That will be enough, sergeant.' Shell was not going to give Katz the opportunity to identify himself and his cause; he had enough Jews on hand doing that without wanting another one in uniform. 'Sergeant-major!'

The broken-nosed sergeant-major thumped his boots in the doorway. 'Sir!'

'Sergeant Katz is under close arrest. He's to be moved to H.Q. Milan first thing tomorrow.'

'Right, sir! Prisoner, about turn!'

Katz stared at Shell. There was hatred in his pale face: it took the plumpness out of it, aged him. He worked his lips and Dunleavy tensed, waiting for him to spit at the British officer. Then slowly he turned about, the slowness of his turning an insult after all the smart boot-thumping of the corporal and the sergeant-major, and went out of the room. He didn't glance at Luise, relieving her of any guilt by association with him.

Dunleavy said, 'As he said, is that British justice?'

'A form of it. You'd be surprised how effectively it works.'

'Who for?'

But Shell did not take the bait. He looked up at Luise, who was still standing quietly in front of his desk, composed and aloof. There was another empty chair in the room but he did not offer it to her. English gallantry seemed to have run out for the night.

'Miss Graziani? You're supposed to be an Italian, is that right? How well do you speak Italian?'

'Perfectly well,' said Luise in Italian. 'How well do you speak it, major?'

'A little better than you, I should think.' Shell's Italian was almost perfect, the accent just right. 'I always had a gift for languages, particularly the Romance ones. Do you want to keep speaking Italian? Or German? Or English?'

'My compliments, major – we'll use your language,' said Luise in English. 'My name is Luise Graz. I am an Austrian Jew, formerly of Vienna, Auschwitz and a Displaced Persons camp in Major Dunleavy's area in Germany. I'm afraid that's all I'm going to tell you.'

Shell looked at Dunleavy. 'Anything to add?'

It was Dunleavy's turn to be frank. 'Just that I've known those facts about her. Does that make me an accomplice or something?'

Shell ignored that. 'How long have you known her?'

'Six months.'

'Intimately?' He looked from one to the other, the shadow of a tired smile at the edges of his mouth. 'I'm sorry, I don't mean *that* way.'

'Not intimately,' said Dunleavy. '*That* way or any other.'

'Do you think she has any connection with our friend Keppel?'

'She was in the party that he brought down here.' He didn't look at Luise, but he could feel her watching him. He felt awkward, talking about her as if she were not present, but it was Shell who held all the cards. 'But I don't believe Miss Graz or any of the others had anything to do with the killing of our two men. Technically, I guess they're accessories after the fact. But I'm not going to press that.'

'Has Miss Graz caused you any trouble in the past?'

'None.'

Shell looked back at Luise. 'Would you step outside, please, Miss Graz? Sergeant-major!' The boots thumped in the doorway again. 'Get Miss Graz a cup of tea, would you? I'll have her back in here in a few minutes.'

When he and Shell were alone, Dunleavy said, 'Okay, what're you building up to?'

Shell leaned back in his chair, put his hands behind his head, blinked once or twice as if his eyes were sore. He was too tired now for anything but candour. He was beginning to appreciate how easy the war had been.

'We have three hundred Jews in a camp over near a place called Sarzana. There are Christ knows how many more on their way down out of the hills, all of them coming from outside Italy. In the next few weeks there is going to be a confrontation here in La Spezia — we've had the word, and nothing short of handing over Palestine holus-bolus is going to stop it. There's a ship already out in the harbour, the *Fede*. If they manage to get aboard it — and I don't think the local police are going to do anything to help us stop them — it will put out to sea and then the whole world is going to know about it. There are a couple of Royal Navy ships outside the gulf and they'll either board it as soon as it's in international waters, or they'll shadow it halfway to Haifa, then make it put into Cyprus. Where all the poor bastards aboard will be taken ashore and will be put in camps with the hundreds of others we have there. Nobody will be happy about it, neither the Jews nor us, and the propaganda from the Jews in your country will put England's reputation down to about the level of that of our late enemies.'

'That's your problem, not mine.'

'Agreed. Perhaps now you can see why I'd like to be accompanying the Contessa to Tibet or anywhere else where they haven't heard of Zionism or the Balfour Declaration or our debt to the Arabs.'

'Go on,' said Dunleavy, not helping him: the problems of the British were not his. Nor America's: like most Americans he had known nothing of the Middle East, Palestine or the Arabs till U.S. forces had landed in North Africa in 1942 and the map of the Americans' world had been enlarged. Once he was back in the States he knew that he, like most of his countrymen, would not give a thought to that part of the world again.

254

'One way of keeping these people off the ship out in the harbour would be to send them back whence they came.' Shell smiled tiredly at his tired joke. 'The Shelley influence – one gets poetic occasionally, living in his house. Whence they came. Or is that biblical?' He was talking with the looseness of the tired man or the drunk. 'Anyhow, if we have to do it, it will be one bloody great bind. Because everybody is going to insist on being sent back to exactly whence he came. Are you getting my point?'

'Not exactly.'

Shell sighed again, at the obtuseness of Americans. 'Even one DP taken off my hands would be a relief.'

Dunleavy stood up, getting the message. 'Okay. Do I have to sign for her or anything?'

'I have never believed in paper-work unless it is absolutely necessary. One day the world may run out of paper – though I doubt it. It's a staple need of our existence now, like bread and water – they'll find some means of creating it, at the expense of something else.' Shell stood up, stretched. 'She is a remarkably attractive woman. You should take her to Tibet.'

'I'll ask her,' said Dunleavy. 'Thanks.'

Shell accompanied him out of the office, down the corridor to a large sparsely furnished room where Luise and the Contessa sat drinking tea out of thick mugs, each of them nervous and upright on the stiff-backed chairs set against one wall. Both women looked up as the two men came in, eyes painful-looking with queries, the tea mugs held before their lips like bowls of hemlock to be gulped if the verdict went against them. Christ, thought Dunleavy, I'm getting morbid. Luise would never commit suicide. Not while he was around to stop her.

'Ah, Contessa.' Shell was polite, smiled at the older woman: she was no longer his problem, he hoped. 'What is Lieutenant Taviani going to do with you?'

Taviani, as if he had been waiting outside for his name to be mentioned, came in, awkwardly and reluctantly, like an actor who was not quite sure of his lines.

'What are you going to do with the Contessa?' Shell asked.

Taviani spread his hands, an Italian actor. He had looked

young and handsome out at the Villa Fontana, but now he had
his cap off: he was bald and middle-aged and had the unhappy
eyes of a man who had forgotten the meaning of responsibility
but was still saddled with it.

'What can I charge her with?'

'Major Dunleavy tells me she had some Germans in her
house, besides the Jews.' Shell and Taviani were speaking in
Italian. Luise and the Contessa listened intently, without
moving; but Dunleavy stood awkwardly by, reduced to the
near-idiocy of the man with the alien ear. He smiled reassuringly
at Luise, but she wasn't looking at him. 'Isn't there something
in the law that covers that?'

'The new laws haven't been printed yet, major. We Italians
are bad enough with our red tape, but the English have made it
worse. I thought it would be best if the Contessa went home –
she can report to me every day until we find a law to charge her
under. Would that be agreeable, Contessa?'

The worry went out of the Contessa's face and she smiled,
liking men again. Well, some men. 'I shall report every day.
Faithfully.'

Shell turned to Dunleavy, who concentrated, knowing he was
now about to be re-admitted to the circle. 'Seems that the
Contessa is also going to be set loose. How would you like to be
her parole officer? You and Miss Graz can go back to the villa
with her. For tonight, anyway.' He looked tired again, blinked
once more as if his eyeballs were coated with grit. 'Will you
come back and see me in the morning?'

'What about the others?'

'I sent them over to Sarzana. I'll worry about them tomorrow.' He nodded to Luise and the Contessa. 'Goodnight,
ladies. Don't give Major Dunleavy too much trouble.'

Going back to Lerici in the jeep Dunleavy said, 'Contessa,
we know about the Germans you have been sheltering. Including the ones who were there in the villa tonight.'

The Contessa sat beside Luise in the back of the jeep, silent,
fat and uncomfortable on the narrow seat. She had been almost
gay as she had said goodnight to Shell and Taviani, but as they
got closer to home she had turned sullen, as if she had only just

now begun to realize that Luise and Dunleavy might be her jailers, more so than Shell or Taviani would want to be. She was suddenly afraid of the Jewish girl beside her, peered ahead as if expecting the jeep to be ambushed by *Bricha* men.

'The man there tonight killed Fräulein Graz's mother,' said Dunleavy; and Charlie Lincoln, rounding a curve in the road, was distracted and almost drove them into the sea. 'Watch it, Charlie, for Christ's sake!'

'Yes, sir.' Charlie looked over his shoulder. 'I'm sorry to hear about your mother, miss.'

'Thank you,' said Luise; then looked at the woman beside her. 'I'm not blaming you for what Dr Besser did, Contessa. Unless you believed we Jews should have been exterminated?'

The Contessa was not evil, just greedy. 'I didn't ask any questions. I did it for the money.' She was honest enough not to make any excuses for her reason: she believed money was an honest enough reason for anything. 'They paid me well. Better than your people.'

'Jesus!' Dunleavy wanted to reach back and hit her. 'Is that all you have to say?'

'No.' She was looking at Luise, not at him. 'I am sorry for what happened to your mother – to all the Jews. That is the truth.' Then she looked at Dunleavy, as if expecting him to make some other charge against her. 'I do not apologize for Il Duce. His only mistake was in becoming that other man's partner.'

'Hitler?'

'I never say his name.' But she nodded.

'Then why the hell did you hide the men who worked for him? The SS – the worst of the lot?'

'I told you – for the money. I thought an American would understand that.'

Christ, thought Dunleavy, is that all the rest of the world thinks of us? Abruptly he wanted to go home, even back to Beef City, which he thought he had left forever; foreigners, goddam them, forced isolationism on people like himself. But there was Luise in the back seat, the only girl he had ever loved. Though as far as he could see, she also didn't have a very high opinion of Americans. Nor did Charlie Lincoln, another American.

They pulled up outside the villa and Corporal Taylor and the other three picquets appeared at once. Dunleavy said, 'The two ladies are released in my custody, corporal.'

Corporal Taylor hid his contempt: these bloody Yanks could get anything they wanted, especially women. 'Yes, sir. We'll be going back to La Spezia first thing in the morning. Taking the taxi with us. Good luck, sir.'

'Good luck?'

'With the ladies, sir.' The corporal's face was blank.

You son-of-a-bitch. And we're supposed to be allies. 'Thank you, corporal.'

Inside the house Giulio and his wife looked apprehensively at Dunleavy, as if he were now the master and the Contessa a guest. But the Contessa wasn't going to give up so easily, not on her own ground. She doffed her cloak, waved a jewelled hand.

'We'll finish dinner, Giulio. Warm everything up again and re-set the table.'

Dunleavy looked into the dining room, saw the table had been cleared, the cloth and cutlery and glass put away. 'Do we need to eat in there?'

'When did you last dine in nice surroundings?' the Contessa asked Luise.

'Are you trying to make amends, Contessa?'

'Yes.' Her honesty was as simple as her greed; she knew when it profited her. Dunleavy, disliking her intensely, found himself admiring her.

Luise smiled, with the same feelings towards this woman as Dunleavy had. 'I should like every Jew who has passed through your house to be sitting down with us. But that's not possible. So Major Dunleavy and I will accept your invitation as their representatives.' She looked at him, smiling at him, too. 'Shall we, major?'

'Sure.' It was late and he was tired, but he knew he would stay up all night with her if she asked him. He was not sure how many more nights there would be with her and he had to stretch the hours.

'Rosanna will run a bath for you,' the Contessa told Luise.

'I am sorry I cannot lend you a dress. Ten years ago – ' A hand ran regretfully down over her plumpness.

'The bath will be enough,' said Luise. Then, as if putting the events of the evening out of her mind, deciding to be nothing but a woman enjoying the small pleasure offered her: 'And perhaps some make-up?'

Long after that night Dunleavy would look back on it with the refracted memory of a man who wasn't quite sure whether he had experienced something or dreamed it. He enjoyed the evening, despite his tiredness; but there was a nagging sense of guilt, as if they were celebrating their ability to turn their minds away from what this house represented. He was not given to thoughts of ghosts, but as he raised the wine glass to his lips he felt the mouth of an SS officer inside his own mouth. The wine tasted sour and he put the glass down.

'Not drinking, major?' said the Contessa, diamond-bright in several ways at the end of the table. Rings sparkled, her conversation had been light and gay and occasionally funny. She conjured up her own ghosts, the guests who had sat around the table in the days before disaster.

Luise, sitting opposite him, smiled at him. 'I don't think Major Dunleavy has your and my talent for adjustment, Contessa. It is a European thing,' she explained to Dunleavy, 'we have inherited it from our history. You will have to adjust to it, you Americans.'

Don't you start baiting me, he thought. She looked beautiful, her face glowing from the bath, her hair shining beneath the crystal sun above the table. She had applied her make-up with a good deal more restraint than the Contessa; her eyes looked larger, the lids more pronounced, and her lips more delectable, inviting kisses. *Christ, if you only knew how much I loved you!*

'We're all going to have to learn a thing or two.'

Coffee and liqueurs were served in the main salon. It was no more than a simple progression from one room to another, but Dunleavy, all at once watching Luise with an acuteness that hurt, saw how she moved from the dinner table acrgss the entrance hall to the couch in the salon. She did it naturally, gracefully, with the air of a woman who had been dining in houses such as this all her life. He was aware of his own awk-wardness, treading in the social minefield; Europeans, he knew, placed great store by the correct thing to do. Till he had come to Europe he had never had coffee anywhere but at the table where he ate. He laughed at himself, making mountains of difference out of molehills of manners, as if any of it really mattered. But he saw the difference and wondered about him-self and Luise.

The Contessa sat down at a grand piano dull with dust and age.

'When the Count was alive we used to have musical *salons*. He would bring a quartet down from Milan or sometimes from Venice. Never from Rome – he always said the Romans knew nothing about music. Sometimes I would sing.' She began to play a Mozart piece, with a good ear but with fingers that were no longer supple. 'Do you sing, major?'

'No. But Miss Graz does. She was in opera in Vienna.'

The fingers struck the keys in a discord of surprise. 'No! What did you sing?'

'I was just beginning,' Luise said modestly. 'Just small roles. But I had hopes –'

'Didn't we all?' said the Contessa. 'Would you sing some-thing now?'

Luise looked at Dunleavy with amused irritation, as if he had played a joke on her, and he grinned.

'You'll have to adjust some time,' he said. 'Why don't you make a start now?'

She got up and went determinedly to stand beside the Con-tessa at the piano. 'Can you play something for two voices? I'll need support. It's been so long –'

'Who doesn't need support?' The Contessa was becoming more honest as the night went on.

She played a Schubert song, light and not too testing. She was a contralto, though not heavy, and her voice blended well with Luise's. Each knew the song well; their only hesitation was in their confidence in their voices. The music filled the room, creating echoes of the past. When the voices rose together on a high note, the singing suddenly broke off in mid-note as they knew they were not going to reach it without straining. They laughed together in embarrassment, like schoolgirls.

'We still have a long way to go,' said Luise.

The Contessa closed the piano. 'Not me. I've been – there's no voice left. But you are still young enough. Isn't she, major?' She shouted at Dunleavy, the old Contessa again; her voice might be finished for songs, but not for commanding attention. 'She should take up singing again, don't you think?'

'Sure.' But Dunleavy knew Luise had other priorities.

When they went up to bed another day was already two hours old. Dunleavy was almost out on his feet; perhaps that was why he was so gentlemanly when he said goodnight to Luise at the door of her room. He lifted her hand and kissed it, neither awkwardly nor with embarrassment. They wouldn't know me back in Beef City, he thought.

'Better than the cellar, eh?' He looked past her into the big bedroom. It had the sumptuousness of a high-class whorehouse he had once visited in St Louis, all brass bedstead and rich red drapes; he wondered what sort of *salons* the dead Count had held in this room. 'You should sleep well tonight.'

'I hope so.' He was still holding her hand and she made no attempt to withdraw it. 'But a lot has happened tonight. If I can stop myself thinking –'

'Maybe the Contessa has some sleeping pills or something.'

'No, that's the easy way. I learned to sleep with things on my mind when I was in Birkenau.' She smiled wryly, looked over her shoulder at the big comfortable bed. 'Perhaps it may be more difficult now that conditions are better.'

He gazed at her a moment, then leaned forward and kissed her softly on the lips that had been tempting him all night. 'Goodnight, Luise.' Exhaustion, or inexperience in gentle declarations, made him say bluntly, 'I love you.'

She took her hand out of his, but not to break the contact between them: that was there in the air around them, soft yet electric. She gazed just as steadily at him as he at her, then she raised her hand and touched his jaw. 'It's too soon –' She laughed softly and in his ears it was more beautiful than her singing. 'I don't even know your name.'

'Matt. Matthew. And it's not too soon. You should know better than anyone that time doesn't have much meaning these days. Sleep tight.'

'Do you expect me to? After that?' She turned quickly and went into the bedroom made for love, closing the door gently in his face. He wondered whom she was afraid of, herself or him.

3

When the girl (he did not know her name, did not want to: that would only add to the burden of memory in the future) escaped from the cottage, Besser's first reaction was to rush after her. He had no idea what he would do if he caught her. Certainly not kill her: the gun in his pocket was a threat, no more. He had never actually seen any of his cases die; he had never been near the gas chambers, and the drugs that had killed the 'useless eaters' had been administered by nurses. He had killed by remote control and now, faced with the possible necessity of having to kill someone directly, stand there and watch them die from a bullet from the gun he would be holding in his hand, he knew he could not do it.

He was prevented from racing after the girl by Ilse. She grabbed his arm, hung on to him desperately. 'Let her go! We don't want her!'

'She'll bring the English! I've got to get her back –'

But he knew he was arguing only half-heartedly; he didn't even try to free his arm from her grip. He went back into the cottage with her, letting her take control. She was tense, frightened, on the verge of hysteria; yet somehow she disciplined herself and him. She was housekeeping, becoming adept in the routine of escape.

'I'll wake the boys. We must leave right away.'

'What about Ricci?'

'We can't wait for him to come back. Perhaps we can leave a message –' She looked at the two old people standing by the kitchen table, the old man grinning toothlessly at the sudden turn of events, the old woman looking half-pleased and half-frightened. 'No, we can't trust them.'

'We can trust no one,' he said bitterly, all at once aware that they were in a world of strangers. But she had gone through into the bedroom, was waking the boys. He followed her to the doorway, keeping one eye on the old couple. 'We'll have to leave the bags.'

'Must we?' But she nodded, slipping shoes on to the grumbling sleepy boys. 'Ricci can bring them to us tomorrow.'

'I'll get in touch with him then,' he said; but a sense of hopelessness was creeping over him. 'Hurry!'

'Where are we going, Father?' Even half-asleep, Hans had questions. 'Are the English after us? Father – ?'

They left the old couple still standing in the middle of the kitchen, the old man grinning as if he and his partisan comrades had scored some sort of late victory in their private war. Ilse felt in her purse, put some lire notes on the table, thanked the old woman in German. The old man reached across, picked up the money and flung it back at Ilse. The notes fluttered to the floor and Hans bent down and picked them up. Ilse closed her eyes for a moment, as if the money had actually hit her in the face; then she took it from Hans, put it back in her purse to use to better purpose than gratitude. She repeated her thanks in German to the old woman, ignored the old man and followed Karl and the two boys out of the cottage.

'Where do we go?'

'We must stay somewhere around here,' Besser said. 'We can't get too far away from Ricci.'

They walked down through olive groves, the boys stumbling along, Paul complaining that he wanted to go to sleep. They stayed above the village, came out on to a road that ran south in twisting curves above the sea cliffs. The road swung away from the cliffs, pushed back by a low stone wall beyond which they could see a black overgrown garden and the dark shape of a house against the silver sea.

'Wait here,' said Besser.

He slid over the wall and went cautiously down through the garden towards the house. As if by instinct he took the gun from

263

his pocket; he might not kill with it, but it offered reassurance. He skirted the house, a low villa with a wide front terrace that looked out on the sea. The shutters were closed on all the windows and doors, but that meant nothing; he tossed stones at two of the shuttered windows and only when they caused no disturbance within the house was he certain it was empty. He went back up the road.

'I think this must be a summer place. We'll stay here tonight.'

He found a loose shutter on one of the windows, prised it off with a length of wood, smashed the window and opened it. He climbed in, went through the villa and opened the door that led out on to the terrace overlooking the sea. Ilse and the boys entered the house cautiously.

'It's wrong,' Ilse said. 'Breaking into someone's home –'

'I know,' he said for the benefit of the boys: Christ knew what they thought of the example he was setting them. Then he thought of the other example he had set them and hoped to Christ they would never learn of it. 'But we'll do no harm. It's just a place to stay tonight and tomorrow.'

The mattresses on the beds in the two front rooms were musty but not damp. Ilse could find no sheets, but she found blankets. She opened the windows and shutters in a room, put the boys to bed there; they went down without complaint, too exhausted to be afraid of their strange surroundings. Ilse and Besser went to bed in the room across the hall, the window open to let in the reflection of the moonlight from the sea. Ilse took off her skirt and jumper, laid them carefully over the end of the iron bedstead.

'You'd better take off your clothes. We may not be able to change for a day or two, not till we get our suitcases again.'

'Always the hausfrau.' But he did what she told him: he was content, *glad*, to have himself organized. She had run the small things of his life so well before the war.

They lay side by side under the blankets, which smelled of the dank winter months; perhaps dank winter years, Besser thought. God knew how long this villa had been closed up. The owners might never come back to it: where lay the man now who had lain in this bed? Houses all over Europe were full of the ghosts of people who would never return to them. Including their own house in Würzburg.

'What sort of house would you like in South America?'

She turned towards him, put her leg over his, buried her face against his shoulder. 'A safe one.'

Besser woke early, as if in his sleep he had been afraid of daylight itself. He got up, closed the shutters in both bedrooms, pulled the blankets up over the still sleeping boys. He stood above them, looking at them as if for the first time (perhaps it was the first time. Had he ever stopped really to look at them before?). Paul's face was smooth, innocent of expression; he was a willing total victim of sleep. Hans lay beside him, just as deep in sleep; but his face was pinched with doubt, he dreamed questions. Besser looked at them for understanding of himself, but that was years away, he knew. If ever.

When he went back to the other room Ilse was sitting up, white and frightened. 'I didn't know where you'd gone!'

He sat down on the side of the bed. Reassured by his presence, the colour came back into her face. Beneath her slip he could see the curve of her breasts, the emboss of her large nipples against the cheap ersatz material; between his legs he felt a response. He stood up, turned away from her and began to dress. He still could not forget Gerstein, the fifth columnist in his bed.

The boys woke at nine o'clock, complaining of being hungry.

'I'll go down to the village and buy something,' Ilse said. 'No one should take any notice of me. And I might even see Herr Ricci.'

'I was going to wait till tonight, go back into La Spezia to that bar where we picked him up in his taxi. Someone there should know him.'

'I wasn't going to go *looking* for him,' she said defensively; she was beginning to wish they had never heard of *Spinne*. 'But we do need something to eat.'

'Be careful,' he warned; he still loved her, even if he couldn't make love to her. 'I'll take the boys outside, let them get the sun.'

Ilse found a basket in the kitchen of the house, took it with some misgivings. This was another woman's house, probably a woman richer than herself, with servants who would do all the shopping; but it disturbed her that she should be intruding on another woman's possessions, using something for which she had not obtained permission. She felt she was looting, turning over the lingering presence of the family who lived in this house in the summer.

She kept to the road finding her way back down into Lerici; staying in the open built her confidence. She had a small pre-war Italian phrase book that she had bought when the *Spinne* man had told her she and the boys would be meeting Karl in Italy; she had not known how long they might be alone before Karl turned up. She kept glancing at it as she walked down to the village; by the time she had reached the main piazza she had memorized the words for the basics she would need. But she knew her accent would give her away in the intimacy of a village shop: she had never spoken Italian in her life before.

She was relieved when she saw the market that was being held in the piazza. Stalls dazzled with the colours of spring vegetables and fruit; at the waterfront end of the piazza fishermen stood above benches of gleaming silver; behind them their nets made latticework of the sunlight. The market was thronged with shoppers, crowded with noise; when the clock on the church tower struck the sound was pushed up by the clamour from below. Voices, let alone accents, were going to be difficult to distinguish in this hullabaloo.

With finger signs Ilse bought food, wine and *ersatz* coffee, loading herself down, carried away by the sheer pleasure of being a *hausfrau* again. Then, as a treat for Hans and Paul, she bought several bars of chocolate, at a price that made her feel guilty. She passed a man selling ice-cream, remembered how much Karl had liked ice-cream in their happier days; but there was no way of getting it back to the villa before it melted and she reluctantly shook her head at the smiling badgering seller. She wandered through the market, enjoying the moment; then she looked up at the clock, saw she had been in the piazza half an hour. Again she felt guilty, as if she had been deliberately careless.

266

She hurried up out of the village, took the road back along the sea cliffs towards the villa. Once she heard a car coming up the road behind her and she ducked into a narrow side lane, afraid that someone might offer her a lift. When she reached the villa she was shocked to find it empty. She went into the garden on the run; then slowed, remembering that Karl had said he would take the boys out for some sun. But as she went searching for them down through the wilderness of shrubs and trees, not seeing or hearing them, she began to panic. Sobs built up in her throat, she wanted to scream their names on the still morning air.

Then she came to the top of a long flight of steps that led down to a tiny cove. She paused as if on the edge of a cliff, the steps falling away steeply before her; she felt the temptation to step out into space, to end everything. Then down below she saw the three swimmers in the clear blue water at the edge of a sliver of beach.

She went down the steps, treading carefully, all her suicidal despair suddenly gone. She sat down on the steps at the top of the last flight, looked down at Karl, Hans and Paul plunging and splashing like porpoises in the water that seemed to shine twice as brilliantly through the prism of her tears.

Chapter Seven

'I'd like to go to the camp at Sarzana,' said Luise. 'Does my parole allow that?'

'Sure, why not? I think we trust each other now, don't we?'

'I hope so,' she said slowly. She had, after all, slept well; but there had been a dream in which Dunleavy and Besser had stood side by side at the top of a long flight of stairs and beckoned her, both of them smiling with all the friendliness in the world, smiles that she had trusted; she had been halfway up the stairs when she had woken. She gazed steadily at one of the smiling men now. 'Last night – ?'

'I meant what I said. I *had* to say it – just for the record, if you like. If you leave here in the next couple of days, I'd never be able to write and tell you how I felt. And so I'd have been stuck with it for the rest of my life, like something in my throat I couldn't cough up.'

'You mean love is phlegm?' But she smiled, put her hand on his. 'Matt – Matthew –'

'Take your pick. My mother used to call me Matthew when I'd get in her hair.'

'In her hair?'

'Annoy her. I'm going to have to teach you English.'

'I know so little about you. Or America, either.'

'Both of us can be learned – me and America. You might never know everything about either of us – but will I ever know everything about you? Does anyone ever know everything about another person? The person without mystery can be pretty dull. Am I dull?'

'No, I don't find you dull at all.'

He grinned. 'That's enough encouragement for now. Okay, we'll take you over to the camp. Charlie and I have to go into La Spezia. But first I've got to see the Contessa.'

The four British soldiers had departed early, driving away in the abandoned taxi. That left only Dunleavy, Luise, Charlie Lincoln, the Contessa and the two servants in the villa; Dunleavy felt they could be rattled around in the big house like dice in a box. He hoped for a lucky throw, one that would give him Luise.

The Contessa was not yet downstairs and Dunleavy went up to her bedroom and knocked on the door. She answered his knock, asked him to wait and it was five minutes before she opened the door. She was in a dressing gown, but her hair had been done and her face made up. But she had not had time to fit herself into her corset and he was embarrassedly aware of all the flesh loosely contained in the worn silk dressing gown.

He apologized for disturbing her and she waved a naked hand; the plump fingers showed the marks where the rings had been. 'Major Dunleavy, I am your prisoner –'

He shook his head. 'Not mine, Contessa. I'm about the only one around here whose prisoner you're not.'

Working hurriedly, she had put on too much make-up: the powder cracked as her brow furrowed. 'I don't understand –'

'Don't play dumb, Contessa.' Last night he had been courteous and friendly; but this morning he had to go back to playing provost marshal, being a cop again. 'Major Shell is interested in you. So is Lieutenant Taviani, even though he didn't seem too enthusiastic about it. Then there's *Bricha* – they're not going to be happy about you two-timing them, sharing your premises with Nazis. And last of all – and I'll bet not least – there are the Nazis. You've got jailers north, south, east and west of you, ma'am.'

'What are you then?'

'I could be your legal adviser, sort of.'

The Contessa had not got out of the chorus at La Scala and as far as this by turning a blind mascara'd eye to hints. She had had to take advantage of every opportunity; her one compulsion was to survive, preferably in the best of circumstances.

269

A hand strayed of its own accord down over her body, as if searching for the slim girl underneath who might have had less serious problems but much less reward. If she were still that girl she might have been able to make another start. But not now: fat middle-aged widows in defeated countries had to be practical.

'What would you advise, major?'

'Just sit tight till I get back. Don't attempt to get in touch with anyone. Take a lesson from Sweden and Switzerland – the only countries in Europe right now without any real problems are the neutrals. Be neutral, Contessa. At least till I'm on my way back to Germany.'

'I was always neutral,' she said candidly. 'If that means being interested only in my own survival.'

He had to smile at her honesty. 'You'll survive, ma'am. Your sort always do.'

When he went back downstairs Luise was waiting in the jeep with Charlie Lincoln. As he got in, Giulio came down the steps, coughed nervously, looked back up at the villa to see if his mistress was watching him.

'Herr Major? Did you tell the Contessa I told you about the Germans?'

'No, Giulio.' Dunleavy recognized someone else who was interested only in survival; if he lost his job there would be nowhere else to go. 'There's no need for her to know where I got the information. You're safe.'

The old man smiled gratefully. 'You are a kind man, sir.'

'Am I?' Dunleavy looked at Luise.

'Yes.'

Dunleavy nodded doubtfully, wondering if kindness, in certain circumstances, was a weakness. 'Giulio, be my watcher.' He didn't have enough German words, wasn't sure how many Giulio had; but he didn't want Luise to translate for him, he knew the old man wanted the direct contact between them. 'If any strangers come, tell me when I come back.'

'Yes, Herr Major.'

A new signpost had been put up at the junction of the roads above the village, pointing the way to Sarzana; the war was

270

over, the enemy no longer had to be confused. Charlie Lincoln took the jeep up over the ridge behind Lerici, bowled down the road between steep hills on which villages broke the skyline like friezes chipped out of the yellow rock.

'Did you sleep well, Charlie?'

'I always sleep well, major. Ever since I got into this man's army, got m'self three squares a day and a pay cheque, I been sleeping like a baby.'

'Even the nights before you went into action?'

'I never been in any action, major. They drafted me, they didn't say I gotta fight – I don't remember 'em saying that specifically. So I always volunteered for the back areas, the rear echelon. I like that rear echelon bit – it's got class.'

'Another survivor.' Charlie looked blank, but Dunleavy did not enlighten him. He looked back at Luise. 'That's how we won the war.'

'The best way,' said Luise.

They dropped her at the gate to the camp, an old army establishment from which the homeless in bombed-out La Spezia had been evicted to make room for the homeless foreigners. Surly Italian soldiers lounged about outside the perimeter, uninterested in the hundreds of Jews on the other side of the barbed wire. Two carabinieri stood at the main gate, equally bored. The British corporal who came forward was the only man who didn't look fed up, but his interest was aroused by the sight of the pretty girl getting out of the Yank jeep.

'Miss Graz is an UNRRA welfare officer from my area,' said Dunleavy, ignoring the looks Luise and Charlie Lincoln gave him. 'I've seen Major Shell about her. She has his permission to talk to some of the DPs who were brought in last night.'

'You have a pass, miss?'

'We left it at headquarters last night,' said Dunleavy. 'I'm on my way in to pick it up now. But to save time maybe Miss Graz can start talking to those people while I'm gone. They'll be going back to my area in Germany in a couple of days. See you later, Miss Graz.'

He nodded to Charlie and the latter caught the hint: they

drove off before the corporal could raise any objections. A hundred yards down the road, when he looked back, Dunleavy saw that Luise and the corporal had disappeared into the camp.

'Those DPs really going all the way back to Garmisch, major? Jesus, what a life!'

'Somehow I think they'll get where they're intending to go. Whatever is going to happen to them, they know the worst is behind 'em.'

Major Shell, looking a little fresher than last night, was in his office when Dunleavy walked in. 'I went for a swim this morning. Just like the cold showers they used to make us take when I was at school – makes the mind sharp and pure at the expense of one's privates. Can an emasculated moralist offer you a cup of tea?'

'I'm sorry about your balls. Sorry about your morals, too. I'm looking for a practical-minded son-of-a-bitch this morning.'

'Try me. The circulation is coming back into the affected parts. I think I once read there's no morality in the blood.'

'Who said that – Shelley?'

'Probably his chum Byron. What's on your mind, Matthew? I take it this is going to be a man-to-man, first-name talk?'

Dunleavy sat down, looked around the cheerless office. 'Do you enjoy all this?'

'That's a stupid question, Matthew.'

'Matt. The other sounds too biblical. Look, Pete –'

'Peter.' Shell smiled. 'I don't mind the biblical touch – especially since we're dealing with Palestine, even if at a distance. Upon this rock Westminster will build its policy ... Though I must say the rock is coming close to crumbling.'

'That's what I'm hoping – that you're crumbling, I mean. Look, last night you said it would be a relief to have even one DP taken off your back. I'll take all those others off you, too, the ones from Garmisch.'

'What will you do with them?'

'You give me the papers and I'll see they get back to Camp 93. I don't think they want to be shoved into *any* camp.'

'I can't supply you with any transport. I was going to send them all back by train.'

272

'I can get transport. There must be guys around here who'd take on the job. I'll only need one truck and some chits from you, so we can pick up gasoline along the way at your supply dumps. I'll pay for the truck, but I think the British Army ought to pick up the tab for the gas.'

'You won't pay for the truck out of your own pocket?' Shell could never contain his amazement at the way Americans threw their money around.

'Uncle Sam will pick up the tab eventually. There are ways and means of being reimbursed.'

Shell nodded, pleased to see an American who was not too profligate, at least not with his own money. He opened a drawer in his desk, took out two sheets of paper, handed the top one to Dunleavy. 'Camp 93, Ulmburg, Garmisch Partenkirchen. Twelve bods, including the rather attractive one of Miss Graz. I got all the particulars last night, just in case. There's your movement order. I was hoping you'd ask.'

'Only two copies? In our army we got to have five at least, sometimes six or seven.'

'In five, ten years' time, who'll be reading it all? I told you, I'm fighting the day when there'll be a paper shortage.'

'What if I lose my copy? Or you lose yours?'

'Exactly,' said Shell. 'What?'

Dunleavy stood up, folded the movement order, put it away in his tunic pocket. He and Shell walked out into the bright Italian morning, smiling at each other, conspirators in the Italian style, allies whose alliance had nothing to do with what their governments had decided. Each man, without telling the other, felt lighter in heart. A funeral went by, the black plumes bobbing on the horses adding a dark gaiety that contrasted with the grief-bent mourners in the procession. Dunleavy and Shell swallowed their smiles.

'Do you ever envy the dead, Matt?'

'Not so far. But then I don't think I've ever met anyone who died happy.' Mike and Mary Dunleavy certainly hadn't. And he didn't think Roy, knowing his job had not been completed, would have been happy to die at the moment he had. 'Do you envy them?'

'Not really. I'm a cynic who, unfortunately, happens to be afflicted by hope. Dreadful split in one's character. Oh, I forgot to tell you – we picked up the owner of the taxi out at the villa. Chap named Ricci.'

'What'd he have to say?'

'Nothing. One always tends to think of Italians as garrulous. They can be as close-mouthed as anyone. But we found out where he spent his off-work hours. A bar not far from here, up near the station. We've closed it down – for the time being. Eventually, of course, we'll have to let Ricci go and let them open the bar again. But we've put the wind up them – and the Nazis, too, I should hope. That's all I need to make me wish for the graveyard – half a dozen wanted Nazis on top of the two or three hundred Jews I have.' He shook hands, his grip firm. 'If you should lose your friends, do me a favour. Don't lose them in my area.'

'If I do, I'll eat the movement order. Good luck in India.'

'I'll probably need it. Awfully nice knowing you. Oh, there are a couple of brothers named Giuffre – they have a garage out on the road near the shipyards. They hire out their truck occasionally, and don't ask questions so long as the money is negotiable. Say I sent you. Then they'll raise their price only a hundred per cent instead of two hundred. The victor in war always pays through the nose.'

'Shelley?'

'Shell,' said Shell. 'When are you leaving?'

'This afternoon, I hope. I'll come through town and pick up the gasoline chits, okay? Can I draw rations for them out at the camp?'

'Why not? I feel I'm getting rid of them cheaply. I hope our Foreign Secretary, Mr Bevin, appreciates it. I often wonder what he has against the Jews.'

On the way out of town Dunleavy stopped off at the Giuffre garage, made a deal with the brothers that made him wonder who indeed had won the war. They wanted an immediate deposit, but he told them they would get it when he came by this afternoon to pick up the truck and whichever brother would be driving it.

Dunleavy got back into the jeep. 'Charlie, I think those two guys are the James brothers.'

'Jesse and Frank? Major, didn't you know – Europe is fulla outlaws like them. There ain't nothing we can teach 'em. Guys like them two Wops gonna get rich much quicker'n you and me.'

When they came into Lerici they had to slow to skirt the crowded market in the piazza. People looked at them curiously, wondering what Americans were still doing in the area; some of the young men shouted at them, showing off their colloquialisms. One older man, the sort who always had to out-do the younger ones, stepped right in front of the jeep and shouted with a wide grin, 'Twenty-one skidoo!'

Charlie looked blankly at Dunleavy. 'Twenty-one skidoo? What the hell's that?'

'I think it's twenty-three skidoo. I heard it when I was a kid, in a Clara Bow movie.'

'Who was Clara Bow?'

Then Giulio appeared beside the jeep, running alongside it on legs that threatened to collapse at any moment. Charlie eased the jeep to a halt and at once the crowd closed in on them, everyone ready to hear what was exciting Giulio. The old man leaned against the side of the jeep gasping for breath.

'The woman, major –!'

The crowd pressed in even closer, faces and ears wide open. Dunleavy pulled Giulio into the back of the jeep, nodded to Charlie to get moving again. The crowd, disappointed, fell back, shouting their borrowed slang again, some of it obscene. The relic from the Twenties slapped Dunleavy on the back, raised the ante: 'Thirty-one skidoo, old buddy!'

When they were out of the piazza and Giulio had got his breath back, Dunleavy told Charlie to pull up. 'Okay, what's the matter, Giulio? What woman?'

'The German woman, the one who stayed at the house last night –'

'Frau Besser?'

Giulio shrugged: he never knew, never wanted to know, the names of any of them. 'She was with the German and the two

275

children – they were a family. I saw her shopping in the village.'

'Where is she now?'

'I followed her. She and the man and the boys are in the Villa Indira on the Fiascherino road.'

Dunleavy was about to ask the old man why he was telling him this; then stopped himself. He would be gone from here this afternoon, he hoped; tomorrow at the latest. Giulio's eager proffering of his information might be no more than a simple attempt to ingratiate himself; or it could be some trick on the part of the Contessa. In any event Dunleavy knew he could not turn his back on what the old man had told him. He had come all this way chasing a man who had killed two Americans; he could not say it was none of his business when he was told of a man who had killed hundreds of Jews. He was being educated in the unlimited magnitude of crime. As Charlie had said, there was nothing they could teach the Europeans.

'Okay, take us there, Giulio.'

They parked the jeep in a side lane a hundred yards short cf the Villa Indira and walked the rest of the way. Dunleavy took off his cap, jacket and tie, left them with Charlie; then, hoping he might pass for a local workman, he moved down with Giulio through the neighbouring olive groves parallel to the villa. They came to the edge of a cliff, the sea suddenly opening up before them beyond a thin screen of oleanders. The first thing Dunleavy saw, far out at sea, were two warships, grey jackals waiting for the DPs' ship to come out of the gulf.

'There they are,' said Giulio, uninterested in the larger scene, and pointed down to the tiny beach half-hidden beneath the headland.

The four people sat on the pebbled strand, picnicking. The man and the boys looked to be in their undershorts; their skins were as white as their pants. The woman sat against a rock, her face turned up to the sun. The man raised a bottle of wine, saluted his wife and drank from it. One of the boys, his meal finished, stood up, began to skim pebbles out over the water, shouting with proud delight as one bounced several times before finally sinking. The woman stood up, began to tidy up

276

the remains of their picnic. The man lay back soaking up the sun.

'You're sure that's the man, Giulio?' It was impossible to imagine what a mass murderer should look like.

'Certain, Herr Major. They came to the villa last night with the taxi driver Ricci. He has brought other Germans.'

Dunleavy pondered a moment, ashamed of the scheme that was forming in his mind. Two days in Italy and already his mind was working like that of – Machiavelli, was that the guy? 'Stay here, Giulio, watch them. If they come up from the beach, go out on to the road, just sit there – they won't take any notice of an old man sitting in the sun. I'll be back in a little while.'

'Where are you going?'

'To the Contessa.' Dunleavy watched the old man carefully.

'She doesn't know!' Giulio was suddenly scared, his fear naked and innocent; Dunleavy knew then that the old man was no party to one of the Contessa's tricks. 'That was why I waited for you in the village –'

'Don't worry, Giulio. I'll tell her I discovered them myself – I bumped into you and asked you to keep watch for me.'

The old man nodded, but still looked apprehensive. Jobs were hard to come by, and Il Duce was no longer alive to look after the poor.

Dunleavy went back up to the jeep, took his cap, jacket and tie from Charlie but didn't put them on. The sun was warm, but he was also sweating from excitement.

'What we gonna do, major?'

We: Dunleavy felt an unaccountable reassurance from the young soldier's commitment. 'Charlie, I'm gonna be a son-of-a-bitch.'

Charlie Lincoln waited for the son-of-a-bitch to elaborate. Then, when no more was forthcoming, he said, 'Sometimes there ain't no other way, major.'

'Maybe,' said Dunleavy, not convinced, though he wanted to be.

When they reached the Villa Fontana the Contessa was standing on the terrace looking up at the villa's façade, faded and ravaged by the syphilis of time and war. 'I think I shall sell it and go back to Milan. Giulio can make a start on cleaning up the gardens today, then I shall find a buyer –'

'A good idea,' said Dunleavy. 'Make a clean break. But before you do –'

He led her into the house, telling her he had found the Bessers. 'I want you to bring them back here, Contessa –'

'I can't!' Her fear was as expressive as Giulio's had been; but she had more than a job to lose. 'The Jews would kill me!'

'Sure,' said Dunleavy matter-of-factly. 'But I'm not going to tell them and I'm sure you won't. All you have to do is co-operate with me.'

She squinted at him, suspicion making her plain, almost ugly. But she could not resist listening to a proposition: her life was milestoned by them. 'How?'

'Where's Giulio?' he asked innocently; she shook her head. 'Okay, I'll find him. I want him to go to the Bessers, tell them that you want them to come back here, that the British have gone and everything will be safe till you get in touch with your German contacts.'

'I don't know any contacts. Signor Ricci was the man who came to me.'

'Major Shell picked up Ricci during the night, so you don't have to worry about *him* coming back. I'll tell Giulio to tell Besser what's happened to Ricci. That'll make him feel isolated, maybe convince him you're the only one he can turn to.'

'Perhaps he won't risk it?'

'He doesn't have much choice, unless he goes all the way back to his last contact, wherever that was. Merano, I think.'

'What are you going to do with him?'

'I don't think you need to know that. You just think about selling the villa and going back to Milan.'

'What if the Jews come back while he's here?'

'They won't,' he lied.

'I'm not sure it is safe –'

'Contessa,' he said with cold impatience; he was past arguing with her now, 'you're like Besser, you've got no choice. You've

two-timed everyone but the Pope, and maybe him, too. It's
about time you started paying a debt or two.'

'What do I owe you, major?' There was still spirit left in her.

'You may owe me your life, Contessa.'

He and Charlie went back in the jeep along the Fiascherino
road. They pulled up in the side lane again and Giulio, who
had been sitting with his back to a wall up near the Villa Indira,
came trotting down to them.

'Herr Major, they are up in the house now. They look as if
they are going to stay there, perhaps till tonight.'

Dunleavy explained to Giulio what he wanted him to do. The
old man squeezed his face with his hand, wrinkling it with
doubt and apprehension.

'What if he attacks me? He may not believe me.'

'We'll be watching, Giulio. If he attacks you, Private Lincoln
and I will come running. But I'm sure he will believe you – you
have an honest face.'

The old man grinned: he knew the truth of himself. 'I am
also a very good liar.'

He went away up the road, only once glancing back, as if to
make sure that Dunleavy and Charlie were not driving away
out of the lane and leaving him to face the fury of a German who
might kill him.

He went in the front gate of the villa and Charlie Lincoln
then backed the jeep further down the lane and into the gateway
of another empty villa. Dunleavy got out, went some way up the
lane, climbed a wall and sat down against its base beneath the
shadow of an olive tree. Through the grove he could see the
road and the occasional truck or car as it passed. The air was
perfectly still and somewhere there was the faint chirping of
a bird, like a nervous tic of the silence itself.

It was ten minutes before Giulio appeared in the roadway
and by then Dunleavy had begun to sweat. The old man came
walking down the road ahead of the Besser family, looking
back at them and urging them on with a snap of his hand, as
if trying to convince them they were doing the right thing by
following him back to the Villa Fontana.

2

'Our ship isn't in La Spezia harbour,' said Keppel. 'That is the *Fede* and we were never intended to go on that. Ours is in a small cove down near Bocca di Magra. The English warships are so busy watching the *Fede* they haven't noticed ours yet.'

'What sort of ship is it?' asked Joachim Winter.

'A fishing trawler. It will only take a hundred and twenty of us and we're going to be packed tighter than the fish ever were.'

'When does it sail?' said Simon Berger.

'It goes tonight, with or without us. The other groups are already on it – they went on early this morning, when they came down out of the hills. They are just waiting for dark and then the captain says he is taking her out. He can do no more than eight or ten knots and he wants to be past Livorno before dawn. That gives him no more than eight or nine hours of darkness.'

Everyone looked at Luise. They were all gathered in a corner of the camp; the familiar spiky buds of barbed wire blossomed above them. The men squatted on the rough stony ground, idly scratching patterns on it with sticks or rusted bolts. The women sat on the rough blocks of concrete that are part of the Italian urban landscape, like fragments of ruins ready-made for the future. The sun beat down with an intensity that belied the season, spring disguised as summer. It was a foretaste of what Palestine would be like.

'How do we get out of here?' Luise said.

'I got in here easily enough,' said Keppel. 'The Italian soldiers don't care about us.'

'All right, so we all get out without trouble. But how far is it to the ship?'

'Fifteen kilometres, perhaps a little more.'

'Ben – ' Luise stopped for a moment, knowing how pessimistic and unconstructive she must sound. 'Ben, we can't expect the children to walk all that way. They'd never make it in time, not over those hills.'

'We'll carry them,' said Joachim Winter and looked at the men who had neither children nor wives. They all nodded, even David Weill who looked as if he would have difficulty in getting just himself over the hills to the waiting ship.

'We can't let them send us back to Germany.' Noah Malchek shaded his eyes against the glare, but it struck him from all angles and he looked bewildered by it. Already his pale scalp had turned pink and he had put a handkerchief over it, adding to his feminine appearance. 'Anything is better than that.'

'I'll walk all the way to Israel if I have to,' said Anna Bork.

Luise smiled at her, certain of the woman's friendship now. 'Across the water? I thought that was only a Christian talent.'

Anna returned the smile: her face looked attractive when she put away her scowl. 'I'll join any faith that will get me to Israel.'

David Weill shook his head in despair at the lightness with which some people took religion. 'That won't do, Frau Bork – we must all be Jews if we are to succeed – '

'I'm Jewish,' said Anna emphatically. 'But I don't need prayers to tell me. The rest of the world will always be ready to let me know what I am.'

'That's what we face if we go back,' said Simon Berger. 'What if they keep us in those camps for another year, two years, five? I'd already begun to feel I was living in another ghetto.'

'We must go,' said Hilde Klein and Judith Winter together with the desperation of mothers who saw no other future for their children. They both looked physically and emotionally exhausted, ready to surrender themselves. But they could not surrender their children: that would reduce all the past years of suffering and degradation to nothing. 'We'll get to the ship somehow.'

'I'll get a truck,' said Keppel. 'We'll need it if you are to take your baggage, too.'

'Oh, we take that!' Anna Bork almost shouted: she couldn't arrive in Israel empty-handed.

'How long will it take you to get a truck?' Luise said. 'If we do have to walk, we'll have to leave very soon. With the children and the baggage, we shan't average much better than three or four kilometres an hour. With rests, that means about five hours. What's the time now?'

'Twelve-thirty,' said Noah Malchek.

Ben Keppel stood up, suddenly looking young again and defeated. 'Then there isn't time for me to go looking for a truck. If I didn't get one, we'd have lost valuable time.'

'Unless we started off on our own – ' Luise also stood up, feeling positive again; depression dropped from her, like the small pool of shadow at her feet. A part of her mind was sufficiently detached to remark the irony that it was her father, the Gentile, the Aryan, in her, who was giving her strength. Her mother, who for so long had done her best to forget she was Jewish, had bequeathed her only the worst of Jewish traits, pessimism. 'Tell us the way to go, Ben, and we can get started. If you find a truck, you can pick us up along the road.'

Keppel produced a map, showed the route they should take. 'You'll have to slip out in pairs, the way you did at Ulmburg. There's a gate at the other end of camp, opens out into a lane. There's a guard there, an Italian, but some money or a packet of cigarettes will get him to wander away. The problem is getting your baggage through the camp down to the gate. If the English see you –'

'We'll have to leave it then,' said Simon Berger, who long ago had lost any feeling for possessions.

'It would just hinder us.' David Weill needed only his shawl and his book, the baggage of the devout: the Lord would provide, one trusted in Him.

'Horseshit,' said Anna. The other women had gone and she could speak frankly, man to man; she seemed to take it for granted that Luise would not be offended. The men looked at Luise, embarrassed, but she turned and gazed down towards the end of the camp, as if she hadn't heard Anna. 'We need our things. We have to show when we land in Israel that we've brought something besides just ourselves, that we intend to contribute.'

'We can contribute with these.' Weill turned over a pair of pale soft hands.

Anna laughed, careless of other people's feelings, especially men's, when the truth was needed. 'They're only good for praying, Herr Professor. You couldn't make one good fist out of both of them.'

'I wasn't intending to fight anyone,' said Weill mildly. 'I hope all that is behind us.'

Luise turned back. 'No baggage. I'm sorry, Anna – ' She made her voice soft and pleading; she knew she was going to need Anna Bork on the rest of the journey. The rough peasant woman had become the one she found herself turning to, even more so than to Simon Berger, the strongest of the men. 'If you think you can smuggle out your case without being seen, well and good. But the rest of us will have to go without our things.'

Anna nodded, mollified. She tried to sound amenable, but the soft voice was not her sound: it came out as just as a rough mutter. 'I'll be careful. Trust me.'

Keppel folded up the map, handed it to Luise. 'I'll pick you up in an hour, either on foot or with a truck.'

'How's your leg?'

He still limped, but not so much. 'It gets better the closer we get to Israel.'

'Will you be happy there? I think you enjoy all this – getting people past the English, risking being caught – ' He said nothing and she knew she had guessed the truth. He wanted life to be a series of journeys, he needed risk and uncertainty like a drug. 'Take care, Ben.'

They had walked away from the others. Some of the men from the groups who had been rounded up yesterday were playing *boccie* with a couple of the Italian soldiers; the wooden balls clicked together with a sound like that of knocking bones; there were skeletons at the game, but the players turned a deaf ear to them. Luise and Keppel passed by the men, who all looked carefree, as if nothing but the result of the game concerned them. Then one of the men caught Keppel's eye, winked and nodded, his face sobering. There were still secrets, determinations, behind the apparent laughing resignation.

'I'd like to take care of the Contessa,' said Keppel. 'When you told us all about Besser being in her house – *at the same time as us –* ' He darkened with anger, as if a cloud had passed over the sun; the balls clicked-clicked loudly behind them. 'She should be punished.'

'How?' But Luise didn't press the question; without seeing it, she knew Keppel still had his gun. 'Besser is the one who should be punished. But he's gone now – ' She was amazed at the chagrin in her voice: she sounded as bitter and angry as Keppel.

Then Hilde Klein came running up to them, thin legs twinkling like a child's but her face old and worried. 'Major Dunleavy is at the front gate – with a truck and papers! He is taking us back to Germany – *now!*'

Keppel cursed, unmindful of the two women. 'You'll have to stall him! Tell our people to lose themselves somewhere in the camp!'

'It's no use, Ben.' Luise felt sick; she had trusted Dunleavy and he had betrayed them. 'This camp isn't built for hiding in, they'd find us all in ten minutes. You'd better go, make sure you get away yourself. Where will you be, just in case we get rid of Major Dunleavy?'

'There's an empty guest-house in the grounds of the Contessa's villa – I stayed there last night. But I'll wait outside the camp, see if he does take you away.'

'I'll try and talk him out of it.' But Luise knew she sounded hopeless. 'Frau Klein, get everyone together. Bring them to the front gate. Tell them not to try anything foolish until we see exactly what Major Dunleavy has in mind.'

Hilde Klein went running away and Keppel said, 'Give him no concessions. You can't trust any of them.'

'If we don't see you again – good luck, Ben. Perhaps – next year in Jerusalem.'

He melted away, the glare and the crowd combining to absorb him. She had a last glimpse of his angry disappointed face, a boy destined for defeats. She felt sorry for him, wished that she had some of his fierce devotion. Then she turned and walked towards the front gate and Dunleavy, already prepared to compromise.

Dunleavy and Charlie Lincoln stood by their jeep. Behind them were a ramshackle truck and its young driver in oil-stained trousers and a clean white shirt. Hilde Klein had collected the rest of the group, except for the children, and they stood in a tight circle around Dunleavy.

'Miss Graz – ' He smiled at her, formal and polite. She nodded, suspicious of his official manner. 'I've just been telling the others – Major Shell has given me permission to take you all back to Camp 93. I thought you'd prefer that to being shoved off to any old camp.'

'If we can't go to Israel, we'd prefer to stay here,' Luise said, and the others muttered agreement.

'I'm afraid the English won't agree to that. You have no alternative to this.' He slapped the single sheet of paper he held.

'We do have an alternative – '

'Don't tell him!' Anna Bork guessed what she had in mind. 'You can't trust any of them!'

'We have to trust *someone*, Anna. As the major says, our only alternative is going back to Germany. Who wants that?'

She looked around her and everyone shook his head. Then Anna said reluctantly, 'Then don't tell him too much.'

'We have a ship waiting for us,' Luise said to Dunleavy.

'The one out in the gulf? Not a chance.'

She shook her head. 'Another one, somewhere else. If we can get to it by nightfall, we shall be gone from here, no more worry for Major Shell, by daylight tomorrow.'

Dunleavy looked around the group. 'How will you get to this ship?'

She said boldly, trusting him completely now, 'You could take us in your truck.'

There was a gasp from some of the group at her risking so much. Those that didn't understand English looked at those who did, guessing they were being endangered.

Dunleavy said nothing. The rest of the camp had gathered in the background, their resentment silent but apparent. The Italian soldiers and carabinieri stood off to one side, being as obviously neutral as they could be. The English corporal and another soldier had come out of the gatehouse, but they had not approached. The corporal could see the Yank had some sort of problem, but he was not paid to take on any more problems than he had; and he had enough, three hundred of the buggers all standing there ready to start a bloody riot. For the present he wanted to be nothing more than a spectator.

Dunleavy put the movement order away in his shirt pocket, buttoning the flap. Luise felt a lift of joy: he was on their side! Then he said, 'I've got a proposition.'

He addressed them all and it was David Weill who answered for them. 'A proposition, Herr Major? But we have nothing to bargain with.'

'Yes, you have. I want Ben Keppel. I know he's around here somewhere. He's been in touch with you, otherwise you wouldn't know where that ship is.'

'What's your proposition?' Luise was suddenly cold. 'Ben Keppel for the use of your truck and our freedom? Is that what you mean?'

'That, plus a bonus,' said Dunleavy. 'I know where Besser is. You can have him, too. All I want is Keppel.'

'We don't know where Herr Keppel is,' Luise said abruptly.

'Just a moment!' Noah Malchek took the handkerchief off his head, all at once business-like and not prepared to dismiss a proposition out of hand. 'You really know where Besser is? I don't care, myself. But if he *is* your bonus, then some of us might be interested in your proposition.' He spoke in German to the others.

'I'd give anything to get my hands on him!' Anna Bork's hands came up in front of her, ready for strangling.

'I owe him to my wife and kids,' said Simon Berger, and for the first time Luise saw him frail and vulnerable; he began to sweat, his face shining as if he were starting a fever. 'We can't let the bastard escape!'

'What's escape?' David Weill spread his hands, one of them clutching his prayer book. 'You think he can forget what he's done? He must go to bed each night with a hundred thousand ghosts haunting him. Who knows, perhaps six million.'

'Not him!' Anna Bork looked around the small circle, beyond

286

it, as if looking for Besser so that she could kill him *now*. 'Tell the major he can have Ben Keppel – '

'No!'

Everyone looked at Luise and Hilde Klein said, 'I agree with Fräulein Graz. I want to go to Israel, to take my children there. My husband – ' Her voice faltered. Standing in the blazing sun, she felt the chill of the mountain pass where Michael Klein would lie forever, never seeing the dream. 'He wanted the children to go there. But not if we have to sacrifice anyone. Not Ben Keppel.'

'What about Besser?' Simon Berger persisted. 'He killed my wife and children. You have your kids – I have nothing – '

Charlie Lincoln, not understanding enough German, looked at Dunleavy and saw the unexpected agony the major was trying to hide. Dunleavy was not catching every word that was being said, but he knew enough and the words he caught were hurting.

'I don't care about Besser,' said Judith Winter. 'All I care about is getting *my* children away from Europe, to Israel. If Ben Keppel is the price, then the major can have him.'

'Where is he?' said Dunleavy in German, but his voice was tight and strained, as if something, decency or conscience, had closed his throat.

'I think we should vote.' David Weill put his hands together, looked ready to pray. 'But why anyone should vote on a man's life – ?'

'It is our lives, too,' said Noah Malchek. 'If Ben Keppel had asked us about killing those two Americans, we'd have stopped him. But he didn't ask *us* for a vote.'

'Vote,' said Dunleavy in English; and Charlie Lincoln, alert now to the pain in the man, heard the silent *For Christ's sake!*

Luise said, 'All those for giving up Ben Keppel?'

Four hands went up: Anna Bork, Judith Winter, Noah Malchek and Simon Berger each for his or her own reasons gave up Keppel. None of them looked at each other or at the other four Jews: they all stared at Dunleavy, as if they felt he was the only one who would not condemn them.

287

Luise looked around at David Weill, Hilde Klein and Joachim Winter. 'Do we protect Ben?'

Weill and Hilde Klein nodded. Joachim Winter looked at his wife for forgiveness. 'I'm sorry,' he told her, then looked at Luise and nodded.

'Four to four,' said Luise and turned to Dunleavy. 'I'm afraid this time the deciding vote is yours, major.'

Get out of that, Charlie Lincoln told the major.

'Herr Keppel can be picked up easily enough,' Luise went on. 'But I shan't ride in your truck – not to the ship nor to where Dr Besser can be found. I'd rather be sent back to Germany.'

'I, too,' said David Weill.

'And I,' said Hilde Klein, on the verge of tears for what she was sacrificing. She looked around for her two girls, for Rebecca who, when she was older, might ask questions that would have the hurt of a knife.

Joachim Winter moved closer to Judith, put out his hand. She hesitated, then took it. They stood close together, two thin figures throwing a single shadow; somewhere behind the still watching crowd a child shrieked with pleasure in some game. Joachim lifted his wife's hand, pressed his lips to her knuckles, was about to surrender.

But Dunleavy, bitterly moved, feeling that in some way he was betraying Roy but unable to avoid it, surrendered first. 'I don't want to know where Keppel is. I'll take you to the ship. And you can have Besser if you want him. No charge.'

Then the British corporal, sensing that something was brewing here that might blow up in his face later, at last came across to them. 'You having trouble, sir?'

'Just a discussion, corporal. Everybody has decided to accept the move back to Germany. I'll take them out now, try and get as far as Genoa by dark.'

'You'd do better if you head towards Reggio, sir,' said the corporal, glad to be rid of even a few of his charges. 'It's a straight run north once you get over the mountains.'

'I'll do that, corporal. Can I draw some rations?'

'We're a bit light on, sir. Will three days be enough for you?'

'Okay?' Dunleavy looked at Luise.

'Everything will be welcome,' she said smiling at the irony, hoping the corporal would never be blamed for what he was unwittingly doing.

The corporal whistled up the second British soldier and an Italian. The children were rounded up, the group's luggage collected, everybody and everything was loaded aboard the ramshackle truck. The driver stood by, unhelpful, careful of his clean white shirt, once running an unnecessary comb through his immaculate hair. The crowd had not moved from the background but its sullen resentment had disappeared from its collective face: the whisper had gone through it, last night's newcomers were on their way to Israel. As the last of the group climbed aboard the truck a voice suddenly rang out in Hebrew: 'Next year in Jerusalem!'

Anna Bork and the others stood at the back of the truck as it went out the gates. Dunleavy and Luise, each silently wary of the other, rode in the front of the truck with the driver. Charlie Lincoln brought up the rear in the jeep. The two vehicles drove out of the gates, turned towards the north.

'I thought you said you would take us to the ship? It's south of here!'

'Relax.' Dunleavy didn't mean to sound sour; his tongue was still tasting the callousness of what he had attempted back at the camp. 'I can't head *south* now, not when we're supposed to be heading north for Germany. Tell Angelo where you want to go. He'll find a way of getting there.'

Luise, squeezed in between him and the driver, found it difficult to look squarely at Dunleavy. She stared straight ahead, wanting to thank him for what he was now doing for them; but the memory of what he had tried to do back at the camp kept her silent. He had been prepared to trade in human feelings, all in the cause of what he would call justice.

She took out the map Keppel had given her, showed it to Angelo Giuffre. He looked at it, frowned in puzzlement, then swung the truck sharply into the side of the road in a cloud of dust. There was a screech of brakes from behind as Charlie Lincoln just managed to avoid running into the back of the

289

truck. Anna Bork yelled and someone beat with his fist on the back of the cabin.

Angelo had said nothing from the moment he had driven the truck into the camp almost half an hour ago. Now, when it looked as if he was going to be cheated out of a profitable deal, he became terribly voluble, shouting across Luise at Dunleavy.

'He says you promised to pay him so much for taking us to Germany,' Luise translated. 'He says he is not interested in small deals like this, it isn't worth his while. He says he'll report you to the police and the English for trying to swindle him.'

'Good old Jesse James.'

'What?'

'Nothing.' Dunleavy looked across her at Angelo. 'Tell him that if he doesn't want to finish up in jail for profiteering and black marketing, he'll do what I tell him and he'll take what I pay him. It won't be what he'd have got for taking us to Germany, but I won't gyp him.'

'Are you sure he's been profiteering and dealing in the black market?'

'Major Shell knows about his profiteering. So do I – he took me on the deal I made with him. I'll take a risk on the black marketing. Any guy with his knack for gypping strangers wouldn't pass up any chance of making a buck, legitimate or otherwise.'

Luise conveyed Dunleavy's threat to Angelo Giuffre. He glowered, chewed on the words he still had stored up, some of them coming out as a dribble down one corner of his mouth. Then he snarled something and Luise translated. 'He wants to know how much for today's job?'

'Tell him I'll give him fifty dollars.'

'Fifty dollars! That's far too much.'

'Look, who's paying?' They were like husband and wife arguing about how much to tip a taxi driver. 'If I give him fifty, he'll know it's more than the job's worth. It'll help him keep his mouth shut, at least for a day or two. By then you'll be out at sea, on your way to Palestine.'

Luise made Angelo the offer and with a grunt he subsided. He rudely took the map from her, looked at the spot she pointed to, then shoved it back at her. He started up the truck again, drove on for a mile or so, then turned up a narrow side road that led towards the hills hiding the sea.

They passed no other vehicles on the road. Once they had to slow to move through a grazing herd of goats. A boy lay against a rock and gazed after them with a blank stare on his dream-bound face, as if their passing had not disturbed his siesta. The truck climbed a series of S-bends, groaning and wheezing, Angelo working hard on the loose clutch and the even looser gear lever; everything in the truck seemed ready to fall apart, and Luise wondered if they would have made it to Germany if they had indeed headed north. They came to the top of a ridge and the truck, trembling and gasping like a dying animal, came to a halt. Angelo grunted and pointed.

'It's down there,' Luise said. 'He can't take the truck any further.'

'How much further?'

Luise queried the driver. 'He says two kilometres, no more. We'll have to trust him, I suppose. I can't see the ship from here.'

'They've probably got it tucked close in-shore. Okay, we'll walk from here. But tell him – if he's doublecrossed us, I'll be in to see him this evening and I'll belt the bejesus out of him.'

Everybody got down from the back of the truck, looked around apprehensively as if fearing treachery. They had heard tales of Jews who had been taken to lonely spots in trucks and then massacred; not by Americans or the English, certainly. But the others had also been just ordinary men. Or had posed as men.

'Tell them not to be afraid,' said Dunleavy, feeling the chill of their fear even in the heat of the day. He spoke a little louder, for Charlie Lincoln's benefit: 'I've done my son-of-a-bitch act for the day. They've got nothing to worry about from now on.'

'Except the English.' Luise pointed out to sea and to the north. One could just see the two Royal Navy ships standing off the mouth of the gulf, stuck on shoals of sunlight.

'I can't help you there.'

'You have helped enough,' said Luise and forgave him fully.

Dunleavy paid off Angelo Giuffre and the Italian took his money and his truck back down the road, driving away without a farewell to the Jews or a backward glance. Fifty bucks didn't buy his sympathy, distract him even for the moment from his own problem of making the best living he could.

Charlie Lincoln parked the jeep beneath a solitary olive tree. Then he picked up Hilde Klein's suitcase, took Rebecca by the hand and moved off down the road, following the line of the cliffs. The others fell in behind him, Dunleavy and Luise bringing up the rear. The bright sun pressed down on them all, turning their pallid skins pink and shiny; it bounced back from the yellow earth like a second blow, shutting their eyes. They had forgotten what cold was like.

'It's so hot,' said Judith Winter.

'It will be worse in Israel,' said her husband. 'Or better. I'll be happy to be warm and sweaty for the rest of my life.'

Dunleavy noticed no one was calling it Palestine any more: it had become Israel, the Promised Land was at last in sight. They went down a dip in the rough track and the British warships were lost from view.

'What will you do about Besser?' Luise said.

Dunleavy shrugged. 'What can I do? I don't even know if he's on the Wanted list back in Germany. I can't ask Shell to arrest him, just on the off-chance. Not unless you and the others are prepared to come back and give evidence against him.'

'I want to. He should be punished for what he did – not just to my mother but to all the others. He's not the only one – there were other beasts I remember. But – ' She wondered what compensation revenge would give her. Revenge is sweet, especially for a woman: some poet had said that, probably a man who had felt a woman's retaliation. But she didn't believe it: not for herself. Whatever her reaction, it would not be sweet-tasting: nothing connected with her mother's death, even so long after, would ever have that taste.

She took another tack, wanting to be totally honest with him: 'I hated you back there at Sarzana.'

'I hated myself. But I just couldn't forget Keppel. Or my brother. Even if I weren't a cop, I just couldn't walk away from that.'

'You weren't thinking of revenge?'

'Maybe. But any cop who thinks that just puts cracks in himself. Someone once said that justice is society's vengeance, but I think it's more than that. It's a – a yardstick.'

'What to?'

'I don't know.' He had the small town man's fear of sounding glib. 'Truth and decency, I guess. It's the *means* of justice that sometimes fall down. I wasn't being very decent back there at Sarzana, offering you that deal for Keppel. But I've come a long way for him – '

'And you couldn't stand the thought of failure?'

'It wasn't that. I just can't forgive him for killing someone like my brother. There are a lot more people still in Germany who Roy could have helped – *wanted* to help. I don't know what's going to happen to you all when you get to Palestine, but hard-noses like Keppel will always be a problem for you. If ever you get *Israel* started, you'll need sympathy and support. You got it now, I guess – from everyone except the English. But eventually the world will forget it owes you a living. And guys like Keppel, the hard-noses with a gun, are going to help the world forget.'

'I don't believe in the gun. But it may be necessary in Palestine – if we are to have Israel.'

'I'm not arguing that. But sometimes a little talking does the trick better than a gun. And I think – I *know* – Roy would have listened to some talking that night when Keppel shot him.'

They walked on in silence. The realization slowly began to dawn on her that very soon she would be saying goodbye to him forever. She glanced sideways at him, took in his strong profile and the bulk of his tall strong body. But when she tried to look *inside* him, at the core of him that needed to be known if she were to love him, she failed. She had caught glimpses, even in the conversation they had just had; he was struggling to broaden the vision that his background had for so long limited. When he went back to America, he, too, would be starting a new life: he had told her that. On opposite sides of the world each of them would be stepping into a new world; it would be just as difficult for him, she guessed, as it would be for her. But she needed to know more of him if she was to love him: all she had gleaned from him so far was surface pleasure and only hints of what lay beneath. And felt disappointed, in her own failure to know him more than in his inability to reveal himself. He had tried, exposing himself with that candour some Americans had. But she was still locked in within herself, still trapped in the defence that had kept her sane in Birkenau: never look too deeply into the heart of another.

For his part he could not believe that he was going to lose her, that she was just going to sail out of his life on some broken-down boat for a destination that was a gamble. He felt a fierce urge to hold her and yell at her that she could not go; but that would be too primitive, he told himself, for a girl like her. Every minute he was with her he was aware of the difference in their backgrounds; it didn't deter him but it made him cautious. The speckled fruits of his experience with women told him that love could not be argued intellectually; but it should not be argued with a club, either. All he had to offer her as argument was himself and, like most men, he was inarticulate in the declaration of his virtues. Vices were another thing: they exposed themselves. And he was damned sure she would not fall in love with any of his, whatever they were. He felt utterly depressed, about to lose the only true love of his life.

The track narrowed, began to descend steeply; they saw the ship below them, tucked in beneath the cliffs. *Ship* was too complimentary, Luise thought: that suggested something larger, more substantial than this floating *wreck*. Everybody stopped suddenly and stared down at it, stunned by the sight of what was to take them the rest of the way to Israel, the most dangerous part of their journey.

'Not in *that!*' Anna Bork shouted from the head of the line.

'Ben Keppel said perhaps a hundred and twenty of us.' Noah Malchek shook his head; the handkerchief, which he had re-donned, fluttered as if he had been scalped. 'We'll be hanging over the sides.'

Only the children were excited; even young Ruth Winter, whose coughing, with the warmer weather, had almost stopped. They clapped their hands, chattered among themselves. Until yesterday morning none of them had ever seen the sea; they looked out on the vast shining blue world with awe. And now they were going to ride on it – in a ship!

'Goddam,' said Dunleavy. 'How can they take you in *that?* I wouldn't sail down the North Platte in it.'

Luise didn't ask him what the North Platte was. She was staring down at the fishing trawler, sick again with disappointment and with apprehension. Not for herself: the thought of danger and discomfort to herself no longer occurred to her. But she worried and feared for the others: they did not deserve to have to face this final bitter joke of a test. She looked at David Weill, the man who believed in God, but refrained from asking him what he thought of God now.

The captain of the trawler was waiting on the narrow shingled beach for them. He was a short wiry man with a wall eye and a broken nose that ran askew down his face; one had difficulty in focusing on him. His name was Drumo and he was the first Italian Jew whom Luise and the others had met.

'Don't worry, don't worry.' He spoke English with an American accent, his gestures were Italian: everything about him seemed askew, not just his face. 'I been fishing forty year and never lost a boat.'

'Where did you fish?' Dunleavy felt suddenly responsible for the group; or anyway for Luise.

'Out there.' Drumo waved a vague hand at the sea behind him. 'Don't worry.'

'Have you ever sailed as far as Haifa?' Luise asked.

'Never. But don't worry, don't worry. The sea, she the same wherever, all you gotta do is read her. Don't worry.'

Christ, Dunleavy thought, optimism like that is a crime.

'Where is Signor Keppel?' The captain swivelled his good eye up towards the cliff path.

'He's not coming,' said Luise, careful not to look at Dunleavy.

'Why not?'

'Because I'm here,' said Dunleavy.

'I wonder about you, you know? When I saw you come down the path, I give 'em the signal out on the boat.'

Dunleavy looked out across the fifty yards of water at the trawler. He had seen the people crowded on the deck, like holiday-makers ready for an afternoon's cruise; now he saw the four men lying on the roof of the superstructure, each with a rifle pointed in at the beach. He looked back at Drumo, the optimist who covered at least some of his bets.

'I'm a friend,' he said. 'Don't worry.'

Drumo turned his good eye on Luise. 'He okay? Then why's he stopping Signor Keppel from coming with us?'

'It's a long story,' said Luise. 'I'll tell you on the way to Haifa. When do we sail?'

'Soon's the sun goes down.'

'Do we have to go on board now? I understand we are going to be very crowded.'

'You said it, you gonna be crowded, all right. But don't worry – I aint gonna let any you suffocate or anything like that. But it's better you get aboard. You stay here, everybody else gonna wanna come ashore. Place is gonna look like a goddam picnic park. We better take the bags out first.'

The baggage was put into the skiff drawn up on the beach and a seaman took it out to the trawler. Now that the moment had come for them to take the last step, a curious quiet had come over the group. They looked up and around them, but this tiny cove wasn't Europe: there was nothing here to say farewell to. Not the cities and fields and the mountains they had known, that they wanted to remember. They were saying goodbye to the wreck of a continent, the ruins of a life and a people, their own. But these Italian cliffs, rocky and bare, were as alien to them as the cliffs that would greet them, if they were lucky, almost two thousand miles to the south-east. The beach was a plank between two lives and for the moment they were afraid.

All but Anna Bork. She bustled up to Luise and Dunleavy, eager to go: there was no need to tell her not to worry.

'Goodbye, Herr Major. Thank you for bringing us this far,

As for Besser – ' Something struggled in the broad aggressive face; she was beset by a sense of loss. Her two children were ashes scattered somewhere on the winds of Poland; the monster Besser had scoured her, dried her womb for future births. 'Please see that he is killed.'

'I can't do that,' said Dunleavy, feeling the woman's pain as if it were his own. 'Someone has to testify.'

Anna looked out at the trawler, one work-scarred hand gently stroking a cheek; a dead child's cheek? 'I don't know. He should be punished – he should not be allowed to go free. But we are needed in Israel.'

'I feel the same way,' said Simon Berger behind her. 'What do we owe ourselves to – the past or the future?'

'The future.' David Weill and the rest of the group had congealed around them; old nationalities were forgotten, they had a commonalty of blood. 'That's all that should count with us from now on.'

'Yes,' said Hilde Klein, holding her two children to her.

'But what about the dead ones?' Joachim Winter said. 'Will they forgive us for letting their murderers go? I only ask,' he said apologetically to his wife. 'We were the fortunate ones – we must have a conscience.'

The skiff was coming back in. Voices came across the still water from the trawler, indistinct and disembodied, like voices from the past: something was going on.

'I'll go back and testify,' Luise said abruptly.

All of a sudden Israel was a concept she could not quite comprehend; in her heart she knew now it had always been so. A new nation to be built out of blood and a sense of history, a rejection of endless persecution, a desire to come home to Jerusalem: none of it touched her deeply enough, there was not enough Jew in her. And yet the Jew in her told her that Besser had to be punished.

'No!' It was the first time she had seen David Weill excited; he clamped a frail hand on her arm. 'You must come with us!'

'Yes!' echoed the others: suddenly they were all one, and Luise was touched by their feeling.

But she shook her head. 'Perhaps next year – ' She could not say *in Jerusalem.* 'Don't worry about me. I have Major Dunleavy – ' Even she wasn't quite sure how she meant those last words.

'Sure.' Dunleavy's face was a mass of joy and relief: he wasn't going to lose her after all, at least not for a while.

'I promise you Besser won't get away.' Luise was fully committed now; her voice strengthened as her resolve did. 'The Agency in Haifa will tell you what happens. He'll be arrested, perhaps be back in Germany before you get there – '

The captain came up the beach, good eye squinting with perplexity; the wall eye gazed out unperturbed. 'I think we better up anchor. The English destroyers are moving up the coast, past the gulf – '

'How do you know?' Dunleavy asked.

'We got guys watching 'em – they radioed us. They dunno what's happening, but if them ships move even six kilometres up the coast, they aint gonna be able to see us. Give me more time to get past Livorno. More time I got, further south I gonna be when the sun comes up. Okay, everybody?'

The beach was suddenly a chatter of farewells. The children came up to Luise, kissed her. 'Why aren't you coming, Fräulein Graz?' asked Rebecca Klein, but it was a question Luise couldn't answer to a child.

Hilde Klein, the Winters, Noah Malchek said goodbye. Noah kissed her hand, was unexpectedly gallant. 'Israel will miss you. Every country needs its beautiful women.'

'Herr Malchek.' Luise leaned forward, kissed the forehead beneath the fluttering handkerchief. 'May you have the best china store in Israel.'

'A chain of them,' said Malchek.

David Weill took her hand sadly, his dark eyes glistening with tears. He had begun to love this woman as he might have a daughter; but he doubted that he would have told her so. All he could say now was, '*Shalom.*'

'*Shalom*, Herr Professor.'

Simon Berger said goodbye, and then there was only Anna Bork left. She put out her hand hesitantly, the first time she had ever attempted any physical intimacy; Luise took it firmly, held it between her own two hands. Tears were in the eyes of both women: they had glimpsed friendship and wept that it would never flower properly. They were from different worlds, but social distinctions meant nothing: the human touch, a compassion, a sharing of a common grief, would have united them. In Israel they would have led separate lives, seen each other only occasionally, but the meeting would have warmed the heart of each of them.

'Take care,' said Anna, harsh voice just a murmur.

'And you, too.' Luise pressed the rough hand again. 'Plant a rose or a tree in Israel for my mother.'

'I always had a green thumb,' said Anna. 'All I'll need is good horse –' she remembered to be polite ' – manure.'

The skiff went out, sunk low in the water with its load. Dunleavy, Luise and Charlie Lincoln stood on the beach and waited till the anchor of the trawler was drawn up. Then the boat, un-safe looking, ungainly, reminding one of a crippled water bird, headed out of the cove. Farewells came back across the gently lapping water, a final cry *Next year in Jerusalem!* like the weeping of gulls on the still, shining air.

'Christ,' said Dunleavy, praying, 'I hope they make it.'

'All that way,' said Charlie Lincoln, eyes glistening in his young bony face. 'It don't seem possible.'

'Anything is possible,' said Luise, 'when you have been through what they have been.'

The trawler went round the corner of the cove and there was then only the sea, stretching away till it faded into the limitless sky. Both sea and sky glittered with light, the face of God that no man could read.

'Now let's find Besser,' said Luise.

3

'You'll be safe here,' said the Contessa and managed to hide her doubt.

I wonder, Besser thought. *Spinne's* route was linked with safe houses – but what house anywhere was safe? He had begun to have doubts and fears, confronted now with a larger picture than had ever occupied him back home in Germany. The world was owned by landlords demanding their rent: governments, dictatorships, churches, cartels: nowhere was safe for the man who had to place his trust in strangers. South America had suddenly become a vast frightening new world and he had lost the confidence to face it. He longed for the comfort and security of pre-war Würzburg, to be once more just a doctor whose world was bounded by his family and his patients. He almost wept at the regret he felt that he had been forced to flee Germany.

'When will you get in touch with your friends?' The Contessa had given them lunch downstairs, eye and ear cocked all the time for the return of Dunleavy. Then she had brought them up here to the largest of the guest rooms on the second floor, offering them better accommodation than the attic they had occupied last night, as if in compensation for the treachery she was committing.

'This evening. As soon as it is dark I shall go into La Spezia. Unless Herr Ricci comes back during the day.'

Then he remembered what the old man, Giulio, had told him when bringing him up from the beach. He had been suspicious when the old man had come to him with the Contessa's invitation and he had made his way up to the Villa Fontana with Giulio to check first that no trap had been set for them. Only when he had satisfied himself that there was no one in the villa but the Contessa and the two servants had he gone back for Ilse and the boys. But it had upset him to learn that Ricci had been picked up; that meant the English were not confining their round-up just to the Jews. He could feel his nerve going and he did his best to sound calm and resigned.

'Of course – he won't come back, will he? The English won't let him go.'

'Not at once.' The Contessa had been told by Dunleavy how to act her part. All her married life she had had to play a role, coached by her demanding, critical husband; she knew better than anyone that the Count had felt he had married beneath him. But he had never threatened her with any danger and she had often fought him. She knew, however, that she could not fight the circumstances that now engulfed her. She could only do what she was told and trust to fortune. 'But you don't have to worry about Herr Ricci. He will not tell the police or the English anything.'

'Perhaps we should have stayed at the other villa,' said Ilse.

'It wouldn't be safe. The Rossanos may be back at the Villa Indira any day now – they only have to come from Carrara. No, it is best that you stay here. And it is more comfortable, is it not?'

'Oh, yes.' Ilse had been pleased when they had been shown into this big room and the boys put in another room across the wide corridor. There were things she wanted to say to Karl, she *had* to say, and she did not want to mention them in front of the boys. 'You have been very kind, Contessa.'

'One does what one can to help,' said the Contessa, but she did not miss the momentary sardonic look in Besser's eye.

'Mother – ' Hans and Paul came to the door of the room, restless at having been kept in the house. 'Why can't we go back to the beach?'

'Not today. Perhaps tomorrow.' How much must I lie to them? Ilse thought.

'Do we have to stay in the house? We want to go outside and play.'

The Contessa was standing by the boys; she put out a hand and stroked Paul's blond head. That had been another of her sins in the Count's eyes, that she had not been able to give him children. 'Giulio is going to work in the garden, to start cleaning it up. Would you like to help him?'

'May we?' The boys looked at their mother, who looked at their father.

'Will anyone see them out there?' Besser asked.

The Contessa shook her head. 'None of the villagers ever come into the grounds. If the English *should* come back, Giulio will hear them coming up the drive. The boys will be safe with him.'

'All right,' Besser told the boys reluctantly. 'But don't wander away. Stay where I can call you.'

The Contessa took the boys along the corridor, holding a hand of each of them, laughing with them as they tried to pull her at a run down the stairs. As her voice died away, an aunt with two suddenly acquired nephews, she was promising them ice-cream for supper.

Ilse wandered about the big bedroom, running a finger over the dust on the huge walnut chest of drawers, straightening a wrinkled rug beside the bed, a *hausfrau* with nothing to do. The shopping basket stood on the floor beside the bed, but she could not even busy herself with that; the Contessa, with a disapproving glance at the basket, had told them that her cook would prepare their meals for them. The windows and shutters had been opened and Ilse paused by one of the windows and looked out.

'The view is beautiful from here.' Then she turned back to Besser, sitting like a disconsolate old man in an armchair beside the bed. 'Nothing looks good, does it?'

He shook his head, being honest with her. 'If there is no one at that bar in La Spezia tonight –' His voice trailed off.

'Let's go back home,' she said suddenly. She had woken during the night and thought about it, but had been afraid to mention it to him until now. She argued quickly, before he could interrupt her, 'We can change our name – we can be the Ludwigs, just like we are now. We can find somewhere else to live – we don't have to go back to Würzburg –'

'I wish we could –' For a moment he felt a lifting of his mood. 'We could settle in Austria. The Tyrol is beautiful – the boys would like it there –'

Out of the corner of her eye she saw movement down in the garden. The boys were following Giulio down an overgrown path, Hans pushing an ancient wheelbarrow, Paul carrying a rake over his shoulder. The old man said something to them and their laughter floated up, as wounding as the pangs of childbirth.

She moved across to Karl, went down on her knees between his legs. She noticed the slight hesitation before he put his arms round her and drew her to him; she knew that he needed her and the ghost of Gerstein could be forgotten. She put her hand on him, stroked him gently, but he shook his head, smiling at her.

'Not now. Tonight.'

'Don't let's stay here tonight. Don't go looking for anyone in La Spezia. As soon as it's dark, we'll go into the station and catch a train for the north. We'll go back to Austria, like you say. Our papers are all right – we're supposed to *be* Austrian. If they hold us up at the border, we can say we changed our minds, we've decided not to emigrate. We'll find a place to live – '

He marvelled at her optimism, allowed it to infect him. 'It will mean starting all over again, but we'd have to do that in South America, too. If we're careful, there's no reason why they should ever catch up with me – ' He saw the shadow cross her face. 'Promise me something. Never ask me about the war. I want to forget it all. Everything.'

She nodded, but bargained with him: she wanted to guarantee their future happiness: 'If you'll forget Heinrich Gerstein.'

'Agreed.' He kissed her, felt himself rising against her softness as he pulled her into him. 'Are you wearing your thing?'

'It's in one of the suitcases. Damn!'

He kissed her again, smiling. 'We'll wait. We don't want you pregnant again, not yet awhile.'

'I love you.' She moved her lips against his, wanting him so much she ached with the hunger of it. 'We can still be happy, despite everything that's happened.'

Then through the open door of the bedroom they heard the raised voices downstairs. Both tensed, stood up. Besser moved to the door and out into the corridor. He could not distinguish the words, but the argument downstairs between the Contessa and the man, whoever he was, was in German.

'Who is it?' Ilse whispered behind him.

He shook his head, went back into the room and took Ricci's gun from the pocket of his overcoat. He saw the puzzled, frightened look on Ilse's face and he pressed her shoulder as he went past her on his way out of the room again.

'Just in case.' He had no intention of using the gun; but he was surprised at the confidence it abruptly brought back to him. Perhaps he was meant to kill, after all . . . He hastily put that unwanted thought out of his mind. 'I'll find out who it is. It could be one of our friends.'

'It could be one of the Jews, too.'

'Be ready, then. We'll go down the back stairs, get the boys and go into La Spezia at once. We'll have to risk trying to get an afternoon train.'

'Be careful, darling.'

He went along the corridor, treading lightly on the balls of his feet so that his heels would not click against the marble floor; he remembered how they had been able to follow the progress of the English soldiers last night as their heels hammered throughout the house. The voices got louder as he got to the top of the stairs; the Contessa and the newcomer were still arguing in the entrance hall, the argument booming up through the two-storied chamber. He went cautiously down the stairs, keeping against the wall, came to the gallery that ran around the hall at the first floor level. He stood behind a statue of a god (Apollo? He knew none of the southern gods; his mythology was rooted in the mists of the north), looked down past the marble muscles at the two figures in the hall.

The Contessa was shouting even louder than usual: it was hard to tell whether in fury or to warn him and Ilse. The stranger certainly was furious: Besser could see him gesticulating, hear clearly now the fierce words he was spitting out.

'Don't deny it – you were sheltering Nazis!'

'I'm not denying it!' the Contessa shouted. 'They came to me the same as your friends did – both of them forced me to let them use this house. I had no choice!'

'We never forced you to do anything – all we had to do was show you our money! How much did the Nazis offer you?'

'It wasn't the money!' Her voice rang through the hall; she had never sung with as much passion as this. 'You are all the same to me – '

'Where is Besser?'

The stranger seemed to scream his demand: Besser had never imagined that his own name could shock him. It soared up to the high ceiling of the hall, brought Ilse running down the stairs from the hall above. He heard her heels clattering on the marble, went as cold as the statue on which his hand rested. He spun round to tell her to go back, but he was too late.

Keppel abruptly left the Contessa, came racing up the wide main stairs to the gallery, his gun in his hand. He fired as he saw Besser still half-hidden by the statue; but he was running and his shot went wide, the bullet clipping the wall just by Ilse's head. Besser, not knowing who the stranger was, knowing only that the man had to be killed if he and Ilse and the boys were to escape, stepped out from behind the marble-eyed, indifferent god. He pulled the trigger of Ricci's gun as a reflex action; it was the first time he had fired a gun since his first days in the SS. The sound of the shot was like a crash in the sound chamber of the hall; Besser didn't hear Ilse's stifled scream, just felt her pull the gun out of his hand. He turned to her, shaking his head wildly but not knowing what he was denying.

Out in the garden Giulio and the boys heard the shots.

'Something's happening!' Hans cried; and Paul whimpered in fright. 'We must go in!'

Giulio grabbed both boys as he heard the car or truck coming up the drive.

'No, stay here!' He knew it was not all over yet; there could be more shots. The children had to be protected; the old man suddenly hated their parents for creating this sort of situation. He dropped into Italian, his German forgotten: '*Aspett'!* *Aspett'!*'

4

'You mean Dr Besser is *here*?' said Luise. 'He's come back?'

'He was here when I left.' Dunleavy turned to Charlie Lincoln. 'Better stand by, Charlie, just in case.'

Charlie reached under the seat of the jeep for his holstered pistol, strapped it on. 'You expecting trouble, major?'

'I don't know. I've never come up against an SS man on the run before.'

The three of them went up the wide front steps, crossed the terrace and Dunleavy took a large key from his pocket.

'You have a key?'

'I didn't trust the Contessa. I didn't want her to keep us locked out while she let Besser get away.'

In the moment that it took Dunleavy to unlock the front door of the villa, Luise had an overpowering urge to turn back. Punishment of Besser was necessary; justice demanded it. But suddenly she could not be the instrument of vengeance, she could not condemn another human being to death.

'I can't!'

But Dunleavy had already opened the door, flinging it wide, and the Contessa stood there in front of them in the middle of the hall, staring up at where Keppel lay sprawled at the top of the staircase. Dunleavy went quickly in past the Contessa and up the stairs, his gun now in his hand. He bent over Keppel, picked up the gun lying on the top step, looked down at Luise who had come in to stand beside the Contessa.

'He's dead. Contessa – ' She didn't appear to hear him and he raised his voice: 'Contessa! Where's Besser?'

The blank look left the Contessa's face, as if she were focusing it from inside herself. She was not a woman who would remain in shock for long; one always had to stay abreast of events, or better still a little ahead of them. She had some catching up to do.

'He's still here! He shot Herr Keppel – ' One witness against her eliminated; now Besser had to be got rid of. She could handle the men from *Bricha* and the Nazis when they came again: already she was looking to her defence. 'He's upstairs somewhere – the second floor – '

Dunleavy called down to Luise, 'Stay there.'

But she could not let him go searching for Besser alone, not if the latter had a gun. She ran up the stairs as Charlie Lincoln moved in from the front doorway, stood guard beside the Contessa. She paused for a moment by the body of Ben Keppel, looked down at the young face that looked puzzled and irritated, as if it could not believe it was dead. Then she

306

ran on, along the gallery and up the stairs to the second floor. Dunleavy heard her coming, waited at the top of the second flight for her.

'I told you to stay downstairs.' He sounded angry.

'Why should you risk being shot? He's done nothing to you –'

'You can't mean that – not if you think about it.' He spoke over his shoulder to her, looking down the long wide corridor upon which a dozen dark doors were closed. 'Besser! It's all over – finished!'

His voice thundered down the corridor, died away. But no door opened, and he cursed softly. 'Stay here,' he said, and this time she knew better than to disobey him.

She watched him as he went down the long hall, pushing open each door and standing back to avoid the expected blast of gunfire. As each room proved empty she moved cautiously down the corridor after him, but keeping well behind him. She glanced into each room as she passed it; it was like looking at the empty life of the Contessa. She could hear the faint squeak of her shoes on the marble floor, but no other sound: the corridor was just a long tunnel of silence.

Dunleavy came to the second last door, flung it open, stood back. She waited for the explosion; the silence suddenly became a pressure. Then Dunleavy stepped into the doorway, stood there a moment, then moved slowly into the room. Still cautious, she went quickly down to the open door.

Besser and his wife sat side by side on the bed, a shopping basket on the floor beside them; they looked like a worn out couple just returned from an exhausting shopping excursion. They held hands and Ilse sat with her other hand in the pocket of the brown jacket she wore.

Besser had been staring at the floor, but he lifted his head as Luise appeared. He looked at her and he had the same expression she had just seen on Keppel's face: he was not dead, but he looked puzzled and irritated, as if he could not quite believe what was happening.

'I didn't mean to kill him,' he said quietly; all the volume had gone out of his voice. 'It just happened –'

307

'I don't think that's what you'll be tried for,' said Dunleavy, 'Fräulein Graz has got some prior charges against you.'

'Please –' Ilse looked at Luise.

'I'm sorry, Frau Besser. I *have* to.' Faced now with the murderer she could not back down: a vast horde of ghosts stood behind her. 'I promised other people – your husband killed their relatives, too. He killed Herr Keppel's brother –'

'Keppel?' Besser frowned.

'The man you just shot. We all had names, Herr Doctor – none of us were just numbers to each other. But perhaps that was the only way you could count us – there were so many –'

'Please –' Besser flinched, but none of the others could tell whether it was at Luise's remark or the sudden fierce clutch of his hand by Ilse.

'Frau Kogan's children – the same age as your two boys, Herr Doctor. And Herr Berger's wife and children –'

It was Ilse this time who said, 'Please –'

Luise looked around the room, back across the corridor at the room opposite. 'Where are your children?'

It was as if Ilse had forgotten them: her head jerked up. 'They are out in the garden with the old man. They haven't seen – ?'

'No,' said Dunleavy. 'My driver will keep them outside. He won't let them see Herr Keppel. But that's as far as we can protect them –'

'Will everything come out?' Ilse's hair had fallen down about her face, her body was slumped and shrunken; she looked sick and middle-aged and hopeless. 'I mean, at my husband's trial?'

'Yes,' said Dunleavy. 'It will be necessary. It can't be allowed to happen again, not what he and the others like him did.'

Besser shuddered and Ilse looked at him. 'I can't believe it, Karl. Why? Why?'

He shook his head, having no answer, not even for himself. Then he lowered his head and began to weep quietly and without restraint. Ilse clutched his hand and looked up at Luise and Dunleavy.

'Could you leave us alone for a moment? Till he has recovered. I don't want the boys to see him – not like this. They love him so much.'

Dunleavy looked at Luise and she nodded. She felt the other woman's pain: this was the sweetness of revenge and it was a terrible, terrible thing. She looked at Besser and tried to hate him; but couldn't, too many years had gone by since her mother had died. She felt nothing positive against him: only the pain of loss that he had caused her.

She went ahead of Dunleavy out of the room. They were halfway down the corridor when the shot rang out behind them: muffled, as if the barrel of the gun had been pressed against or buried in something. They spun round, ran back to the doorway.

Besser lay back on the bed, one hand clutching his side. Ilse still sat on the bed beside him, the gun held primly in her lap. With her free hand she stroked Besser's face, as if trying to ease away the still puzzled look that creased it. She was talking to him, even though he was far past hearing her:

'I'm sorry, darling. But I couldn't let the boys know. Please forgive me.'

Chapter Eight

===

'I'll have Lieutenant Taviani arrange the burials and all the paperwork,' said Major Shell. 'He's not going to query it if I tell him each shot the other. That's what you want, isn't it?'

'Don't you reckon that's best?' said Dunleavy. 'I don't want to put Frau Besser on a charge, not unless you do.'

'My dear chap, don't you think I have enough on my plate? Where are your DP friends, by the way? You haven't mentioned them.'

'They're on their way.' Dunleavy waved vaguely. 'I still have their movement order.'

'Frame it. But don't hang it where any official eye can see it. There are still an awful lot of bureaucrats around, demanding the letter of the law. I sometimes think we fight wars only for them.'

'My sentiments exactly.'

'Where are Frau Besser and her boys now?'

'Still out at the Villa Fontana. The Contessa will look after them until after the funeral. She's not such a bitch, after all.'

'Oh, she's a bitch all right, make no mistake. But even the worst of us has some compensating factor, I suppose.'

'You'd have a hard job convincing me about Besser. I never knew the guy, but in my book he must have been bastard all through, every slice of him.'

'His wife must have loved him. But then there's no knowing with women, is there? How's Miss Graz?'

'She's on the movement order. I'm taking her back to Germany this evening. The sooner we get away from here, the better.'

'I'd better make out a separate order for her.' Straightfaced, he added, 'Just in case you lose those other bods between here and the border.'

Five minutes later they both walked out to the jeep waiting outside headquarters. Shell saluted Luise, who sat in the back of the jeep, and nodded to Charlie Lincoln behind the wheel.

'Do you have to go back to the Villa Fontana?'

'No,' said Luise. 'I couldn't face Frau Besser again.'

The scene at the villa had been too harrowing. Giulio had not been able to restrain the boys and they had come plunging up the front steps and into the entrance hall. Charlie Lincoln had intercepted them, but they had fought him, screaming for their mother and father. Ilse had rushed out of the bedroom and down to them, leaving Luise and Dunleavy with the dead Besser still staring in puzzlement at the ceiling.

Dunleavy had crossed to Besser, closed his eyes. 'We better go down.'

'What are you going to do with – him? And Ben Keppel?'

'I'll have to turn them over to the Italian police. Corpses are their responsibility.' He didn't realize he was talking like a cop; only an instinctive bow to her feelings had prevented him from calling Besser and Keppel *stiffs*. 'I'll call Shell first. He can have Taviani handle it.'

'What about Frau Besser?'

'How much of this do you want to come out?'

'None of it, now. What's the point?' She looked at the body on the bed: if there was a hell, Besser was already there.

'Okay. I'll fix the story with Taviani.'

'What about the Contessa?'

'She won't give us any trouble. Any story we dream up, she's going to swear it's true.' He closed the bedroom door. 'How do you feel?'

'Empty. I know I should feel something else, but that's all – empty.'

He nodded sympathetically, took her arm and they went downstairs. Charlie had left the two boys down in the hall with their mother; the Contessa was just leading the three of them into the main salon. Giulio had come into the house

311

and now was helping Charlie lift the body of Keppel off the top stairs.

'Put him in one of the bedrooms,' Dunleavy said. He stared for a moment at the man he had pursued; but, like Luise, he, too, felt empty. 'Besser's up on the next floor. Bring him down and put them together.'

At the bottom of the stairs Rosanna had come from the kitchen, stood bewildered and frightened. From the salon came the sobs of the two boys, the weeping murmuring of their mother and the occasional word of sympathy from the Contessa.

Dunleavy asked for the phone and Rosanna led him away down the corridor to it. Luise braced herself and went into the salon. The Contessa, standing behind the couch on which Ilse sat holding the two boys, looked at her enquiringly.

'Major Dunleavy is calling the police. You have nothing to worry about. Neither of you,' she said as Ilse lifted her head. 'Herr Keppel and Herr Besser – ' she looked at Hans and Paul, then decided there was just so much they could be spared – 'shot each other.'

Hans lifted a tear-stricken face to his mother. 'Why did the man shoot Father? The war is over – '

'It is.' Ilse's voice was no more than a croak. 'It was all just – just a terrible mistake.'

Luise turned away, went quickly out of the salon. She felt Ilse Besser's pain, understood why she was trying to protect her sons; but there was a limit to the lies one had to listen to, to support by one's silence. The Contessa followed her.

'What do I do with her and the boys?'

'They can go home to Germany, I should think. Perhaps Major Shell will arrange it.'

'Will there be trouble for me?'

'That's up to you, Contessa.' Dunleavy came back from the phone. 'If you stay in this game, running a safe house for anyone who meets your price, sooner or later you're going to have trouble. Sell the place or close it up, Contessa, and go back to Milan. They might still have a place in the chorus for you.'

He wasted no sympathy on her: she would survive. He turned away from her as Charlie Lincoln and Giulio came down the stairs. Luise, suddenly feeling unconnected with the whole business, as if some sort of umbilical cord had been cut and now she was alone and adrift, walked out on to the front terrace.

Then Charlie came out with Giulio and they both went down to the jeep. 'We gonna pick up Frau Besser's luggage. When I get back, the major says we better get moving. You coming with us?'

But he didn't wait for her answer, was gone down the driveway in a spatter of gravel, Giulio hanging on to his seat for dear life. Then two local police cars from Lerici, told to get there ahead of him by Lieutenant Taviani, came speeding up to the villa. Policemen jumped out and ran up the steps; men took over the house, uniforms asserted their authority. Luise felt more and more isolated, longed for Dunleavy to appear on the terrace: he had become her only point of reference. But he, too, was busy, another uniform with authority.

Charlie and Giulio came back in the jeep, unloaded five suitcases, among them the Vuitton. As they were carrying the luggage up the steps, Ilse came out on to the terrace, Hans and Paul on either side of her. She looked at the suitcases as Charlie and Giulio took them in past her; then she said something to her sons, left them and crossed to Luise. The latter knew what Karl Besser's widow was going to say.

'Fräulein, do you want your mother's suitcase? I can't take it – it would always be a reminder –'

It will be a reminder to me, too: but perhaps she had learned, better than the other woman ever would, to bear such memories. 'Yes, I'll take it.'

Ilse had one hand in the pocket of her jacket; the other worked nervously, as if she were trying to rid it of cramp. Luise wondered if that was the hand that had fired the gun.

'Will you ever forgive him?'

'No,' said Luise. 'Will you?'

Ilse said nothing, but turned her head and looked across at

313

her sons standing still and apprehensive, waiting on the future. She looked back at Luise.

'No. But I still loved him. Goodbye, Fräulein.'

And now the Bessers, Luise hoped, were behind her forever, she was sitting in the back of the jeep, the Vuitton case beside her, and Dunleavy was saying to Shell, 'We'll stay somewhere up the coast tonight. Somewhere quiet.'

'Are you disappointed at not making it to Palestine this time?' Shell said to Luise.

'It was somewhere to head for,' she said, feeling no disappointment at all. 'One needs a destination.'

'How about America?' Dunleavy smiled, all those marvellous teeth showing again; he was something like the old Dunleavy, the man she had known at Camp 93. But he would never be completely like that man again: she had found another person altogether behind that smile and the casual easy-going air. 'It was good enough for Columbus.'

'I thought he was looking for India, wasn't he?' she said, returning his smile. 'I shouldn't like to find myself heading in the wrong direction.'

The thing is, she thought, I have to build my life *somewhere*. An old woman stopped by the jeep, a skinny child clinging to her black skirt. She held out a claw, croaked an appeal past two yellow teeth; the child, thin and starved, was a miniature of its grandmother. Shell waved them away, his voice gently gruff.

'Eventually you have to tell them all to shove off,' he said apologetically. 'One's charity gets diluted after a while.'

'What will happen to them?' Luise looked after the two figures shambling down the street, the child as rickety on its legs as its grandmother.

'The amazing thing is, they survive. Don't ask me how. Perhaps it's just willpower.'

That's what it is, Luise thought. Nothing else but that had kept her and Anna Bork and David Weill and all the others alive.

'Or maybe it's love,' said Shell. 'The Italians have a marvellous capacity for that. That old woman would never let that child die.'

314

'Not only the Italians,' said Dunleavy. 'Frau Besser has a pretty good talent for love, too. She's going to spend the rest of her life protecting those boys of hers from the truth.'

'Perhaps the next generation of Germans will want the truth,' said Shell. 'It's our only hope, don't you think? And theirs, too.'

He said goodbye to them, an old-young man heading for future wars so far undeclared: he looked as if he wished he had chosen other destinations.

'I hope you get to India soon,' said Dunleavy. 'Before you have to round up any more Jews.'

Luise sat back in the jeep as Charlie Lincoln took it through the city and began to climb up towards the coast road. The breeze blew in her hair, washing away the heat of the day. It could not wash away the blood and pain of events: the texture of her feelings was too dense, it would be weeks, perhaps months, before she could unravel them into some sort of acceptance. In the meantime she had to go on building her life.

'Are you gonna stay in Germany, miss?' said Charlie Lincoln. 'Or go back to Austria?'

Dunleavy looked back at her for her answer: in his face she saw love, and strength she could borrow, if she wanted it.

'Not Austria,' she said. 'Austria for me is Vienna, and I couldn't go back there. Germany? I don't know. There's not much future there, won't be for a long time yet.'

'Not for opera singers,' said Dunleavy.

'What about America? I used to read about the Metropolitan Opera in New York. We were very snobbish about it – we used to think the only *good* opera was in Europe. But things may change now –'

'I could come up from Washington.' Dunleavy was smiling, but his eyes were serious. 'Maybe it's time I started listening to someone else besides Maxine Sullivan.'

'There's Ella Fitzgerald,' said Charlie Lincoln. 'And that new guy, Sinatra.'

It's another world, thought Luise. She looked at the back of Dunleavy's head; he had turned to face forward again as Charlie took the jeep round some sharp curves. *He's nothing*

315

like any of the men I once knew; and will New York or Washington ever be like Vienna once was? But the old Vienna, and that old world of which, for her, it had been the capital, that was gone forever. She had to start again somewhere –

'What are you thinking?' They came out of the curves, the jeep straightened up and Dunleavy looked back at her.

'Where will you go to law school?'

'Depends where I can get in. Depends, too, whether you want to go back to singing.'

'I think I shall. Will you mind?'

'No,' he said.

Both of them were aware of the presence of Charlie Lincoln. All she could do without embarrassment was lean forward and put her hand on Dunleavy's shoulder and press it lovingly.

'I think we may both be very happy.'

'I hope so for both of you, miss,' said Charlie Lincoln, young and inexperienced but not blind to love.